Loon

Glossary

Ashwagane	Ash-wa-GONE-ee
Wendaban	Wen-DAW-bun
Achinike	A-CHIN-i-kee
Gahbodnay	Ga-BAWD-nee
Shagonash	SHAW-gan-osh
N'Daki Menan	Da-kee-Meh-NAN
Majukimo	Ma-JUKE-i-mo
Osatig	O-SAW-tig

Dedication

This book was finished in early December, 1991. Two weeks later, I was sitting on a verandah in the early mornings dividing my time between watching the gentle breakers rolling in on the west coast of Barbados, and reading *The Great Code*. One morning my wife asked me if I would like to go swimming in the ocean. I replied that since 7 a.m. I had been swimming "for my life" in Northrop Frye.

A week later, under a Christmas tree in Vancouver, I received "from Santa" *The Double Vision*, and on Boxing Day morning, again about 7 a.m., I was again swimming in Frye, this time a bit more leisurely with more flotation.

Since 1959, I have read most of Frye's books and lectures, and in my teaching and writing he has always been there, a kindred spirit, formative teacher and pathfinder for me. Alas, I knew him only through the printed word. But as I came face to face with him again in Barbados and Vancouver, with *Loon* still fresh in my mind, I had a strange experience of déjà vu. I wondered how much Frye was in the novel, and began to wonder if the answer wasn't a great deal.

I suspect he may be Catherine's spiritual godfather, the antitype to Dr. French. But when an author is asked about the sources of the webs spun from the imagination, he is best to respond with the road grader at the roadblock: "Don't ask me, ma'am; I just work here."

This book is dedicated to
a great pilgrim and tourguide on the paths
of our imagination and mythic heritage.

NORTHROP FRYE
(1912 - 1991)

vi

Caveat

An early reader of the following story, when it was circulating in manuscript, was sure he noticed a resemblance between the Wendaban Band of the Ashwagane Indians in the story, and the Temagami Band of the northeastern Ojibwa of Ontario. That being so, he figured Achinike must be Temagami, White Falls, New Liskeard, Almaguin, North Bay, and Huronia City, Barrie, Ontario. Incoville perplexed him.

Even if such foolhardy resemblances were to be entertained, who then, pray, is Catherine Saltonstall, Conk Seguin, Zellie Rabinovitch and Sammy Osatig? And where, oh where, is Ashton's Cave? Obviously, this early reader had stars in his eyes and an historical imagination beyond the reach of common mortals. Needless to say, any resemblance between the fictional characters, places and events in the following story, and real live equivalents, is purely hypothetical, unintentional, coincidental, and, in general, ridiculous. Ask anyone who was on the roadblock if that isn't so!

Author's Foreword

President Dave Marshall, Jim Puddister and Frank Ciancio, all of Nipissing University College, provided generous use of and technical assistance on the faculty computers for the transferring of *Loon* from typescript to disk. Joan and Peter Moes and Arthur Perlini read the manuscript and offered valuable suggestions. An author must ultimately do his own thing, however, and I did not follow all their suggestions. So the book's shortcomings are all mine.

Brian Moulder of the MNR in Temagami searched his slide collection and came up with the gorgeous photo of Henry (or is it Henrietta?) for the cover. Bob Gareh of Lakeland Airways in Temagami, Richard Smith of the Graphics Division, Canadian Forces Base, North Bay, and Dick Scott of Railton's Camera Centre, all searched their personal collections for the picture of the Stinson, and I am very grateful for their efforts. Just any old bush plane wouldn't do. The astute proofreading eyes of Lois Pollard at the Highway Book Shop saved me from several infelicities I should not have wanted to make public.

I should like to thank a small island in a remarkable lake for the opportunity of peace and quiet and concentration. If Conk can talk to his airplane, I don't see why I can't thank an island.

Finally, Niki Plumstead's presence is everywhere in *Loon*. She was a captive audience all those mornings during its writing, and offered wonderful initial reactions and suggestions; she painstakingly transferred it to Wordperfect 5.1 and "saved it to DOS;" she has been a constant source of encouragement.

Chapter I
HAROLD

The first faint streaks of dark blue and orange light came into the dawn across the dark lake outside his window. There were flecks of October frost on the pane. A hand was gently shaking the young boy's shoulder as he slept. "Harold," the old man said, "get up. Harold!" He opened his eyes. The grizzled deep-lined face of the old chief looked down on him. "Harold. Up! You must come with me. Dress quickly now. I will wait for you down by the canoe."

Within the hour they were inside the inky blackness, a single smudgy flame spluttering from the bear grease lamp the old man had brought. The boy sat shivering on the rock ledge beside the black water as the old man stood beside him gazing up at the wall of ancient paintings. The boy thought he had seen little piles of something whitish behind him on the rock, but in the dimness of the light he could barely make them out. He would not ask. He would watch and listen. Something unusual was going on. The Chief had never taken him aside like this before. Something important, strange, was going to happen.

The old man stood gazing up at the pictures spread across the rock, outlines of men and women, birds, animals, the sun, canoes, strange shapes. He was silent, contemplative. Then he turned to the boy. "I have brought you here because I will soon die. I will join our ancestors here." The musical, deep sounds of the Ashwagane words made the young eyes grow big. "This is our most sacred place in n'Daki Menan," the Chief said. The dark orange and yellowish flickers of light played over the prickly face. "He has not shaved for several days," the boy thought. "Why will he die? How does he know? What has that to do with me?"

"Look," said the old man. He moved closer to the huge wall of ancient figures in reds and rusts, blue and yellow. "This is Ogima. He is the young Ashwagane Chief. He never dies. He is chasing Geezhigo-quae, the earth mother. See?" The boy squinted up at the chiaroscuro of flickering light. A man was chasing a woman who was chasing an animal. A wolf, he thought. The old man moved his finger to the animal. "This is Maninganaki, the life of the land," he said. "He is the wolf, the favorite of Kitchi-manitou. The running man is the Wendaban. Geezhigo-quae is our land. Maninganaki is the spirit of life. They are running together, trying to catch each other." He turned, and slowly squatted down by the boy, tucking his old legs close in to his body as best he could. He looked into the young one's eyes.

"You are of the clan of the mank," he said, "the sacred totem of the Wendaban in ancient days. I have talked with your father. We are agreed. You will be the next shaman of the Wendaban. You must get ready, my son. You will carry the soul of our people forward, our wisdom, our history, our medicines." He reached over and put his hand on the boy's shoulder. Harold shivered. "You must promise that you will protect the land. It is ours. It has never been traded away. The new Chief will tell you. You must work together. You must help him train the young and tell them all the stories. You must protect this place. Only you and the Chief shall know about it and you must never reveal its whereabouts to anyone. Here you can talk to the spirits. The pictures will talk to you too. They will tell you as they have told me. Protect the land and her spirits. Never let Shagonash take it away. He may borrow pieces of it but it must never be traded away. The gods are in the land as well as the sky. You know that. You must promise—here, now."

He tried to reply but his throat was dry and the words caught in the roof of his mouth. He thought there was a chilly numbness in his spine. Suddenly he stood up. He looked down at the old man for several seconds. "Yes, Pashawonaby, I promise," he said.

Harold was only twelve then. But he would never forget the saying that he had said. The words in the flickering rays of the lamp singed his mind for ever. "I promise," was his innocent pledge to the unknown; but he knew he must say it. What would it all mean? He knew then that he would never forget to be finding out and to be telling the stories so many of which he already knew. He must learn and teach the medicines. He would be a healer. He had a destiny. He was a marked man. He was proud.

Chapter II
THE DISSERTATION

i

She had always loved the deep sounds of the bells as each morning, exactly at 9:00, they sent out their slow pulses of sound across the campus and down the streets and alleyways of what her neighbors still called the "town." Living a few blocks from the College, she had heard the morning bong, bong, bong, for as long as she could remember, and even as a little girl she had fancied that the great bells somehow had a meaning for her future life.

Her parents early instilled that future meaning, not as a dream or wish, but a taken-for-granted fact of life, for it ran in the family that she would, like her parents and her cousins in Boston, and their parents, and her great-grandfather, go to college, the female version of the older patriarchal one she was now attending. "That's what it's there for," her father had said, as if he were a part owner. All through prep school in Connecticut it was understood that the prepping was not so much for life as it was for the College back home, and the sounds of the bells when she returned home for vacations assured her that her College was waiting, the ivy-colored buildings only four blocks from Harrington Lane. College had been part of being a Saltonstall for three hundred years.

She couldn't have asked for a finer day, in late March, with the last traces of snow a memory and the campus coming up green, some daffodils up already in front of the Houghton Library, and the feel of spring and the end of classes in the air. For most students, the long winter's haul was just about over and the robin's warble, drowned out by the bells for a moment, announced that time was also of the future. Life was coming into full bloom.

She walked between the old administration building and Leonard Hall and came out in the centre of the yard in front of the huge Library, with its high Grecian pillars and forty-one steps (Zellie said that by the time you climbed them you were too tired to read) and headed for Winthrop Hall for her first appointment. She had timed it just right, for the last of the nine strokes of time echoed off into the distance as she passed the Library. She knew she should be concentrating on the interview ahead, but her emotions were running high—was it nostalgia, she wondered? It was supposed to have been only four years at Radcliffe, but it had now grown to seven, with an extra three as a graduate student at Harvard, and she had tried to follow Professor Greer's advice to live just a day at a time, to deal with just tomorrow's assignment, and not worry about degrees in the future. So she was now almost done, one last hurdle to put behind her. She looked forward to the dissertation; it had been the earlier qualifying examinations that her friends had warned would be the big hurdle, the torture chamber. But they were behind her now, in December, and she had been awarded high honors, and Professor French had been very pleased. As much as the gentle man had herded her through the ordeal with all the care he could muster, he could not stop his colleagues and the outside examiners from pushing her "to the frontiers of her knowledge" as he later put it, with the kind of question that went beyond what it could be expected that she should know, into areas of speculation that maybe even they didn't know much about. She had smiled slightly, paused, and then in her modest, gracious way, had sent them scurrying into hypothetical possibilities that they were unprepared for from such a pert little twenty-five-year-old who hadn't even decided on her dissertation yet. Professor Gurnz from Sociology had looked over at her above his dark-rimmed glasses and inaudibly wondered how Anthropology, the weak sister of the social sciences, could attract such remarkable and lovely talent.

As the last echo of the bells faded, she still tingled with the sound, for the bells meant stability and tradition, never more so than on this day. Many of her friends, little tots in the Yippie days of the 60's, had developed an indifference to the tradition of the old school and the burdens of being a New Englander. Even Zellie, for all her brilliance, took the three hundred-plus years of the College's past with a grain of Bronx salt, and once wrote a dirty limerick about the formerly all-male school which shocked her. But she had had no inclination to scoff, had found little to interest her in the notion that old families and inherited privilege of ancient descent, and old schools and names and ways and thoughts to be defended because they had been there for so long, might not be adequate to face up to the new times ahead. The bells had brought comfort, stability, a feeling of belonging, of being a part of something much older and steadier than she, something solid she could count on. She was traditional not by default but by adoption.

She rounded the corner of Winthrop Hall where she had spent many hours in classes and seminars and bounded up the six little marble steps with her new blue and white pinafore dress swishing out in front of her, darted through the glass door and into the hallway. This morning she stopped to look at him. Normally she just breezed by with a barely audible "Good morning, Ralph," or sometimes, "Morning, Waldo"—hardly ever glancing his way. He was her funny friend, always there, funny because it wasn't quite normal to greet a statue every morning; but then, nobody ever noticed. On occasion she would stop and take a curious look, for the darkened bronze face sitting on top of the long darkened bronze body in the darkened bronze chair played tricks with her. Ever since she had become bewitched by his writing, she had noticed the wry humor, the old Yankee deadpan, and there were times when she thought the statue's mouth had just a nuance of a curious grin. At other times, however, he seemed deadly serious, the wise old sage. She glanced down the hall; it was empty. She stood directly in front of him. "Ralph," she said, "I am going to have to make a decision in the next few days. Today will bring the two alternatives into sharp focus. Are you going to help me decide? I think I already know whose side you are on." She screwed up her lips into a round O as if she were about to kiss someone she wanted to keep at a distance, and watched the corners of his mouth, but Ralph's steadfast gaze was today like the Sphinx. She screwed up her nose and headed down the hall to Room 133, Professor French's office. She glanced at her black and white watch on the narrow leather strap. It had all twelve numbers on its face. She was two minutes late. She knocked.

Normally Professor French called out "Come in," but this morning there was a bustling noise and then he opened the door. "Good morning, Catherine, please come in," he said. He gestured her into the chair opposite his desk. How often she had loved to come into this old office, she thought; when she took her first class from him she used to fantasize that he would pick her out for something and ask her in. It had a certain odor, not musky exactly, but of lemon oil and old leather. It was dark, in part because the office faced up against another wall close by, but also because Professor French had blinds on the one window, little slits stacked in a row that let in very little light. He had one shaded lamp on his desk. She had been here many times since that first visit three years ago; she was looked on as one of his special students, perhaps his last, rumor had it, for he was already emeritus and had cut back on his graduate student load, though he still insisted on teaching the eager young faces in the freshman introductory course about the wonderful world of anthropology. If the freshmen did not register in the first day they would be out of luck, his course filled up so fast. It was the most sought-after freshman course in the College, but everybody knew there were days now when the deep powerful voice would waver, stop, then begin repeating again.

He got up from his chair and went over to the old high desk beside the window. "I have something for you, Catherine;" he rolled up the wavy sliding top of little slabs of oak, and took out a paper. She had marvelled before at the lovely old desk; as she watched him she thought of a Norman Rockwell sketch of American village post offices of the past, with an elderly man with spectacles and a green cap talking with youngsters in front of just such a high wooden wavy desk. "I have kept this on file all these years, but it seems appropriate now that you should have it," he said. "It's a photocopy of a long note that Ashton made up in Canada. He did not use it in his published work, for he thought it too speculative, too, ah. . . well, perhaps romantic, and he was such a stickler for verifiable fact. But it is a clue, perhaps a major piece in the puzzle, Catherine, if you could ever get to the bottom of it." He handed the paper over to her with a look of quiet joy, the twinkle still evident in the eyes under the heavy grey eyebrows. As he returned to his writing desk, she noticed he still wore the black boots, as she called them, soft dull black leather, well worn, with high ankle sides laced criss-cross from metal eyelets. She wondered if you could buy them anymore. "Ashton only mentioned this reference to a panograph once, but he was very excited about it. In all the time he was up there, he said he heard it referred to twice, but one of the references was from the old Chief Whitebear, who was a vast storehouse of information and legend." Professor French's face grew serious and he leaned forward a little toward Catherine. "Ashton was sure this silence on the matter was not because they did not know whether it existed, or where it was, but because of religious taboo. Whitebear wouldn't tell anything about it. Ashton suspected that it was for them like a holograph manuscript of a part of the Bible would be for us—a treasure of incalculable value. He inferred that it was probably a panograph somewhere, on several adjoining rock faces, a series of visionary paintings about their history. As you know, Catherine, only two panographs are known in the entire northeast, and both of these are Inuit in northern Quebec. If it exists, its location has to have been handed down from chief to chief, shaman to shaman. I'm sure they are still guarding it. If you got lucky, it could help confirm what we are learning about their origins and beliefs." He settled back in his chair which tilted slightly, and looked above her into the dark recesses of the office ceiling. His face was still clear of heavy wrinkles and struck her as almost beatific as he reclined further and laced his hands behind his head. The silver cuff links stood out against the white shirt and grey flannel sleeves. The soft, sloppy hand-tied red bow tie seemed to perk up a bit as he stretched back. "I am not asking you to don hiking boots and wade through marsh, or dive to secret caves or anything like that,'' he said, ''but if you take this dissertation on, you should try very hard to locate this panograph, if that's what it is. You have been following Rita McDermott's new digs in the area and you know what exciting new stuff is turning up. Thanks to Ashton and others, we know a great deal about the last four hundred years; but you know, Catherine, I have spent most of my life exploring the deep culture of this aboriginal people, and the missing pieces over the last two thousand years may finally elude me. I have decided this is my last year of teaching, and yours, my last dissertation to direct.'' He paused for a moment, still looking up at the ceiling. He continued. ''The modern descendants of these Indians are under such pressures nowadays, with their court cases for land, social workers trying to better their lot, governments deciding where to cut trees, dam the rivers, mine the ore, and harvest the animals.'' He stopped, then looked straight at her and leaned forward again, rivetting his eyes on hers. ''But for so many of them, their deep past is sketchy, unknown, misunderstood.'' His eyes shone. ''So much of the original mythologies and tribal interconnections, their roots, Catherine, are dim or lost, and they badly need them back. The new wave of the natives' sense of themselves and where they are going recognizes that now, as it didn't fifty years ago. That is why your study is so timely. You can do your bit to assist them, you know.'' He looked away again into the dark corner of the ceiling. ''And it will help us, too. It is what we cultural anthropologists are still all about.'' He fell silent, contemplative, as if waiting for her to respond.

How often she had heard the story, in his classes, seminars, books and articles. His great dream was almost in place. He was respected, widely known, an aging man of lifelong devotion to his students and his conviction that in the northeastern tribes at the dawn of the Christian era there had existed an extensive civilization—he never used the words wandering tribes—an interconnected league of peoples who grew into a thriving culture across the wilderness, and that this league was starting to break apart before the Europeans arrived to finish it off. "We have to know more," he would say to his classes; "we have to learn to interpret, we must sense where pieces of old cohesive legends have fragmented into today's stories, we have to learn how to interpret the animal world as symbols, as they saw them, we have to dig, explore, interview, read, and we have to be imaginative," he would say, with a sweep of his hand across the front of the amphitheatre where two hundred eager faces seemed mesmerized by his words—"we have to relearn how to think mythically as they did. Our computers can store the information for us, but our task here is imaginative as well as scientific, to recapture the mind of a successful unmechanized life adapted to the land and to the seasons." The students, some recording him on unnoticed little black tape decks, loved it, and now she was to be in the vanguard, grabbing the banner, marching off to see if she could fill in a few more pieces of the great puzzle, the great code.

She glanced around the office. Still no word processor, she thought. The stuffed thing on top of the bookcase hadn't moved since her last visit. Hardly visible on top of the glass bookcase against the dim back wall, the specks of what she assumed were once white were dulled grey, and the protruding beak seemed much too far away from the feet stuck under its back end. The taxidermist must have had a problem, she thought, for where he put the webbed feet was impossible. Anybody could see at a glance it could never walk like that. Dust abounded everywhere in that corner of the spacious office. She remembered the eye from an earlier visit when she had shuddered at the image of the little piercing purple orb—or was it ruby? It reminded her of Poe and some ghoul-haunted weir. Professor French had once mentioned it, a gift from Ashton, he had said, but for all his respect for his former teacher and mentor she thought it odd that he didn't at least dust it off now and then, or throw it out. She darted a glance at its head; its red eye was watching her.

She turned to him. "I have assimilated everything I have done so far on the Ashwagane into the proposal, Doctor French, and I have tried to suggest what we need to find to pull the new information together. Do you like the proposal? Will it do to get the dissertation started? Do you have any suggestions?"

"We have read your proposal, Catherine, and it is fine as is. Professors Benson and Greer have assented, and here are their notes of suggestions and caveats." He handed her several sheets of paper. "My notes are there too. But the proposal as is can be filed with the Dean tomorrow with your consent. I have been out of touch recently with the Wendaban Band, but I am sure Mr. Gahbodnay is still their Chief, and I can make arrangements for your accommodation on the Reserve. We have a good track record up there, but with so much national publicity over their land claim they have become something of a hot spot. I know they are guarding themselves against invading snoops and do-gooders. But I don't see a problem. My last correspondence with the Chief was cordial and he hoped we would pursue this research, for it helps them build their case for their right to the land."

He took another sheet from his desk drawer. "I have saved the best to the last, Catherine." He smiled and handed her a letter. "I know you are considering another dissertation possibility under Professor Zukawitz, and you have to do what you feel is right for you and your career. You have been one of our best students in a long time, and your future is very bright. You must weigh things carefully." He paused and held his hands out as if asking for a blessing; the cuff links picked up a ray of reflected light from the desk lamp. He started to chuckle. "You understand, of course, that I would be the last one in this great institution to ever be accused of undue suasion or anything even remotely resembling such devious tactics as blackmail," and here he paused and laughed a little laugh. "But the truth is, Catherine, that for you, my last student, I used all the influence I had, against some pretty strong competition, to get you the Joseph L. Larson Scholarship in Anthropology, the most prestigious scholarship in our field in the country. You have it. That's the Dean's letter of acknowledgement. For the Ashwagane study. Nine thousand dollars will go a long way towards getting you up there and suitably ensconced for a year. And it is renewable for one second terminal year." He looked deep into her eyes again, smiling. "But we are worth it, aren't we!" She caught his emphasis on the "we."

ii

Zellie Rabinovitch was Catherine's closest friend. From such different backgrounds, the one Bronx Judaism, the other Boston Puritanism, they had been thrown together on the same day in the same place for the same reasons at Radcliffe, to prove to their respective parents and communities that they were properly entitled to be at the prestigious College and to take back home the right to due adulations and romances and even careers befitting the baccalaureates of such a famous institution. But graduate school? That was never part of the plan. Four years, even five (allow for a fling or two) were sufficient to win the credentials, to get cultured enough to get on with one's life. What was it that lured both Zellie and Catherine into further study at Harvard, requiring so much more money, time, and knowledge, all quite extraneous to their families' traditions? The Saltonstalls had been a force to contend with in New England history, but no one could remember a female with a PhD; that was a bit much for a Cambridge lady, a bit on the too ivory-towered side of a long line of social butterflies, too much blue in the bluestocking. The Rabinovitchs could not understand Zellie's announcement a week after the elegant graduating exercise that she had been invited by one of her teachers to apply to graduate school under her sponsorship, and she was going to do it. "In what?" Mr. Rabinovitch had asked. "Anthropology? And what is this, Zellie? Anthropologists in our family there have not been, and no one has missed them. What do you do with this anthropology business? How is it you use it? You will put your mother and me to shame, such a nice girl getting so much in her head." He could not find "Anthropologists" in the Bronx yellow pages. Very baffling.

The truth was that the girls were both very bright; too bright not to taste the adventure of further knowledge, too smart and energetic not to see past what was required of them into what they wanted to try and to succeed at.

So it was natural that Catherine wanted to have lunch with Zellie on her "dissertation day." She wasn't sure why she had all along seen this dissertation business as having to be pushed to a little crisis—the two teachers, so different, the two proposals, so at odds with each other, so contrasted in methodology and procedure, squared off on two ends of a late March day. French in the morning, Indians in Northeastern Canada; Zukawitz in the afternoon, computers in Cambridge. She guessed she wanted to confront them directly, to have a last chance before deciding to see and hear them together, as it were, obviously each trying to clarify the starting position and the amount of time, strength, cash, and patience required to finish. It was a ridiculous situation, she knew, almost a farce. But she had genuine interest in both projects, excellent relations with both teachers.

Zellie had managed much more sensibly. She got her dissertation out of an early paper for another professor; they had talked over its possibilities for expansion for the past year, and Zellie was now well into her research. Mr. Rabinovitch still did not understand what it was all about. "For $12,000 a year, something good must come of it, eh Zellie?" was all he could say, forgetting that for two years she had been on substantial scholarships. Mrs. Rabinovitch's problem was that to her friends she could only say that Zellie was still working away. She carefully avoided using the word "doctor" in explaining her daughter's prolonged absence at school in Boston for fear her friends would somehow think Zellie was mixed up in medicine, and since Mrs. Rabinovitch did not really know what Zellie was mixed up in, she preferred to say that she was still "just working away at it." This was troublesome because her friends' daughters had graduated three years ago and were now properly pregnant. Was Zellie having difficulties? they asked.

Zellie was sitting at their usual table in the cafeteria, alone, with a book propped up in one hand and a straw

stretching from a coke can to her thick flaming red lips.
She looked up. "How'd it go?" she said. "You look
okay. Will he accept the proposal?"

"No revisions required," said Catherine, "and a
bonus to boot. The old man wants me to go north, that's
for sure!"

"A bonus?" said Zellie. "C'mon, Cathy, tell me, tell
me. He's arranged a young handsome Indian Chief to be
your bonded slave!"

"Nine thousand dollars called the Joseph Larson
Scholarship," said Catherine; "it's mine if I do the
Ashwagane study. What do you think?"

"What?" yelled Zellie. "Faaaaaantastic! So you *did*
get it! Oh Cathy!" and she jumped up and threw her arms
around her and hugged her close. "I'm so excited. Can we
tell everybody?"

"Not yet," said Catherine, adjusting her dress. "I
have to give him my assent, and I am not going to do that
until I have seen Madeleine this afternoon and seriously
weighed the issues."

Zellie sat down, frowning. "How dumb have you got
to be to turn down nine grand for a year of mounties, pow
wows, adventure, handsome Indians and voodoo magic!"
she said. "And you think you might want instead to sit
here in riot village and pound computers for a year? Come
on, Cathy! I've been for the Canadian project all along.
And now the most prestigious scholarship in our
department, and you're not packing your bags? Wow! You
sure you're feeling okay, Cathy? I'm available as a
research assistant, you know. I'd phone Zukawitz right
now and tell her you've contracted computer's disease,
and all your fingers have turned orange and twisted. The
scholarship alone is worth a job." Zellie was usually
excited, and although she could write the clearest, most

professional prose of anyone Catherine knew, in conversation she was always just Zellie, from "NeYauk." Catherine cherished her humor and vigor. Zellie continued: "Wanted: will do research on northern Indians. Employer must provide northern lights, handsome mounties, curried beaver stew, dry tents, the complete Boston Pops on compact disk, and free condoms. Employer to provide immunity from mosquitoes and four legged wolves. Apply: Zellie Rabinovitch, 1385 Adams Street, Apt. 103, Cambridge, Massachusetts." "I would probably answer your ad, Zellie," Catherine laughed, "but I'm not sure about those guarantees. Anyway, I have to see Madeleine first. You have to admit, hers is a much more manageable project. And I have Dawson for the cold nights. Mounties I do not need."

Zellie screwed up her nose into wrinkles. "I'll predict what she'll say. She'll tell you that French is an old ass and his project a stinking job up in the boonies where you'll spend a year swatting flies for every tidbit of information you'll find. And she'll pull the cutting edge shit on you. Her variety of social anthro is where the action is, baby, and the jobs. And if she's really uptight, she'll get off onto her new chauvinism kick; we, Cathy, we cool chicks have the future à la main. Generalissimo Catherine M. Saltonstall, PhD, the new woman, the new leader of the troops, engaged in the new battle to push men off their towers. Yuk!" "I wish you were interviewing her," said Catherine; "it would be hilarious." "I'd plant a *Playgirl* in her bookcase and then discover it during the interview," said Zellie. "'Why Professor Zukawitz, I do believe this journal is misfiled with articles on computer modelling.'" Catherine laughed. "Phone me tonight and tell me all about it," said Zellie.

The office of Madeleine Zukawitz was across Brattle Street in Harvard's newest building, a bright creamy affair with large square sealed windows. Funny, she thought, as she climbed the steps to the glass front doors, how her anthropology teachers were so scattered in different buildings across the campus, French in the oldest, in the old yard, Madeleine in the newest along with psychologists, sociologists, two historians and an economist. It would save a lot of student shoeleather if the school could get them grouped together.

Madeleine Zukawitz had been one of Cornell's most brilliant graduates, and after a stint at Michigan State, where she published a quickly-acclaimed text on computer modelling for ethnic communities, Harvard had decided that this was where the future was going to be defined in Anthropology, and lured her east, four years ago. Catherine's two classes with her had opened up the precise, neat methods of computer modelling. Madeleine had put her onto the Irish in Boston for one project because the data bank of information was so extensive, but Catherine had managed to coax the computer into some questions which hadn't been asked in the same way before, and produced a profile of the Irish in Boston, 1945-1955, that convinced Madeleine that here was someone to keep her eye on.

There was an elevator, but she decided to use the stairs. Madeleine was only one floor up. "It's so good to see you, Catherine," she said at the door; "please come in. I've been expecting you." As she sat across the desk from Madeleine, she couldn't help noticing the contrast with Dr. French's quarters. The walls here were of light cream, the room bright, the curtains partially pulled back admitting the smoggy sunlight of a fresh spring Cambridge day. In the corner were a word processor and computer, and beside them on a little table a fax machine. Nothing stuffed. Madeleine was very high tech. Whereas French wrote letters by hand, or dictated them to the pool secretary for mailing, Madeleine Zukawitz zapped material from processor to printer to fax and could have a reply within the hour. French swam in the mythic voids of legends, myths and artifacts; Madeleine punched in figures and key word types based on statistics, measurable performance and polls. What statistics to look for, where to find them, how to get them out if they were locked inside people, or needed to be compiled, this was her methodology. Then came storage, electricity, regrouping and assembling, megabytes and nine-millisecond disks. Finally, came interpretation and publication. The process could always produce.

"We had a meeting just last week on your dissertation proposal, Catherine," she said, looking up from the file on her desk. "It's going to work out quite well, we think. Professor Tillson raised some queries which we think need addressing, and I've written notes on them for you. But it's nothing serious. It will take you two, maybe three days to research them and work up a revised proposal. The committee said that if I were satisfied that their concerns had been addressed, we wouldn't need to meet again and your revised proposal could go directly to the Dean's office to be registered." She handed Catherine a few pages. "You're practically ready to begin," she said, looking at Catherine intensely, with a smile. "Your study of the Italians in Melwyn Heights in the 30's and 40's leading up to and into the war, is a sure bet for publication, maybe by our own press. I will certainly push it for you. The data is just waiting for someone of your abilities."

Madeleine Zukawitz then got up and came around to Catherine's side of the desk. She pulled over a chair and sat down close beside her. Catherine was a little taken aback. The perfume was now pungent. She could feel the warmth of her skin as Madeleine placed her arms and folded hands on the desk. "Cathy, I've given considerable thought to what I am about to say." She turned from looking at her hands and looked at Catherine directly. "We must be frank with one another. You have had two classes with me, and I feel we know each other well. I want to talk with you as a friend, not your teacher. You have an important choice to make. It's not just a matter of which dissertation may be easiest to do, or which might be the more rewarding. There are deeper issues at stake."

She rose, and went to the window, pushed the curtains even farther apart to let in more sullied yellow sunlight. "I've had a tough fight here," Madeleine continued, looking out across the street. Then she whirled and faced Catherine. "The point is that we're women. We are career professionals in a male-dominated profession and institution. Wherever you teach it will likely be the same. You must think of your future. Professor French is one of the grand old men of Harvard, loved by the undergraduates, generally respected in his field. The Dean likes to think that French lends national visibility, as he calls it, to our sagging reputation in the last few years. I lost my recent battle with him, because I dearly wanted the Larson Scholarship for your study with me, and he got it. He has had his way here for years. But Catherine, you must understand that his is a dying world. Women like Weston gave the field some early shining lights, but his kind of cultural anthro is a man's world. The aboriginal past has always belonged to the men; cultural heritage is a guarded world where male chauvinism researches and protects the very thing that gives it strength. But it has had its day, not just because of the male problem, but the new anthropology, the cutting edge of our profession today, has moved into social research. The computer has given us the tool that the old culturalists did not have, and as we work with new models of communal behavior, it's like exploring space. The sky's the limit. Your Italian dissertation will show how true that is, and will be a model for a long time. Job opportunities in the new social anthropology for a smart girl like you, Cathy, are going to be plentiful in an increasingly tight market. I'm not sure that would be as true for a student of French's. You have to weigh these considerations very carefully, with your head, not your heart.''

She came over and sat down by Catherine again. This time she reached over and put her hand on Catherine's arm which was resting in her lap. Madeleine drew very close. ''Cathy, this is a bit hard for me to say, it sounds so uncouth. But we must be realistic. French is big stuff here, but he has his detractors, you know that. You were at the New York convention two years ago and heard the paper denigrating his whole thesis. I have a good friend at Chicago who tells me that this northern league stuff two thousand years ago is pure poppycock. It would be nice if it were true, but the farther back you push it, the more it just dissolves into speculation. It's been so hard to get evidence, Cathy, because there is no evidence. My friend is convinced that the northeastern aboriginals were just a foot shy of being cave men, the most basic type of scavenging existence based on hunting only—no farming, little mythology, no art, no music, no sophisticated costuming, no masks, no interconnected languages or trade. He says that compared with some of the southern civilizations, in Mexico and parts of Asia, for example, the northern aboriginals were barbarians with a culture, if it can be called that, not worthy of the word civilization. They got their biggest boost when they encountered the Europeans. The thesis of a deep northern aboriginal culture two thousand to three thousand years ago is simply dead duck.''

She took her hand away from Catherine's arm and walked to the other side of the desk. "If you embark on the French dissertation," she continued, "you become embroiled in a thankless controversy, which little you can accomplish will settle. You will spend a year or two of your young life up there in probably pretty sordid conditions, for meagre results. Ashton got as much as he could fifty years ago; what's to say that your sifting through his coals will yield much more? And suppose you do get a dissertation out of it—if it's less than something pretty impressive, your pick of jobs will be jeopardized. I hate to see your brilliance thrown away. A dissertation for French will do more to enhance his reputation than it will to announce the arrival of Catherine Saltonstall. You will always be his student, the second-class girl. An even less brilliant dissertation for me will make you your own woman in a new field. I have found a few thousand dollars in our faculty research funds which I can redirect your way. The whole thing can be done here in Cambridge, with just a few side trips. With hard work, you can wrap it up in nine months. Think it over very, very carefully.''

Chapter III
SALTONSTALL

She crossed Brattle Street, went up the little curved
street around the Theological School's houses onto
Chauncy, passed the Longfellow House, and turned up
Winthrop towards 33 Harrington Lane. She couldn't get
Madeleine's intense grey-green eyes out of her mind.
What was happening, what was going on here? Her day,
anticipated as a kind of high point in her life as a graduate
student, when she would sit down with two of her favorite
and admired teachers in America's oldest school to
discuss intelligently the merits of her two proposals, had
not gone well. The stuffed thing's pallid red eye had
thrown something weird over the sweet old man's charm,
and his putting her in the position of crusader, of "doing
something for them" gave the Ashwagane study a twist
she didn't relish. She was no crusader.

And Madeleine! Why was she so uptight lately? Was
her dissertation the latest pawn in the rivalry between the
new social and the old cultural anthropologists? Was she
the middle of the rope in a departmental tug of war? She
glanced up the street. The sun was still high, but far
enough down the rim so that long shadows from the elms
threw soft, dull patterns on the houses, and a few were
completely in shadow. One more block and she would be
home, and there would be questions and opinions and
maybe nastiness if they thought she would go off to the
north, for there had already been discussions and mother's
views were clear.

Thirty-three Harrington Lane was not an outstanding
old home only because those around it were equally
impressive. They were all originals. If old New England's
upper-class architecture were one's hobby, Harrington

Lane, Cambridge, would be a welcome find. Three storeys, gables, white wood clapboard with grey trim, four bedrooms, three fireplaces and a recent solarium adjoining the library, the Saltonstall residence was vintage New England stability. The property had been in the family for generations, dating back to Judge Thrumpington Saltonstall who came out from England forty years after the *Arbella* landed in Boston harbor in 1630. He moved the family to Cambridge upon retirement, and Saltonstalls had lived on the property ever since. The core of the present house was early nineteenth century, for the house before it, the second one of colonial wood, could not make it through the end of the eighteenth century and had to be torn down and replaced by John Saltonstall's great-grandfather. A half acre in the back yard, now sprouting apple trees, was all that remained of the original estate.

It was all Catherine had ever known of home. Aside from her years of prep school in Connecticut, and once a summer visit to cousins in New Jersey, her life had been here. Of course, she had had frequent shopping trips to New York with her mother, but they had always returned less with the goods that they thought they were going to get than with the feeling that it was good to get home and that Boston had just as much to offer. Catherine early realized that these Manhattan jaunts were not of necessity but part of a game, the expected and proper little sorties that Cambridge ladies were required to do so that they could keep New York in its proper perspective, that of an elegant Vanity Fair which one just must swirl through from time to time in order to keep things in their larger, proper perspective. She had loved the Cape, the open spaces and miles of sand and sea, the walk along the beach with the chilly ocean nibbling her toes as the sun was coming up. Unlike so many of her acquaintances, her parents did not have a summer place on the Cape, or on the Islands, so her visits there were confined to invitations. But if she loved the sea and sand, she had always worried a little over the night life on the Cape, and once she had a bad experience with a blind date who tried to seduce her. From then on, the Cape for her was a world of radiant daylight and brilliant blue; soft nights didn't exist. She still had a little piece of Cape Cod seaweed in a bottle on her dresser alongside a companion bottle of what was now very brackish-looking water which she had taken from Walden Pond. These were the extent of her environmental menagerie.

Never for a moment had she had a pang that she might be too secluded or provincial a Cambridge lady. Ralph had said that travelling was a fool's paradise and for all she knew he could be right. The libraries, her acquaintances, the timeless world of her reading, her journal, Dawson—her world was rich and cosmopolitan enough for her, and her ongoing engagement with the world's cultures and the so various ways peoples cohered and created societies and behaved with one another filled her days and kept her mind fresh and adventuresome. Cambridge was her outpost in the Republic of life.

Zellie had been to Israel once, Germany once, and Barbados—was it three times, with her parents?—and once, last winter, when she was in the doldrums of preparing for her qualifying exams, she suddenly did what she had always threatened to do, and got on the plane early Friday morning with a girlfriend (Catherine had declined) and left Logan Airport at 1:35 a.m. (American Airlines Red-Eye Special), arrived in Los Angeles before the sun was up, and was back in Professor Greer's seminar at 2:30 p.m. Monday, looking very mischievous. Zellie's accounts of her travels were sparse on geography and architecture and culture and rich in her love affairs. She didn't exactly chide Catherine about being a stick-at-home, but a few times she had tried to pry out of Catherine if life with Dawson were all that exciting, because she hardly ever mentioned him. Catherine had learned to sidestep the issue, and Zellie respected her enough to pry only occasionally.

As she entered the house, she smelled the cabbage. Corned beef and cabbage, she thought, her father's favorite. For years they had had a housekeeper ("Never refer to Rose as a maid," her father once said to her; "she's like a member of the family and is due our full respect"), but Rose was getting on and came now from her brother's house in Dedham only three times a week to clean. Tonight Lydia was cook, one of her life's passions, and Catherine relished the upcoming meal served in the dining room on the large mahogany table with napkins and silverware the way it always was. (Her mother had been christened Lydian, but had been Lydia for as long as Catherine could remember.)

As she was going upstairs to her room, Lydia called out, "Is that you, dear?" Catherine paused on the stairs. "How did it go? I've been thinking of you all day." Lydia came out into the hall and looked up at her daughter. "You poor thing," she said, "you look terrible. Wash up and have a bit of a rest if you like, and then you can tell your father and me all about it at dinner. About half an hour, darling." She disappeared back into the kitchen.

Catherine put her briefcase on the floor beside her desk and lay down. The poster on the ceiling directly over her seemed even more banal than usual tonight, a line drawing of a busty Marilyn Monroe with accented red lips and incredulous smile and "FLOSS DAILY" across the

bottom. Lydia got it on one of her dental trips and
Catherine supposed her father had taped it to the ceiling,
but no one had ever mentioned it. Her mother did,
however, continually remind her of the merits of flossing.

She wished the half hour would never end. She was
confused, tired, not ready for further discussion. Perhaps
Zellie could come over and play decoy. She had a touch
of headache, but dinner would surely fix that. She had for
years practiced the arts of "fudge" (as Zellie called it)
with her parents; little subterfuges, dodges, changing the
conversation, throwing up the old smokescreens to those
who said they loved her so much: "Oh now, daddy, don't
get your old banker's brain so fussed about it, it's just a
trifle;" or "Mother, you mean to tell me that Mary thinks
I'm off the track? Well you just tell her that she has as
much faith in me as an old hedgehog. Trust me, I know
what I'm doing;" or on occasion, the old standby: "Now
daddy! You don't want to open that old can of worms, do
you?" She had had to protect herself. As the crack
widened between their expectations for her, and her own
desires, she needed space. She didn't want to hurt them,
but she couldn't travel on their road; she had to plod on
on her own.

"I don't understand you," her mother would say,
more and more often now. "You have had a good
education, which your father and I have given you. You
have a wonderful future husband in Dawson, a fine,
caring, upstanding young man with solid business
connections. You won't want for anything. But you persist
in pushing on with this education business past all
reasonable limits. How long is Dawson to wait? You keep
putting him off and it's not fair, to him, or to us, or to our
grandchildren. You know how I'd love a granddaughter,
Cathy, and you know how tempus fugits. The world is

simply not going to sit still while you grow older trying to
tax your little brain to the limit. It's not like a Saltonstall
woman to cram in all this education at the expense of
everybody else. It's just gone too far, dear, and now you
tell us you have to put in another year or two of hard
work. Where's it going to lead, Cathy? Lay it aside,
darling, let it rest awhile. Marry Dawson and we'll have
such fun planning the wedding. Your father and I can help
you get a good house close by. You so love the
Cambridge setting. Oh Cathy, Cathy,'' and she would
reach out and pull her head against her and stroke her
auburn hair.

Lydia had never thought much of Catherine's shy
attempts at keeping a boyfriend. She had been pleasant
enough with them in a matronly way, but none was good
enough, or pure enough, for her only daughter. Discussion
of sex was not on the list of Saltonstall discussables, but
on a few rare occasions her mother had landed on the
subject tangentially. The word vagina was not in her
vocabulary; it was, rather, ''down there,'' and lovemaking, whatever that was, was ''naughty'' or ''dirty.''
Young men had one goal in view, and that was to
deflower the virgins, and Catherine had been guarded for
as long as possible from these defoliators by the usual
regimentations of early curfew, father's driving them and
picking them up, no drive-ins, no drinking, no nail polish,
or perfume, or mascara, and very little lipstick. The boy of
her second infatuation had said she was so beautiful
because she didn't wear makeup and he wanted sex only
with a ''natural girl.'' She didn't tell Lydia of that one.

Dawson Penhurst III had been on the scene for a long
time—prep school friend and casual date, friend of the
family. The two sets of parents saw one another socially
and while there had been nothing so improper as

discussion of an arrangement, the two families didn't miss an opportunity for Dawson and Catherine to get together in the hope that two rocks of old New England stability might become cemented together. Now it had grown to a love affair, and Lydia had finally decided that her only child, at twenty-five, was ready to leave the nest as long as she established a very similar nest close by.

She heard the grandfather clock in the livingroom chime six times, one of her favorite sounds, a soothing steadfast sound of repose touched with challenge. Zellie would have run away from this home, she thought, but she still liked it in spite of the growing tensions. "You're twenty-FIVE!" Zellie had said to her recently. "Way overdue. You have to get out of there, Cathy. Come live with me." Catherine wasn't interested in discussing it further; there were no 150-year-old grandfather clocks in Zellie's apartment.

"Darling, we're ready in a few minutes," her mother called up. "Yoo hoo! Cathy, are you awake? Dinner!" The last word was sung out in the rich soprano that still caused Lydia's friends to ask her to sing at their parties.

Catherine splashed some water over her face in the peach bathroom adjoining her bedroom, smoothed her hair, looked in the mirror. She thought she looked fine, but at the last moment she changed into an old pair of jeans and her favorite short-sleeved light red shirt. If there were going to be discussions, she was going to look relaxed and feel comfortable.

Lydia had excelled herself tonight. The settings were perfect, with delicate pink napkins and sparkling silverware, recently polished. The two mustards were in their little silver bowls with the fluted rims and dark blue glass linings, home prepared hot for John, creamy, garish yellow for Lydia. Catherine thought tonight she would try a little of the hot. There was a glass plate of slivered carrot sticks, green pimento olives, and finely-cut celery. Lydia had prepared the plates in the kitchen, the pale pink slices of brisket, the cabbage chunks steaming just the way John liked them, and tender small new potatoes in their speckled spice-colored skins, four on his plate, three on theirs, the large Limoges china plates solid ivory in color with one curved stem of grain for a pattern, barley or oats Catherine thought, but she had never been sure. John laid the napkin over his upper leg without unfolding it, glanced at them with a gentle smile, and said, "Shall we?" She looked down but didn't close her eyes. "For what we are about to receive, the Lord make us truly thankful. Amen." John's grace never changed by a word; no new inflections ever entered, none departed. The angle of his head, the drone of the voice—the ritual was as old as she could remember, as reliable as the chimes from the livingroom clock. Lydia never forgot to wind the clock; John never forgot to say his grace. He was an elder at First Congregational, where several Saltonstall names appeared on dingy plaques, one of them a minister during the American Revolution. He wore his religion lightly, but was pleased when they asked his advice on church matters, and a few times he had even discussed these matters with his family at the dinner table. He was honored to play his little part in the ongoing work of the Lord. The church was a local business to be run as efficiently as possible, and his talents in finance were not kept under a bushel, but neither were they aggressively paraded for power or display. He was content to leave matters of divine grace and salvation to those who knew more about them than he did, "Probably," he would say, "to be decided on the last day." Who would decide and on what basis were left obscure. His one maxim on these matters was: "I had nothing to do with where I came from and I shall have nothing to do with when, or how, I shall leave, or where I shall go." That said it all for John Pendleton Saltonstall. She could hear the earlier Puritan Saltonstalls turning over in their graves and shaking their fingers at him: "Ichabod! Ichabod!"

Normally Catherine was pleasantly sedate at the dinner hour. She could count on John's cautious ramblings about the ongoing mess in the Massachusetts Assembly (though, as far as she knew, he continued to vote Democrat), the ups and downs of stocks and mergers, international trade, the damnable demands of the unions who were bringing the country to its knees. Lydia knew when to be silent and attentive, and when to take up the torch of pleasantness with the latest on the Children's Relief Society and the deteriorating state of parking in Boston. Catherine took it all in pleasantly, but went out of her way to keep her academic affairs anecdotal and light, the excitement of her mind veneered by cheery quips about this and that, her deeper concerns buried. As Zellie would say, why rock the boat?

Tonight, however, she took the offensive. "I had some good news today, daddy," she said, looking at John. Then she turned to Lydia. "Professor French told me I have been awarded the Lawson Scholarship which can become effective immediately. It pays nine thousand dollars for research, and is renewable for a terminal second year." "Why Cathy, that's excellent," said John. He came over and gave her a peck on the side of the forehead, and returned to his chair. "I was just reading somewhere recently that this year Harvard exceeded all previous records for scholarship donations. It's a great tribute to them." John had done his business degree at Yale and still obliged them with a cheque now and then when pressed, but his association with the school was perfunctory, to keep its name and a few contacts handy for business use. "I'm so proud of you, darling," said Lydia. "How will you use the money?" "Well, there's the hitch," said Catherine. "It's mine if I do the Ashwagane study under Dr. French."

She could feel the chill. She pushed on. "Professor Zukawitz has also offered me some research funds. I can't go wrong, can I! They both liked my proposals, although for Professor Zukawitz I have some minor changes to make. But nothing serious." She tried to smile her usual casual way. "Have you decided yet, dear?" said Lydia with icy sweetness. "Well, it's just come to a head today, and I want to sleep on it," said Catherine. "I wanted to get their reactions to my proposals first. I was hoping one would look better than the other to them, which would make it easier to decide, but that didn't quite happen." She flashed a smile at John. "Maybe I should do them both, and pan one of them off for a second degree in human relations." She tried to laugh. "Have you talked with Dawson?" said Lydia. "Will you see him tonight?" "No," she said, "Dawson and I have a date for tomorrow evening. I suppose we'll get into it then. I just wanted to relax and think tonight. It's been quite a day." She was feeling beleaguered, like a little town on a plain, surrounded by an army.

There was a long silence, broken only by Lydia's slight sound as she sipped her glass of water. Catherine felt the old tiny twitches of her stomach muscles. She kept the antacid tablets in her desk drawer. She would have gas tonight. Lydia's face grew serious, her voice a bit louder. "Well, I suppose there's no use going over it again, darling," she said. "Your father and I simply cannot understand why you would want to go up among those

Indians. You'll miss Cambridge so much—our shopping sprees you enjoy so much. Dawson will find it very difficult without you after you have hung onto him for so long. I wouldn't blame him if he looked on this as your not caring for him anymore. Maybe he will find someone else. And we just don't know what effects this will have on you, dear. I mean, there's a lot of drinking up there. They don't have good work habits like we do and they sit around a lot on dole as I understand it. It's not a wholesome environment for a young girl still in the formative years of her life. God knows there could be smallpox and lice and all kinds of terrible diseases you hear about, and no sanitary conditions or nurses or doctors for miles. You know Mary's nephew's experience with dysentery in Mexico last summer. He was four months getting over that." She paused and looked at John. Then back to Catherine. "And what about us, Catherine? You know how much we love you and want the best for you, but you seem to be turning your back on everything your father and I have taught you since you were a little girl. Think of us sitting here night after night worrying about you. You have no friends there; you'll have to live with them, I suppose. We'll fret and. . ." Lydia grimaced and looked away. She uttered a sob. "They don't think anything of ruining young innocent white girls, Cathy." Her breath was coming in short gasps. "Deep down I'm sure they hate us and the thought of you. . ." Her face was reddening, and she began to sob openly. Her chest heaved. She cradled her forehead into her hand with her elbow on the table. "I'm sorry," she whimpered, "but I can't. . . I just can't. . ." and she broke into uncontrollable sobbing. John came round to her and put his arm around her heaving shoulders, and stroked the greying hair. "There now, my dear, there now," he said, "Cathy doesn't mean to hurt you and she'll make the right decision." He looked at her with a bewildered expression. Her stomach muscles had gone into a steady rhythmic twitch. She pushed back her chair and went upstairs.

She was going to call Zellie but threw herself on the bed. Her headache was still there but no worse. She took deep breaths. "Turn down the knobs, Cathy," she said to herself, "turn them down, down, away down. Listen to your ears. Down. Down." She got up and went over to the desk and sat down. She reached down into the lowest drawer on the right and took out the brown leather-covered book, lightly lined. She had looked many places but had found only one store, in Boston, that carried anything like Ralph's old cracked ones she had once held in her hands at the Houghton Library. She gazed at the cover for a moment. "Vol VII" it said in faded ball-point purple, in large caps. "Five years, seven volumes already," she thought. She stared for a moment at the calendar on the wall over her desk. It was from the stationery store, and this month's picture was of a little yellowish-cream chick breaking out of a white cracked egg. She looked at it blankly for a moment, and began to write.

Tuesday, March 29.

As long as I work in my own backyard, things go well. I sow and tend my plants as it beseems me they require, and they grow. But when I look over the wall into my friend's backyard, I see that her plants droop and struggle. I am chagrined. I tell her how I tend my plants, hoping she may pick up a point or two. But I would not make my way prevail. She must raise her plants as it

befits her so to do, and if they insist on drooping, I have
done my part. Perhaps her soil is less fertile. Perhaps the
rains that visit me stop at her wall. Perhaps her seeds have
suffered. Perhaps the rock beneath her soil puts up a
barrier to deep roots. I will take her in and share my
plants. But I am not able, in spite of all I do and all I
know, to make her plants prevail. They become her plants,
not mine, I say. How do they belong to us both?

She wonders why her plants are sickly. She becomes
jealous of my plants, uneasy that try though she will, hers
do not respond. My ways do not work on her side. I do
not know why, and wonder who has placed the wall. I say
to her that we should take down the wall. She replies that
good fences make good neighbors. The poet says we
should like to know what we were walling in, or walling
out. But I know that roots and vines can smash a wall.

In the successful cultures I know of, fertility, of plant,
mind and body, is the icon of life. To produce new life
and allow it to grow as beseems it, is all we have to do. I
have reached a wall. I must seek to go around or through
that wall, to grow further in my own way and put down
yet deeper roots. Love is freedom to grow and bring on
new birth. She resents my growing. She cannot grow with
me. She has arrived at the rock. I smile. I will not defy,
will not hurt or condemn. But I shall tend my growth as
my own pattern and needs require. I shall pray for rain
and reach higher than the wall, lower than the rock. To
stop growing is to die.

Chapter IV
PENHURST

i

Dawson Reginald Penhurst III was a very nice young man. All the major events and directions in his life, mostly planned, some happenstance, had conspired to produce a very very nice young man, at twenty-nine, one of "la crême de la crême of our Cambridge bachelors," Lydia had once put it. Catherine didn't know many of the other bachelors, so she couldn't form a judgment, but she allowed that her mother might have a point.

The original of this patrician line of American Penhursts, Dawson's grandfather several greats back, had come to America in uniform, a Colonel in his Majesty's Royal Fusiliers, to help Burgoyne put down the American Revolution. He was strictly a military man and did what he was told, but secretly he tended to side with Burke's notion that the colonies had had a bit of a bad deal and that King George and his ministers were probably biting off more than they could chew before exploring other possibilities. He led his troops commendably through the campaigns of Ticonderoga and Saratoga in New York, but had discovered in the siege of Boston that the New Englanders were as hardy a stock as the old Englanders, especially one Priscilla Secord, who was the daughter of the keeper of the Old Stone Mill Inn on the Pike from Manhattan. Plotting their demise by day, Colonel Harrington Penhurst wooed soft lips by night. He returned to England a chastened soldier, and decided that a future with his demented Dutch Majesty's Fusiliers was less appealing than the awakened desires of the American Dream, where a very pretty face and a few hundred acres would probably see him through. Father was at first recalcitrant, but Harrington eventually wore him down, and in 1787 he returned to America with some of his leveraged inheritance in the form of solid British pound notes, won the amazed Priscilla away from her Yankee betrothed, and settled down on two hundred acres of rolling farmland at Quincy, not far from the Adams, with whom he was soon on tolerable terms for a retired British Colonel. The Quincy acreage grew more valuable as the years rolled on, and in spite of voracious spending appetites, the subsequent Penhursts knew where their bread was buttered, sold off very little, and watched the American Dream grow from orchards into their own office buildings and elegant homes.

Dawson's father had not needed an MBA from Harvard to rise quickly in one of Boston's oldest firms of chartered accountants where his father had been a partner, a firm chartered, he sometimes thought, in the original one by King James. There were now so many partners in it that it took a half page in the yellow pages to list them all. Normally the switchboard operator's abbreviated response was: "Clive, Lowell, Penhurst—may I help you?" but recently the "may I help you?" had been dropped to save time. His Amherst degree in economics had been quite sufficient, and his stories of fraternity antics and visitations both coming and going from Holyoke and Smith Colleges for women so inspired the young Dawson that there was little persuasion needed to convince the latest Penhurst clone that he should follow in his father's footsteps. Unlike his friend John Saltonstall, Dawson Penhurst II was an ardent alumnus and football devotee, and the family's yearly return on Alumni Weekend to the little town with the orange and red flaming leaves was a

treasured event, eagerly anticipated each fall by young
Dawson III.

There had been a few dates with Catherine in his first
Amherst year when she was still a junior at the Arabella
Coddlington School for Girls in Connecticut. She could
remember travelling the Pike on the green and white bus
for two hours, and Dawson meeting her with his red
Mustang. There were kisses and dancing and football
games and once a hockey game at Orr Rink with raccoon
coats. Then she was at Radcliffe and Dawson was a
junior. He was drinking more now, but still
conservatively, and she could remember his remarks to his
friends, when they pressed him to take one more of
whatever it was, that went something like: "You fellows
just load it on, I'm saving myself for more important
things," and he would wink at her. He managed to stretch
a bottle of Genesee to incredible lengths, and she couldn't
remember him much more than tipsy once or twice. He
was well liked by his friends. He loved fun but guarded
his caution. He didn't expend himself, he didn't
overindulge in pride, highway speed, or prejudice. He
didn't belittle, swagger, swear, or denounce. And he was a
fine dancer. His father prided himself on his big band
collection which occupied three rows of shelves in the
oak-panelled library—Jimmy and Tommy Dorsey, Glenn
Miller, Sammy Kaye, Duke Ellington, Guy Lombardo—and
without lessons or fanfare, Dawson III mastered the
foxtrot and waltz when rock was taking young America by
storm. He prided himself on gracefully leading Catherine
in and out on the danceroom floor, and on occasion he
could pick her off her feet and swirl her round and round
until she was dizzy. She began to acquiesce in his notion
that rock was really a conspiracy financed by the

deodorant industry. What was remarkable was that when occasion demanded, he could rock with the best of them.

It was in his final year that the dating turned serious. He said he was in love and she thought that he was right and wondered if she were too. She said she thought she might be, but he was older and knew more, and give her another year or two and she would know more too. So they pledged their little troth, that they wouldn't date others and that they would probably marry in a few years, and that they would give their love first place in all they did, and that they would hold fast to each other because so much of what they both liked was so sensible and healthy and solid and so much of the rest of the world seemed so messy.

That fourth year had been her annis mirabilis. Love was blossoming, Amherst was winning on the football field, Professor Jane Robinson was opening up the world of New England literature for her at Radcliffe, and Dawson was growing impetuous. She had to come up every weekend, he insisted, and when she said she really should stay and study, he would turn up in Cambridge in the red Mustang, and once, simply swooped her up and took her back to Amherst. She enjoyed the frat parties and was now known as Dawson's girl. She was a bit shy, but only enough to suggest a certain reserve by deliberate choice, not a temperamental deficiency, as if the last word wasn't in yet. In matters of drink, food and clothes, she was glad they agreed on moderation, and they fell into a predictable routine. In matters of sex she was demure but never cold, in discussions of family, politics, war and peace, she was reserved, tentative, more questioning than convinced, never cynical. If she and Dawson had their preferences they wore them lightly; deep prejudices they came to realize weren't worth the effort of defending, if even to hold, for the time being at least. They made friends wherever they went.

One weekend was very special, her grand awakening she would later call it. Dawson phoned her to suggest that instead of her taking the usual 4:30 bus, they'd both skip their Friday afternoon classes and he'd meet her off the 1:30 bus. He had never showed her the Emily Dickinson house, and they could catch the mid-afternoon tour. Then he wanted to take her to a new seafood restaurant he'd discovered in Holyoke before the Psi Beta Chi party. He had made the usual arrangements for her to stay in the dorm the College set aside on weekends for visitors. She couldn't resist. She'd do it.

It was unusually warm for November. The sun was high and the leafless Hampshire hills looked ready for snow, but here and there the rock cliffs reflected the warm shafts of sunlight back at her through the bus window. There's a certain slant of light, she said to herself, and she was certain that was from Emily. She had read Dickinson before somewhere in school, but now in her course in New England writers she had become a rapt devotee of the Amherst poetess. She awoke to the rigorous freedom the mind could play in, the flashes of intuitive probes in Emerson, the strong reliance on the sufficiencies of one's own powers if alert and free, Emily's crisp condensed imagination.

They arrived at the house for the 3:00 o'clock tour, Dawson discreetly parking his flaming red vehicle a block farther down the street in the parking lot of the Congregational Church where the Dickinsons had once worshipped. She quickly warmed to the old house, its kindly austerity and dusty smell, Emily's bedroom, the old copper spigots with the five finger knobs, and pictures of ancient grim-faced divines who she was sure would have helped stir Emily's mischievous spirit. As the guide pointed to the white shroud which she wore daily in the later years of her reclusive life, Dawson squeezed her hand and whispered in her ear: "That must be a fake. If it was her real shroud, she'd be buried in it, wouldn't she?" But no one heard or guessed a hint of cynicism from them as they tried to look awesomely impressed. Catherine often recalled the uneasiness that crept over her that afternoon. She had come not to worship at a shrine, but to explore, not to idolize but to deepen her acquaintance and find out new facts, suggestions, possibilities. She wanted the sanctimonious guide to take the tourists away and leave her to poke, to handle, to open books and closet doors and feel the bedsheets and long crinoline dresses, and to get to know the house as a house. She whispered to Dawson: "They're not showing us her bras or underwear, are they!" He gave her a momentary grimace as if to say "Sssshhhhhh," and squeezed her hand tightly. Then he leaned over and whispered with a wicked grin: "Maybe she didn't wear any."

Outside, after the tour, she pulled Dawson away from the group and around to the side of the house, and gazed up at Emily's bedroom window. The sweet smells of hyacinths and honeysuckle were in the air and she could hear the voices of children at play. Suddenly she knew that the lady in white was there. She had for a moment left the windowsill. She waited, and then the white shroud appeared, shadowlike, and a white arm swept out over the sill and threw down to her a folded sheet with a flower petal attached with a little pin. She caught it and opened it and saw several lines in a tiny script, a fine-nibbed poem. But she couldn't read it. Whether it was her tears or the smallness of the script, she could not see to see. It had always been mixed up in her mind with several years later when, on a whim one day in graduate school, she asked her friend Jane who worked on the rare book library desk to let her into the Emily Dickinson Room, and after stretching her wits as to what to put down on the required research form she must fill in, something that had anything to do with anthropology (never mind the Ashwagane) and Emily Dickinson, she just scribbled "Working on editing problems of old manuscripts," and hoped no one would enquire into what problems and what old manuscripts. It worked, for Jane was soon unlocking the door of the blue room, with Emily's mahogany desk and bookcase and wick lamp, and she was soon poring over the little packets of poems neatly bundled up with blue ribbon, in such a tiny neat hand. She had learned from her class at Radcliffe that Emily was an editor's nightmare. She would write a few words in a line of her poem, then above the next word she would stack two or three alternative words, and maybe several below, as if she couldn't make up her mind. None of them was crossed out. Editors pulled out their hair wondering what Emily's final intentions were, or whether there were five different poems here. But she knew exactly what Emily was up to, that she wanted the simultaneous experience of multiple possibilities, that at a sudden juncture in the road there were many routes to take, that the world was forever asking for final intentions when sometimes only proximities would do. This multiple possibilities theory was only one theory about Emily, but Catherine knew it was the truth. She often felt the way Emily did. Dawson still had hold of her hand but as she gazed back up to the window the shroud was gone. She felt a chill, a constraint of breath that wasn't fear, nor joy, but that shock of recognition she had heard of, the profound conviction that something of Emily was inside her, and she inside Emily.

She certainly wouldn't be as reclusive, she knew, and for a girl who in only a few hours would be dancing the night away, she didn't see herself as preferring an imaginative love affair to the real thing. It was the mind. It was that untradeable irrevocable energy of the mind that was so awesome in the lady of the shroud and that she was awakening to in herself—the terrifying power of the imagination and intellect that no room or shroud or manuscript could bolt down, that could at times, she feared, drive her like a demon.

Dawson must have felt the shudder. He turned to her. "You're as white as a ghost, Cathy," he said. "Are you sure you're all right? We'd better go and sit in the car."

The seafood at Holyoke was as good as he had promised. They had early discovered a mutual addiction to the food of the sea, though her paradise served fresh Boston bluefish baked in a creamy wine sauce, whereas his had lobster served daily, great big red lobster in the shell. On a date once in Boston she had seen him emerge from his usual reserved shell when a two-pound very red and ferocious-looking lobster was placed in front of him. The way he looked at it started her fancy about Henry VIIIth and raw duck torn in the fingers and the bones hurled over the shoulder after a sufficient amount of fat and gruel were allowed to collect on the lower lip. Dawson's cracking the claws caused her discomfort for she was sure it sounded like gunshots echoing around the diningroom, and she noticed an unusually heavy amount of butter stain on his napkin that night. Tonight in Holyoke they both had his recommendation: fried oysters, and fresh Boston scrod in a tomato and light garlic sauce. He was right, as usual; they did know how to prepare fish here. Her day was practically complete.

But Dawson had a finale planned. They danced with the orange and green balloons popping one by one, till after midnight. His confreres at Psi Beta Chi indulged his love of big bands, and tonight there was plenty of Tommy Dorsey and Glenn Miller. Dawson was especially solicitous, drawing her close during the dreamy Miller, and he swayed through the whole of *Tuxedo Junction* with his lips pressed gently against her forehead and his left hand rubbing the back of her bra. She got the message.

They had had sex several times in this remarkable year, the first time in the red Mustang which they later agreed was not engineered for such activity. He had begun as he always did by nibbling the lobe of her left ear, like a puppy dog; then he was kissing all her face not just the lips, and then undoing the blouse buttons as he whispered in little gasps, "Do you want it, Cathy? Do you want it?" But as he was undoing her bra he blurted out, "This old car's upholstery is pretty dirty and I don't know whether our vital parts should touch it." Her growing rapture suddenly ceased. It was so like Dawson, she had often thought since, the rational guardian always waiting in the wings. It wasn't so much that the upholstery might be dirty, or how they could possibly keep their vital parts from touching it; it was the "vital parts." Where had that phrase come from, she thought, and what parts were so much more vital than others? She supposed he meant her vagina, but the way he had handled her he must have meant her breasts. She thought her rear end was also very vital. He had had his satisfaction that first night, and she faked that she had too, without saying anything. But she couldn't get past the upholstery and the vital parts.

But now in November, full of oysters, scrod, and the gentle swaying of Glenn Miller, she knew it would be better. As they drew away from the fraternity house, he reached over and tried to pull her over close. At first she mildly resisted. She had never liked to sit close to a boy driving. Dawson had always respected her for that. From early teens she had thought how silly the two looked, two heads showing through the window like siamese twins where only one should be and the rest of the seat so empty. She associated such displays with teeny boppers and beach boys, cigarettes and coke and little kisses at stoplights, and acne. It wasn't that she had anything against sex; she had decided early that it was here to stay in spite of Lydia's warnings. But not in cars, not show-off stuff which wasn't affection at all but a phony mating game that any decent girl with her head screwed on right would not call respectable. She had always wanted to be decorous, to see things as others would see them.

On this chilly November night, however, she let him have his way. "Cathy," he said, "we deserve better than this old car for our love. You are so beautiful tonight." She thought she was going to get a fine speech but he grew silent and gently rubbed her shoulder. She soon concluded that the night's passion had begun that morning, because that's when he engaged the motel along the lonely road to Leverett, one of the less travelled routes into the upstate rural towns. "This is a college area," he said as he produced the key; "they get hundreds of these room engagements all the time and never blink an eye." Somehow that seemed to lower it to the mundane, she thought. She wondered if he had registered just himself, or Dawson R. Penhurst and Catherine Saltonstall, or Mr. and Mrs. Dawson Penhurst III, or Dawson and Cathy Penhurst, or some fictitious names, but before she could fully savor the various possibilities and make her own choice, they were in the shower "washing off the Psi Beta Chi smell of burnt popcorn," he said. He stood behind her, foaming her breasts in bubbly soap, and he went after the old preferred left ear. The play of the warm suds and his arms around her melted the final drowsiness of the day into soft loveliness and she turned round and gave him a long kiss on the mouth, rubbing the back of his neck. He mushed his lips all over her ear, barely whispering the inevitable "Do you want it, Cathy? Do you want it?" as if there would never be a giving or a taking without permission first. Their satisfaction was mutual this night; she savored her relief and amazement at how ecstatic love's gift could be. As she drowsed off with his arm around her he whispered, "It was good tonight, wasn't it!" She didn't reply but touched her tongue to his left ear lobe. She thought she would dream of knights and shining armour and there would be one who stood out above all the rest: emblazoned on his banner was "Dawson Penhurst III, the nicest, kindest, sweetest man in all the world." She snuggled her vital parts down deeper into the clean sheets.

ii

Recently, their lives had settled into routine. During her three years at graduate school, Dawson was a constant presence, a reliable friend, supporter, lover. They enjoyed the seafood houses, the theatre, the Boston Pops (he bought them season's tickets). They tried opera. It didn't grow on them but they stuck with it. They sampled ballet, and returned for more. They both adored book stores and art galleries and by now they were sure they knew every nook of an artist's exposure within fifty miles of Boston. He took her to the Cape on weekends, to New York, and once she joined him for a week's business trip to London. They had sought out every seafood house from Bangor to

New Jersey and all the big dance halls. He was gradually winning her over to a little scotch with water, but she still preferred champagne in small glasses, or one caesar, rarely two. He had become a connoisseur of white wine, but she said she just liked it dry, and would leave brand and country and date and bouquet up to Dawson.

But she wouldn't leave to Dawson his mastery of her in football. They had been several times to Fenway Park, but he couldn't get as enthused about baseball as he was about football. It was his passion and he was always explaining it to her. She decided she preferred baseball, and in typical Catherine Saltonstall fashion she unobtrusively started to buy books on the Red Sox, yearbooks on both leagues, biographies of managers and players, histories of the game. She studied, she watched, she memorized. It came easily. He could not convince her that football was an intellectual game. "Whether it comes from the coach on the sidelines, or out of the quarterback's head, the play is not just a gamble," he would say to her; "it's a carefully calculated move chosen according to how the game is going, who's on the ball, what weakness has been detected in the other's defence." "Pooh!" she would reply. "There isn't a play down there that doesn't depend on how hard one Neanderthal can push the other Neanderthal. It's a muscle game. You can hear their grunts up in the stands. As long as they know the plays by rote they can leave their brains in the dressing room. In a perfect game of baseball, there's very little body contact. Even the slide into second base has the runner low and the second baseman high in the air, or just touching him with the end of his glove. There's the odd crash at home plate, but the perfectly executed out is just a kiss of the glove." Dawson looked incredulous.

Three months after she began her baseball studies, an occasion presented itself when she thought she would try her new wings. It had not been one of Boston's better seasons and in the top of the fourth inning it was already 5-1 for Oakland. The starting pitcher had retired to the showers and the reliever Jones, after a routine fly ball for the first out, was facing a tough Chessman who had worked the count to 3 and 2. Catherine leaned over to Dawson. "Even if he strikes him out, Calder will bring in the lefthander O'Toole," she said. Jones delivered: called strike 3. The crowd came alive. It was Dawson's turn. "Jones is doing just fine. He's got 2 out of 2." They were sitting along the first base line so they couldn't see the Boston dugout. She decided to push on. She leaned over once more. "Calder's just putting down the phone from calling in O'Toole from the bull pen. Watch!" Soon the manager came out and walked slowly to the mound, took the ball from Jones, and they chatted until the little cart dropped off the lefthander, O'Toole. While the new reliefer was taking his warmup pitches, Dawson turned to Catherine. "How did you guess that?" he said. She looked at him. She had him. "I didn't guess," she said. "It's logical." She put her lips close to his ear. "Intelligence, remember? That's what this game is all about. Consider. The next batter is their superstar, Slayer. He slammed Jones over the fence in Oakland last time they met, but he has had trouble with lefthanders. A .321 hitter, he's only .140 against O'Toole. What would you do?" He thought for a moment, then bent slightly towards her. "May I be so bold as to ask, Dr. Saltonstall, your prescription for getting us out of the mess we're in in this game?" She consulted her program as if going through numerous calculations, then moved her mouth back against his ear and whispered, "Rain. Lots of it. Soon.

Our batters are in a slump." "Oh!" he retorted, "then you admit there's some mystery to baseball, that logic has its limits, even here?" She couldn't believe how easily she had him again. She put her lips to his ear once more and tried to sound deep and sexy. "There's mystery in everything, my dear Mr. Penhurst, from mythology to baseball. Logic and mystery; but no shoving."

So he gave in, and added the Red Sox to his list of routines, and the following year presented her at Christmas time with a season's subscription, fourteen rows up on the first base side right between the plate and the bag. Jason Weir had pulled some strings for him. She was delighted. Their lives now had a sporting challenge for all but three months of the year. "Maybe she'll take up hockey," he thought. "I wonder what she'd do with the Neanderthals on ice?" He didn't pursue it.

iii

Tonight he said it was to be dinner at Sweeny's and dancing at Pier Eleven. He was working late finishing "a very big deal" and wouldn't have time to go home, but he'd pick her up at seven.

Father Dawson Penhurst II had decided that before taking his son into the firm, it would be good experience for him to be farmed out to a prestigious rival firm for a few years. He could then be brought in seasoned, so that father could cut back a bit and not have to be confronted by his peers complaining about a greenhorn's performance. Dawson had rented a townhouse overlooking the Charles River on the Cambridge side, midway between his downtown office of Young, Weir and Crandall, and 33 Harrington Lane. If working late, he had a closet downstairs at the office, with his squash clothes, suits, ties, fresh socks and linen handkerchiefs, towels, and Maid o' the Mist soap and shampoo with conditioner. The bottle of Exterminator after-shave lotion and his electric razor, he kept in a bottom desk drawer. He had a key to the office of Jason Weir, his closest friend among the senior partners, and could use his private shower when need arose. Once they met, Jason coming out as Dawson was going in, and he couldn't help noticing the large black mole on his boss's right shoulderblade. Jason was over sixty, divorced, and still, so rumor had it, quite a womanizer. He joked with Dawson that perhaps he should post a shower schedule in his office and Dawson quipped back that then all the secretaries would want to be on it, but he wondered later if the old man was telling him to check carefully and not come too close until Jason was dressed and gone.

So Dawson had come tonight directly from the office, showered and looking relaxed in a soft, light brown cotton shirt with matching tie of light summer colors, dark grey flannels and brown loafers from his uncountable collection. Catherine had threatened to come and count them some day, so she'd "know what she was getting into;" she had but five pairs of shoes. Lydia showed him into the livingroom and tweedled in high soprano up the staircase: "Cathy. Dawson is here." Then she turned to him and changed quickly into the earnest, serious mother of her only child.

"I hope you get into a good talk tonight, Dawson," she said. "This dissertation thing has come to a boil. You'll hear all about it. That rascal old professor of hers has offered more money if she'll work under him on the Indian affair." She sat down beside him on the sofa, folding her hands in her lap. "I know we agree, dear. It's

just contemptible that such a fine old place as Harvard
College would stoop to such a thing, to try to buy a pretty
young girl like my Cathy to go off a thousand miles away
into God knows what kind of stinking Indian Reserve. We
have to be firm, Dawson. The time has come to put all the
cards on the table, and you hold the trump. John and I
have talked to her until we're blue in the face, and she just
says that she will have to do what is right for her and that
she wants our support. Support! All her support is here!
How can we support her up there? She doesn't need any
more support, she needs some common sense and to
realize who are the ones who love her. Maybe she's had it
too easy, Dawson!'' She got up and stood directly over
him. "Remember, you hold the trump!'' she said. "Talk
some sense into her. Get her to commit herself to a
marriage date within the year. Harp on the tempus fugit
business. You can't wait another year! My gracious!'' and
she looked out the window. She turned wistful. "I seem to
have lost my baby somewhere, Dawson. I can't talk to her
anymore.''

The maitre d' at Sweeny's knew them well and always
seated them at their favorite table for two in the corner,
looking out on the harbor. The Wharf, three ship berths
down the harbor, was the more famous restaurant, four
times the size of Sweeny's, but they found the crowds
oppressive. If you hadn't made a reservation, you had to
sit in the Wharf's bar for from twenty to forty minutes.
Just when you were trying to think of something romantic
to say at the Wharf, a loudspeaker would announce:
"Your attention is directed to the cruise vessel just
passing in front of us, the *Lady Julietta* registered out of
Amsterdam, of the Holland Line, just leaving with eight
hundred passengers for New York, Atlanta, Miami, and
Havana, after docking with us for two days in Boston.

Thank you.'' Whatever it was he was going to say had to
be brought back into focus across twelve hundred miles of
seasickness, for he had had one miserable experience
when a little boy on a cruise ship to St. Thomas with his
parents, and he swore then that once was enough.
Sweeny's had a smaller menu, but was much quieter; the
food, they thought, was a touch better, and there were no
announcements.

"Do you have any of the 1971 Chardonnay left,
Gaston?'' Dawson asked. "If not, the Riesling will be
fine.'' "Yes, Mr. Penhurst,'' said Gaston with a slight
bow. He lit their candle, removed the two larger wine
glasses from the settings, smiled at Catherine, and
disappeared. Catherine had her eye on the bluefish
hollandaise, but when Dawson suggested bouillabaisse for
two, she agreed. Sweeny's bouillabaisse was out of this
world.

Gaston brought the Chardonnay, the shrimp escolaise,
and eventually the bouillabaisse in steaming deep white
porcelain bowls. They talked casually of the flotsam of
their last few days, the outlook for the new Red Sox
season, the Patriots' recent trade with the Vikings,
whether the new Perestroika in Russia would lead
anywhere, Mrs. Reagan's recent blunder when she asked
on a television talk show what the AACP stood for. "I'm
sure it was just a little lapse in memory, don't you think?''
she said, sipping the wine. Dawson had on his new brown
rim glasses, and looked at her over them. "You know
what I think,'' he said. She wanted to be easy, pleasant,
relaxed, but she was sure Lydia would have given him a
pep talk, and the inevitable hung over the first delicious
sip of her bouillabaisse.

Dawson surprised her. He reached across the table and
held her left hand briefly. "I have something to tell you,''

he said. "I haven't bored you with the details before now, but our firm was engaged several months ago by Wilson Candell, the pulp paper and wood products giant, to explore the possibilities of a merger with Nesbitt Sinclair Corporation of Minneapolis. They make scotch tape, all kinds of wire, rocket components, a lot of computer bits—a huge conglomerate world-wide. We're talking mega dollars, Catherine, very big dollars. Anyway, for some reason that still baffles me, Jason put me on the team preparing the proposal. As luck would have it, Nesbitt Sinclair engaged Dad's firm. The problem with these big mergers is communication." She noticed out the window the twinkling lights as a liner moved slowly out to sea. "The big boys on each side deny everything publicly, and actually seem to be trying to hate each other. Neither wants to admit to, or allow for, the slightest advantage or disadvantage. Neither is in trouble, neither needs the other, the advantages all seem speculative, the disadvantages real and apparently insurmountable. Dad and I got together early on this, and started swapping all kinds of secret stuff that often gets swept under. The members of our team couldn't believe what I was bringing into the office; I was presenting Dad's ideas along with mine and he was doing the same thing for his team. The result is that Dad and I came up with an unbeatable deal. Our firms presented them with our packages a few days ago. Wall Street is just holding its breath for the news. Dad phoned me this afternoon to say it's a sure thing. We had only to tidy up a few points of clarification, which I've done. Both clients are ready to sign. There will probably be a love-in between the two company presidents on Monday, but the real winners are our two firms. I can hardly let myself believe it." He sipped the Chardonnay and smiled at her. His soft cobalt eyes met hers and she felt the old comfort, the tenderness of his caring. "As far as we're concerned, Cathy, it's going to be a good boost to my resources. I was talking it over with Jason just before I left, and it looks as if my commission will be substantial"—he paused—"about equal to my yearly earnings." He reached over again and took her hand. "Why don't we make plans now for that trip to Europe we have talked about, a trip just for us, Cathy—no business—and not just for a few days but a few months—to Paris, Florence, Rome, the galleries and museums, the art shows. We could take it all in, Cathy, before settling down. We could start by tracking down the Penhursts and Saltonstalls in Britain. I've got relations galore over there and we could let them show us a good time. Then we could do your Browning tour of the galleries in Spain and Italy, that you've often talked of. You could bring your dissertation with you and maybe the change of climate would help you to write it. We'll come back refreshed, and you can finish it off, and we'll be married. Let's indulge ourselves a little, Cathy. God knows we've earned it, and waited long enough." He looked at her tenderly, pleadingly.

"It's wonderful about the merger, Dawson," she said. "You never cease to amaze me on how calm and casual you are about these big matters, for you didn't mention a word about it even when you were in the middle of it." She smiled and whiffed the Chardonnay from just above the glass rim she held in front of her, her elbows on the table. "The trip sounds wonderful, and I suppose I could bring the one study along with me." She paused. "But not the Indian one." She tipped the glass slightly and tasted the cool white wine again. "Yesterday, Dr. French accepted my proposal for the Ashwagane study, and Dr. Zukawitz likes my proposal for the Melwyn Heights study, with minor revisions. She thinks the Ashwagane year might produce only limited results, and whatever I come up with would be a feather in Dr. French's cap, not mine." "What do you think?" he asked. "I'm really not sure," she said. "With Zukawitz, you know pretty well what's to be done before you do it, whereas for French you don't know what you'll find until you get there." She paused again, and tipped the rim against her lips. Another liner was drifting out to sea. "But the studies I have done on the Ashwagane suggest we have just scratched the surface. There are digs going on up there right now. A lot of the information that has surfaced in the last twenty years hasn't been pulled together. The Ashwagane study is riskier, but if I could pull it off, it would be far more significant and satisfying than the other one. It would be for me, like your merger, a triumph." She paused a long time. It seemed to her that seconds turned into hours. Her glass was almost empty. Dawson looked at her. She could see he knew. "Could the trip wait a year, Dawson, until after I return from Canada?"

"Cathy, you know me about as well as I know myself," he said. "The trip would be nice, but what I want so desperately is for us to be married and have children. I know your mother is scared of the culture shock you will encounter up there, and that the Indians won't be nice to you, or for you. Frankly, I think that is just her perception and her way of dealing with her only child. For her, the umbilical cord never got cut. You'll probably love the north and find a warm and friendly people. You'll do a brilliant study, there's no doubt in my mind. French has been around a long time, and he knows who to put his money on. I'll miss you. Oh, how I'll miss you. Bouillabaisse alone at this table is an intolerable thought. But I've never been one to be pushy. I can push, and push hard, at the firm, but not with the one I love. I respect you for what you want to do and I'll support it all the way. I have for three years; another one won't kill us, I suppose. Maybe I can visit you and you'll have to come home at least once to see your mother, and time will fly by. It will fly by only if I could be sure you'd marry me when you get back.''

Catherine prided herself on being the last to cry at weddings and funerals and movies, but tonight she was helpless. The corners of her eyes moistened. She would never have that dream of Sir Dawson Penhurst in silver armor because dreams were about what might happen in an unreal world and this man was sitting before her in the flesh, his banner flying high for all in Sweeny's to see: "Sir Dawson Penhurst, Knight of the Round Table, the kindest, sweetest, nicest man in all the world." "Dawson," she said, "thank you. It's settled. You give me all the space a woman could ask for, and more." She went over to him and bent down, and kissed him hard on the mouth. "Isn't that sweet," she heard a lady say at the next table.

She lay in her bed a long time without sleeping. Her light was on. She looked up at Marilyn for some time but as usual didn't get a message. Then she realized that there had been an oblique connection with Camelot. Princess Marilyn did not make any sense. Then she wondered if Queen Marilyn was looking down at the Lady of Shallot. Her mind was doing crazy things. She got up and went to the window, opened it. Cambridge lay quiet in the chilly darkness, the traffic on Harrington Lane stilled in the first hour of the new day. The lights of Boston in the distance reflected off the heavy cloud cover, but she could see the slivered moon peeking at her and then disappear. Something inside her had changed, not an earth moving change but a small, slight shift, an adjustment of some chemistry of emotion that she couldn't taste but knew was there. She was very tired, but she sat down at her desk and reached below for the thick leather book. Yesterday had been the storm. Tonight the skies were clearing; the smell of new life drifting up from the lilac bushes beneath her window blended with her sense of relief.

Wednesday, March 30

We talked of roots tonight. Of going back to the beginnings, tracing the lineage of Penhursts and Saltonstalls. And that, I guess, is what makes the difference. Without my roots I am nothing. Without the chimes of the ancient clocks time becomes only a now and not a continuity. For sacred time is not of time but of a human eternity, and that is all we are given to understand. The only Republic we can ultimately give up our lives for is the republic of community, the ageless ways in which people have lived and loved and created rituals of what was important to them since the dawning. For we are all pieces of one mythology and the clock strikes but a new version of hidden originals. Roots grow deep, hidden from view.

I did not want to see it, but my life has a calling, as strong and deep as for a nun. I shall have little to do with doing good, for doing good so often ends in doing wrong. But it shall have to do with finding roots, uncovering the downgrowing spirals of meaning and fulfillment. I am weary, but joyous. My dissertation conflict is settled and tomorrow will bring its good or bad; I am ready.

But will they have me? Who am I to assume that the Wendaban will welcome me with open arms? I show them my credentials: all they see is a little white girl from

Disneyworld come to study them some more. I have no medicines in my bag, no balm for their hurt, no food for their tables or music for their souls. I have little to trade with. I know about fifteen words of Ashwagane and am not sure how to pronounce even them just so, for my ear has never listened. All my knowledge of the Wendaban is from books; I see no real faces, hear no real voices. Why would they open their treasures to another white—a member of their problem for so long—for yet another study? Dear God, please may Dr. French pave the way. Maybe I can help them, show them more of their central stream. Can I discover more? What more is there to discover? Can I convince them? Will they be honest? Can they see me as honest? And there will be no Dawson's shoulder to lay my head on in the evenings when days run rough. But I shall have thee, my little journal, the only savings account I treasure. My old security, growth investment. I suspect my cloistered self-reliance will now be fully tested. I can pass Harvard's, but can I pass their exams? If I can keep my self together, can I gain their trust, their respect? One decision made, only opens up new casements onto the unknown. What lies ahead? We shall soon see—ten weeks until I leave will fly by. I must prepare. I am a single stem of maturing wheat in a great field of rusty gold. The gentle breeze blows, and I bend toward the Ashwagane.

Chapter V
THE WENDABAN ASHWAGANE

i

The last of the glaciers moved slowly through its receding across the northern cap of the continent, slowly, majestically. As if it knew it was the last of its kind, of its ultimate capitulation to the greening and warming scheme of things, it gave up not easily. As it retreated to its Arctic lair of perpetual ice, it fought back, stalling, grinding, crushing, gouging out small and large erratic holes for water, shearing off cliffs, seeping into crevices and then with swelling power widening them into chasms and caves. It was determined to leave its mark forever. It would tolerate little earth. It picked it up and washed it into rivers and down to the coasts. If warm alluvial earth was to engender the dawn of new life, the last bastion of ice would see to it that roots would have to grow wide, but not deep, to clutch the oldest rock exposed on the globe's surface by its persistent scraping. Geologists would call it the Precambrian Shield; fur traders would refer to it as "the badlands;" but for the Ashwagane, it was "n'Daki Menan," the motherland, eventually rich in animals, minerals, trees, fish, plants, water and sunshine, a good land to live on.

Their ancestors had come from Asia thousands of years before, pushing across the Bering Strait when it was still land and the continents were joined, spreading south down into Mexico, some staying north to live along the edge of the ice pack. As the ice retreated, they followed it north and developed a network of tribes or "Bands." Before Rome became an empire for Nero to fiddle away, these bands had developed a language and mythology, dances and masks and drums, stone implements with which to hunt and farm, bone hooks with which to fish, wooden and clay dishes to cook in and eat from, bark canoes to travel in, skin and fur clothing, beading for money and decoration, collapsible bark pointed tents and more permanent log houses, the art of painting with dyes made from barks and ochre from rock, and an extensive mythology of gods and spirits, passed down in stories from generation to generation. They had their hunting territories staked out, for the band as a group and for individual families within the band. They assembled in spring and summer at central lodges; they spread out to their hunting grounds during the winter. The land sustained them. The Ashwagane, from Manitoba to Quebec, were "the people of the Northeast."

By the time Samuel de Champlain was exploring the waterways of the Ashwagane's homelands (and Shakespeare was strutting across his "wooden O" outside London), one band of the Ashwagane, calling themselves the Wendaban, or "coming of the dawn," had chosen a large lake as their home base and called it Achinike, "the lake of clear water." With over one thousand islands, Lake Achinike provided sand beaches for easy beaching of canoes, abundant fish, and summer hunting close to the water. In the fall, although some stayed behind to hunt out of the village, most of the Wendaban bid one another goodbye and set off for their winter hunting grounds, to the north, west, and south, for the beaver and moose that would see them through the winter for food and clothing. They would return to the village during the melting of the snow for the annual spring festival of the Majukimo. They fought off Iroquois incursions into n'Daki Menan from the south. They greeted the early white fur trader with emotions of friendliness and disdain, but they refrained from collective attack. They called him Shagonash. They, the "children," were invited to sign a treaty by the Great White "Father" who wore a crown of gold. Soon after the turn into the twentieth century, they saw Shagonash building houses on the shore of Lake Achinike, then on the islands. Then they were told that the Father with the Crown wanted them to move their settlement to an island reserved for them in the centre of their favored lake, named by a white trader after its beach on the east side, "Sand Island." It was a time of blood counting. Adolf Hitler would destroy adulterated Jewish blood and raise up unadulterated German blood. The Ashwagane were given new status, a number assigned by the Crown for each member issuing from unadulterated male Ashwagane blood. Then came little red plastic ID. cards with their number and photo which would excuse them from paying retail sales tax as compensation for their being inaccessible to the modern world.

ii

Harold Kenebek was now the oldest man on the Sand Island Reserve, their shaman, or medicine man, hand-picked when he was twelve by Chief Pashawonaby, when he said "I promise." He had kept his promise. He was looked upon by all the residents as the final authority in Wendaban culture, the keeper of the old ways and legends, of what juices healed what ailments, of what times in the year were best to hunt what animals, of where the sustaining life of the land came from and of what Nanabush might next have up his sleeve. He was eighty-three now, and crippled with rheumatism, but his voice was still deep and musical and his memory rich.

Getting Harold to talk was no more difficult than asking him a question. Chief Philip had equipped the Band Office with computers, but he sometimes wondered if these new wizards of stored information had as yet developed the data bank capacity of Harold's old head, where names and dates and ancient hunting territories popped out on request with little effort. Uneducated past grade two (so he recalled), unable to read or write, Harold lived in a world of sight and sound, of observation, thought and memory. He spoke fluent Ashwagane, good English, pieces of French, and his ear picked up from his beloved television set the new words and new nuances of the old words with the astuteness of a Cooper Indian who heard twigs crack a mile away.

Harold was known throughout the area for his fiddling. As a young man he had mastered the art of the violin and was for a time part of a group that played for dances at hotels on the lake and dance halls along the highway. Of recent years his fiddling had been confined to the Saturday night dances at Sand Island, to which summer tourists and cottagers flocked in large numbers to hear him play the likes of Fisher's Hornpipe and Money Musk. Many an older businessman grown sedate in his ways gave in to the urge and threw himself in a frenzy around the sweaty hall covered in unstained natural plywood, here where you could let your hair down in the wild fantasy north of the aborigines. Wives gaped in amazement as fathers and grandfathers overexerted themselves to the flinging rhythms of Harold's bow. Now, his rheumatism had won the day and his public fiddling was done.

He lived with his granddaughter, Angele, in a small two-bedroom wooden house, made of large rough-sawn thick planks, never painted and now weathered black. Little crevices between the planks had been plastered with grey clay which was now falling out. Harold had been offered one of the new government-funded houses, but had declined. "I moved into a house just down the path," he said, "and helped my dad build this one. This is home. You can build Ann a new house when I'm gone." (He had dropped the second syllable of her name when she was a baby.) But he did not object to a new lining of insulation and pine panelling and rewiring for electric heat. The iron wood stove in the living room with the kitchen on the end could now die down on cold January nights and hydro would keep him and his granddaughter warm.

She was eighteen. Her father was Harold's second son, killed in a mining accident when she was three. After that her mother drifted in and out of affairs on the island; then one day she was gone with a new face from a reserve to the south, and Harold and his wife took over. When Harold's wife died seven years later, Angele was old enough to look after filling her grandmother's shoes, especially in the kitchen, for Harold's second love after his Ann was beaver stew, the dark brown meat chunks smothered in vegetables which they grew behind the house and stored in a root cellar under the house.

She was trying to finish her high school diploma and perhaps go to college. Six miles by boat every morning to the landing, then fifteen bumpy miles by a small yellow bus down the gravel road to the town of Achinike, then thirty-four miles north in a bigger yellow bus to the white man's school in White Falls. Sometimes in the fall, early-morning fog would be so dense she would have to creep along the shoreline in her boat, taking longer to get to the landing, and though she would leave earlier, at 6:00, there were times when Mr. Towser, the school bus driver, who was supposed to leave the landing for Achinike sharp at 7:00 to connect with the bus going north, would peer out into the fog listening for the first sounds of an approaching motor, and wait an extra few minutes. With his help, she rarely missed the bus.

When the summers came, Angele worked at the grocery and gift store on the Reserve, as a clerk. Many a tourist and cottager would remember the raven hair and dark brown eyes of the little Ashwagane smiling one, who could add so well and change the register tape and whizz the articles through so quickly without a hitch.

As she grew up, her love for her grandpa matured and her care of the household and his needs became the passion of her life. "I think I learn more from grandpa, me, than from school," she said one day to Chief Philip. He had his eye on her for a position in the Band Office someday and then, hopefully, on Council. Harold had not set out deliberately to train her in any devised plan of studies, but as the gregarious fiddle player was slowed down by his rheumatism, his commentary on what he saw and heard and his love of telling old stories about the Ashwagane and its folklore, seemed to grow. She would eagerly await the ending of *Family Ties* on the television, one of Harold's favorites. The rabbit ears on the ancient set picked up only one channel from Incoville to the west, and the antics of the Keaton family were routinely followed by *Guns of the Old West*, which Harold once tried to throw his crutch at. So she would turn it off, and try to entice him into more remembrances of his family ties in the past, and in the days before them, as Harold was told by his parents. She would crouch at the side of the large worn green easy chair that Harold practically lived in now, and he would sometimes stroke her long black straight hair with his gnarled brown hands that still seemed to her so veined and powerful looking, and he would reminisce and chuckle and compare the times, often slipping in and out of the musical Ashwagane tongue.

So she heard and learned, of their dress, their hunts, their marriages, the festivals and the drownings, the good times and the bad times, the fight for survival, for food and money, for respect and for pride. And always there was Nanabush, the delight of Harold's timeless vision, the ancient trickster of Ashwagane spirits, Satan, Robin Hood and Puck all rolled into one. She was sure his imagination took much license with the handed-down tales, and on occasion when he had had an extra (or even extra extra) glass of Branvin sherry, which was now the last staple of his spiritual life (''one small glass each night, Harold, just one now, or you're going to be in real trouble, beyond my help,'' the doctor in White Falls had said), he would report with a stern look at Angele that he had seen Nanabush recently, and then he would concoct what Conk would call ''a Harold Bruiser,'' for Conk had been on several fishing trips when Harold was still guiding, and had heard him talk around the shore lunch fire, when the deviltry of Nanabush and Harold's gratuity grew in direct proportions.

She had early learned that her grandfather was, however, a different Indian from the other elders on the Reserve. He was rarely bitter. Underlying the love of fun and adventure she had come to associate with her friends on the ghetto of Sand Island, was a resentment she felt too, the unspoken depression which could bubble up in a fist fight or retreat into drunken sickness, the resentment of defeat, a dull anger over the patience required, the opportunities shot down, the pity proffered, the claustrophobia of a little world so enticed at school and on the colored screen to be part of the bigger scene, so often shut off from it by intangible walls of misunderstanding and the indecisiveness of bewildered political power. The words racism and hatred were never used. How could they be the truth?

But Harold was different, a beacon of light in the dark. He would scoff and chuckle at the Shagonash world. His years of guiding white trophy hunters had given his ample mind food for one hundred years of yarns; he had the ancient mariner's compelling eye, but nothing of his curse. He had looked on the white man's world that had come his way with the interest of a spectator at a circus. They were performers, sometimes in their dances drawing his applause, sometimes his boos. They were both models of accomplishment and freaks of nature. He had too much strength in his own sense of race to let them get to him. He could take them or leave them, charm them, fiddle for them, dance with their wives and bait their hooks, laugh with them and at them, admire, resent, and tell a few to go to hell and move off. Always there was a barely detectable distance, a strange quiet nobility that never flaunted itself but was always there for the discerning.

So Angele was quietly trying to reconcile that nobility of grandpa with her sense of living in a cursed world. For him, Ashwagane problems were mostly self-inflicted. "We shoot ourselves in the foot," he would say to her, "and no good woodsman does that." That the Ashwagane tongue had not been taught in the little school on the Reserve until recently, when it was finally introduced after Chief Philip's four year prodding of the School Board on which no Indian had ever sat, struck Harold as incredible. But there was no one to teach it except some parents, who rotated their services for four classes a week. That the youth cared no longer for Indian games and played television games instead struck him as betrayal. It was a matter of debate in his mind whether Tylenol was a better pain reliever in certain circumstances, sciatica for instance, than some of his bark juice medicines. Chief Philip was trying to bring back some of the old rituals and festivals, but the Sand Islanders were slow to respond, quizzical, perplexed, as if they were being asked to tie their shoes with gloves on. Beadwork was sissy stuff and too unremunerative for the young girls who preferred to watch television which he was sure was even less remunerative. Canoe races had turned into splashing contests; tea boiling without matches was now looked upon as analogous to pulling a white bunny out of an empty black hat. Harold and Chief Philip and Matt Commanda huddled. Cultural decay was not inevitable or necessary. Other Indian bands were meeting the challenge of survival across the country. Much could be done, though the odds seemed insurmountable. Taking a leaf from Harold's book they would not be bitter, cynical, or sanctimonious. They laid plans. They knew that the ancient Ashwagane ways as stewards of the land (Shagonash's new buzz word was "sustainable yield," which wasn't new at all) would ultimately come to the rescue of colonial thinking about resources. They agreed that they should be suspicious if not hostile to scientific planning processes. There was a new day coming. They could feel a new importance. Could they be ready? There were exciting times ahead. As they talked they watched Harold's eyes shining.

iii

There was only one suggestion in the circumstances surrounding the birth of Philip Gahbodnay that he would one day be a leader of his people—his mother. The fourth of five children, Philip spent an uneventful youth. He played and hunted and fished and stole cigarettes from the store, like all the other boys. His father Charles was a fishing and hunting guide who found it difficult to refuse offers of Shagonash firewater, and early developed a love of whiskey. Spasmodic drinking played a small part in Charles' summer life, for he took his guiding seriously and was one of the best, in constant demand. Rarely did he miss a day. He managed to build up enough money to almost see his family through the winter. But after the hunt was over in late fall, Charles would disappear for days at a time, and as the children assembled for supper their eyes conveyed that they knew he was gone again and they secretly prayed there would not be an accident. While he was away nothing was said about his absence. When he would return, looking haggard and thinner, nothing would be said about where he had been or why. He would return to wintry days of cutting wood, ice fishing for some family food, cards in the evening with his friends for several weeks—then he would be gone again. Their three huskies rarely got any special attention from him, nor did the children.

Philip's schooling in the one-room schoolhouse was typical, the indigenous despair of generations of Sand Island youth, the problem he would later discuss at great length with Matt and Harold and the Band Council. To be isolated by geography and race on an island Indian reserve with twenty-seven students to teach in grades one through eight, at the bottom of the pay scale (if you were new at it), with little to do when winter darkness was ink black soon after the school day ended, and transportation to the mainland (which was miles from anywhere when you did get there) was a matter of begging and luck—such considerations did not add up to an enticing prospect for young graduates of teachers' college. If they couldn't get a job elsewhere, young teachers might settle for Sand Island rather than nothing, and consider the job temporary until something better turned up. Sometimes they left for another position before the school year was finished. There was little continuity. In the forty years since the school had been built, there had not been as yet one native Wendaban teacher. Philip saw six different teachers come and go in his eight years of school. But he was fortunate. There was so much failing at the school, that what should have taken eight years, frequently took ten or eleven. If the students did not care, they failed in the teacher's eyes; if the teachers did not care, they failed in the students' eyes. But it was the teacher's marks that counted and went to the School Board for the next teacher to wrestle with. The school was a day-care centre for youths who wanted to put off as long as possible going to high school fifty-five miles away, when, after they would drop out at the usual age of sixteen, there was likely little for them to do.

In Philip's fifth grade, the well-meaning young man gave up serious teaching after Christmas, and Philip and his friends learned how to make paper airplanes (eventually with wooden frames and elastic bands) go around three sides of the schoolroom. In grade seven he was singled out for a special commission. Each noon he tidied up the teacher's apartment adjoining the school, neatly stacking the erotic magazines and tabloids of the sensational scattered across the floor, emptying the ashtrays of butts and washing the dishes, for $2.00 per week. He was on his way.

His mother, Patience, knew Philip was being poorly treated, but like other parents who cared, she felt powerless to change the system. But she was not helpless. From Philip's earliest days she had sensed something special in the boy, an unusual inquisitiveness, a temperament of concern. Because her family could not afford the daily travel to school in the village of Achinike during the War, she was unable to read or write. But Patience Gahbodnay had received a rich upbringing in the verbal folklore of the Wendaban, and she took every opportunity to tell Philip her own stories, usually at bedtime. By the time he was ten, she had a better idea. With other parents, she approached Harold. He was delighted to hold weekly Sunday afternoon meetings in various houses around the Reserve to tell those who came to hear about old days and customs and to tweak their young ears with the native tongue. It was at one of these Sunday sessions that Harold explained that the Wendaban had never signed the 1850 treaty. Philip stared at him with intense eyes. He asked questions. He wanted to hear more. "You mean the land is still ours?" he asked. "Only we think so, so far," said Harold. Under the young boy's prodding, Harold talked well into the supper hour that night. Philip became his star pupil. Harold knew a future chief when he saw one, and he said so to Patience. Her eyes grew bright. From then on, she had one mission in life.

By the time he was sixteen, with his mother's urging and Harold's coaching, the future chief was proficient in Ashwagane. Now, there was other help. Patience had been firm but not pushy, for she had simply assumed from early days that Philip would travel the daily one hundred and ten mile round trip to the high school in White Falls. His father had been told in clear terms that there were going to be extra costs involved and he had stodgily gone about trying to save more money each year. So when the time came, it wasn't that he should have to go, or must go, only that he would go, as if going off to White Falls High was no different than learning to shave. Philip had accepted that, and was looking forward to learning more about the Shagonash world which he knew he was going to have to deal with. Little did he know that he would have to deal with it as no Wendaban Chief had done before him.

He met Willard Gilman on the first September day of class in grade ten. Willard had two daughters, one just beginning and one just finishing universities in Toronto and London. He had always wanted a son. As the senior English teacher at White Falls High, he had had several surrogate sons. There were always one or two in his class in whom he took special interest. He pampered his dream that future prime ministers and leaders of industry and great teachers and scholars were sitting staring up at him, hungering for direction and inspiration. He had taught several young Indians, but had not discovered one who might enter the class of his special sons, until Philip. His was an eagerness so unlike the usual Wendaban cynicism, a drive to learn so unlike the usual indifference. His writing was atrocious. How could earlier teachers have passed him on like this? Willard decided to try to fix that, to take him on as his first Indian challenge.

By mid-October Patience was distressed over the amount of daily homework Philip was struggling with and his yelling at his siblings to accommodate him and shut up. The noisy, cramped quarters of the little house were not suitable for this new scheme of things. She called Harold and her friends together. He told them what to say, and they petitioned the Council, and within a week the Band Offices were opened for quiet study from 7:00 to 9:30 each weeknight, with parents supervising. Philip was a regular. He wrestled with grammar. He did all the exercises in the assigned book, then those in an extra one

Willard had lent him. He studied the model essays in his text and traced the line of development by diagrams as Willard had shown him. He built up a list of vocabulary and reviewed it each night, adding one new word each day, and Patience then traced over his answers trying to see if they were right. He wrote his own essays, two for every one assigned. For description, he did a moose pasture; for narration, he did a moose hunt; for argument, he defended an Indian's right to hunt out of season. But the harder he worked the more passion built inside him to argue the claim that the land was still theirs. He couldn't shake the possibility of that unbelievable injustice from the forefront of his concern. He would write little paragraphs about it, then crumple them up. A larger essay was welling up in his mind—it was becoming an obsession. He knew what he wanted to say but he couldn't prove what he wanted to say. He felt it, but didn't know enough about it. His heart was aching but his head couldn't keep up. He kept pestering Harold for more information until the old man knew that at last their advocate had arrived.

Just before school ended for Christmas in his third year, Philip got his chance. Willard Gilman had started an informal, voluntary class in elocution several years previously. He had tried to introduce a class in public speaking into the curriculum, but with so much new material bombarding the three R's after Sputnik, the speaking class was left on the shelf of permanent consideration. Still, six to eight boys and girls came out for the voluntary sessions twice a week at noonhour. By the end of the year, each would have had a chance to deliver three speeches. For the final meeting before the holidays, Philip Gahbodnay and Mary Jane Shawcross, the two best in the current group in Willard's opinion, were to give talks. For this occasion, Willard did a little extra scrounging. He usually tried to round up one or two guests to listen, in addition to the class members. For this day the ranks were swelled: Elsie Fairweather, his colleague in English; Dick Forman, his friend in Shop Studies; Jim Delisle, deputy manager of the local Regional Department of Lands and Forests; Eric Forchesne, the Principal of White Falls High; Dither Gotsenberger, President of the White Falls Chamber of Commerce. They each had a bag lunch, ready to enjoy a different kind of lunch-hour diversion.

Philip was nervous, but he had it all written down. He had spent the last three evenings with Harold, polishing and pruning the details. He told Willard that his topic was "Indian Land" and Willard introduced him with that title. Mary Jane Shawcross had just returned to her seat flushed from the warm applause for her eloquent description of the value of the annual White Falls Fall Fair to the community. With the taste of pumpkin pie in their mouths and images of red ribbons being pinned on the halters of clean big white and black holsteins held by proud youth in white from the Junior Farmers Club, fourteen eager faces looked up contentedly as Philip mounted the podium on the little stage set up in the gymnasium, anticipating "Indian Land"—perhaps the reds and yellows of fall leaves crunching under moccasined feet, or the crisp feel of the paddle cutting a clean blue northern lake in a birchbark canoe, or the loud smash of the beaver's tail as he dives with his fresh cream-colored twig of poplar towards his new house abuilding.

Philip had other ideas. He briefly described the events leading up to the treaty of 1850, in which the British Crown had to purchase the land rights to the northeast draining into the Great Lakes, rights granted to the natives by the Royal Proclamation of 1763. Chief Chickchick of the Wendaban had received notice of the treaty assembly at Sault Ste. Marie, over two hundred miles away, too late. Whether this failure of adequate notice was because of unintentional human error, bad weather, or cunning, was not determined. Chickchick and three fellow travellers hurried towards the meeting, but arrived two days after the negotiation was concluded. The treaty gave the Ashwagane a lump sum of £2,000 to be divided among fourteen bands, a promise of reserves, some gifts, and an annual payment of $4.00 per Indian. "Quite a deal for millions of acres of the richest iron, copper, nickel and gold deposits in the world," the young Philip said, barely looking up, "never mind the timber and animals." Neither Chickchick's name, nor that of the Wendaban, appeared anywhere in the treaty. Chickchick was outraged and told the Crown representatives that the Wendaban would continue to regard their hunting territories as excluded from the treaty and still theirs for future negotiation. "Not so," said the Crown. Its representatives replied that the Wendaban were understood to be part of the Band at Almaguin, and that they were covered by the treaty. When Chickchick returned, he called his people together and informed them that they must fight to keep their land.

That was over one hundred years ago, the eighteen-year-old said, but to this day the matter was unresolved despite numerous attempts by former chiefs to have the matter addressed by Ottawa. In the meantime, the reserve promised by the treaty was slow in coming, and when it finally came, it was a little island of about three hundred acres. From forty thousand acres rich in resources, they now had under their jurisdiction only three hundred acres rich in raccoons, skunks, and one bear which no one was allowed to shoot because it ate thirty-four times its weight in garbage. This very high school and the Shawcross Construction Company were sitting on Wendaban land. Mary Jane, whose father owned the Shawcross Construction Company, was gazing out the window. Eric Forchesne cleared his throat. He had heard enough, but how could he interject? Where had all this stuff come from? He looked at Willard with a furrowed brow.

Philip was concluding. The one hundred and thirty-two townships, still claimed by the Wendaban, must now be adjudicated. Canada had been built on the notion that there were two founding nations, ignoring the third that had been here long before the other two arrived. Injustices must be addressed. The time had come. There were new days ahead. Indian Land must be cared for, for the future generations of all the people.

There was polite applause. Eric Forchesne looked at Willard. What the hell was going on here? What kind of nonsense was he tolerating this year? He would have to have a talk with Willard in his office, and he would be sure to get back to Jim and Dither this afternoon. They should understand that such drivel had nothing to do with the School. Deputy Jim was pensive. It had been a hell of a speech. He might be Deputy Forester for the area, but he had never heard of an 1850 treaty. When he got back he would see if there was a copy at the regional office; if not, he'd order one in for the library. He'd like to have a look at it. This kid sounded serious. Thank God there were only two of them from outside the school. Suppose the newspaper got wind of it! How serious was this kid? Had earlier chiefs really made such a claim? It was preposterous. It couldn't be true. He had never heard anything about it. One hundred and thirty-two townships! An eighteen-year-old on a fantasy trip! But it was a hell of a speech.

Dither looked over at Jim. He would talk to Jim afterwards. Twenty million dollars of commercial property in White Falls was sitting on Indian Land? Oh, come on, now, let's be serious, he would say. Where was this kid coming from, anyway? Was it a joke? He'd have to talk to Willard and Eric. Speeches like this should be censored before they could go before the public, or the school could get a very bad name. He was on the School Board. Thank heavens this was just an informal little group. Suppose it had been a public speaking contest, with one hundred parents and maybe the press! He shuddered. He would have to talk to Eric and Willard very seriously. The whole idea in the speech was utterly preposterous.

iv

With Harold and Patience his mentors, Philip had finished his grade thirteen matriculation, the first Wendaban boy to go the route since Alex Osatig twelve years earlier, who went on to medical school and was now a doctor in Huronia City. At nineteen Philip debated about going to University, which is why a student would take the extra thirteenth year, and Willard Gilman had already written a fully documented letter of recommendation that bristled with both solid accomplishments and superlative opinions. He was ready to send it off to whatever universities Philip chose. With Philip's marks, Willard was sure he would be accepted somewhere, but being Indian, before it was prestigious for institutions of higher learning to carry Indian students, Philip would need solid recommendations. But the young Indian could no longer put off his sense of destiny, that he must be up and doing for the days ahead. By day he worked for Gerald

Commanda's construction company on Sand Island, building, altering, repairing all over the Lake, and developed a lifelong friendship with his son Matt who shared his vision that there must be better days ahead. By night he read. His was a familiar face in the Department of Lands and Forests office in Achinike (before it was changed to the Department of Natural Resources), to read, borrow and purchase studies, pamphlets, bibliographies, books—anything he could get his hands on that had to do with the rules and regulations and other aspects of the Department's management of the land they thought was theirs to manage—the fisheries, wildlife, hunting, mines and minerals, forestry. Little did the government men of Achinike suspect what he was grooming for.

He and Matt spent hours talking about what was wrong with Indian life and where the evils lay. The government's policy of assimilation was mischievous and soul killing. Yet they had to come to terms with the modern world. What was the answer? Philip continued to buy books, and built an addition onto his house for a study, the first residential study in a private home on Sand Island. His father thought his son "had a screw loose" and didn't help him buy a board or hammer a nail. He and Harold dragged out boxes of old documents and photos and letters packed in the basement under the rickety old wooden Band Office, and lamented over how much was unknown, uncatalogued, unappreciated. He and Harold talked into the night about the problems of what an education should mean for a modern Wendaban. Harold suggested they rejuvenate the Majukimo and get somebody to prepare a history of the Band. Television was king: get the youth involved in acting and film-making. Boredom was queen: stimulate new clubs in native studies and explore new opportunities for employment by the Band. Alienation was the joker: developing faith in oneself and having a strong cultural identity would win the hand.

Two years later, on October 14, the Wendaban voters elected Philip, twenty-one, their new Chief, the youngest recorded in Wendaban history. On October 25 the Council applied to the Department of Indian Affairs for a grant of $500,000 to build a new office and library, equipped with the latest technology, including funds for training in the new gadget called a "computer." Philip had decided that if they had to regain their past, they could not be caught napping by the future. There would be times to appear one thousand years old in feathers; there would be times to appear modern in dark business suits with feasibility studies in hand. He would try to carry the Wendaban backwards and forwards at once, though it seemed a difficult task. How could he sell such a contradiction? What was the formula?

They got the grant. "It's about time you guys got off your butts," the government official said to him privately when he came to the Island to review their needs as outlined in the application. "You'll never get what you don't ask for." Philip tucked that little message into his own organic computer and would bring it up onto his mind's eye screen many times thereafter. He would call it, as if it were a piece of music or a poem, "Invitation to a Shagonash Dance." Unsolicited assistance, he decided, was not a white government's virtue.

It was on a grey, drizzly Thursday afternoon in November, scarcely a month after his election, that the lanky young Chief took the first step, at 4 p.m. (because he couldn't get an earlier appointment and he was hitching a ride with Matt since he didn't have a car yet), which would soon escalate the Wendaban from a small unknown Indian Band to a position of national prominence.

The law offices of Cohen and Smith in White Falls were drab and simple, one waiting room with one secretary and one typewriter and three plastic chairs, one office to the rear on the left, Mr. Cohen's, one on the right, Mr. Smith's. Situated on the ground floor of a small two-storey unpainted cement block office building on a side street, the rent was low and they enjoyed the prestige of being housed with the local radio station, the Department of Health's Sanitary Division (septic tank applications), a real estate firm, a dental surgeon (from whose office the occasional shriek escaped), and the local dairy marketing board. Jerry Cohen had grown up in White Falls, and after his good friend in law school in Toronto, Hamlin Smith, had finished articling, he persuaded him to come north and to pool their resources and purchase, by way of a mortgage, his father's law practice in the healthy farming and mining community. Divorces, small suits, wills, buying and selling of properties, automobile collisions (especially if alcohol was an alleged factor)—the law practice was modestly busy and fairly routine. They joked about waiting for their first murder case and what they would do with it if it ever came along. They had the respect of the community and the local judge. Jerry Cohen was a Rotarian, member of the School Board, and one of the few regular worshippers at the only synagogue for eighty miles in all directions. Hamlin Smith was a Lion, hockey coach, member of the local Welfare Board, and could be seen with his young family at the United Church at Christmas and Easter.

All that Philip Gahbodnay was seeking was some legal advice. The Band had authorized no more than $250 for one visit and a follow-up letter or two. Philip's sister-in-law said that her brother, charged with shooting a moose "out of season," had hired Smith to defend him, found him helpful, and he was instrumental in getting the charge dropped. So, with a sheaf of papers in hand, Philip went for his appointment and made sure he was there before 4:00 p.m. Hamlin Smith moved some papers aside on his laminated desk and beckoned his client into a chair. "What can I do for you today, Mr. Gahbodnay?" he asked, anticipating another out-of-season or drunk-and-disorderly charge.

Philip began slowly. He retold the story, going back to the treaty of 1850. At first Hamlin just looked at him, waiting for him to get to the point. Then Philip handed him a map of the motherland, the ancient hunting territories he and Harold had worked so hard on over the years since he was sixteen. From the look on Hamlin Smith's face as he studied the document, one might have thought that the young Chief had just handed him the original manuscripts of Genesis, Leviticus and Deuteronomy. It suddenly occurred to him that he was talking to a duly elected Indian Chief about a land claim that involved one hundred and thirty-two townships which the Province of Ontario assumed it owned and on a piece of which were situated not only the law offices of Cohen and Smith but the house he had just bought two years ago, which was mortgaged for $75,000. He grabbed his pen and started writing quickly. After ten minutes he interjected. "Excuse me, Mr. Gahbodnay," he said, "I can't keep up with you. This is very interesting to me and important material. Our secretary is occupied this afternoon preparing documents that have to go to court in the morning, so I can't ask her to come in and take shorthand. Would you object if I turn on this recording gadget here, and I'll make a tape of what you're saying?

That will help me considerably. It's in complete confidentiality, you understand." "No, I don't mind, and you can call me Philip," he said. "I have to stop and think who Mr. Gahbodnay is." Philip smiled. Hamlin smiled. An eleven year friendship began. Hamlin started the machine. Philip started speaking. Over one hundred years of Wendaban frustration poured out. They closed the office together at 7:45. Matt was still waiting.

One week later Hamlin Smith phoned and asked to see Chief Philip in his office at his earliest convenience. Philip was there the next morning. Hamlin had discussed the matter with his partner at great length, but with no one else. They had arrived at a procedure they were now recommending. On behalf of the Band they would register cautions against all the Crown land in the one hundred and thirty-two townships, about 90% of the total claim as far as they could determine, in the Land Titles Office in Almaguin, without any previous announcement to anyone. He explained that a caution was a legally recognized caveat attached to a registered property, warning subsequent interested parties that there was a cloud of uncertainty over the ownership of the parcel of land in question. Such cautioned parcels could not normally be sold until the caution was lifted. Registering a caution was at the discretion of the local registrar of land titles. The Wendaban claim, in their view, fulfilled the requirements of a bona fide caution. All they had to do was show that certain legal conditions were met and properly articulated and the registrar must register the cautions. Judging the merits of the case was beyond his jurisdiction. In this case, the courts would have to settle the claim before the cautions could be removed. That would allow ample time for a defense. Filing individual cautions on every piece of privately-held property in the one hundred and thirty-two townships would take years and a huge sum of money. Cautions on the Crown land, however, could be ready, if fast-tracked, in about a month. A fee of $3000 would cover out-of-pocket expenses and extra secretarial help required. The rest of the fee, many times that amount, would be sacrificed by the firm vis à vis the recognition that such a case would bring them, and on the understanding that the Band would retain their firm at least up through the first court hearing.

Chief Philip returned to Sand Island elated. Not only had they received advice; they could within a month be embarked on a course of action which would force the issue onto the government's table after one hundred years of promises and fog. He summoned the Council the next morning. The vote was unanimous. He returned to Hamlin Smith the following afternoon with a letter authorizing the firm to proceed, in strict secrecy, and he brought extra documents that Hamlin had requested, as well as a cheque for $1000.

Four weeks later, as the Land Titles Office in Almaguin was preparing for a Christmas party the next afternoon, Cohen and Smith walked in at 9:30 a.m. with two bulging briefcases. By 3:30 p.m. the cautions were registered and notice sent to Queen's Park in Toronto. By 6:00 p.m. it was on the Almaguin evening newscast. By 7:00 a.m. the next morning it was reported in all the Toronto media. The Attorney General of Ontario was told the afternoon the cautions were registered just as he was rushing out for some last-minute Christmas shopping. "What!" he bellowed. "They've got to be kidding! That's going to tie up development up there as of today. It's ridiculous. It's got to come off. We'll get to work on it first thing tomorrow. Why didn't the Registrar contact me, the idiot! I'd have never let him do it." Such response was typical of that of the media, government, and befuddled public. Scrooge had struck again!

That was when Philip was twenty-one. Now, seventeen years later, the Registrar was still Registrar, Philip was still Chief, the cautions were still registered against one hundred and thirty-two townships, but the Attorney General had long ago receded into history. Few could remember his name. Such is the wonder of democracy. Such is the wonder of Philip Gahbodnay's drive for justice.

v

He pushed the curtains back as far as they would go to let into the crowded little office as much of the bright April morning sunlight as possible, then started to read the mail. It had built up for three days and Gisele had said he must get at it. Some items needed immediate attention.

As soon as he had finished reading Dr. French's letter, he called Harold. "Can I come over?" he asked. "Something's come up." "Sure," Harold said; "I was just going to take apart an old fishing reel and see if I can get it to work. I won't be going anywhere."

As he walked the path towards Harold's house the Chief was musing on this new possibility. He thought they probably owed Harvard a favor. Of all the research done over the past seventeen years for the claim, Ashton's study done in the 30's out of Harvard had been the key document—so helpful, authoritative, so crammed with observations and interviews that fifty years had now seasoned into gems. Now there was so much more to fold into the bigger picture.

"How long did he think she'd need?" said Harold again—"eight months to a year? Why so long? Most of them are in and out in two days." "That's not for us to know," said the Chief. "The point is, she could be here for almost a year, and I am wondering if she could stay here with you? She could discuss her work with you and she could help out when Angele is at school. Maybe she could draw off some of your time from that damn TV set. You're becoming a couch potato, Harold! What do you think?"

Harold was silent for a minute. "It might work, if she doesn't mind sharing the small bedroom with Ann," he said. "She sure ain't gonna share mine! And, only if she's nice. If she's an old bitch, out she goes." "Fair enough," said Philip; "but she's only twenty-five. You wouldn't think she'd be some old colonial know-it-all at that age, would you? She might be good company for Angele." "We'll see," said Harold. "But why should we be doing this? How much are we going to let her see? The whole thing? What about the new pictograph? And we're still agreed, aren't we, that we'll keep the old taboo secret for a while yet? Although, I sometimes wonder, now, what's the point." "Absolutely," said Philip. "But we can't afford not to give her a good look, at least, Harold. You know how valuable the Ashton stuff was when we came to put our claim together. Her teacher says she's dedicated and will see her work through to the finish. That's important. She's got to be able to stick with it. We don't need any more weekend specialists who plug us into their national grids on what Indians are supposed to be like, for some brownie points. We've already had two whites who want to write up our history, and we've been cool to both. And I don't see any of us doing it in the immediate future. Do you? Let's face it, Harold, how much longer are you going to wait around? So let's play it by ear. We'll look her over for awhile and then decide whether to open up the archives to her. We'll tell her that she comes up on spec—no promises. Let's ask her first to interpret all the pictographs. Sure. Why not the new one? Maybe she'll have some good ideas. Apparently she already knows a lot about us. I wonder if she knows Rita? She's an anthropologist—so was Ashton—and she's from the same school. Maybe we can get her involved in the Majukimo. She could be helpful, especially if she can get along with the kids. You know how much we've all talked about trying to get our heritage back into our bloodstreams. And how tough that is. Remember too, Harold, that with grant money so hard to get these days, she comes for free. Maybe we could support her with some room and board." He paused. Harold was frowning. "So, will I write her teacher to let her come?" Philip asked. "As far as I'm concerned, you've got a veto. You're still Shaman. I'll discuss it with the Council tomorrow, but they'll only want to know what you think. I'm sure they'll support it as long as somebody will be responsible for her and keeps an eye on her. Can I tell them you and I and Giselle will sponsor her?"

The old man sat another minute in silence, pondering. There wasn't even the tick of a clock to be heard in the little house. "If she's nice, I'll do what I can," said Harold, slowly. "I'll have to talk to Ann first. She probably won't mind. She's got to share her room for a whole year. Twenty-five, eh? From Boston. Maybe she likes baseball. Tell her teacher she'll have to like baseball. The Jays are going to take it all this year, you know." He chuckled. "At least she's a woman. I've been so turned off by the government guys lately, eh Philip? All the answers. All the answers. Input. Input. That's all they talk to us about. I wonder if they eat input for lunch? And then when we give it to them, they screw up their noses as if we'd just tossed them a sack of week-old fish. Their minds were made up before they asked us. You can see that. Why don't they ask us earlier?" He pulled his crutch over and slowly pulled himself up, and grabbed the other crutch. Like some behemoth of old he struggled to the window and stood, hunched, gazing out at his beloved lake. Would the lady from Cambridge be thwarted by the men from Achinike? "But you're right, Philip," he said to the window. "I would love to see our history written up before I croak. Wouldn't that be something! If she could only feel it from the inside. Be one of us. Feel the power. It's not gone yet, Philip. But maybe it's too much to ask anymore." He turned round to the Chief. A slight smile crossed the lined face. "Let's cross our fingers," he said. "Maybe she'll be a godsend. Ann and I will know soon enough."

"Yes, Harold," said the Chief. "We haven't much to lose, and maybe something to gain, if it goes well. Speak to the spirits. And speak to Angele. We don't want to go against her wishes. Yes, we'll hope for the best, Harold," he said as he rose to leave. "Who else is showing enough interest to stay a year? I'll get the letter off this afternoon."

Chapter VI
CONK

i

"Jesus Christ!" His head was stuck down inside the raised cowling of the old plane so that his voice boomed out as if from an echo chamber. They heard it next door in the office and Freda looked at Ted and muttered, "Good Lord!—now what." Earlier in the morning he had pushed the button on the hydraulic winch and watched the stubby Stinson come slowly up out of the water on the railway, into the metal hangar, its dulled yellow paint on the aluminum still able to reflect shafts of the brilliant June sun. Now he was standing on the stepladder with his head buried down beside the engine. He pulled back, straightened up, holding up a little screwdriver in his hand. "God damn it!" he cursed. He jumped to the floor and walked quickly across the boardwalk to the adjacent office on the second floor over the storage room. He bounded his large six-foot frame up the stairs and burst into the office, holding up the screwdriver by its tip as if it were a little reptile. "Can you believe it? Can you honestly fuckin' well believe this?" They waited, Ted and his wife, for they were used to his outbursts. It was all in a day's work. "That jerk," he said, "that stupid idiot jerk." Ted was seated on the stool in the corner under the high peaked gable roof that slanted right down to the floor so that roof and walls were all one. His head barely touched the roof, lined with photos in frames, screwed against the wood, of men holding strings of fish, lots of men, a few women, and strings and strings of fish, men in red flannel shirts posed smiling, with guns in their hands, beside dead moose and black bears, float planes of various kinds and colors, taking off, in the air, water-bombing, landing against evening skies of blue, crimson and gold. Ted looked up casually. "So?" "This morning on the Nelson trip I heard a funny rattle in the engine," he said. "Clankety clankety clankety. So when I got back I checked it out and look what I find." He held it up again. "A goddam fuckin' screwdriver lying in the bottom of the engine casing. Suppose that thing had worked its way up into the starter housing?" Ted still viewed him casually. "With all the other rattles in that thing, I'm surprised you could pick up a new one." Ted was not checked out for the Stinson, nor was the other seasonal pilot, Bill, but he had ridden in it enough times in the spring and after the fall moose hunt, when they cleaned and organized the outpost camps, to know what he was talking about. "No one but you would have noticed." "That's not the point and you know it," he said, scowling. "Why my plane, that little twit."

Freda looked up at him. She kept her voice low, unemotional. "Conk, I don't want to make a big thing of this, but you really have to watch your language around the docks. You know my feeling on this. You never know where passengers may be, even up here in the office. When you yell it's a public announcement all over the place." He ignored her, still intent on forcing the screwdriver into Ted's comprehension. Ted was the idea man, advertising and marketing, reservations, schedules, weather, public relations, employee relations, inventory, and some flying. Conk was senior pilot and mechanic. He kept the three planes flying, and knew every marsh and peak within a two hundred mile radius.

"Where is he? He worked last on Cloudie, not me." "Mike?" said Ted. "He's uptown delivering some luggage to the station. Shouldn't be long." "Well, you can bet I want to talk to him when he gets back,'' said Conk. ''This is like leaving the scalpel inside a patient. Three months later he bends over to tie his shoe and cuts his balls off.'' Freda kept typing but shook her head. ''You took him on, not me,'' said Ted. ''After all, Conk, he's only a student. You said just last week that this training program from the College had its benefits. We get him cheap with the subsidy and get a good chance to look over a possible future employee. Besides, he's your man. You're supposed to be training him. Why didn't you check over his work like you said you would?'' ''I did,'' he said, ''but I never thought I should be looking for a stupid lousy fuckin' screwdriver. Jesus! He just left it in there. Must have been dreaming about a broad, or something.'' He got up and went back to the hangar, climbed up and gently put down the cowling and snapped it shut, went over and pushed the button and watched her slowly move out into the sunshine and down the incline into the blue water.

Flying was his love and his life and she was his mistress. She was old but still powerful, and the most manoeuvrable of the three planes, maintained with his loving care. Parts were hard to get and they had built up a good inventory, but the summer before he had had to have a bracket machined, and when it wasn't quite right, although it would work, he had insisted on sending it back to be redone even though the down time stretched into the second week. Ted was upset. ''How can we make money when a third of what makes us our money sits idle in a short season, waiting for repair? We should sell it. We need new equipment,'' but as he said it he knew the bank would never go for another plane when they had just bought the Cessna the year before and were still deeply in its debt. But he also knew that if it went maybe Conk would go too, for the way he talked he sometimes thought they were married. His flying talk about himself and Cloudie had become legendary at the airways. The passengers would notice it and smile. "I can make her do anything I want," he would tell them, "but she's very demanding. She's a good woman, though. She keeps her mouth shut and gives me a great ride every time." Sometimes he could feel a woman bristle with such talk. Freda was reminding him that these were new days and it would be diplomatic to curb such suggestive language about riding and controlling and handling the "parts" of objects traditionally referred to in the feminine gender by the males who use them. He would just look at her and say, "I couldn't give a shit. If they want to ride in my airplane and pay the bill, that's fine with me. If they don't, they can swim." Freda kept on trying.

His bravado was in his talk, his manner, his style and view of things, joking, scoffing, never looking at anything as too big for him to handle, too dangerous for him to try, or too serious for him to meddle with. He was a perpetual, confirmed, anointed flirt. "You're the most spiritual man in town," Freda had once said to him, "but they're all animal, those spirits." She was, unlike Ted, a devout Catholic.

But his powerful hands were now gentle at Cloudie's controls, his bravado restrained to expertise. In the earlier days, sometimes when he would be alone heading back to the base, he had buzzed friends he would recognize in canoes or boats below him on the lake, and once, when one of his dalliances with the daughter of some tourists from Montreal blossomed into an affair, he spotted them out on the front dock among a group at the Silverwoods Resort and he dropped Cloudie down fast and aimed right at them. "My God, he'll crash!" the mother had screamed, and as the roar came at them like a rocket they scattered like flies, all but his sweetheart who stood quietly beaming up at him with her hands folded in front across her breast, the willing target of Cupid's mating call. Someone reported him and he was scheduled for a hearing in Almaguin by the Department of Transport, but after he wrote them two letters (it was Ted who dictated and Freda who typed), the charges were dropped with a stern warning.

But it was the following fall he remembered most of his youthful braggadocio. A father and his young son had gone in fishing for a week to a remote lake to the north, and their return pickup was scheduled for Saturday at nine. The fall colors were at their peak, the first Saturday in October, but the day had dawned grey with a mist of rain. It was a heavy low that would be around for at least another day. The Cessna was booked to get them, but as the weather worsened, Conk said he'd do it. They had cancelled the rest of the flights, but he took Cloudie up for a quick check. When he returned he said visibility was "the pits" but he would follow the lakes, flying low. Of the two of them, he knew the route better. They were waiting for him at the appointed spot. When they were airborne the father leaned forward from his rear seat on the canvas cradle and yelled into his ear: "I can't thank you enough for coming for us; we thought you wouldn't come. My wife didn't want us to come on this trip and she's very nervous." "That's okay," said Conk, who usually had few words in matters of sentiment, humility, or returning thanks. He looked over at the little boy who had pulled himself up almost out of his seat by the handle on the high dashboard to look out the front window, and said, "I thought junior here would enjoy the ride." He had had little to do with children. The ones he had known best were dim memories and those in the present, passengers mostly, were usually a nuisance and frequently puked. He had never changed a diaper nor fed a bottle; babies and kids he would suspend judgment on until they grew up. He looked again at the boy beside him, about nine or ten he figured, a few freckles on his nose, blue eyes and blond hair, squinting out the front window, then turning sideways to look down out the side window, then back to the front window again. "Geez, we're low," the boy said. "Once back there I could see the yellow leaves on the trees right at the end of the wing." "That's the only way I can know where we are," he said back to him. "If I go much higher we'll lose sight of it all. Do you like it?" "You mean you recognize all these lakes?" said the boy. "Geez. Sure. This is great." The blue eyes were so big he thought they covered his face. "Especially when you turn and go between the islands," the boy said.

So turn they did. Cloudie seemed in great form that day and he figured that if the dad really was grateful he wouldn't report him if the flying turned out to be a bit more than required by the call of duty. For forty minutes the four of them flew, without a word spoken, like the charmed falcon of legend, gliding in and around islands, turning almost on their sides, patches of yellow, gold, and bits of red shooting up at them, glancing off the wing tips, the rippled water coming up at them as they dropped low over a lake, only to fall away as they banked pushing against a face of rock and up, and over, and down again, curving, dark black marshes flecked with green and brown flotsam of lily pads tilting into jagged jack pine, suddenly then green white pine tops and more golden birch, a kaleidoscope of color never still, always tilting, an endless sensation of color, sound and sway. As he slowed into the final channel at the base he suddenly thought that he hadn't smelled any puke. Cloudie rocked back and up as she slowed to a crawl and the engine lowered to the idling punka punka punka punka when you could hear every heartbeat. "Geez, dad, maybe I'll be a pilot," the frecklednose had said as Cloudie drifted into Ted's waiting arms. But he wasn't looking at his father but at Conk, the eyes not much smaller, the worshipper so close to his god. "Geez, that was great, mister." Conk smiled a big grin at him. "Yes, it was great, wasn't it," he said.

He couldn't remember precisely where the "Conk" had come from, for he was christened Joseph, but he thought it was from the day Jimmie and he went fishing in the old cedar strip boat at Gawa. He was eleven then, and had already decided that his life would be spent out-of-doors in the bush country, and that fishing, even through the ice, was something special. It had been a lazy day in August and they had meandered in and out of bays casting for bass. He had caught more keepers than he could ever remember and decided he should start throwing all the rest back, for the heap on the boat's floor was beginning to look ridiculous. When they got home Jimmie said that Joe was charmed that day; he just kept "netting them, and unhooking them and conk on the gunnel, and netting them and unhooking them and conk on the gunnel," and he gestured with his right hand as if swatting a fly. The next day Jimmie called him the conker, and then it was just Conk. So after flying school when he applied to Lake Islands Airways in the small wooden office where the hangar now was, he told them his name was Joseph Seguin, but they could call him Conk. That was ten years ago when he was twenty-one. The Stinson was already over thirty years in service even then. He was trained to fly it that first summer, and by July was certified and flying fishermen and hunters, government officials, prospectors, Indians and two men from Natural Resources on the annual moose count. He had learned to tie a canoe onto the left pontoon and with a full load of passengers calculate the extra half mile he would need to get off. "Come on, baby," he would mutter in the odd tight spot as the ear-splitting noise of the nine pistons shattered the stillness of the peaceful lake, "you've got to make your own breeze today," and he would taste just a tinge of iron nails in his mouth as he would gently, gently ease her up onto the steps, trying to gather speed, "just a bit more, baby, come on, a little more, come on," as the treeline ahead came at them.

He had had close scrapes, and had learned that his great foe was not the one they had warned him of, the mirage of where the air appeared to end and the water begin on a calm cloudy day, so that you could suddenly slam into the water when you thought you were still fifty feet above it; the greater foe was taking Cloudie and conditions and his pride and talent for granted. He learned to fight against the easy assurance that because they had always done it before they would again, that Cloudie had no limits to her strength, her amazing agility. He would hold in reserve her limits for a needy day and he began to regard each day as his last, each flight as a crash in the making. He learned caution and respect.

It had been just "the Stinson" when he first arrived, but he soon learned it had been used in the war film *Captains of the Clouds*, filmed on the Lake with James Cagney in the 40's. When he finally saw the movie on the late TV that first year he so loved her looks (she was much younger then) that he christened her in a private ceremony the next day and secretly promoted himself to tenured Captain. At first they didn't take to the name; "It sounds like grey and not good flying weather," the owner had said, but he replied that when you spelled it his way it meant that she loved clouds, white billowy clouds, to fly through. She was a captain of the clouds. A month later they let him have her name painted in white letters with grey outlining just beside the doors behind the ladder. He put up a picture of Cagney in the office.

Ted and Freda arrived three years later, to help out the aging owners with a growing business, and the following year the three of them decided to pool their savings and take a mortgage and buy Lake Islands Airways. They added ski service on the original Cessna the following winter as the iron mine grew in both its needs and the huge hole in the earth up behind the airbase.

What no one could figure out was his craze for photography and loons. When asked, he couldn't shed much light on it, only that a man had to have a hobby besides women and beer, and his course in photography at the community college when he was getting his basics for pilot training had "really interested" him.

But his interest in loons was a puzzle even to him. As a boy he had hunted and plucked grouse, conked fish, and once helped his father quarter a moose, and each time all he could think of was the good meal as long as he didn't have to cook it. Surrounded by wildlife all his life he had, until recently, scarcely noticed it.

After he became a pilot Aunt Jane sent him an illustrated book on loons one Christmas because, as she wrote on the card, "They're such terrific flyers they're supposed to make a stunt flyer jealous." It sat unopened for two months and then he picked it up, and then he couldn't put it down. He learned that their greatest flying antics occurred at mating time, in the early spring, "often in troughs of open water in lakes still icebound." Incredible, he thought. If it skidded onto the ice the loon would have trouble getting airborne again because it couldn't walk on its large webbed feet. They were placed too far back on their bodies, which was one reason they were such powerful swimmers, divers and flyers. Placed so far back, their landing gear could be tucked up well into the rear fuselage; loons were very aerodynamic, with flight speeds up to one hundred miles per hour, which was as fast as Cloudie went when she was burdened with a canoe. These "flypasts," he thought, had all the right stuff. Orgies. The men parading their flying skills to woo their women to bed, swooping, diving, turning upside down, flying sideways, heavy landings with blasts of flying spray, taking off again, all the while singing their heads off. But if they miscalculated—if they put a bit too much show for sex above their navigational instincts? "It would be pretty dumb to kill yourself against the ice even for a good screw," he said to himself, "or worse yet get stranded on the ice and have to sit there helpless with a hard on while the others all laughed at you. Grounded."

A few days later he had a flight to Sand Island Reserve, and after the government people got out at the dock down the hill from the Band Office, with their square black cases, wading cursing through the snow drifts in little inch-high rubbers made for Toronto afternoons, he radioed the base that he was going to take a half hour off. "Roger," said Ted, "but keep in touch. There's a front moving in in about an hour." "I'll be back by then," he said. He got out and poked around the skis with his foot just to make sure there was no slush in the area, then headed up the hill to Harold's house. He had fished with him years earlier and knew that Harold was wise in natural matters. Harold came to the door, on only one crutch then, and slowly recognized him. "Come in, young man, come in," he said, pointing to a chair with his crutch. "Did you bring me a package, eh?" Harold dropped into his green recliner. "Sherry, maybe?" he chuckled. "That can be arranged," Conk said, "but I've come to pick your brains, Harold. I've heard that the loons put on a pretty good show at spring mating time. If I could find some before the ice was out, I'd need about a mile of water to land in. I want to get some pictures. Got any suggestions where I'd try?"

The old man grinned. "You'll never know how we men can fuss over a woman until you've seen their mating dances. Very competitive." He looked out the window. "We're going to have snow in about an hour. You can't stay long. I won't get out the sherry." "Beer," said Conk, "but not when I'm flying." "I haven't seen their mating games for years," Harold said. He paused. "Keewaydin Bay. That's where I'd go. They bunch up there usually by mid-April, depending. The channel is likely open now. Bad ice all winter. Too much current. It curves. About one hundred feet wide I guess. You could probably land, though I've never heard of anyone doing it. Afternoon'd be the best time." He chuckled. "Before bedtime."

So it was that April, the 19th he would remember, that he watched, crouched unseen among the pines, bewitched. Ted didn't want him to go. "Ice isn't very kind to pontoons," he said. Conk just looked at him. "If Cloudie and I can't make a perfect landing, we'll come home. We'll be fine."

It had been a warm spring, and although the main lake was still ice-bound, the bay at town had just opened up the day before. They had dragged the three planes out onto the ice two weeks earlier from their winter perches on shore, and he got airborne that first day of open water, darting down the lake, crossing back and forth, letting everyone know they were flying again. He swooped down over the ice-bound resorts, and circled Sand Island. "I'm back," he shouted; "send me your women, send me your men, I'll fly them to heaven, I'll fly. . ." He couldn't think of a rhyme that made sense. He circled low over the Keewaydin Bay Channel twice, pretending he was going to land. "I can just make it," he said aloud to himself, "with a nickel to spare." He counted four loons. The others were off reconnoitering, he thought. "The fun begins at 4:00."

The next day at noon he landed, the loons scurrying like little motorboats up on top of the water off to the sides of the channel. He came to rest about twenty feet from the ice pack. He paddled Cloudie into a shaded nook, tied her to a tree, removed his camera, tripod, and sandwich. He worked his way through the underbrush to a point at the middle of the channel. He was prepared to wait. He counted six loons. They would have to get used to the floating plane. They'd surely remember that it was okay, he thought. Might it spook them? Would they get a message to the sky raiders that an alien was present? Would they postpone the flypast? Cancel it?

He ate his sandwich and waited. There were no bugs out yet, but it was awkward squatting, then sitting cross-legged, then kneeling. The bush had him boxed in and twist or squirm as he might, he was uncomfortable. He had several scratches. He had checked his sight lines through the camera on the tripod a hundred times. The six loons swam placidly, dipped and doodled, snapped up some fish, but otherwise seemed bored. He didn't want them to see him. He glanced at his watch. Almost 4:00. "My luck," he said to himself. "These are probably six old pensioners past childbearing and the rest have gone off on a spree somewhere else." There was a faint whiff of chill air from the ice down channel, and as the breeze came up he could hear a symphony of chimes and tinkles as the tiny needles of melted ice fell off from their mother and played a last tune of joyful sprites against one another.

Suddenly a sound sent a chill up his spine. From high overhead he heard one high-pitched laugh. Then came the squeaky pumping of wings, hundreds of them he thought, right on top of him. He looked up. They were zigzagging right over him, coming in low. Then the air exploded in sound, shrill laughing yodels, piercing, intermingling, the sounds crashing against the channel rocks and echoing back at him. They dove. There must be twenty of them, he thought. Black bodies speckled with white, their necks and pointed black heads stuck out straight in front, they pulled out of the dive only seconds before the crash into the water, the cascading pulses of shrieking laughter getting louder. Then came great splashes. They were landing, scudding in on his left and right. He could hardly see them for the spray. Some rose straight up, flapping. A few dove directly into the lake like rockets, sending up a wall of spray. One pair came right at him; both were on top of the water crashing their wings down onto the surface in a frenzy. As they veered at the last minute and headed back out into the channel, he looked directly into the round red eye—no lid, no eyebrow, a tiny black pupil. Noise, spray, the flapping sound of the wings on water, then the leathery sound of the airborne wings beating against his temples till he thought they would burst. He realized he was shaking a little. "Suppose they turn on me," he thought, "or Cloudie."

As he tied up the plane at the base the sun was setting. He was still tingling with an emotion he couldn't describe, a sight he would never have thought possible, flying that had defied broken necks and battered wings. Ted had locked the office so he walked up the street wearily to his apartment, dangling his camera and tripod, his head still full of the loons' piercing laughter. He laid the camera on the couch, rummaged in the freezer compartment for a pizza, and turned the microwave knob to 3. As he stretched his long legs out in front of him, and looked out at the sunset, it suddenly occurred to him that he had not taken a single picture.

ii

But now it was different. Over the last three years he had built up what he considered must be a remarkable collection of loon photos. He was sure he noticed a trend towards loons—on sweatshirts, coffee mugs, calendars, posters, telephone books, TV ads. Maybe he was coming into a good thing, he thought. He had bought two more books on them from the bookshop on the highway, and he figured that he must be becoming something of an authority. Freda could see at a glance the pattern in the reservations book; every Tuesday morning between 6:00 and 9:00 Cloudie was booked in for "loons," always in pencil because he insisted that if a trip came along that required him he could switch to another time or cancel the looning for that week. He tried to keep it all very low key, almost secretive, and when Ted occasionally kidded him about it he would shrug and mumble something about keeping fit and that without a wife to worry about, what else was a guy to do in the boonies during the best hours of the day. Twice now, known only to herself, Freda had turned down early Tuesday bookings when the other planes were busy. "He's a good mechanic, pilot, and friend," she said to Ted, "and if he's a cowboy and a bit loony we can forgive him, can't we?" she said smiling. They agreed that he kept them on their toes; they all worked hard and the business was growing.

Now he had a new venture. He had noticed that there was a great deal of knowledge about loons in the air, on the nest, on the water. Their powerful flying was matched by their gentle manners as parents, and unlike the mergansers who parted after he had had his fun, they stayed together as a family all summer and raised the babies until it was time to fly south to the ocean by the Carolinas and down the Florida coast. Like the dolphins of the sea they had several voices, an intricate communication system, and they called and yodelled and laughed and crooned to one another under the stars across miles of silent dark lake that few animals save the wolf could bridge with sound as well.

But there was little said about loons under water. As flyer, lover, parent, singer and fisherman, they were well known. As diver, submarine and torpedo, there was hardly a photo, scarcely a word. From the canoe he had had rare glimpses of them down through the water streaking against ducks and beaver silly enough to invade their territory, but he wanted to photograph them under water, to follow them. Their dives were routinely short, about one or two minutes; but once in a while he was sure one would disappear somewhere, as if off on a special underwater adventure. Their long necks and sleek bodies would show up under water in the same positions as they assumed in the air, but encased in bubbles. He wanted to record that too.

So the last year had been expensive. First the scuba lessons in the Y pool at White Falls, then the new equipment and underwater video camera. He had never paid much attention to money; there had always been enough even for the odd trip south to the big city, skiing in Quebec, and once, when Ted agreed to a short time off in the busy spring season, three days of salmon fishing in New Brunswick. He knew nothing about investments and whenever he had an extra grand, he bought another bank certificate, GICs they called them, which is what the bank suggested he do the first time, seven years ago, and now he had thirty-six of them. The little branch was so sure of his intentions, the staff just rolled the GICs over for him without even notifying him that they were coming due. But last year the underwater loons had made their claim, and he thought he had bought only three new certificates. He had the receipts along with all his financial records in the old box the telephone had come packed in; they had left it behind on his kitchen table when they installed his phone six years ago. It was getting full.

He stood on the pontoon in his rubber suit and a heavy knit grey sweater. He had pulled Cloudie back into the water lilies and tied her to a tree with a long rope. The sun had lit up the tops of trees on the opposite shore with the warm rich gold of morning, but wasn't high enough yet to light up where he waited. The shoreline was alive with early-morning birdcalls, arpeggios and chirpings, piccolos, oboes and flutes, and one high soprano practising her octaves. Recently he had been going down into Shiningwood Bay where there were two nests. This morning he was back to his old haunt, the original place, the backwater bay inside the curved channel to Keewaydin Bay, the nesting home of Henry and Henrietta. He wanted some balm this morning, some of the relaxed feeling of familiarity. Yesterday he had had to chew out Mike over the screwdriver, and the young student had looked aghast and had apologized, but he had kept pushing and haranguing and swearing over the need for care well after he knew the affair should have been over and done with, to the point where he found himself trapped in a performance, the big angry boss and headbasher. Mike had looked as if he were going to cry and asked, "Do you want me to quit?" It wasn't his style, and he smarted over it later. Exuberance, yes; arguments, confrontations, no; walk away from them had been his motto. He could count on one hand the times he had let himself work up into such a snit. Once he had walked away from a bar fight before it got going; "I could pound the shit out of you but it's not worth it," he had said, and no one present even hinted that he was a sissy or afraid because they knew he was right. He made it sound right. He was above petty fighting.

This morning, then, he would try again. He wasn't sure it was going to work, but he was bound to try it. He had brought a small plastic bag half full of fresh minnows, half full of air. Yesterday afternoon between flights he had experimented with a little polypropylene rope attached to the bottom of the bag and to a weight, so that the minnows would hang suspended about seven feet above the bottom. He figured he was going to be in twenty feet of water. Henry, the script called for, would spot them, dive for them, and he would record the whole thing on videotape. But this morning he had a funny feeling. He was sure Henry knew him now in this third year of his being among them, and Henry was very bright. "He'll probably say to himself, 'Look at this idiot. He's got a bag of fish and I'm supposed to dive for it. What he doesn't know is that I don't take my fish prepackaged in plastic when I can get them *au naturel*.'" The shoreline across the bay was now fully lit with a golden film. Then he heard him, from farther down the bay. Henry was fishing for mother's breakfast while she sat on the nest. "Who," came curtly across the water, barely audible. "Who. Who." He crouched down, pulled himself into deeper water sliding on his stomach, and slipped beneath the surface, clutching weight, minnow-bag and camera tied together. He swam quickly to where he thought would be about the right place, and surfaced. He was about one hundred feet from him; Henry was floating silently. The red eye saw him, he was sure, but Henry did not move. He dove down and put the weight on the bottom, carefully letting the bag rise to the full extension of the rope. It was perfect. The sun's rays were now hitting the clear water and it was translucent all the way down. The minnows were lively. They looked as if they were enjoying it, he thought. "My God, what a breakfast, Henry," he said to himself. He swam to a spot about twenty feet away and waited. He looked at his watch. He had thirty-five minutes of air left. The water was still. There wasn't a sound. "Come on, Henry. Mother's hungry and here's God's aplenty." He checked his camera. All was ready. He waited. He swam in little circles to keep the stiffness from setting in. He waited. With only five minutes of air left he surfaced. Henry was nowhere to be seen. He waited for him to surface. Nothing. Henry was gone.

As he headed back to the airbase, he pondered. There had to be a way. Was it only a matter of time? He'd just have to be patient. Should he look into some kind of underwater sound device that might attract him? He noticed a heavy cloud bank to the north, deepening into storm clouds at the horizon. He glanced at his watch. Bill had a flight up there to Sable Mountain. Maybe he had delayed it. He landed and taxied up to the dock and cut the engine. Ted grabbed the wing and pulled him in. "Freda wants to talk to you, Conk. You'll have to do a

run for Bill," he said. He walked into the office and gave
Freda a smile. "What's cookin', good lookin'," he said.
They tolerated his teasings but he was careful to go no
further. They were a good team. "You'll have to do Bill's
sched," she said. "There's a storm up north. Bill got in
okay but he's going to sit it out. Let's see," and she
glanced down at the book. "One passenger and luggage.
Meet the *Northlander* and bring her here; she's going to
Sand Island. From Boston. Cash deal. Miss Catherine
Saltonstall." She looked up at him. "Says in her letter
she's doing research on the Reserve for a university."
"Aha!" he said. "One of those!"

The *Northlander* was only fifteen minutes late this
morning. Lately it had been running as much as an hour
behind. He met it, or waited for it, regularly. June brought
the campers who in spite of the bugs were going to renew
their souls in the pristine wilderness that the margarine ads
pictured so beautifully, and the train had to wait for
chartered buses and airplanes and connecting trains, some
boarding in Toronto, arrangements having been made
months in advance. The ultimate lure was James Bay, but
Achinike had long been an internationally-known
wilderness haven from the days when the old railroad
advertised it in the *National Geographic* in the 20's as the
true virgin Canadian wilderness, and ladies came up in
long dresses and high heels to dance the nights away at
the two famous lodges down the lake. There were only
two trains now, each of four cars, each with a locomotive
pointing forwards, as well as backwards, depending on
which direction it was going, so that heading north the
front one pulled the one sticking out back, and then it was
vice versa on the trip south, so that the train had no
forwards or backwards and it never had to turn around. If
the front engine failed, the back one could push, and no
one would know the difference. While one train was

heading north from Toronto the other was heading south from James Bay. They had managed to pass one another at the appointed siding at precisely the appointed minute the schedule called for only three times in the last four years. But then, they catered to the individual needs of all sorts of bushwhackers.

He watched the first passengers get off, trying to spot a university researcher. He didn't have a clear picture of who he was looking for other than her gender, but he supposed a brown tweed skirt, spectacles, 45ish, hair in a bun, silk stockings and brown-laced leather shoes. The platform quickly filled, some getting off, others getting on; there were dirty brown and orange knapsacks thrown here and there and kids running, and a canoe struggled forward with hairy legs sticking out from under it, searching for the baggage compartment. He lost sight of the conductor at the train's door behind the wall of people. He looked down. Lots of low-cut sandy-colored leather boots with heavy dirty white socks, jeans and sneakers, wallabies and roeboks with neon purple and pink and green stripes. No silk stockings yet. One pair of bare, tanned female legs caught his eye and he followed them into the washroom. But she wouldn't arrive in shorts, would she? he wondered.

"Excuse me, would you be from Lake Islands Airways?" she said. He turned to the soft voice at his elbow and looked down into her hazel eyes. "Sure am, honey," he said. "You Miss Saltsmill?" "Saltonstall," she smiled. "Catherine. I'm afraid I have two very heavy bags." He grabbed one in each hand trying to let on they were not that heavy, but she was right. "Follow me," he said. "A perfect load," he thought: "Cloudie, me, Miss Boston, and three hundred pounds of iron ore."

As he drove the Jeep Cherokee the short distance to the base he pointed out some sights for her— the Shell station which served the best hamburgers in the north, the new senior citizens' home, the Welcome Centre with its library and displays, the Waterfront Pavilion which held a canoe collection, dances, and fish derbies. He looked over at her and took her all in. She was on the smallish side, had on a very fresh-looking pair of jeans and clean white sneakers. Her checkerboard red and white blouse showed off her smart figure, "ample but not stacked," he noted; her shoulder-length auburn hair had a sheen to it. He didn't think he could smell perfume, but there was something there, perhaps fresh soap. She seemed relaxed, friendly, smiling, yet somehow a bit distant, erect, her white teeth perfect, no lipstick or makeup, her skin hardly tanned. By the time he and Mike were unloading her bags down to the plane, he had decided she was really very attractive.

While he gave Cloudie some gas she went up into the office and paid Freda her fare, in Canadian dollars. "That storm's going to stay north of us, heading east," said Ted coming up to him; "there's some rain coming but you'll be okay. Almaguin says we'll be clear by 1:00 o'clock." The bags were loaded, he climbed in and Ted helped her up the ladder into the other front seat. Conk pulled the door shut and fastened the latch. Normally he let passengers buckle themselves in, unless they were having trouble, but now he reached up and pulled down the buckle and strap, across her front and down into the latch. He wanted to touch her, but somehow he managed not to. "Wouldn't want you to fall out on your maiden trip in the northcountry," he said; he was sure he was going to say virgin trip but he said maiden. She smiled, very faintly. "Meet Cloudie," he said, giving the dashboard a little slap. "We've been together for many years. I work her hard but she rarely complains. She's a good woman. She gives me a good ride every time," he said, not looking at her. "I'm sure she does," she said. "Any woman would be crazy not to give you a good ride every time, now wouldn't she!" She looked at him without smiling. He looked at her, without smiling. "My God, I wonder if she thinks I'm a jerk already," he thought. "This could be interesting."

Whanga whanga whanga whanga; the high-pitched starter sang his favorite song. Cloudie's engine caught with sharp explosions of sound. They moved out slowly into the bay. He did his routine check, adjusted the prop blades for takeoff, raised the rudders, checked behind as he worked the flaps. One of Cloudie's signs that she was a pioneer they had never updated; the wing flaps were still raised and lowered by cranking a handle in the cockpit ceiling. She said, "What's that for?" as he cranked them down. "That winds up a big rubber band back there," he said, looking straight ahead. "Oh, then I was right," she said. He looked at her. No one had ever said that before! "If you wish, you can grab that handle in front of you on the dashboard," he said, pointing. "Some people like to pull themselves up so they can see out the window during takeoff. Or any other time. Sometimes it gets bumpy. It's going to be bumpy today, likely, but it's only twenty minutes to Sand Island." He smiled at her. "Thank you," she said. He turned Cloudie her routine turnaround, once, glanced at the heat gauge, pointed her straight down the channel and slowly pulled out the throttle handle. Cloudie roared into deafening sound and gathered speed quickly. He never looked at his passenger during takeoff. It was a critical time. A log could suddenly appear out of nowhere, or some crazy boater, trying to prove something, dart across their path. Years of flying had given him a sensitive feel for when he could trust her to air, when she was high out enough and fast enough to leave the water and become a bird. The takeoff was his favorite moment of flying, the sensation of power, the crashing noise, the gradual pushing of his back into the seat, the feel of the lift, the winning of the challenge, the receding spray, the water and islands slipping away below as if falling off the pontoon into a mirror, the throttling back to a steady hum. The islands spread out before them as in a huge puzzle for the gods. He never got tired of looking at it.

"It rattles a lot, doesn't it," she shouted over to him, leaning his way a bit. "I can't hear myself think. Is it always this noisy?" "You get used to it," he said back to her in a raised voice. "Remember, you've got nine pistons and no muffler, right under your nose." "Oh!" she shouted. "Look down there," he said, pointing. "That's a log boom. We're one of the last places in North America to still haul logs by water. See the little rope attached to the tug? They're cutting up at Sharp Narrows and it takes him three days to pull the boom down to the mill in town. Reads an awful lot of novels, he told me. There's enough logs in that boom to last the mill only about three weeks." "Oh!" she shouted. "What kind of research are you doing?" he asked. "Welfare?" "I'm trying to find out more about their history," she shouted. "It is going to take a while just to get a handle on things." He looked over at her and thought he'd like to handle her things. "Can't help you there," he said; "I live for the present only." "I am sure you do," she shouted; "but if you continue to fly this thing, there may not be much of it left." He decided to shut up until they were parked at the Band dock.

Freda had phoned ahead and there was a welcoming party waiting—of one—the Band Secretary, Giselle. The Chief was busy. Pleasantries were exchanged. The Chief had made arrangements for her to stay with Harold and Angele, and Giselle concurred that it was an excellent choice. "I hope you like sherry, TV and baseball," she said to Catherine. "Those are his favorite pastimes these days." "Well, we will not have a problem with baseball anyway," she said. "I hope no one has objections if a Red Sox fan comes onto your Island. Do you get the Sox games up here?" "Only when they play the Blue Jays," said Conk. "You'll get a few." He saw no way out but that he would have to lug the two bags of iron ore up the path to Harold's house, but the researcher grabbed one and surprised him with how well she managed. Angele had stayed home from school to greet her, and shook her hand warmly, but was shy and quiet. As soon as Harold saw how young and pretty and fresh his new house guest was, he mellowed; when she responded to his question about baseball, his apprehensions disappeared. He thought that after such a long trip she might like some sherry. "The Chief has booked an appointment with you for Friday; in fact he's pretty well set the whole afternoon aside for you," said Giselle. "We'll be in touch. Angele will show you around the Island and help you get settled. But she has to go to school, so if there's anything I can do, please call; our office is just down the path, there, and I live down by the store." She shook hands again, and left. Conk lugged the suitcases into the tiny bedroom and could hardly fit the bags between the beds, or the bed and the wall. "Oh well," he thought, "she just sleeps in here," noticing how small each bed looked for one, never mind two. If he ever got her to bed, this was not the place, he decided. He hoped she would follow him into the little room because he wanted a private word with her, but she didn't. When he returned she was declining sherry, and he went over to her and said in a lowered voice, "Would you like me to check in on you in a day or so? I mean, they'll treat you terrific here; Harold is a fantastic old fisherman and he'll have stories to make you laugh and cry. He's God's aplenty, alright. I just thought you might like someone to talk to who you know." He thought it sounded a bit odd as he said it. She looked perplexed, then turned to Harold. "Do we have a phone, Harold?" she asked. "Sure. He knows the number. Get him to show you his loons," said Harold, chuckling. She looked back at him and said, "That would be nice, then. But give me a while, anyway, to get the ringing out of my ears."

As he untied the pontoon rope, he had already decided against his earlier idea to go all the way down the side of the island and round to the back bay where the sand beach was, so she would hardly hear the takeoff noise. That would take an extra fifteen minutes; then she probably wouldn't hear it at all if Angele was talking to her, just a little hum off in the distance. No, he'd taxi down the lake a bit, just far enough so that he'd be getting airborne as he passed directly in front of Harold's house. The noise would be deafening for a moment. "Those old windows'll rattle," he said to himself. "She might as well get used to it. She's in the northcountry now." He pushed the heavy bird out into the lake and jumped up into the cockpit. "We've got our work cut out for us, Cloudie," he said as he latched the door. "How can we get Henry to take those fish? And how can we get Miss Saltonsmill to like us? Both of us!" It occurred to him that he hadn't told her his name. But then, she hadn't asked. "She has an odd accent," he thought; "doesn't seem to get her r's out right, especially when she says Harold. Saltonsmill. That's not quite it. I'll have to check the book when I get back." "Whanga whanga whanga whanga," said Cloudie.

Chapter VII
N'DAKI MENAN

i

The first few days flew by. She thought she would feel strange and awkward for a while, but it didn't happen. How quickly she would begin to feel comfortable was evident the first morning. She knew that in spite of the journey she would not be able to sleep much past her usual early rising hour. She had decided she would slip out and walk around for an hour or more before breakfast, though she knew from their walk up the path the day before that there were a lot of barking dogs around. But they'd better get used to her, she thought, "and me to them."

Dawn was her favorite time of the day, and she wanted to be alone, to steady herself, to contemplate an agenda in her new world. Angele and Harold had done much to wash away her anxieties the night before, but there was still so much ahead. She would need all her reserves, her strength, her determination. And her guard. She must get right to work as soon as she saw the Chief; he could open many doors for her—or not. She had two days to reconnoitre and plan her strategy, pinpoint her needs.

When she woke and glanced at her watch she couldn't believe that Angele's bed was already empty. Then she smelled coffee. It was 5:15. Angele was at the only table in the little house, reading, a notebook and coffee cup beside her and a pink highlighter in hand. She looked up. "You said you'd be up early, but I didn't think it would be *this* early," Angele said in a hushed voice. "I'm so glad. After I get done with school we'll have the mornings to talk and explore, before I have to go to work. I had to find extra quiet time this year for studying. Exams start next week. Grandpa loves his TV at night and it's harder to study then. I started getting up at 4:30 last October, and now I love it. I have to be gone by 6:30 to catch the bus. Grandpa will be up about 7:00, and I'll leave his breakfast ready." "Well, don't pay any attention to me," said Catherine. "I'll grab a coffee and go for a little walk. I'll be back before you leave. You can tell me what he likes to eat and I'll get his breakfasts."

She stood outside the door, looking down on the lake, full of new sensations. Her first was that she was already not just pleased but baffled about the coffee in her hand, that she had had to come up into what some of her friends had portrayed as savage if not brutal country, to taste at 5:30 a.m., better coffee than she made at home. Was it the altitude or air or what? She had fallen into the habit of making instant, and here her dark-eyed Wendaban had made perked coffee before she was even out of bed, sending the rich aroma all through the little bungalow, not specially for her new houseguest but for herself. And she likes the early mornings, she thought. They would get along just fine.

The light was different, too. She thought of Emily. She knew that the farther north you went, the earlier and later there was daylight, especially with the solar mid-year only days away. But she wouldn't have believed that only eight hundred miles could make such a difference. It wasn't just the quantity of it, but the color of it. It seemed different. She'd have to study it more. In Cambridge, there would by now be signs of the dawn, but only a faint lightening. Here it was already daylight and although she was looking northwest, she was sure the sun must be just ready to slip above the treeline behind her. The lake lay still, stretched out before her below, so blue she thought of Van Gogh. The birds were making a cacophony of sounds. She would have to inventory them, later, for her journal. "I wonder how many Cambridge birds I'll find up here," she thought. A dog barked.

For the next two days, until her meeting with the Chief, she thought that with Angele at school, she'd have to look for things to do, but she was almost swept off her feet. If Harold had limited access to his bowed legs, he compensated with his access to the telephone, for he had one of the few private lines on the Island. Most of the others were party lines of two, three and four houses per line. He knew every phone number on the Island by heart, and she was no sooner out the door on one visit than he was lining up another, spreading the good news that his new visitor must be made welcome. As far as he could detect, she had nothing to do with any government, he said, and being from Boston she was a Red Sox fan, adding some spice to life. He had never heard of Cambridge, and Harvard hadn't sunk in yet. She didn't have to explain about the big net in Fenway's left field; Harold had often chuckled over it, especially when George Bell drove a ball up there as he could do. She was invited down to the store where Angele worked on weekends, and met Diane Friday, postmistress. She learned about the receiving and sending of mail on an island by boat and snowmobile. She visited the schoolhouse with its twenty-four students spread out from grades one through eight, all in one room, and she talked to them for half an hour about Boston and her trip to Achinike by plane and train.

Giselle had a day off, and invited her over. Her husband, Matt Commanda, had inherited his father's business and was now the most prosperous contractor on the lake. Their house was one of the finest on the Reserve, two storeys, with central oil heating and vacuum outlets. Giselle didn't serve her tea, but "anibiwanagek," a blend of plantain and bark juices with hot water, which she only served on special occasions, she said. Catherine decided that if she could not get a job as anthropologist, she would open an anibiwanagek shop in Cambridge, with fresh hot buns and an adjoining used-book store. Giselle said she would come down and help her set it up. She must be the new Indian woman, Catherine thought as they chatted— attractive, well educated, holding down such a responsible job, in the driver's seat of their land claim, dealing with lawyers and negotiators and other band representatives, tourists and do-gooders. "We had a good one a few days ago," said Giselle in her warm husky voice. "He was very thin and wore a black wilted suit and black tie, and his white shirt had been washed too much and looked threadbare. He looked like a tombstone salesman and he was just suddenly standing there in the office in front of me. No phone call; no appointment. I never did hear whether he came by plane or boat; he came out of nowhere. He looked as if he were going to cry. 'I'm from the Bishop Blakeny Memorial Church in Toronto,' he said in a tiny voice I could barely hear," and she imitated a dry wisp of a sound. "'We made a substantial contribution to the Anglican Indian Freedom Fund last year, with specific instructions that our funds were to go to support your land claim.'" They were both beginning to giggle from Giselle's impersonation. She went on. "'My congregation has asked me to investigate the situation up here and report back to them before we allocate further monies.' I usually try to screen some of the odd ones, who show up once in a while; of course they all want to talk to Philip. But this time I thought I'd better get him into the Chief's office fast before he died on the spot with his money." They laughed.

Giselle already knew Catherine was a baseball fan, and she asked her youngest son Joey to show her the ballfield. "We're a little nuts around here about baseball ourselves," she said. "Of course, it's softball, but it gets pretty exciting. Matt played up until a few years ago, but he can't keep up with the younger ones now. Seems as if I've been a baseball mom since the kids were small, but I love it. Sometimes it's a great release to yell at those Shagonash jocks." She laughed. "You'll get used to us," she said; "our bark is worse than our bite."

So Joey took her up the little path behind the schoolhouse, through the trees, to the ballfield. "We just had it resurfaced in May," he said, looking very proud. "There's usually a good crowd and we just put the lights in last year. Now we don't have to call the games." She figured the wooden bleachers on metal pipes might hold one hundred. He explained how there were five teams in the league, one as far away as Norich Junction, one hundred and five miles south of Achinike, and how they travelled by their own boats and vans and had to pick up each team, and their spectators, and bring them over by boat when it was a home game. Sometimes they couldn't get enough players but they tried never to forfeit a game, and would play with only six or seven players. Last year they had beat Almaguin with only six men because Sammy Osatig, their best player, kept hitting a home run every time up. She decided that as well as keeping Harold company for the TV games, she'd adopt the Wendaban Bears, for their home games anyway. "I'd love to see Mr. Osatig hit a home run," she said to him, smiling.

She arrived five minutes early. Giselle beckoned her to a seat and pushed the intercom button. "Miss Saltonstall's here," she said. "I'll be just a minute," the intercom said; "I've got to move some papers around to get a place for her to sit." "He'll be right out," Giselle said. She was sure in her head she wasn't nervous. She had been thinking about the interview for two days now, and had made some notes which she had with her, just in case she got sidetracked. Already, at only twenty-five, she was seasoned in such matters. She had tried to reassure herself that anyone who had come out of a doctor's oral exam with high honors, where six experts had tried to dissect a brain to see where its weaknesses were, was surely able to press her claims with an Indian Chief.

But her stomach said otherwise. Just after lunch she had had diarrhea for no apparent reason. Her bowels had always been the better thermometer of her state of emotional stress, she knew, from the morning after the seduction attempt on the Cape when she was a teenager and she had wondered if it would end in rape, through some of Lydia's more painful motherly talks on her great expectations for her only daughter.

Now she was an outsider. In spite of the warmth and friendliness they had shown her, she wondered if they were beginning to perceive her as so privileged, so white ("Shagonash," Harold had said, "your first word in Ashwagane"), so terribly Anglo-Saxon. The Chief controlled precious materials she needed. Why should he just hand them over to her? Should she pretend to be the expert, or play the innocent who was ready and willing to go to work? She must not be condescending; she hadn't come up here primarily to help them. She was a professional anthropologist. If her findings were useful, so much the better. She would have to keep her cards up her sleeve, the research and publications which she knew of and he probably didn't. She had her bibliography with her. If all else failed, should she beg? Should she make a donation to their cause in lieu of? How well had Dr. French paved the way?

The door opened and he stood there, slightly smiling. "Catherine Saltonstall, isn't it? From Harvard. You've come a long way. Please come in, and forgive my messy office." He looked at Giselle. "No calls or interruptions till we're done please, Giselle. Probably about 4:00." He turned to Catherine. "Do you drink coffee? If not, we have pop." She wondered if pop was an Indian drink. She said she did like coffee. "Good. We'll keep the pot full. Please come in." She glanced down. It was 2:05.

She hadn't expected to find him dressed in buckskin and feathers, but he had her immediately off guard. He could have been an executive for a shirt company in Boston or New York, she thought. Funny, that in three days on the Reserve, when she had met so many people, she had never laid eyes on him, even in passing, he who held all the cards on why she had come in the first place. She thought he looked young, late 30's, dark hair, sharp features, just a touch Indian-looking if you thought about it, tanned clear skin, jeans, black leather cowboy boots with square-ended toes, light blue denim shirt. The shirt fit him perfectly and looked expensive. No feathers.

He closed the door behind her and she sat down in the one vacant seat. He was right. The office was a mess of files, stacked everywhere, on his desk, on a table, on the floor. The window looked out on the blue lake, and the early-afternoon sun was streaming into the office. There were no blinds, just faded light brown curtains. He got up and pulled one over a little so that she was in the shade.

"How have we been treating you?" he began, as he sat down. "They tell me you're a pretty nice person." He had a mischievous smile. "Is it true?" "That must be Harold," she said, trying to smile. "He seems to have adopted me already and has taken over as my public relations agent. I want to thank you for placing me there. I'm very fortunate." "He's a good man, still very respected here on the Island," he said. "He's our Shaman—I hope not our last one. As you get into our materials, you'll see how much has come from him, a bottomless well of information. His father, John Kenebek, or Whitebear as he was called, was Chief in the 20's and 30's, and was also a storehouse of information about our past. When your predecessor Ashton was up here, he got a lot of information from Chief Whitebear, but it was Harold who identified the old hunting territories for him. But they didn't begin to tell all. Even today, Harold will still pop out a name or story we haven't heard before. He's like a bilge pump in your boat after rain. You think you've got it all and you're just ready to turn it off when out comes another little squirt. But the last dregs of bilgewater are full of air and foam, and I fear Harold is getting that way. I suspect his imagination is now more vivid than his ability to recall fact."

She couldn't resist the temptation. She was beginning to feel at ease. "He's a wonderful host," she said. "I haven't really got him going yet on the old stories; that'll come in time, I hope. But we shouldn't worry too much about his imagination, Mr. Gahbodnay. Myths originate in the imagination. From the beginning they were explanations of the unknown, attempts to deal with and organize systems, some animal or personality that took its place in a larger story about where we came from, and who we are, and where we're going. If Harold has the old

Indian ways flowing in the marrow of his bones, his mind, as the rational part of it fades, may fall back into some basic, primordial associations. Even though he may be making them up, the older civilization may be bubbling up through him like oil from a deep underground reservoir. That's what my teacher, Dr. French, calls deep culture, as opposed, say, to dress and spoons and marriage customs. It's both inside you and outside you, and speaks up onto the surface through the imagination." He looked directly at her intensely. His teeth were set in a little grimace. "My God, what have I done now!" she thought. "I didn't mean to lecture." "I want to hear more about that, sometime," he said. "I want to hear a lot more about *that*." She was scoring, she thought. "I think I just cracked a homer," she said to herself.

He looked down and opened a file. He read out hastily her dissertation summary statement in a monotone. He had her whole proposal in front of him. She was sure she could see several letters. Bless Dr. French. He looked up. "This is pretty important to us, Miss Saltonstall. Pretty important. Harold agrees with me that it's crucial." He leaned back and put his hands behind his head, and put his feet up on the desk. He began the long story, carefully, passionately, in a quiet way, reviewing what they knew from a few digs and pictographs, of their earliest ancestors dating back three thousand years, the coming of the Europeans into n'Daki Menan, their ancestral homeland, the treaty they didn't sign in 1850, which ceded their homeland to the Crown, extinguishing all their rights to it, the subsequent years of disillusion and frustration, to their now being boxed in on a little island reserve where, whenever they stepped off it, they were subject to the laws of Shagonash. They couldn't net fish in their homeland, or they'd be fined, they couldn't hunt moose or trap beaver "out of season," or be fined, they couldn't cut trees for heat and docks and houses, without a permit. They watched the lumber companies clearcut huge tracts of their trees, and the miners dig out precious metals, leaving tunnels and shafts and huge holes under the land and lakes, ravines in the earth, and erosion. The view from the air told it all. "One mine, on Achinike Island," he said, "produced for a few years in the 50's, the second richest copper ore in the world, as high as 33% pure copper, second only to one in South Africa; they scooped it out of an open pit and stockpiled it in a huge yellow mound by the lake until the price was right. Shagonash was getting very, very rich." They watched the tourists arrive in increasing numbers leaving their garbage and helping nature burn down the forest. As the snow melted, they saw strange new patches of black collecting in gullies in the ice, like the swirls of giant cobwebs. On rare days, when the wind was right, they could taste the acrid yellow fog of sulphur in the air from Shagonash's smelter stacks fifty miles away, and they listened in disbelief as the chemists told them that the lakes of n'Daki Menan were going acid, that some were already devoid of life, and that their jewel, Achinike, would die before another one hundred years at the present rate of toxicity. "You've heard all this before," he said, leaning forward. "We can deal with the poison of our motherland. Much of it can be reversed. I, for one, believe that science, with nature's help, can mostly repair what it has broken. What bothers me is the loss of our soul, the poisoning of our sense of ourselves, of our assurances, of our roots. I anguish over whether that may be irreparable. That's the bigger problem."

He paused. She felt she should say something. She was rarely at a loss for words, but she felt crippled. Humiliated. The home run was wiped off the board, replaced by an error. She said nothing.

"We went to court first in 1978. Knowing how tough it would be, we had spent seven years researching our position—it's all in there in the original seven volumes of documentation, four more added since then, in huge binders," and he gestured towards the library. Her heart beat faster. "We backed off from our original position. We realized that if we let relations with our white neighbors in n'Daki Menan sour too much, we would do ourselves a lot of harm. We would have to live with them in the future regardless of the outcome of our claim. So we excluded all privately-held land from our claim, and we adopted a policy that in demonstrated cases of hardship, we would lift the caution on certain parcels of land. We focused our claim on the Crown land, and restitution for its depletion of resources."

He stopped. He grinned at her. "Would you like a coffee, Miss Saltonstall?" he asked. "This is pretty heady stuff and I'm sure you could use one. How do you take it?" "Sugar and a little milk, if you have it, would be fine, thanks," she said. He got up and went out. She wanted to stand up and stretch, but she wondered if her legs were shaking a little. She sat still.

He returned with two white, steaming mugs, "Wendaban Power" inscribed on each with a smiling face. "There are some among us who think the smiling face should be a clenched fist," he said as he handed her a cup. "We sell them at the store. I think we're better off with a smile." He sat down, stirred his carefully, and handed her the spoon. She glanced down: 3:05 already. They each blew against the steaming surfaces, and sipped. It was strong, she thought; it was good coffee.

"We suffered a major blow in our first court case," he continued. "The Crown surprised us. They brought in two American historians—odd, isn't it, that they couldn't find a Canadian to do it—from somewhere in New York State, who testified that the Wendaban Band of the Ashwagane had no connection whatsoever with the earlier civilization so clearly established by the digs. We were apparently descendants of itinerant Indians of no fixed address. They came up with the biggest cock and bull story you could imagine, about how we were a splinter group made up of some renegade Iroquois from New York and Mohawks from the Ottawa Valley. We were bedevilled by a lack of ferociousness and just kept moving about, they said, unwilling to stand and fight, always running out of food. You would have thought we were the founders of the Greyhound Bus Lines, they had us moving around so much. And some of us landed on Lake Achinike just a few years—get this—before the 1850 treaty. Our n'Daki Menan was pure poppycock; we were no more entitled to the land than the mosquitoes. You can imagine my sleep that night of the hearing." He sipped again.

"What evidence did they give?" she asked. "Funny, I'm not aware of their thesis. Have they published it?"

"It's all in there," he said, gesturing towards the library again. "Of course it's not published. Who would print such bird droppings?" He paused again, and took a good swallow. "The judge didn't pay much attention to it in his judgment; he noted it as a theory only, not proven fact; but he ruled that we were party to the treaty, so that was that. The real damage was to us. The theory of our being a wandering bunch of homeless wimps leaked back to the local press and the Reserve, and of course our enemies who wanted the caution removed and our claim quashed made heyday of it."

He studied her carefully. "We're only now recovering. We've tried to get our old mythologies into our school books, but there's very little in print. Maybe you could

help us there. A drama group has produced a play about
n'Daki Menan, with original music and dance, with great
success. They're going to offer it in the Rec Hall this
summer. The young people have really thrown themselves
into it with gusto. Next month, we're going to revive an
old Indian festival of thanks for the coming of the spring,
called the Majukimo. Thanks to Harold's constant
prodding, we got our native language put into the school
curriculum, but we can't find someone to teach it fulltime,
so some of us are pinch-hitting as best we can. But it's
tough going. If our Indian youth wanted to be front-runner
Canadians in the twenty-first century, they should be
fluent in Ashwagane, English and French; but that's too
much to ask. Are they Canadians first and Ashwagane
second, or Ashwagane first? We are now beginning to
understand why they must be Ashwagane first. You have
to know yourself and have confidence in your own culture
before you can be a good citizen of the larger group.
That's why what you are going to be doing is important to
us.''

He got up and went to the window and looked out at
n'Daki Menan. "I want to bring up two more
considerations," he said. He turned to her. "I'm sorry to
be doing all the talking, but I've been doing a lot of
thinking about you, and after Harold and Giselle gave me
the green light last night, I thought I might as well cover
as much as I can today. My job is to make your job as
easy as possible, as quickly as possible. So if you can
stand it, I'll go on."

She didn't know what to say. Should she say she was
interested, fascinated, grateful, excited, honored, appalled,
or fall back on the old American catch-all, flabbergasted?
None of them was alone appropriate; all of them were
true. She looked at him. "Please go on," she said.

"As things moved forward, it was inevitable that we'd have to grapple with questions of civil disobedience and militant action. The world around us was giving us the message." He returned to the desk and sat down. "Planes were blowing up, airports gunned down, the IRA was causing bloodshed in Ireland, the PLO in the east. When I was first engaged in this work, I watched fascinated as the American youth turned their country around on the Vietnam question. There were marches and huge protests, a great deal of civil disobedience. We had an American draft dodger here on the Reserve; he wanted to live with us. Nixon threatened to throw the long-haired punks in jail. You'd only be about ten then, I guess." He smiled. "I was pretty green myself. Anyway, there was growing pressure on the Band Council to become more militant. We had waited so long without tangible results. We were being studied to death; the government gave us a nurse and sent in social workers. We could now apply for drug rehabilitation. But deep down where it mattered, nothing was happening. We became convinced nothing would. How long can one wait? Would they break our resolve with time alone?"

"I had always advocated negotiation, persuasion, legal redress within the system. But I came to see that I was going to have to shift, first a little, gradually, more and more. We were just a willing tool of the Shagonash, I was told by some of our Council members. I was beginning to believe they were right. It was time to protest with all the new proven tactics. The Band insisted on a middle way; symbolic protest, vigorous, precise, well-planned and executed. We would make our statements in new ways. But no violence. We decreed that there should be no guns on the Reserve except hunting rifles, and they had to be registered with our Reserve Constable, Charlie Papakina.

We built a jail. We went into the law and order business while exploring ways of mildly breaking Shagonash law. We netted fish in front of the tourists' eyes, and got charged. We shot moose during the summer, and got charged. We cut trees without permits, and got charged. Our lawyers worked hard. There were backroom discussions in the halls of justice. We were becoming a political liability to the Crown. They didn't want to see us arrested; certainly not fined for catching fish. It made the newspapers. They let us off with warnings. Our strategy was working."

"Our first large-scale act of civil disobedience was a roadblock in 1985. I was reluctant, but gave in. The government had decided to extend a logging road another ten miles, into the heartland of n'Daki Menan. It was used only by lumber trucks and a few campers and fishermen. It wasn't heavily travelled. It was perfect. We staged it as if it had been a play in a theatre: tents, bonfires, blankets, food, placards. We even rehearsed the shouts. The media were alerted. Secretly we talked to the police. We would block the road on the second morning, allowing the first day of occupation for whoopla and pictures and statements. Three TV stations interviewed me. The second day was the actual blockade. We were to sit across the road in tiers, arms folded across our chests. We chose who would participate, a cross-section of men and women, Council, elders and youth. I would sit in front, in the middle. The police would ask us to leave, we would refuse, and they would pick us up. I remember the Sargeant in town telling me that they'd be as gentle as possible, as long as we didn't throw punches or resist too forcefully. We wouldn't resist. They would put a pre-chosen five of us, including me, in their paddy wagon—it was agreed they'd need only one vehicle—take us to town, charge us. No fingerprints, no detention. It would all be over and done with by noon. The five charged would return to the Reserve, the rest could block the road until sundown. We would then clear the road, and keep it cleared. We could keep our tents and bonfires on the roadside as long as we wished, and as long as we kept our part of the bargain, the police would leave us alone. We stayed for two months, on swingshifts. We sang songs, gave out pamphlets, talked to the tourists and the lumbermen, some of whom became friendly and regularly stopped for coffee. We grew in solidarity; we were mobilized. We had joined the 80's.''

"Since then the pressure for militancy has grown and may split us down the middle. More and more we are told to use our fists. Staging symbolic protests is a fraud, the radicals say; if you really believe in something you have to be ready to lay down your life for it. I tell them that if we had adopted that policy twenty years ago, there wouldn't be any of us left. Shagonash would have even this Island by now. Out there right this minute," and he gestured towards the window, "about half the Reserve believes in non-violence. Another sixty aren't sure where they stand. About twenty are ready to break any law by any means, including guns. But I'll get to them in a minute."

She noticed tiny beads of perspiration on his forehead. He went over and clicked on a fan on top of a filing cabinet, pointing towards the ceiling. "The rest of the offices are air-conditioned," he said, "but I don't want it in here. I talk to so many different types," he grinned, "some after our throats, some with bags of money to give away. I don't want to look too comfortable. The Chief should be seen to sweat." He sat down again. "How are you doing?" he asked. "It's 3:45 already and I've still got more I want to tell you. You're bearing up well. Had enough?"

"Graduate seminars used to last three hours, and sometimes Dr. French would get so carried away he'd forget the break. We've got an hour to go." She smiled. "Good!" he said, "that should do it. I hope I can meet him some day." He looked down at the closed file for a moment as if to collect his thoughts.

"I want to explain to you—defend, I suppose, would be a better word—our policy of non-involvement. We have been criticized for it, and our position is often misunderstood. Since we began our concentrated fight for justice through the courts ten years ago, a good deal in the world has swung our way. It must appear to a lot of white people that these are great days to be an Indian. Governments appear to be listening to us as never before. There are enquiries and commissions. We have the media's ear; we're a hot topic. We are invited to Shagonash's big tables in Ottawa. The public has swung round too. Polls suggest that native concerns climb higher in their priorities each year. They want land claims settled. We'll never be up there with job security, but we've come a long way. *The Last of the Mohicans* didn't turn out to be quite true for the Ashwagane; we're rising from our ashes. Shagonash's environmental concerns seem to fit right in with our belief that the land doesn't belong to anybody, that it is on temporary loan to the present generation to use only so as to preserve its use for the unborn. In our fight for justice, the child has gained new importance, the tree has become our symbol for hope."

"Take for example the Achinike Wilderness Society. It has taken as its special mission the preservation of an old growth stand of pine twenty-five miles north of us. Wherever the politicians have gone, someone shoves a poster in front of them about saving the old growth trees of Achinike and, by implication, the Wendaban. Someone said to me recently that preserving these old trees was on a par now, internationally, with saving the rainforests in Brazil. The Endangered Species Society in The Hague has moved it high on their list.''

''The Society came to us expecting, of course, that we would endorse them, join them. Get into bed with them I guess is the expression. We said no thank you. They were thunderstruck. Why not? Our goals were identical in their view. In print, they loved us, we were the saviors of the new dawn. One of their spokesmen, a university professor, began to sound as if he belonged to the Band and was speaking on our behalf, very politically. We objected most strenuously, and forcibly disassociated ourselves from them in print. I hope they still respect us, but some of them will never understand nor forgive us for what they perceived as our inexplicable disdain.''

''The problem is that when you get into bed with someone, you make yourself vulnerable to that person's colds and coughs and more serious communicable diseases—and responsible for—if there are any—the offspring. After the honeymoon is over, there can be painful separation and divorce. Our fight for justice is with the Crown, no one else. It was the Crown that defrauded us in the first place—stole from us—and it is only the Crown that can correct the injustice. We have no grievance with loggers or miners or commercial fishermen, nor have we a special interest in preserving any one stand of old trees, or young ones, moose as opposed to beaver, hummingbirds over butterflies. That one species should be singled out over another is precisely the kind of colonial thinking that has got us into the environmental mess we're in in the first place. Let us have a say in the management of all natural life in our homeland, we say, and all the rest will fall into place. We say to Shagonash:

'Give us a chance to try our ways, now that yours have failed. If your new dawn is rising,' we say, 'the sun is coming up much too slowly. We can't see it move. Nanabush has attached huge weights to it below the horizon. We'll freeze before it gets high enough to warm us.' So we have steadfastly adhered to a policy of non-alignment. Our battle is a single-targetted one with a specific antagonist, the Crown, and all our limited energies must focus on that struggle alone. To join with these other concerns, worthy though they be, would be to water down our case and lend it to confusion."

He paused. "How's your coffee? More?" "No thank you," she said, "but you go ahead. I'm grateful for this briefing. It's very helpful." She decided to stay away from superlatives for the moment. "I'm almost done," he said, "though I have two surprises for you at the end." His face grew serious, his mouth terse.

"Recently, we've had to live with a divisive element. I said there were about twenty militants on the Reserve. It may be only fifteen, or ten, if it came to a showdown. But the hard core is determined. They call themselves the Warriors. We believe they have a cache of guns hidden somewhere, but we can't find them. They meet regularly, secretly, rotating among one another's houses. Apparently they've taken an oath, fingers pricked with blood and all that stuff. We speculate they're getting terrorist propaganda and tactics from somewhere, but we can't be sure. They have vowed to go to next Tuesday's roadblock." He paused, wiping his brow. He looked as if he were in pain.

She was visibly agitated. "I cannot believe it," she said. "Satan in Paradise." "This is no paradise, Miss Saltonstall," he said, "though you've got the Satan part right. But I want to end on a positive note—my two little surprises. I hope they turn out to be as important as I think they are.'' He got up and went again to the window, looked out for a few seconds, then turned and stretched out with his back against it and his arms folded across his chest. He smiled. She was sure she had seen him on a TV ad for blue denim shirts.

"Last year my son and I discovered a new pictograph on a canoe trip to a lake north of here. We were searching every rock and cave in the same area as a known rock painting. It's in very good shape. There are four different symbols or markings on it that I can identify, in three colors, the usual brown, blue and red. I took pictures which you may borrow. In high water it's a bit submerged, but by the fall it's all above the surface. My son has been sworn to secrecy and as far as I know he has kept his word. Of course, I'll report it when the time is right, but with tourists chiseling off bits of the known ones, I have decided to keep it to myself for now. I've taken Harold up to look at it. I'll take you up there this fall if you wish. Maybe the markings will mean something to you.'' She wondered if he could hear her heart beating; to her it sounded louder than Cloudie's idle. "I'd love to see it,'' she said. "In the meantime maybe I can identify some of the markings from the photos.'' He reached over to the top of the filing cabinet, and handed her an envelope. "Don't lose them,'' he said. "That's the only set I have.''

"Then there's another surprise,'' he said. "As you may know, Rita McDermott from McMaster University has been on three digs in the Birch Point and Graceful Lake areas.'' "Yes,'' she said, "I've read her articles. She's excellent and devoted. I was going to ask if you knew whether she was still working on them.'' "Last summer,'' he continued, "she found a new site. It's still secret. It's in a remote little lake, too small to land a plane in, and very hard to get to by portage. If Sammy Osatig hadn't got her canoe in there for her the first time, she never would have found it. She goes in and out by helicopter, now, about once every two weeks. She has a student working with her. She thinks it may turn out to be the best site yet, maybe even in the whole northeastern region. It's all buried in what was an old sand beach, only about ten feet in from today's lakeshore, and it's only a foot deep. It must have been a little village on one of the early travelling routes. She's put up her camp across the lake from the site, to throw off any snoopers from the air, and paddles across each morning in a rubber dinghy which she can hide in the trees. She's found pipes, bits of pottery, and beads. A few clubs." He leaned towards her. "And a mask," he whispered; "the first mask to show up in n'Daki Menan. It's only a partial piece, but it's meant to be worn on the head and has a long beak. She thinks it's of a duck or loon. She's hoping more of it will turn up. I talk to her about every two weeks on the radio. She hadn't had it dated as of last week, but she's sure it's old, three thousand years anyway, she says." If her heart was at idle noise before, it was now exploding in takeoff. She had to stand up. She was breathing deeply. "I can see my surprises interest you," he said. "Good! Let me know when you want to go up, and I'll arrange it. Rita plans to stay up through September and wants to meet you. She knows of your Dr. French and she hopes you can help her identify some of the artifacts." She just stared at him. If Dawson Penhurst, Knight of the Round Table, had walked through the door in full shining armor carrying a baby on a silver pillow laced with gold, she could not have been more amazed. She was speechless. He went to his desk, gathered up some documents, and jammed them into his briefcase. "It's 4:35. Seminar's over, I think. When do you want to start?"

"So I have access to all your archives?" she asked. "Everything," he said, "with full Band support. Giselle will help you with the indexes till you get used to them. There's a bit that still isn't catalogued, and you'll just have to go through that item by item." "I'll start immediately," she said, trying to regain her composure. "Good," he said, coming around the desk and looking directly into her eyes. "We'll give you all the help we can. The Ashton study helped us a great deal in putting together our recent history. I hope you can help give us back our roots." "I'll try," she said. He held out his hand. "Good luck," he said. "Meegwetch, as we say in Ashwagane; it's our equivalent to 'thank you.' We've told Harold that the Band will compensate him for your room and board. So you don't need to pay him anything. You'd better drink some of his sherry though, for he'll certainly claim for lots of it." He gave her hand a slight squeeze. "Goodbye for now," he said, and opened the door. "And don't forget Giselle. She's a powerhouse. She knows more about a lot of things around here than I do." He closed the door.

"How'd it go?" asked Giselle. "You were in there long enough. He wouldn't give the Prime Minister that much time, unless it was for an awful lot of money. It's been almost three hours and there are two people waiting to talk to him before 5:00." "It was very helpful, Giselle," she said. "Are you open tomorrow?" "Saturday? No. Not usually," said Giselle. "I suppose I could let you in, though." "No, Monday will be fine," Catherine said. "See you then." She thought her heart would be back to normal by Monday. "Call me if I can help," Giselle called out the door as Catherine started down the path.

As she walked back to Harold's house she realized she
was exhilarated and confused at once. She looked at her
watch: 4:43. She wanted to lie down. Angele wouldn't be
home from school for at least another hour. She opened
the always-unlocked door. Harold was gone. It was so
painful for him to walk that he kept his visits to neighbors
to one or two a week. He had always been an outdoor
man, and he refused to stay bottled up inside, he had told
her, even though the doctors warned him that his visiting
days were over, at least until he took off another fifty
pounds. He must be somewhere close by, she thought.

She lay down on the narrow bed, but didn't close her
eyes. The little room seemed so small, so bare, save for
Jesus on the cross, crippled, head hanging low, dejected,
oozing dark blood. She looked up. A single fly buzzed,
sole occupant of the pale blue ceiling space. There was no
Marilyn above her, grinning. She thought of Emily. What
were those cryptic lines she had thrown down to her from
the windowsill that day in Amherst? Was it that to stand
off made all the difference? Or had she sent a secret
message to Catherine, that she wanted to jump, to kick
free of the white shroud and dive down into life? Dogs
barked in the distance; the voices of children; the faint
hum of a motorboat out on the lake.

She reflected on the last three hours. The Chief had
been more than she could possibly have wished for. How
lucky they were to have him. Where did he learn to talk
like that? He was a brilliant man. He had written her a
blank cheque to study them, giving her access to materials
not open to the public—some that even the lawyers hadn't
seen. She was miles into the wilderness and she had at her
fingertips a collection richer, for her immediate purposes,
than those of the Houghton and Widener Libraries
combined. Were hers the first outsider's eyes to try to pull

it all into the larger, older scheme of things? The Chief thought they were. He encouraged her. He wanted her to do it. Why the sudden trust, this amazing opportunity? Why for her? What did he know about her? Was it his respect for Ashton? Or Dr. French's recommendation? But they didn't even know each other except by correspondence. It couldn't be the name Harvard. He struck her as someone not impressed by names. What would he know about Harvard anyway? What a responsibility! She must write Dr. French. If clairvoyant, he must be dancing a jig. Zellie too. And then the dig. The pictograph. Promises to take her to special places guarded by secrecy and respect. She remembered Ashton's note on the taboo panograph. Would it turn up? She felt for the first time that a dissertation was out there, waiting for her. The last big doubt was fading. She would start Monday.

But the fear she saw in his eyes, the pain, anxiety. Who were these Warriors? How powerful were they in the community? What would this roadblock accomplish? She shuddered. She thought of Lydia. Suddenly she jumped up from the bed and went to the phone. The Band office would just be closing. Giselle answered. "Hi, Giselle," she said, "it's Catherine again. You said if I needed anything I could call. Could I impose on you? Some questions have come up from my talk with the Chief that I know you could answer, and I would love to talk to you again." Giselle said that Matt and his crew were working late these nights to take advantage of the extra daylight, and he wouldn't be home until 7:00. She'd start making supper in about half an hour. "Come on over. We could have a good hour together, anyway. But aren't you exhausted?" "I'll be right over," she said.

The front door was open, except for the screen door, and Catherine could hear Giselle humming in the kitchen. "C'mon in," she called. The stone fireplace with its huge slab of natural pine for a mantelpiece dominated the attractive livingroom. "In here," said Giselle from the kitchen. Catherine entered and sat down. "Why I decided to dice carrots on a hot afternoon beats me, but Matt loves them, with big chunks of butter. What we won't do for our men, eh? It's crazy." Giselle turned to her with a grin. "Speaking of men, Cathy. . ." She saw how dejected Catherine looked. "What's up?" she asked.

"Who are the Warriors, Giselle? The Chief mentioned them but did not go into much detail. He seemed pretty concerned about them." Giselle paused. "You did get right down to business this afternoon, didn't you!" She put down the carrots and knife and sat down beside her. "They started up last year. It grew out of one family, the Bigtrees. They're a bad lot, the men anyway. The father was in and out of jail, a drunk, on welfare most of the time. He's dead now. The oldest son, Tommy, was trouble from day one. There were a couple of sisters. One's still at home. Their mother worked hard, but just couldn't handle the family. When I was a kid I used to see her in Church, alone, and sometimes she'd be crying. There were rumors she was beaten at home, but there was no nurse then. She tried hard. As close to a martyr as we've had on Sand Island in my day. She's very infirm now, and the daughter looks after her. Tommy's younger brother Ben is just as bad. They've both been in and out of jail, and there's no work for them. No one will hire them. Chief Philip put them on house construction early last spring, and they lasted through the first paycheque, then went off on a binge, and several boxes of nails went missing. The younger boy, Arthur, isn't so bad. He managed to stay in school till about grade eleven. He works for Matt. He does his work well, but he's shy. If he doesn't watch out he may have a drinking problem too; but so far he's been a good worker. He's dating Angele, you know." "No, I did not know that," said Catherine. "Angele has mentioned a boyfriend but I did not know who he was. They are going out tomorrow night, I think." "Angele should be good for him," said Giselle. "Arthur has a heart of gold, but he's stuck in there with his brothers 'cause he can't afford to rent a place of his own. All his money goes to the support of the family; he's the sole breadwinner at the moment. If he and Angele get something going, Chief Philip can get a new house for them, even if they're common law. Anyway, last summer, Tommy and Ben suddenly sobered up. Nobody could figure it out. Matt said that the Catholic Church had finally brought a miracle to the Wendaban after three hundred years of trying. They started talking to certain of the young boys, the listless ones, inviting them over for sessions in group leadership. We figured it had to be a scam of some sort, or a cover up for a drunk, but next morning they were all dead sober. The group got to be about ten, maybe twelve." "Philip said twenty," she said. "Well," said Giselle, "if you put a gun in their hands and said, 'See that Shagonash over there, shoot him, he's the enemy,' I'd say it would be down to about three, Tommy, Ben, and Jimmy Whitebear, who'd pull the trigger. But if you're holding a meeting about discipline and being organized and studying Shagonash duplicity tactics and justifying violence as a political weapon, I guess we're talking twelve, I'd say, no more. Some of them I know are just snooping to see what's up, like Sammy Osatig. Why, if he turned terrorist, our ballfield would jump into the lake. I think it's the notion of the discipline that attracts them, something organized. Now they've got these jackets, deep brown leather, with a clenched fist on the back in black, so that you can hardly see it. They call themselves the Warriors, but they hardly ever use the name. Some think they're sneaky, others think they're training in white diplomacy. The Chief thinks they've got guns hidden somewhere, but I doubt that. They act polite, but they won't say much about their meetings. The parents are concerned, but can't pry much out of them. They're all in their late teens and early 20's; what are you supposed to do, lock them in their rooms? One thing is for sure. Someone's giving them lessons in kung fu or jujitsu or one of those defence tactics sorts of things. A few nights ago, there was a meeting at Tommy's house, and Matt went and stood in the trees across the path from the house, and he said you could hear the bodies falling on the floor and grunts, but he didn't hear a spoken word. It's a bit spooky at this point, I guess. I sort of think it will blow over. Our kids are frustrated, we all are, but there's a rich tradition of family life in our Band. As I said, if it came to a crunch, only about three would report for duty." "That's three too many," said Catherine. "Yes," replied Giselle, "you're right. It's three too many."

"Tell me a bit about our ball hero, Sammy Osatig," she said. "Well," said Giselle, "he thinks he's God's gift to women. But he's a kid in a macho body. He's full of heart. He traps and hunts a lot, has a regular territory, so he's used to guns. He's had his share of fights, some of them on the ballfield. But if he's a terrorist, I'm a witch on a broomstick." They both laughed.

After supper, Angele said she had to study in her room, and would be early to bed. She had to be at the store by 8:30 next morning, and had a date with Arthur that night, so "It will be a full day." Catherine said she would do the dishes, and Harold said he would keep the TV low. "We'll have to get you an earplug, Harold," she said to him after Angele had closed the bedroom door.

"Why, don't you like Matlock?" he asked. "I will only be good through the 10:00 o'clock news tonight," she responded. "After three hours with the Chief, I'm exhausted." "After half an hour of news I'm exhausted," he chuckled.

But she did not make it to the newscast. She was very tired. She closed the bedroom door quietly. Angele was already asleep. It was hot. She undressed and lay down naked on top of the sheet. She closed her eyes and tried to turn down the knobs; "Turn them down, down, breathe deeply," she said, "feel the ends of your fingers, the sound of your ears. Turn them down, down, listen to the silence," she said in a whisper. Then she opened her eyes. "I haven't heard from that pilot," she thought. "The way he was drinking me in, I was sure he would have phoned by now. That was three days ago. Oh well, he has probably found bigger breasts than mine to gaze at." She closed her eyes. She could hear the noise of the plane. Dawson, smiling, was holding a crying baby. She opened them again and stared into the darkness. "What was that he said, that he lived only in the present? That is just my problem! Trying to study their past, I am being lured into their present like a moth to a candle. Ah, dear God, deliver us," she sighed. She heard Angele breathing deeply.

iii

He called the next morning. "I'm sorry I didn't call sooner," he said, "but we've been so doggone busy down here that you can hardly think straight." There were the evenings, she thought. "Anyway, I see they're starting the Saturday night dances up there tonight. You really should take in these famous Indian affairs, you know, as part of your research. I thought you might appreciate an escort. I can borrow Ted's boat so I can get home after it's over." He paused. "Would you like me to come?" It was her turn to pause. She decided to give him a little bit of a rough time. "Who did you say this was?" she asked. "Oh my God, I'm sorry," he said. "I remember I didn't really introduce myself the other day, did I! The pilot. Remember? Conk." "Conk?" she said, trying to sound baffled. "Mr. Conk?" "No, Miss Saltonstall," he said. "I've got your name right now, haven't I! I felt so stupid the other day when I messed it up. No, it's Conk Seguin, C-o-n-k," and he spelled it out for her. "It's really a nickname, but it's all I go by now. I'll tell you the story about it sometime, if you like." "What kind of dancing do they do?" she asked, trying to stall a bit while she decided. "Oh, there's rock, usually, and country, and square dancing." She thought she had square danced somewhere, once. "Do they foxtrot?" she asked. There was a pause. "Foxtrot?" he said; "ah, I'm not really sure." She wouldn't mind some dancing, she thought, foxtrot or no. It would be an adventure, part of her introduction to Sand Island. "Are you still there?" he asked. "I think that would be very nice of you, to escort me, Mr. Seguin," she said. "Is it at the Recreation Centre? I could meet you there." She thought she'd like to avoid being picked up at the house. "Yes, but I'll pick you up at Harold's," he said. "About 8:00. Okay?" At least he has some manners, she thought. "That sounds fine, thank you," she said. "Okay. See you then," he said. "Bye." There was a distinct flirty tone to that last word, she thought as she hung up. He dragged it out and inflected it. Well, at least he'd leave his rattletrap behind, this time. A major improvement.

The dance was a disaster, but Conk Seguin crept up the evolutionary scale, from Pithecanthropus erectus to Neanderthalensis, the smiling caveman. He arrived in clean jeans and solid burgundy long-sleeved cotton shirt and slightly scuffed brown leather loafers. His curly dark brown hair had been freshly washed and spun out in ringlets around his ears. The aftershave was a bit potent. He must have slapped it on just when he got out of the boat, she thought. He had on a blue peak cap, with "Lake Islands Airways" in white emblazoned across a red float plane. She stifled an instinct to giggle when she opened the door. She had never gone out with such a hat before. Her men had never worn hats. But it disappeared for the rest of the evening and she wondered what he had done with it until she found it the next morning on the chair beside Harold's door. "Cleverly forgotten," she thought. Once that evening she caught herself admitting that he really looked rather handsome in a northern bushy sort of way.

The band was not a band but three unpracticed extroverts. The drummer was soon mildly intoxicated and played a bit faster than the others could keep up to. The guitar, tune it though its player might, would not hold, and kept slipping down a quarter tone until screwed up again. The cottagers weren't up in numbers yet and only a handful showed up. The dance was poorly attended. There was quite a bit of drinking, she thought, and a fight broke out. The Reserve Constable was nowhere to be seen. By 11:00 the smell of beer, perspiration and marijuana dominated the stuffy hall. The doors and windows were open but no air was moving. She was grateful for his aftershave lotion, little whiffs of sweetness and light. He managed to walk her through two squares, and she was glad he knew what to do next because the caller slurred his words and was off key, and she found him confusing to understand. Conk was a fair rock dancer and tried to throw himself into it, but the band's rhythm was lacklustre and from time to time out of synch. Dancing under such circumstances was perfunctory. Once, on a twirl, he stepped on her foot and she winced. He felt terrible about it but she smiled and blamed it on the poor beat. Angele and Arthur turned up, briefly, and for half an hour the four of them exchanged pleasantries about dancing and the weather and the coming tourist season. Arthur had a lot of acne and didn't smile much. He had on his brown jacket, and looked uncomfortably hot. She was relieved that Conk dallied over his beer during their conversation, while Arthur consumed one and went for another. She discovered that pop meant soda, and she and Angele settled for that and he didn't kid her about it. But for the first time she felt an outsider, a visitor who didn't fit in. The topic of her research came up, but Arthur seemed deliberately to change the subject quickly. Angele looked uneasy. When they left, Catherine was sure Arthur looked drunk and once she saw him push Angele away.

"Why is there so much drinking, Conk?" she asked, in a confiding whisper. "Dancing's a lot of fun, but not when everyone's tipsy, including the band." "I don't know," he replied. "There's something strange here tonight. I don't get it. Last year these dances were a lot of fun and great music. Maybe it's too early in the season. There's always booze, but I never noticed it as much as tonight. Course, there's so few here it shows more. Still, something's queer. You can almost feel the heaviness in the air. And there is a lot of pot going around." "Are you into that?" she asked, casually. "Who, me?" he said. "Oh, I've smoked some pot just to see what it was all about, but I've never smoked cigarettes, and I'm easy on the booze, and this other harder stuff just doesn't interest me. Flying's too important. It's my life. You're stupid to mix them, even on weekends." "I guess," she said. She asked him if he had heard of the roadblock planned for Tuesday. He shrugged. "Yes, I've heard something. Supposed to be some lumber truckers coming in. I've heard the Indians don't know what to do. Some say they'll join; others, I guess, feel they should leave well enough alone. Are you going? I wouldn't. Might be a mess." She said she had not thought about it—which was a huge fib. "I couldn't go even if I wanted to. This week's booked solid," he said. The topic was dropped. He was right, she thought. There was a strange dullness in the air, wearing down one's will to enjoy. She wondered if it had anything to do with the looming roadblock.

He wanted to kiss her at Harold's door, but she pushed him back gently. "In spite of the band, it's been fun, Conk," she said, "but not tonight, please. You were going to be just an escort, remember?" "That's okay, Cathy," he said. "I understand. Everything must still be very strange to you. It hasn't been an exciting night. I think we'd have had a better time paddling down to the nests in Keewaydin. But maybe we can do that sometime. Goodnight." And he was gone into the darkness. She wondered for a fleeting moment if he would be alright getting home. There was no moon. She turned and went inside. One small table light was on, beside the TV. The house was still, except for Harold's heavy breathing. Angele's bed was still empty. She reached down to the bottom of the suitcase and brought out volume VII. She wasn't fully tired yet. There was a ballpoint pen in a glass jar on top of the refrigerator. She gently closed Harold's door, clicked on the overhead light, sat down at the table and opened the book. She stared at it for a moment. It seemed as if she were in a reincarnated life, and had suddenly stumbled on a piece of her long lost past.

Saturday, June 25.

I have been in my new world four days. I have discovered friends and warmth among the Ashwagane Wendaban. I live with the past and the future, Harold and Angele, he so full of the old days and ways, she trying so hard to find a future. I will learn much from him; Angele will learn from us both. I think I shall grow to love her very much. I want her to accept me as a friend and guide, but I shall not push her. I hope she will come to love me, too. She is so unlike Zellie, my only other esteemed friend.

It is a new world in many ways, but I already feel comfortable in it. I have barely scratched its surface. I have seen some cement in the foundation of the store and houses, but have yet to see one patch of asphalt. The ballfield is surfaced with cinders. I walk so much on wood, the floors of this house, the boardwalk which runs from the store down the side of the island to the Band Office. The island floor is a soft, spongy humus. I have rediscovered the sky. The world here on the island is flat, not perpendicular, one's sense of the day so subtly contained by the sky's message, blue as I have not seen it except at the Cape, with clouds of all sizes and heights constantly over you and in your eyes as if they belonged in some important way to the day's meaning. The light is different, especially in the morning. It adjusts its radiance quickly in and out of shadow, as if there were unseen elves of God constantly turning huge theatre lights high in the sky, pulling out one tinted filter and inserting another,

twisting the great lights now this, now that way, sending a
sudden shaft down between the clouds to spotlight a wave
or tree. I hear the wind more. Around my house at home a
tree is a preserved thing among the ponderous architecture
of man. Here, a home is a little throwing together of wood
and shingles against the mighty panorama of trees and
sky. And as the wind blows, which it does most of the
time, the trees speak. I must learn to interpret their voices.
There are no cars. There is the rusting carcass of one
down on the shoreline.

I came here to piece together more of the story of their
ancient past, back to earliest roots. Already I know that
the project can no longer be just a project, the dissertation
no longer just an academic exercise. What was it Ralph
said about his old problem, of being in it and out of it at
the same time? To understand it all, I must protect myself,
keep my own space around me wide, keep my eyes
trained steadily on the material, as I have been trained to
do. But it will be hard not to be involved. I have walked
into political turbulence, deep culture in disarray, a people
lost and in search of their souls. Their land claim is but
the symbol of deeper claims.

I made the choice. What strange forces, what mindless
collusions brought me here? As I look into the
Ashwagane, do I but look into my own psyche, my own
buried life? I have always felt so settled, so sure, so rooted
in traditions and the esteemed, so safe in the arms of the
tried and secure. I unsettle all things, Ralph said. I thought
Emily's cryptograms thrown down to me from the
windowsill were of roses and lilies. I must look at them
again. Perhaps they were warnings of dark turmoil. We
shall see.

In the meantime, to steady things down, I have
Harold's chronic dry wit and the antics of a new admirer,

Neanderthal Canadiensis, Conk for short. I suspect my bludgeon-toed pilot will not give up easily.

I must rise to the Ashwagane's trust. Can I help heal their wounds when I am a part of that wound? The Chief is right. They only can heal themselves, alone. Perhaps I can hand them a new tool to use in their struggle. We shall see.

Chapter VIII
ROADBLOCK

i

The Robert Sloane Lumber Company had been a mainstay of employment in the town of Achinike for three generations. It milled spruce and pine lumber from raw logs, hauled to the mill by truck or floated down Lake Achinike by boom. Most of the two-by-four's and pine paneling ended up in homes in New England and Virginia. Two other companies took trees from n'Daki Menan, but Sloane was by far the largest harvester. Each year the District Office of the Department of Natural Resources allotted the company cutting areas, always at least four years in advance of their present needs.

But now there were problems. Replanting had at first been discredited, then practiced haphazardly. A harvestable pine took one hundred and fifty years to grow in n'Daki Menan. The new trees were not ready yet. Many seedlings had not made it through the first winter. A crippling fire in 1977 had wiped four thousand acres off the plan. However, if left to their own resources, the government men of Achinike had it all worked out. There was still enough to go around, providing. There were as many projections as projectors, but it was generally agreed that if the mills gradually scaled down, about 5% per year to an eventual 70% of capacity, there were enough trees to last until new growths "came onstream." This "downsizing" could take place through employee attrition. It was the best they could do.

But these were not the times to leave the government men of Achinike to their own resources. The environmentalists were growing in numbers, wealth and power. Rallies were held, songs sung, headlines printed. The forests of n'Daki Menan were being slaughtered, they said. Photos of clearcutting in which hundreds of acres looked as if a tornado had just hit, moved from the third page of the newspapers onto the second, then onto the front page. The forests of n'Daki Menan became a national debate; for some, their preservation a cause célèbre. These were the times to try the souls of the government men of Achinike. Orders came down from Head Office. Elected governments must listen to the people. Some of the finer stands of trees had best be removed from the allocations. Clearcutting must be suspended in all but a few townships. The government men of Achinike scrambled. The immediate cut in mill production must jump to 10%, then, after that figure was barely announced, to 20%. Attrition would have to change to layoffs.

Reforestation was rushed into full production. Students with bags of seedlings swarmed over barren hills. The old growth forest to the north was singled out for special consideration, and select cutting of the oldest trees there was changed to no cutting at all. The government men of Achinike worked late into the night with their calculators. New studies were commissioned. First there was a five year plan; then it was changed to three, then two. The public was invited to give "input," but by the time it tried to understand how one plan was going to work, there was a new plan substituted, calling for more public input. The cottagers joined the chorus. "Save our trees" rang out across the ancestral homeland.

For two years the employees of the Robert Sloane Lumber Company watched with growing concern. Then they began to huddle. Attrition had their numbers down from seventy-one to fifty-five workers. Then ten were laid off. They could see the usual high mound of raw logs out behind the plant dwindling. Unfamiliar trucks started appearing with logs from outside the area, already branded with some other company's mark. There was ominous talk. Next year's allocation was still up in the air, they heard, and they had only enough logs left in the yard for three months. Another ten were laid off. It was only a matter of time. Finally the announcement came: after seventy-five years of continuous production, the Robert Sloane Lumber Company of Achinike would close its doors permanently on September 1. The reason? Insufficient timber supply.

The town felt a dagger blow. The Reeve cried out to anyone who would listen. He talked of ghost towns. The government men of Achinike were quoted as saying that they could provide enough cutting areas to keep the mill open at 50% capacity for at least another year, when new allocations would be determined. The management at Sloane was quoted as saying that the government men were liars. They now had no more than two months of logs in stock and no official allocations whatsoever. There was confusion. There was no confusion about the men's pink slips.

Their roadblock was to be a brief symbolic statement. The lumbermen chose the gravel access road down the side of Lake Achinike to the public docks, ten miles in from the highway. The blockage would inconvenience cottagers, delivery trucks, the Indians, but only for half a day. Truckers rallied from miles around. Radios crackled. Workers from mills as far away as White Falls and Spume River would join their Achinike brethren. If it happened to one, it could happen to all.

On the other side, the Achinike Wilderness Society mobilized a huge rally. Busloads were to travel north to

158

show their support. Other groups also saw an opportunity; they too would participate. Some defended multiple use; it had worked for years in the past, it could go on working. A few more trees saved, perhaps, fewer jobs, maybe, but life should go on as usual. Some thought the environmentalists were the new Ku Klux Klan. There were millions of trees out there; anybody could see that if they'd ever flown to Winnipeg. The Northeast, all the way to the North Pole, was nothing but trees. Jobs were sacred. Bash those tree huggers' heads! Others thought otherwise. If it came down to trees or jobs, trees must be the clear winner. The mill was poorly managed, anyway. For years they had been allowed to get away with tons of wastage, at the cutting sites and at the mill. New jobs could be created. The government had a whole department for that. But the old growth forest, if cut, would be gone forever.

The police knew a brouhaha in the making. This one had all the right ingredients in the right proportions. By Saturday night two cruisers from White Falls to the north had been assigned to join two more from Norich Junction to the south, to patrol the roads of Achinike. With the three cruisers already stationed in town, the total had grown to seven. Major Harrington Gotlieb of the riot squad stationed in Huronia City was called out of bed early Monday morning, and he had his crack troops moved onto the ballfield at Achinike by 4 p.m. That night's game was cancelled. Another ten cruisers were called in Monday. The highway was alive with them. By sundown, seventy-four policemen were billeted in Achinike. The town was tense. "We're under siege," the Reeve said. No ghost town yet.

The sun rose hot on the moist Tuesday morning. By 6:00 a.m., Catherine could see a heat haze hanging over the lake, and it was already 22 degrees on the thermometer outside the bedroom window, which she knew was hot even before she converted the Celsius into her more familiar Fahrenheit. Angele had just poured them each a bowl of cereal. She could sense the young girl was uneasy. She wasn't getting ready for school. "Is there no school today?" she asked. "I don't have an exam," Angele replied, "so I'm not going." "Are you going to the roadblock, then?" she asked. Angele frowned. "I don't know what to do," she said. "Arthur says he's got to go with the rest of them. He's leaving just about now. He said I should stay home. But I'd like to go. I don't want him to get into trouble. Joey was in town last night and he says there's cops everywhere." "Well, they'll keep a good control of things," Catherine said, "so don't you worry." "What do you think I should do, Cathy?" asked Angele. "Let's both go," she responded. "You want to keep an eye on Arthur, and I'm curious. We'll stick together. I don't think I want to go alone. Do you think you could find us a ride?" "Oh, that would be neat," said Angele. "I'll call June. She shops in town every Tuesday morning and she never pays any attention to things like this. She probably figures she'll just drive right through."

The three of them were driving down the gravel road by 8:30. June said her husband had to have a part for his chainsaw from the hardware store. She had to get to town. As they came round a curve, the town grader was parked in the middle of the road. June slowed to a crawl to pass it on the left. There was barely room. "That's odd," she said; "I've never seen him stopped in the middle before. On the side, maybe. And he hasn't been doing any grading. See? The road hasn't been touched. Roll down your window, Angele. I want to talk to him." She stopped the car alongside. "You picked a fine day to be on the road," she shouted up to the operator. "What are you doing here, blocking the middle like this?" "The grading was laid on weeks ago, ma'am, long before there was any talk of a roadblock," he said. "What grading?" June yelled. "I don't see any grading. You guys usually start at 8:00. Have you just been sitting here for half an hour?" He looked sheepish. "Look, lady, I was just told yesterday afternoon to bring it down here and park in the road. Double time. I've been in this thing all night. And it ain't bugproof, either. It's hot up here. That's all I know, lady. Don't ask me. I just work here." "Well, you might at least do some grading on this lousy road," said June. "I'd like to see your car bills after driving over this thing for a year! If you went fast enough, you might make enough breeze to cool off." She drove on.

"Can you imagine?" she said to them. "Double time to sit like a donkey in the middle of the road and do nothing. His motor wasn't even running. He won't last till noon, I'll bet." Discussion of this strange event lasted for the next three miles.

As they came over a hill a mile in from the highway, cars were lined along one side of the road in front of them, and a cruiser was parked across the road, its red and white lights flashing. As they drew up, an officer approached them, radio in hand. "I'd advise you to turn around, ma'am. Everything's blocked up ahead." "Can we park and walk down?" June asked. "I can't stop you," he said, "but I'd advise against it. There's about five hundred people further on at the entrance, milling around. It's mass confusion at the moment." "Well," said June, turning to them, "what will we do?" "Let's go," said Angele. "We can stay together." "I may try to get a ride into town," said June. "If I come back without that part, there'll be hell to pay."

As they walked along, the congestion got thicker. When they reached the top of the last hill, they looked down on a sea of tightly-packed humanity. They worked their way down. "You two stick together," said June. "I'm going to push my way through to the highway and get a ride to town. Let's meet back at the car at 1:00 o'clock. That should give me enough time." "We'll see you at 1:00, then, June," said Angele. Catherine nodded. June disappeared into the throng, pushing hard.

Catherine thought she began to see something of a pattern. Individual policemen were scattered in the crowd, about thirty of them she figured. They had billy clubs, but they were using them just to point, cajole, threaten. There were shoving matches here and there. "Move along, there," she heard an officer say close by; "we have to keep moving along here." She spotted the Warriors in their brown jackets, along the side of the road, higher on the embankment. She counted seven, including Arthur. They were trying to stick together, in a line, parallel to the road, with their arms folded across their chests. But two policemen were onto them and had other ideas. As fast as an officer would move one out of the line, another Warrior would circle round through the crowd to take his place. She figured the police would need seven officers to keep the seven Warriors from regrouping. One tall unshaven one seemed to be their kingpin: Tommy, undoubtedly, she thought. The rest continued to pull in alongside him as if attached to him with an invisible rubber band.

Down in the corner, by the highway, she saw the riot squad. They wore white helmets with curved clear masks in front of their faces, of some very tough substance she was sure. The sun sparkled off their translucent dark green shields. They were just lounging at the moment, taking it all in. Just in from the highway, in the middle of the road, there was another group, about fifty of them she thought, circled around someone in the middle. This group stood out, because it was stationary in an otherwise slow-moving mass. Probably the mill workers, she thought.

She looked out onto the highway. Both sides were clogged with vehicles, cars, transport trucks, smaller half-tons, and huge yellow machines with big tires and metal screening over the driver's cab. Must be something used in the cutting operations she thought. A trickle of traffic was moving south in one lane, and an officer with leather leggings was waving frantically at the slow-moving traffic. She heard a chopping noise and looked up. A helicopter was circling, then it pulled away towards Achinike.

Across from the riot squad, on the opposite shoulder of the intersection, the media had set up. Two TV cameras were perched on two shoulders aimed at two people being interviewed, one a man, the other a woman. Up behind them and stretched along the embankment all the way down to where the Warriors were trying to make their stand, were lines of tourists, bright-colored bands on straw hats, overweight legs and arms, one with an umbrella, the inevitable cameras dangling. The police were allowing them to stay there as long as they just watched. Angele squeezed her hand. "There's Arthur," she said. She waved at him but he appeared not to see her. An officer pushed up against them. "If you want to watch, get over there on the embankment," he said. "We're going to clear this road. C'mon now, ladies, move over there.'' He gave Catherine a gentle shove, and in a few seconds she heard him saying the same thing in a dry, worn voice to some others behind her.

A bullhorn suddenly bleated out over the din. ''Will all the Sloane employees and supporters please group over here.'' It came from the man in the middle of the circle of stationary bodies. As she watched they quickly spread out into several lines across the road and sat down, folding their arms across their chests. It all happened so fast that the few policemen in the area got pushed aside. The leader, seated front centre, started yelling: ''Jobs! Jobs! We want Jobs!'' Within seconds the voice turned into a ringing chant. ''Jobs! Jobs! We want Jobs!'' boomed out. One of the TV cameras swirled and pointed at them. Then a loud voice answered from about fifty feet up behind them on the road. ''Trees! Trees! Save our Trees!'' Soon that slogan, too, grew to a loud chant of over one hundred voices. The rhythmic chants crashed into one another. The battle lines were drawn. There were sporadic little flashes from cameras, everywhere.

Angele meanwhile was gently pulling Catherine across the road, closer to the Warriors. Arthur gave them a half-hearted wave. Just below them to their left was the last row of the sitting, chanting loggers. ''We want Jobs! We want Jobs!'' At the end of the row, closest to the Warriors, was a young blond man, giving the chant all his energy. He was in his early 30's. He wasn't ten feet from them. He had moved to Achinike from the south to work in the mill three years ago, bought a house, and a new daughter had just joined two small brothers. His take-home pay had stalled at $427 per week over twelve months ago. The shutdown announcement was devastating. He had just talked to the bank about refinancing his house; they said that the market value had probably dropped below the outstanding mortgage. His investment might be wiped out.

Arthur was being harassed by an officer determined to break up the line of brown jackets. He pushed Arthur forward. Instead of circling around to retake his place, Arthur decided to work his way towards Angele. The blond mill worker suddenly jumped to his feet. He couldn't take it any longer. Sitting cross-legged was stiffening his joints and his heart was pounding. He had only meant to stretch. He turned and saw Arthur pushing towards him. His emotions were taut. "You're the real fuckin' problem," he yelled out—pointing at Arthur. "You guys think you own all the trees in the country." "We want Jobs! We want Jobs!" pounded across the road. Arthur was now opposite him and stood looking at him, expressionless. Angele pushed forward, pulling Catherine. He had meant only to push Arthur away, on the shoulder, but as his hand came up, Arthur thought he was going to be hit, and parried with his left arm to ward off the supposed blow. The blond man retaliated, clenching his fist, and struck—for family, job, mortgage, life. Angele was straining to get between them, and as the blow landed, it caught her on the side of the head. It glanced off, but pushed her head with sudden force into Arthur's skull. Catherine heard the crack as bone hit bone. She put her hands up on Angele's shoulders and pulled her back. Blood was oozing from a gash just above her eye. Arthur was also cut. Both Arthur and the blond man stood staring.

By the time she and Arthur had half pushed, half carried Angele over to the side of the road, a crowd had gathered around them. They lay her down. Arthur was trying to keep the blood mopped up with a dirty red polkadot handkerchief. The blood was running freely now and Catherine knew they would have to get it stopped soon. Angele said she was fine, but felt a bit dizzy. Catherine detected a faint tremor in Angele's body. Someone thought Arthur had hit her and shouted out uncomplimentary words about Indians and the clenched fist on his jacket. He took it off and laid it under Angele's head. He had nothing on under it. Catherine pulled out a little package of kleenex from her handbag, and handed it to Arthur. His handkerchief was already soaked beyond use. Just as she was deciding to find a policeman, a smiling man in tan shorts and with a black bag crouched down beside them. "Hi," he said; "I'm Doctor James Starbuck from Bethesda, Maryland. I'm up visiting and I brought along my bag just in case something like this might happen. Can I take a look?" "Good Lord," she thought to herself; "when the crunch is on, are there any Canadians in this country?"

She thought she should establish some authority right off. "I'm her guardian and this young man is her fiancée," she said. "Yes, please do what you can." He cleaned the wound and dressed it, talking all the while to Angele. He took a little swab stick and asked her to follow it back and forth, up and down, with her eyes. "She needs about six stitches and she may have a slight concussion," the doctor said. "She needs rest and a blanket. She's close to shock. Can we get her to a hospital?" Her mind was racing. Getting Angele down to the highway through this crowd would be a major chore. The police could call for an ambulance, but could it get here through the clogged road? She turned to him. "Can you do the stitches right here?" He looked in his bag. "Yes," he said, "but I'm not licensed to practice in Canada." She bent closer to Arthur. "I heard him," he said to her. "Please try to get him to do it." Her heart went out to Arthur. He seemed so young. She turned to the doctor still crouching beside her. "We won't tell, if you won't," she said. "Please stitch her up. Arthur says it could be several hours before we can get her to a hospital." Arthur had not said that but it sounded appropriate. She didn't know where the nearest hospital was. "All right," he said; "I'd still like to see her get an exam, though. Concussions can be tricky." Then she heard June's voice. "Forget trying to get anywhere on that highway," said June. "It's plugged solid. Trucks all over, even sideways. Can I help? What happened here? To hell with his saw part. I'm not walking to town through that mess!"

They decided that June and Arthur would stay with her. The doctor said he'd stay too. Catherine would try to get the helicopter in to pick up Angele. Where would there be a flat spot? The police would have to clear one. She turned to leave. On a rock above them a lanky man in a plaid sportshirt and blue wallabies had his camera aimed at Angele. The flash popped. "Oh!" Catherine spluttered, scowling at him. He waved at her.

As she worked her way back into the crowd, the bullhorn crackled again, but louder than before. An electric one, she thought. It was from the leader of the riot police. "We are now going to clear the road," it blared. "Move off to the side. Those remaining will be arrested and charged. We are now going to clear the road." The riot squad was arranged now in a solid line just in front of the highway, facing the crowd and the sitting loggers. The police stood so close together she thought it would be hard to slip a piece of paper between them. They lowered the green shields and held their clubs erect. Slowly the phalanx started to move forward. Someone screamed. "We are going to clear the road. Move aside," the bullhorn blared out in a passionless voice. "If you stay on the road you will be arrested!" "Jobs! Jobs! We want Jobs!" greeted them with renewed vigor. "He won't order me a helicopter," she thought. "He's preoccupied." "Trees! Trees! Save our Trees!" roared out behind her. She looked for a policeman. They had radios. "What am I doing here?" she suddenly thought. "I could be back in the library. The past, remember, Catherine?" "Jobs! Jobs!" pounded in her ears. She was furious. "Why Angele?" she blurted out. "It's so ridiculous!" "Trees! Trees! Save our Trees!" She wished she could get up on a box with that bullhorn. "You all get out of here, you idiots!" she wanted to yell. "Take your jobs and your trees and get out of here. Just get out of here!"

"Cathy!" he yelled. "Over here." She looked for the voice and he was suddenly beside her. "You okay?" he asked. "Let's get out of here." He took her firmly by the hand and started pushing towards the side of the road. "Let us through, there," he said; "'scuse us, out of the way." His large six-foot frame made a good block for her. When they got to the roadside, he turned to her and said, as if scolding, "I didn't think I was going to find you, but Harold said you'd be here." She looked up at him. "Angele's been hurt," she said. "A doctor has stitched her up but he thinks she has a concussion and should go to the hospital." "Christ!" he said under his breath; "I thought something like this might happen. Where is she?" Catherine pointed. "Apparently the road is plugged," she said. "How will we get a helicopter in here?" "The road's jammed all the way to Achinike," he said. "Three miles of trucks parked like you wouldn't believe! We'll fly her up to the hospital. Cloudie's parked down on the lake. It's the only way I could get here. It's about a half mile through the bush to the lake, but it's a fair path. I keep a portable stretcher in her. You stay with them. I'll be back in about twenty minutes.'' He jumped down the embankment, and she watched him disappear, running quickly among the trees. In one leap, Neanderthalensis, the smiling caveman, jumped across 100,000 years of evolutionary time to Yeoman of the Guard, right before her eyes. And, she knew, Yeoman of the Guard was just a little below Knight of the Round Table.

Conk returned with the stretcher. The police were now dragging the loggers one by one, in sitting position, across the gravel to their paddy wagons, which were hot and stuffy and going nowhere. Inside the wagons and on the road the sweaty loggers were still chanting. The doctor bid them goodbye and refused Catherine's offer of payment. Arthur and June said they would head back to the car after Arthur returned from helping carry the stretcher to the plane. Catherine would stay with Angele up to the hospital. Conk said he wanted to keep the load to a minimum.

Angele was made as comfortable as possible on the canvas cradle in the back, and he covered her with a blanket. He pushed them out into the lake. Whanga whanga whanga whanga. Within minutes they were airborne. Conk was on the radio; Freda was to have an ambulance waiting at the municipal dock at White Falls. He would confirm with her in ten minutes. As they were climbing, she reached over and patted the dashboard in front of him. ''Funny, I don't hear as many rattles today,'' she said, smiling at him. It was the first time she could remember smiling in several hours. ''I want to talk with you, a lot,'' he said, ''but we'll leave that till later. It hasn't been fun for you, back there. It's fifty miles up to the hospital—about half an hour.'' She nodded at him.

She didn't think she had ever loved any machine so much, before. She settled back into the frayed grey lumpy upholstery, and closed her eyes. She turned down the knobs, way, way down. The hum was soothing, she thought, relaxing—a lullabye. The gentle throbbing was like a massage of all the senses. How odd. She was dozing off. There were a few little bumps, then it was still again. She felt cooler. She turned and looked back at Angele. A tiny piece of dried blood stuck to the bottom of the bandage. Angele was asleep.

iii

She did have a mild concussion. They wanted to keep her overnight at the hospital for observation. She was now asleep in her room. "June can come up for her tomorrow, if the road is back to normal," she said. "Sure," he said. They walked down the hall of the hospital together, towards the front door. Cloudie was berthed at the waterfront. They had come to the hospital in the ambulance. "I'll phone for a cab," he said. "Why don't we grab a sandwich before heading back. I know a good place." "I'd like that," she said.

Casey's Roadhouse was the newest restaurant in White Falls. It looked out over the waterfront and the berths of power and sail-boats of many colors and sizes; she could see Cloudie resting in unique splendor tied off the outer wharf. Several people were standing looking at her, and some were taking pictures. The walls were lined with the décor of yesteryear: old Coke ads, the cover pages of *Saturday Evening Post*s with Norman Rockwell paintings, and a billboard for Aunt Fanny's Bust Builder, with two wooden cups that looked like large eggcups attached to a crank handle. She turned to him. "Why did you come for me at the road, Conk?" "I was just coming back from a run over to Quebec, so I passed to the south to get a good look at the road before landing," he replied. "I knew from the number of police in town that they were expecting trouble, but I wasn't prepared for what I saw. I couldn't believe it. Cars, trucks and skidders jamming the highway for three miles to the north and two miles to the south. I could see the riot police huddled, and figured it was only a matter of time until they got into the act. The gravel road was plugged with people all the way up the first hill. I figured there must have been close to a thousand. When I got to the base, Ted was huddled over the radio with Freda and three tourists, listening to the police band. There had already been bloodshed, he said, and a lot of scuffles. The riot police had just been ordered to clear the road. When those guys move in, they're like a tank. You either get out of the way or you're forcibly removed. I phoned Harold and he said you had gone to the roadblock. I had a hunch you would. How could I make pleasant chatter with passengers, never mind concentrate on flying? I had seen all I wanted of it from the air, but I had to find out if you were okay. So I told Ted to put my sched on hold, and Cloudie and I took off and circled around into Spooner's Bay, just below the road. I had heard there was a path up to the road from where the creek enters. I found it, and you know the rest of the story."

She was silent for several seconds. "I felt so helpless, so utterly helpless, before you came," she said. "The violence all around me—I mean the noise, the chants pounding at you, the shoving, the indifference of them all. And those green shields advancing at you. I never want to be in something like that again, if I can help it. It was terrifying."

He looked at her. "There's enough violence all over, anyway," he said. "I live with it every day. A sudden storm and wind that come out of nowhere. The fog that hangs over the lake but it was clear at the base. A new noise in the engine. The flaps get jammed. A panic-stricken father had to deliver a baby in Cloudie's rumble seat three years ago. I couldn't get in for them sooner because of the weather. Blood and screaming, and I felt helpless; I was yelling instructions to him from a doctor on the radio. About a year after I first got here I snapped a pontoon and flipped her landing in a crosswind. Thank God I was alone and it was at the base. Heart attack victims, dirt in the gas, rain so heavy you can't see, it's all there just around the corner, all the time." He looked deeply into her eyes. "You play the game with all the care you can," he said, "but sooner or later. . ." He stopped. "Sorry. I didn't mean to get morbid," he continued. "Flying's no worse than that Trans Canada Highway we followed up here. What bugs me is that those guys at the roadblock are making violence—manufacturing it. The other kind is natural, part of life. But for the truckers and tree-huggers and riot police to deliberately line up, knowing they're going to square off at one another—that's stupid. It's lunacy." He paused. "I doubt any loon in its right mind would stand for it." He smiled. His voice dropped a tone. He leaned towards her. "Loons are only violent for love, you know." "For love?" she asked. "I'll tell you all about it sometime. In the meantime, I want to show them to you in their peaceful state. They're nesting now, all over the lake. Do you like canoeing?" "I don't know," she replied; "I've never tried it." "Well, we can fix that. If you're getting used to Cloudie, we'll just have to go down there some morning and take a look. Let's get back." He reached for her hand. She was glad. She had wanted to hold his hand again ever since Cloudie had taken them flying so high.

Chapter IX
HENRIETTA'S BAY

i

They had made all the arrangements. He would bring the canoe and breakfast, she the coffee in a thermos. They were to wear their bathing suits underneath. She had reservations about swimming at 7:00 in the morning, but it was more the hour and the circumstances she thought, than the water temperature late in June. She had already swum out from the sand beach at the back of Sand Island on several occasions, and the clear bracing water of Achinike had won her over. A swim with an unattached male so early in the morning, however, struck her as a bit odd, like wearing high heels and mascara to a football game. It hadn't been part of her routine. She had wanted to read up on loons so he couldn't pull any fast ones on her and get the upper hand, but her first week of research compounded by Angele's accident had been so time-consuming she hadn't found time for it. She had gone in to the library the last two mornings before 6:00, now that she had her own key. "The Chief says it's okay, but just remember to hand it in when you leave us," Giselle had said when she gave it to her. "Even the historian we hired five years ago didn't have one. In the old days, you'd have had to smoke the peace pipe first. Today, you just have to have the coffee on by the time I get here." So she had tried to make up for the lost time; "I'll have to approach these loons dead cold," she said to herself. "Maybe they're wound up with elastics too."

He had called yesterday and asked what she liked for breakfast and before she could answer he wanted to know if bacon and eggs would do. No toast. "I'll make a fire," he said, "but by the time you mess around with cooking toast, the day's half gone. I have to be back by at least 8:45 for a trip, so some other time I'll give you Conk's Great Shore Breakfast, which is brunch and a bit of supper combined." She preferred to skip the bacon, she said, but one egg would be fine. "Good," he said; "I'll scramble them and bring some stuff to put in them. Anything tastes good that time of day." She thought it would be interesting to see what "anything" was; old engine parts, perhaps.

He was at the dock sharp at 6:00 and they were soon in the air. She could see the large brown knapsack in the back, a very black-looking fryingpan handle sticking out. Now that she knew Cloudie's peculiarities of sound did not indicate imminent disintegration, she could relax and take in the view. On her first trip things had been grey and drizzly; on her second, she had dozed off. Now it was the right time of day. She and Conk and Cloudie and Lake Achinike were brimming with life. The first week's research had been good. She was being accepted. The old confidence was back. She was adjusting to the lake's higher altitude, the clear untreated water, the far horizons. The heat wave had passed and a northern flow of fresh arctic air now opened up mile upon mile of clear horizon. The blue water sparkled diamonds up at them. The islands stood out dark green, brown and black against the blue. A tiny boat left strings of white behind it and little widening ripples, like a fly swimming on the surface. Flecks of gull white circled below, gliding, swooping, in slow motion. "See how they glide?" he said, leaning over to her and pointing where she had just been looking. "I've watched them go for five minutes without moving a wing. They catch the currents and ride them." She pondered. Somewhere inside her a memory was reaching for the

surface. Then she had it. "I remember reading a book
about them at prep school," she said. "Livingston . . . yes
. . . Jonathan Livingston Seagull. He was quite the glider,
as I recall." "A book?" he asked with a bewildered look.
"Have you noticed Cloudie's wings? The Stinson's wings
are designed after the gull. We're riding in a big gull," he
said, smiling. "And boy, can she glide! Someday when
we have more time, I'll take you up high and cut the
engine." "You'll conk it, you mean," she said to him. "I
looked up your name in the dictionary yesterday. You're
also some kind of a wart on a tree, and a big seashell."
He was nonplussed for an instant, but kept right on
talking. "If the currents are right, she'll glide us for sixty
miles, conked!" he said. "Without any engine?" she
asked. "Without any engine!" he replied. "But with the
rubber band wound up, right?" she asked. "Of course,"
he said. She looked down again, entranced by the crisp,
clean mirror images slowly passing beneath. This morning
there were no bumps. He had been right; you did get used
to the noise. It was beginning to blend in, retreat back
inside her to a hum of reliance. She thought how for him
it must be like the Harvard bells and the livingroom clock,
sounds of steadiness, stability and joy.

So it surprised her to discover how much he liked
quietness too. She knew the canoe was an Indian
invention, and had opened the north for voyageurs and
traders. Now she was sitting in a dented, dull aluminum
version of the old bark ones, with "Lake Islands
Airways" partially visible in black smudged paint,
stencilled on the sides. He put her in the bow and handed
her a paddle. "Do what comes naturally," he said, but she
watched him for a moment, then she paddled. It was all so
soft, so quiet. The water was soft, the dipping of the
paddle, the gliding. She stopped and laid her paddle over

the gunnels in front of her, and he let his trail in the water, and the huge trees towering eighty feet above spoke to them their noiseless words, and little twisted gnarled trees, "jack pine," he said when she pointed, hugged the bare rock and their roots ran into crevices and disappeared. Everything was soft, the quiet floating of soft, noiseless dreams. The bird sounds were so inside her ears she thought she had headphones on. They drifted towards a fallen log which lay out into the water about two feet beneath the surface. Minnows swam under its shadow. About ten feet out from shore it sent up high into the air two weathered branches, so curved that when superimposed against one another, she saw a graceful duck as they glided towards it, with triangular beak and long slender back, its front billowing out into a pregnant curve before tucking back in at the feet. "Look," she said, "a Picasso duck." "Where?" he asked. "I don't see any duck." He was looking out across the water. "The branches in front of us; see?" she said. "Now the angle is changing. The duck is gone. But that's just the way he would outline a duck." "Beats me," he said. "They're just dead branches. Who's Picasso?" "A great artist," she replied. "He'd go crazy in this country. For a while, anyway. It's so symbolic. I'll tell you all about him sometime, if you're good." "It sounds like a Mafia name to me," he said. "You can tell me about the symbolic stuff too, sometime." He turned the canoe out towards the bay. "Let's see how Henrietta's doing this morning."

He paddled them around an island and into a small bay. Halfway down, he moved the canoe in close to shore and laid down his paddle in the bottom without any noise. He reached into the big brown canvas bag in front of him, felt around, and pulled out a pair of binoculars, which he handed to her. "See the fallen birch across there," he said pointing, "the one caught up in a tree and leaning down on an angle?" "Yes," she said. "Okay, go down to the shoreline right under that tree and slowly move to your left, about fifteen feet. You'll see her on her nest, slightly above the water line." She adjusted the focus and found it. They were powerful lenses and Henrietta seemed right in front of her. "She is very beautiful," she said. "I didn't realize how big they are." She paused. A bullfrog croaked just behind them. "She looks nervous," she said. "Her head is jerking around in all directions." "She knows we're here," he said, "but that's their usual behavior anyway. They've got very herky, jerky heads, especially when sitting on the nest. She won't alert Henry, though, unless she figures it's an emergency. She has faith in her camouflage. If I hadn't pointed the nest out to you, chances are you would scan that shoreline and not pick her up. Besides, she sees hundreds of boats in a season, and it's not as if we were an alien spacecraft or something. Loons are very smart. She'll not move anything but her head, or make a sound, unless she's sure we're intent on hurting her. Then she'll let the old man know, and he'll be over here pretty fast. He's watching us now, somewhere, probably. But she knows me. She knows the canoe. The extra person won't worry her. She's probably saying to herself how nice it is I've found a friend. I'm always alone down here. She won't mind the glint of the sun on the binoculars either. She's used to having them or a camera of some sort aimed at her. Last summer I went in close, within twenty feet. I talked to her all the time and she didn't fuss. I was using a mild telephoto lens, and you should see the shots I got! Maybe she knows she's going to be a filmstar or a centrefold. But I usually try to keep my distance."

"Look, there's Henry now." He pointed down to the end of the bay. "Keep your binoculars on him, Cathy. It may be a few minutes, but eventually he'll come up with a minnow good enough for mother, and he'll swim over and feed her, beak to beak." She watched him. The red eye glared at her. "Good grief!" she said, putting down the binoculars and turning round to Conk. "The stuffed thing. There's an awful-looking big stuffed bird covered in dust in my professor's office back home and I didn't know what it was until now. I'll write and tell him he's got to get it shampooed. It was a gift from his teacher, who was up here doing research in the 30's." She turned back, and put the binoculars up to her eyes again. "There he goes," said Conk. "Watch." Henry swam over to the nest. She could see the minnow hanging out of each side of his beak, still squirming, and Henrietta snatched it, somewhat greedily, she thought, and swallowed it whole. "What an awful way to eat fish," she said; "she didn't even chew it. You have to chew them and savor them in your mouth to get the flavor." "She has no teeth," he said, "but I'm sure she enjoys it anyway. Don't we swallow oysters whole, and isn't the fun of it the slimy feeling as they go down your throat?" She turned around and looked at him. She wouldn't tell him oysters were her least favorite food of the sea. Especially raw. "I prefer Boston bluefish," she said. "That's something I'll have to try you out on, someday, but I won't be able to feed you from my mouth, not in a restaurant, anyway." She turned back and put the binoculars on Henrietta. She waited. "Well," he said, "I'm sure there are other things we can find to do with our mouths, maybe even in a restaurant." Before she could think of a reply, he said, "How about some eggs, à la Conk." She was ready, she said; she was hungry.

He took her to his favorite campground, further up the bay, a promontory of rounded rock jutting out into the water in a smooth rounded curve, like a giant whale's back. There were a few small red and jack pine on it, looking starved and blasted by years of struggle to stay alive. A bit of humus and blueberry bushes covered the rock in patches. "Good place for a fire," he said. "If it ever got going in dry weather, there's nothing much to burn out here. I was the first to use it three years ago, but there have been others since. Not many though. I usually find it just the way I left it. This is a remote, dead-end bay, well off the beaten track." There was a small pit with black ashes, lined by a circle of rocks, and two charred and rusted short iron bedframes, from a child's bed, she thought. A small amount of firewood was placed nearby. "I always leave enough cut for the next time," he said, "hoping that if someone else uses it, they'll do the same. They always have, so far. I think I'd feel awful if I came and the wood was gone, as if somebody stole gas out of your plane. Or car." He smiled at her. The sun was beating down, the rock warming up. It was all so languid, clean, gentle, she thought. She felt relaxed. She looked down the bay; not a sign of anyone or anything human.

At his suggestion, they swam. The water was cold, but she was determined not to let him think she thought it too cold. She splashed wildly until she adapted, then let her feet sink down so she was upright. She could see her toes clearly, only slightly darker and greener in the depths. She had a sudden feeling that a big fish was going to swim up with bared teeth and bite her. But nothing happened. She couldn't associate the green of the depths, with some blue in it, with a color she could name. She'd have to think about that some more. As her eyes grew accustomed to it, she could see the outlines of boulders and logs below, but as she swam out a little they disappeared. There was no salt on her lips.

Earlier that morning she had decided to wear her one-piece dark blue suit. She had a bikini with her, but that was for sunbathing. The white skin she had brought with her was tanning a bit darker, but she still had a long way to go to match his deeper tone. Beads of water glistened on his moustache. She couldn't remember seeing so much hair on a man. He really looked in excellent shape, she thought. Lithe. His arms and legs were full and muscular, but not in any obtrusive way. He must like burgundy, for his trunks were a similar color to the shirt he had worn to the dance. And they were shorts, which she preferred on a man for swimming. The tight bikini-like suits had always struck her as too suggestive, something out of body-building magazines. Bulging genitals and exposed female breasts were not her idea of a day's fun at the beach; such sights were indecent and pained her enjoyment. She had always thought it more fun to imagine what lay under discreet clothing. She had had several discussions on this topic with Zellie, who was of a different persuasion. "I'll just do my usual," he said, and was off, swimming powerfully, his head down in the water, his arched arms coming down rhythmically, with a small unobtrusive flutter of the feet, out beyond what she thought was a safe distance, perhaps half a mile. Soon he was back, and lathered himself with soap, and took another plunge. "That'll set us up for breakfast," he said, as he towelled on shore. She had forgotten to bring a cap. She ran the towel over her hair, then threw her head forward and shook her hair from side to side in the sun. No hairdryer. "I'm becoming a natural woman already," she said. "Nothing wrong with that, I guess," he replied.

He set about his breakfast makings. One by one he produced little packets and utensils and tools from his bag. A magician's bag, she thought. There was a small hatchet, and a file, "in case I screw up and hit a rock," he said, and kindling paper. He produced matches, the wooden kind, in a small round metal waterproof can. "I've seen myself go through a half book of matches trying to light a fire in the wind," he said; "these wooden ones hang in there better." Soon there was a crackling fire, the slivered kindling catching fast in the warm sun. He placed the metal crosspieces across the fire and placed the fryingpan on them. Out came a small jar of yellow oil, and he poured some into the pan. "I usually use bacon fat," he said, "but thought I'd use mazola this morning because I wasn't sure if you had something against bacon." She thought she'd leave her nutrition lecture for another day. Then he produced three neatly wrapped packages of waxed paper: sliced red and green peppers, diced onions and small cubes of ham. "Are you hungry?" he asked, smiling at her, "or does a bear shit in the woods?" "Given that choice, I'll take the former," she replied. "Then you can handle three eggs?" he asked. She couldn't recall ever handling three eggs at once, but this morning was not her usual day; she was going to protest, but suddenly said on a whim: "Of course." He cracked the eggs without dropping a speck of shell into the pan, stirred in the ingredients with a fork, and extracted another tiny bottle from Houdini's bag (was it cream, she wondered, though she was determined not to ask), whose contents he poured in. "Jesus!" he yelled as a bit of the omelette stuck to the side of the pan. She wondered for a moment if he was having the first pangs of a heart attack. "This man is going to take some getting used to," she said to herself.

She knew from the first bite she would eat all the omelette. She had to admit it was one of the best she could remember, but she didn't say anything. Not yet. Or was it the atmosphere, the sun and sky and water and the swim and fire and these incredible little bottles? When he had brought out the tin plates and silverware, both scrubbed to a silvery shine, the last of her reserve melted. "I can't stand plastic out here," he said. "It's not the garbage problem so much as the taste. It just doesn't taste right from plastic." "I agree," she said. "It would be a travesty." The way he looked at her she wondered if he was having trouble with the word travesty, but he quickly turned to his bag again. Out came salt and pepper in the little packages made for restaurants, and a small bottle of "Captain Turtle's All-Spice Flavorizer," which he sprinkled liberally over his omelette. "Want some?" he asked. "It's good." "When in Rome, do as," she thought. "Thank you," she said; "I'll try a smidgeon." Finally out came a small glass jar with catsup. She quickly knew he liked lots of catsup on his eggs. She said she'd pass. "Why the little jars for the oil and catsup, Conk?" she asked. "Why not just bring them in the bottles they are sold in?" "Well, this probably sounds kind of dumb," he said, "but it's habit. It's space and weight. We are always flying fishermen into remote lakes with canoes and motors, and the stuff they bring along you wouldn't believe. Some of them must think we're taking them in military transport planes. Every ounce gets to count. For shore lunches, you learn to pack just what you need in there, not an extra pound. Besides, if its bumpy and the bottles break, you only spill a little instead of a lot." "I see," she said.

She was learning. She had anticipated the wilderness ("the bush," as she was learning to call it) as a release from the tricks and games of her life, but she was seeing now that here, too, were little techniques and points of care and attention that made the big difference, that made life easier, safer, more fun. She would learn a lot from him. She lay back with the towel folded under her head, the sun beating down on her. He had been right; in just under the hour her suit was dry. It wouldn't be a hardship to stay here all day, in lotus land. She looked up at him, so busy, packing up, dousing the fire, splitting some wood, whistling a song she did not recognize. "Conk's song," she said to herself. It occurred to her that he had made no overtures of love. They had been in their bathing suits for over an hour, but he had not made a remark, or gesture, of wanting her physically, other than the crack about doing something with their mouths in a restaurant. She wasn't concerned, she told herself, certainly not insulted or miffed. But she wondered if she might be a little disappointed. No, probably not. But her earlier amusement at him was turning to respect, anticipation. This morning she had felt their magnetism; she was sure it was mutual. It was there in his eyes, the way he looked at her. She hadn't wanted it, certainly hadn't sought it. It had just happened. She had decided after the trip back from the hospital, when she knew she'd like to see him again, to go very, very slowly. She was making such great strides in her research. But somehow he would not conflict or interfere or draw her off from that. He would be someone to confide in, to share with, a counterbalance, though he might have a hard time understanding what she was doing and accepting it as important. But that wouldn't matter. She'd take him on as a freshman anthropologist. Maybe she could open his eyes, win a convert.

She closed her eyes. She could feel her body drinking in the sun. It was narcotic, she thought. The whistling stopped. From down the bay she heard Henry's laugh. Funny, they all called it the loon's laugh; but she thought it tinged with fear. Perhaps Henry wouldn't laugh until the babies were here safe and sound. "Let's go," he said; "we've got to get back to the real world." She dressed quickly.

Because it was so calm, he wanted to strap the canoe on her side of Cloudie, "just to balance the weight a bit." She was learning that a bush pilot's greatest friend was wind, not too much, but enough. So she would have to get up into her seat and fasten the door before he strapped it down. He threw in his bag and gave her his hand as she jumped onto the pontoon. She didn't need any assistance to climb the little ladder, but suddenly his hands were on her waist to help her up. But they didn't help her up. They held her back as she started to climb and suddenly she knew it was now. He turned her around without resistance and enclosed her, his lips coming down hard on hers and the moustache feeling warm and woolly. His left hand slid up her back and under her shining hair into the nape of her neck, holding her close. It lasted, she thought, a long time. She had the faintest taste of catsup. No words were exchanged. She smelled smoke in his hair, and soap.

ii

She had meant to write Zellie for two weeks. She hadn't been ten days on Sand Island before a letter arrived, addressed to:

Miss Catherine Saltonstall,
Achinike, Northern Canada.

Bless Zellie! The smartest, most gorgeous Jew in the Bronx, who could dazzle her professors whether she was reading a paper at the Graduate Club, or submitting one to a learned journal (she had published two, now), could drop in the mail an address like that! Some kindhearted person in the Cambridge Post Office must have been curious and taken the time to look up Achinike, and had added in a different hand, in pencil, the postal code P8H 1H9, and it had made it through. Zellie wanted to know everything, and now there was so much to tell.

The past three weeks for Catherine had been another time of awakening. The Tuesday morning affairs had grown to Tuesday and Friday mornings. Henrietta had just given birth to two tiny brown goslings. He had flown them to many other parts of the lake, and to other lakes, to other nests, flying high in the sky to glide effortlessly in great circles, the wind whistling against Cloudie's silent prop, to waterfalls and sheer glacial cliffs four hundred feet high, to deep trout holes and pickerel beds; but their favorite spot was still Keewaydin Bay and keeping an eye on Henry and Henrietta.

She was learning a lot about loons. She was learning a lot about the teacher of the learning about loons. He was, like her at a younger stage, a student in the bud, self-taught researcher, explorer, experimenter, recorder, all rolled into one consuming passion. On several nights in his little apartment she had gone over with him his collection of remarkable photographs, and listened as he would recall the circumstances of some of them, of what he had learned of the loons' behavior and the nuances of what they were doing and saying to one another. But there wasn't a word written down. Like Harold, he lived in a world of sight and sound and memory, and the words were there, on the subject of loons, anyway, lots and lots of words, but only inside his head and in his mouth, never on paper. "I'm a lousy writer," he had said; "even the inspectors groan at my spelling when they check my flight logs." "But writing isn't spelling, silly," she had said, but dropped the subject for another day.

Could she tell Zellie about their second trip to Henrietta's Bay, as she had now christened it? He had brought along a fishing line this time and a collapsible minnow net. She could recall being in a big launch years ago with her parents when she was very young, at Cape Cod, and someone was fishing, and she had been bored and started to whimper and then she had this big pole in her hands, and was told to "pull, pull, pull with all your might, Catherine," and it was so heavy she couldn't pull, and thought it was going to pull her into the sea, and she began to cry and someone else took it. Other than that fish were served in cream sauce and bouillabaisse at Sweeny's, lightly broiled with chives and peppers at Tontini's, or small pink fillets of trout lying waiting on Lydia's breadboard. She knew that fish somehow got into nets and into boats and then into kitchens and then onto the plates by the window at Sweeny's, looking out onto the harbor, with candlelight and Chardonnay, but the actual transmissions in this process had neither crossed her path nor whetted her interest. This morning she had watched him assemble the little net, the four corners fastened to a wire frame which bent, curved down, when you pulled it up in four feet of water by a cord attached to a pole. He had produced another of his little bottles, this time containing flakes of dried oatmeal for making porridge, which he soaked crumbled in his tanned, hairy fist, and then let fall over the net, the mush dipsey doodling in slow downward spirals into the net. She watched the minnows come over to the net and hesitate, circling, some just sitting watching, then there was a rush and they swarmed, darting at the falling mush and scooping it off the net's floor. He pulled hard, and up came enough, if they were only two feet longer, to make a Cape fisherman ecstatic. They were poured into a little bucket with holes in it and it was tied to a thwart of the canoe, and thrown overboard. He reached in for one and put it on the hook, pushing the barb through under the minnow's back fin. He lowered the line into the water and the minnow swam desperately trying to get away. "Nice action," he said. "It doesn't hurt them when you hook them that way." She wondered how he could possibly know that. If asked her opinion she would have said that it likely hurt a good deal.

He had soon pulled up a small pickerel, a wide-eyed and greenish fish with yellow flecks in its scales, especially down by its whitish underbelly, and he unhooked it and conked its head over the gunnel and after two quick convulsive spasms it lay limp in the bottom of the canoe, its big glassy eyes looking right at her, she thought. "There are only two ways to kill a fish," he said: "the fast painless way or the slow painful way. I prefer the fast way. That's providing of course you're going to eat them within an hour or two." He hooked on another minnow. He showed her the reel tension mechanism, the flip of the bail, the gentle fling of the line "so you don't rip the minnow off," and he let it settle, then slowly reeled it in, and handed it to her. "You try. Let's see you catch one," he said, and she thought it sounded just a bit like a taunt.

She did as she had seen him do and as the line settled she felt a little something and he said that it was just the minnow swimming around. Then she knew it was more than that and he said, gently, "Let him take it, let him take it," and she suddenly wondered why Cloudie was a

she and a fish a he. Then she pulled, and she had it, for it
pulled too, going under the canoe and the line whizzing
out with a high-pitched whine, and he told her to keep
reeling in and not to let out any slack at all, but the fish
said it had other ideas and wasn't coming in yet. It
surfaced once with a splash but she couldn't get a good
look at it. He told her to keep her line high and keep
reeling and her heart was pounding. She had been
determined not to be too excited, but when he finally got
the net under it and swooshed it up fast in one upwards
motion and held it high, she saw how big it was. She
wanted to laugh and sing and shout all at once but she
only blurted out "Golly!" "God damn it!" he said,
reaching into the net and holding it up with his finger
through its gill high against the morning blue. "It'll go
four pounds for sure." He looked at her. "Beginner's
luck!" he said. She smiled at him. "I learn fast," she
said. "Bah!" he said.

It wasn't beginner's luck later, after their swim. He
had wanted to help her dry her hair, he said, and came
over to her with his towel stretched out, but suddenly his
hands were all over her, and she turned to him, and he
pulled her close and kissed her hard, and she could feel
his erection, and then their suits were off. She thought the
bag had looked bulkier that morning, and now she saw a
heavy cotton blanket of multicolored squares spread out,
and he didn't ask for anything, but he didn't need to for
she knew her body said yes. He was rough and powerful
but not awkward, and the power in his hands was a new
sensation. She couldn't believe how quickly the orgasm
came, and for him too, and she wondered if they might
have been simultaneous. She was almost frightened that
their bodies seemed so compatible, beacuse she was used
to his wanting her to be first, and then, on occasion, he

having held it back, it would be difficult for him to get it to come again.

Later that morning in the library she had felt a little burning sensation in her right buttock, and when she went home for lunch she climbed up on the sink in the bathroom with her pants off, and she could see her rear in the mirror with the help of her looking glass, and there was a definite red pattern there that resembled a large hand, where he had held her against him so hard. She had looked up from her reading several times that afternoon, smiling, wondering if it were her scarlet letter or red badge of courage, but it didn't make any difference because no one would ever see it or ever know.

The breakfast that morning had also been unusual for a Cambridge lady, she recalled, for he insisted that they leave their suits off. "We have to tan you up," he had said. She was accustomed to cuddling after making love, to a quiet time of gentle hugs and soft kisses and drowsiness and drifting off in one another's arms. Not this morning. It had seemed less than a minute from their uncoupling, and she was just settling down to feeling the narcotic sun and his assuring embrace, and he had mumbled something in her ear about God's aplenty, when he suddenly pulled out his arm and jumped to his feet. "We've got to get breakfast," he said; "I've got to clean the fish and we don't want to be late." She just stared up at him. She watched him crouched over the fish and a newspaper, and he explained every move of his knife. He had brought bacon for himself this morning, to be fried up after the fish, but she said she'd have "one piece" because she hadn't wanted to allow distinctions between them; they had done everything else together, they'd eat the same food. Would she provide Zellie with a sketch of the two of them sitting there on their towels on the rocks, naked in the blazing sun, eating fresh-caught fish and fried bacon from tin plates, drinking her perked coffee from tin cups, their bodies a mixture of cool depths and hot passion and ravenous hunger such as she had never known in the mornings, with the smells of coffee and pine trees and shampoo and the sounds of Henry and Henrietta and the chicks, who sat out on the lake watching them, uttering their gentle calls of "who? who?" "What's he saying, Conk?" she asked. "Well," he said in a drawn-out way, and she knew there was another Conkeroo coming; "when you're better tuned in, you'll understand, but for now I'd say, very loosely translated, that he's saying, 'Jesus! Conk, what a babe!'" and he came over and kissed her hard before she could swallow the bacon and she dropped her plate.

Her research in the library had been going very well. She had carefully read every word of six of the eleven volumes, and kept her laptop busy recording data. She studied over and over again the five known pictographs, including the Chief's new find. Many more stories and myths had been collected and cross-referenced than had been available to Ashton, and she had already had Harold starting to winnow the seed from the chaff, as far as he was concerned. She had been in touch twice by radio with Rita McDermott at the new dig, and kept track of her findings and got them into the computer.

Something strange was shaping up, an irony that could only have been planned by the fates, she thought. The more she learned about loons in the mornings, the more importance they were assuming in her studies during the day. They were in the mythology, the pictographs, and now, apparently, in the dig. The recent pictograph was crucial, for it alone had the clear red dot for the eye, made from a rock's dye over two thousand years before. She had shown the pictures to Conk and asked his opinion. "Well, if those branches sticking out of the water in Keewaydin Bay are a duck," he said, "then these are loons. If you asked me to draw the outline of one, I couldn't do much better myself." That was all the authority she needed. The shapes in the pictographs, and Henry and Henrietta, blended in her dreams.

So she had to pick and choose for Zellie, from so much to tell, a bookful, she thought. She pictured Zellie sitting in the cafeteria at the College. They appeared so unlike, on the surface, she all body and heart, Catherine all costume and head. But it was only a matter of style and temperament, she knew, for underneath they were much alike. Zellie loved to "let it all hang out," as she said, because that's what honesty was all about, and any good scholar couldn't be honest about some things which she had to be if she were going to be a good scholar, and not about others. "It's not a matter of honesty at all," she had said to Zellie, "but style. All style's a mask, you know that; it's just that you all agree that some things aren't put on centre stage as much."

So now she had decided to concentrate on her new sense of herself, the Catherine of Henrietta's Bay. She, too, would let it all hang out. She would try to preserve something of the old discretion, if she could, but she must probe the new Catherine Saltonstall. Zellie was the only one in the world she could tell. "Move over, Zellie," she said to herself; "I'm overlapping into your preserve."

Tuesday, July 24.

Dear Zellie:

There's so much to tell you I don't know where to begin. First, you were right. This new country is kind to body and soul. I haven't grown tired of its freshness yet. The

Wendaban are warm and kindly in spite of their having deeply entrenched reasons for resisting Shagonash, their word for a white person. Some of them have married whites, but I'm the only visiting white living on the Reserve at present. They have graciously made their archives available to me, including new pictographs and unpublicized digs. I can feel you squirming with envy. I'll have a good dissertation, and figure I'll be here until next spring.

I miss Fenway, but they have a good substitute here and I've become a fan of the Wendaban Bears softball team. Their superstar is Sammy Osatig. His family name means crooked tree, but when he stands erect at the plate, he's six-feet-three, and he sends a lot of balls out over the fence. He's what I guess you'd call a hunk, and when he swings the bat I sometimes think his muscles will pop out of his arms. He either hits home runs or strikes out, the proportions depending on what he's been into the previous night. Right now he's batting .390, but with the Majukimo coming up, that may drop considerably. The Majukimo is an ancient Ashwagane fertility ceremony. Don't worry about me. I'll batten down the hatches.

And now for my bombshell. I may still marry Dawson, but at the moment I'm quite swept off my feet—literally. He flies a yellow bush plane he calls Cloudie. He takes care of it as if he were Henry Ford looking after the original model T, and it's just about as original, too. Look up "Stinson Reliant" in an aviation encyclopedia, and you'll see what I mean. I think there are about five of them left flying in the world. Anyway, I've gone loony. He's introduced me to the fascinating world of loons, and it's great relief from my Indian studies. His favorites he calls Henry and Henrietta, and she has just hatched two little balls of brown fluff which ride up on her back and

then tumble off into the water and hide up in behind her
tail feathers and you'd never know they were there.

Now hold onto your chair. I kid you not. My pilot is a
bit rough in some aspects, but for zip and get up and go,
he has no equal. I know your morning begins at 10:30
when your hunk brings you breakfast in bed, and that your
day slowly rises to a climax about midnight. Well, try this
on for size, because it's just the opposite. He picks me up
at the dock at 6:00 a.m. in yellow bird. I have fresh
perked coffee in a thermos, he a bag of breakfast goodies.
Then we fly, high, low, gliding, on our sides, not yet
upside down, thank goodness. Then we're into a canoe
and my insides start to settle. We fish. I usually do better
than he does and he gets mad and I'm glad, 'cause I love
to see him worked up. Then we go over to the campsite
and undress each other, and it's off for a swim. Nude. No
sex in the water; it's sort of religious for him, I think. We
swim hard, a half mile out into the lake. I keep right up
with him. When we return, it's love time. The swim has
us both horny and we know what's coming. I'm near
exhausted, but the old body's tingling and we go to it. He
brings the blanket. Now he's very sexy. He's powerful
and just about crushes me, but lately I've been handing it
right back, and I'm beginning to see a little bump of a
muscle in my arm in the mirror. Then, as if a school bell
had rung, it's breakfast time—eggs, bacon, fish, sometimes
pancakes, lately a few blueberries, prepared by my nude
gourmet chef over an open fire. He brings out amazing
little bottles of this and that from his bag to garnish the
meal. Have you ever watched a nude six-foot hairy man
crouched down over an open fire turning fish fillets,
singing all the while, at approximately 7:30 in the
morning? Try it! I find it very exhilarating. Twice we've
made love a second time, and once I thought I was going

to puke I was so full of fish. But usually it's wash up, tidy up, cut some wood (I now know how to wield an axe!) and then load into yellow bird, tied down by the shore. He drops me off rarely later than 8:30, and so I hie me off to the library. Can you blame me if I sometimes try to sneak a little nap at noon? I never knew I had such a body until now. I eat bacon and drink homogenized milk because he can't stand 2%, and I haven't gained a pound.

Please give my love to mom and dad if you hear from them, and tell them I'm doing very well. I've written them twice. I haven't told them about my pilot yet, because I think for now no news is probably the right news.

Oh, I don't think I mentioned his name. It's Conk! Isn't that bloody ridiculous?

Write soon!
Love,
Cathy.

Chapter X
THE LIBRARY

i

As he fed the gas into Cloudie's gull wing, standing up on the strut, he looked skywards. Now, with only a few days remaining in July, the early daylight of June was beginning to recede. It was barely light. A dull grey drizzle had settled in and he could feel it on his face. The weather office at Almaguin had told him on the phone that the low wouldn't pass through before evening, and it looked to him as if they were right. There would be just enough visibility to fly low. Heavier rain was on the way. He pulled the nozzle back towards the storage room, dragging the long line of hose behind him, then laid it down on the dock. He went over and clicked off the pump. Bill would be gassing up about 7:00. He returned and untied the lines, gave her a little shove by the strut towards the lake, jumped on the pontoon, climbed in and secured the door. He was restless. The air was still and heavy.

Cloudie drifted only a few feet before gradually coming to rest. She seemed to be waiting for the electric signal. He buckled his belt. Everything was still and quiet. Then a transport rumbled around the curve in the highway, barely slowing down for the deserted streets of Achinike. He turned on the wiper, but after one pass cleared the water-pebbled glass with a little whining noise, he turned it off. He opened the side window. He placed his feet firmly on the flap pedals and gripped the half wheel with his hands. The window was water-pebbled again. He relaxed.

This morning would be different, he thought. He was looking forward to it. She had suggested over a week ago that when the first inclement Tuesday or Friday morning came along, she would show him the library, the documents and photographs and the work she was doing. It would be her turn. She would provide the breakfast, too. She wouldn't be standing down on the dock with her thermos waiting for him this morning. He had planned pancakes, and packed it all up the night before, but the big dunnage bag and the blanket were still on the table in his apartment.

His recent days had been like nothing he had ever known. Freda and Ted sensed his perturbations even though he thought he had succeeded in not showing so much as a flutter of anything unusual. They had been used to his little escapades, and once, several years ago, a blond girl they had never heard mentioned arrived unannounced and stayed with him in his apartment, and then she was gone. Without a car, his weekend overnights to Almaguin were sporadic, and when he did go down to the little city with friends, or by plane, he was always back on the job the next morning, hardy and chipper. They could count his obvious hangovers in six years on one hand. He rarely uttered a word about his private life, except when he would want to use Cloudie or take time off. He had never taken either for his own use without consulting with them first. He enjoyed his women, his male cameraderie, the pubs and the good times. But his only love had been flying and nothing had as yet come along to enter into that sacred domain. He had pals in town, but he had no close friends, no shoulder to cry on, no intimate to confide in. His joy had been spattered on people and events who simply came and went; he took what he needed, gave what he could, and walked away from them with the fresh innocence of a child. There were moments when Freda and Ted envied him. After his last flight of the day, he walked off the base as free as a bird. But of late they sensed something just a little different, that wouldn't go away. They had discussed it without being able to put their finger on it; was it the look of his eyes, a slight urgency to his actions, a huskiness in his voice, a slight flush to the cheeks? "I think he's in love," Ted said.

He looked at his watch. He wanted to get going, but he knew he should wait another few minutes until the grey drizzle lightened up another tone. He wanted to see her again, just to look at her, even without touching her, to drink her in with his eyes. Lately she was going everywhere with him inside his mind, to Red Pine Mountain, Norich Junction, the outpost camps, riding in his fantasy in the next seat as he pulled the seismic bulb swung out behind Cloudie on a long rope to pick up ore concentrations, up and back, up and back, slicing off another quarter mile each time as he worked his boring way across the little piece of map ruled in long parallel lines from the mining company. He couldn't leave her behind at the base or in his apartment. This had never happened before. If she were suddenly to leave, would he follow her?

He thought how odd it all was. He had never had a preferred type. The women he had known had generally worn their hearts on their sleeves, had pretended to travel in the fast lane. Fun was to be quickly pushed to its extremity for it was foreknown that time would soon be up. The tourist girls were always on vacation, on deliberate escapes from their other lives, ready for adventure. Pilots and planes and easy access to lakes and beaches attracted them. So now comes onto the scene this demure little Cambridge lady of auburn hair and hazel eyes who wants to study documents and photographs and old maps and diggings in beach sands for ancient junk, who sees ducks in dead branches and once saw a dead lady in her white funeral dress throw her a piece of paper out of a window. She would go out of her way not to appear sexy, wouldn't wear a bikini in public though she had nothing to be ashamed of, shied away from holding his hand in public, had never worn makeup, regularly talked like a British Queen, and on occasion looked at him as if she had just detected him letting a noiseless fart. With luck she'd be a doctor in little more than a year, but she couldn't take out an appendix or stitch a cut, and what she would be a doctor in he had never heard of before and still didn't know what you could do with it or why anybody in his right mind would consider calling it by the word doctor in the first place. It certainly didn't pay like a doctor, she had told him.

But she had come round to him, he knew. The mystery was that she was doing it without shedding any of her reserve, without adjusting her temperament or changing her tune. She wanted to fish, swim and canoe with him; she loved now to fly, glide, study his maps. Nothing escaped her. He couldn't appal, bore or outsmart her. He couldn't find anything she didn't want to try. She had won friends on the Reserve, was as interested in Henry and Henrietta as he was, and had joined his determination to catch them diving on tape. She had become his lover with ardent joy and was giving him back anything he could dish up. He had never known such compatibility in two bodies. She had adjusted to his life so easily, entered his secret places so happily, without fanfare, with acceptance and respect, and always that indestructible smile.

Was he in love? he wondered. He was already thirty-one, and had never thought much about love. He

thought maybe he had been in and out of it several times.
Maybe Freda's and Ted's kind of relationship was just a
matter of deliberate determination to fight the clock and
stretch out an initial attraction to a much longer time, for
better or for worse, rather than a matter of a different
degree of attraction. Now he would have to reassess that
question. Or, you did it for children. That reason was not
high on his list.

It was still barely light enough. There was no breeze
through the window. The grey peacefulness was heavy,
clammy. Cloudie would surely be thinking something very
odd was up. He patted the dashboard. "We'll just sit here
another minute or two," he said. "It's okay. I guess I
pushed us off a bit too early." Could he come round to
her? That was the bigger question. Could he enter her
secret places with as much ease and understanding as she
had his? Their bodies said yes, but their minds, their
backgrounds, the things they held important, seemed to
him, at times, so different, so removed as to be seen
across a great gulf. It wasn't that she was so educated, and
he a dunce; or that she was so sophisticated and he a
baboon. That didn't bother him—wasn't his concern. He'd
put his upbringing in the practical life of getting people
and freight moved against great odds in the northcountry
against her life of books any day. She said that what she
was working on would clarify the past. So what? Who
needed it clarified? The past was over and done with.
Could he change her deeper tendencies, to align them with
his? Could she change his, to align them with hers? What
were his deeper tendencies? Had he already shot his load,
he wondered, exhausted his bag of tricks, whereas she was
still a mystery, with so much still in reserve. Should he try
to understand, to move over, to admit that his was just a
little piece of the life he might know, could know? He

couldn't ever just allow her her different ways, the way you could allow an elephant to sit on its hind end. And certainly, he couldn't forgive her for them, or just tolerate them. That would never work. How could he close that gulf? He had the sneaking suspicion that it was his gulf too, his to close. "My God," he thought, "here I'm thinking long term. I've never thought long term about a woman before. Jesus! The considerations!" He was swimming in dark uncharted seas. He looked down at his watch: 6:25. She'd be wondering where he was. "Let's go," he said.

ii

He was wrong. She was waiting for him, standing alone in the drizzling dawn with a yellow rain jacket and floppy hat, but no thermos. She waved. They had soon joined hands and were walking up the hill to the house. She opened the door and reached inside for a large plastic bag on the chair. She gently closed the door and they went on to the Band Office and into the library. "I decided not to try and cook eggs in here," she said. "This is going to be more like my Cambridge breakfast, the easy kind. I hope it will get you by." She produced two white porcelain bowls, a box of raisin bran, spoons, a plastic litre of milk, and two wet-looking peaches wrapped in wax paper, which she had already skinned. She cut up the peaches with a paring knife, letting the juicy slices fall scattered over the cereal in each bowl, and threw the pits in the garbage basket. She handed him the milk. "I hope you'll forgive me for the 2%," she said, "but it's all Angele keeps in the house." "It's white and cold," he replied; "it will do just fine." She brought out a little plastic envelope with sugar in it. "I try to keep my loads light," she said, smiling. He took some. Then she produced another little plastic sandwich bag sealed across the top with three unglazed donuts in it. "She must have noticed I like donuts when she was at the apartment," he thought. "I baked a dozen last week," she said; "my first attempt. I froze them. I hope they're up to snuff." "They'll be the best donuts I'll ever eat," he said, the big black moustache spread out across his grin, "in a library at least." They laughed. The last items to come out of her bag were two paper napkins. "You call these serviettes up here," she said, handing him one. "At home, we call them napkins." "We call them serviettes, because we use them for serving up and wiping off food. I believe napkins can be used in other ways, in other places," he said. "Oh, I see," she said, starting to tidy up and put the used bowls back into the bag; "I'll try to remember the distinction." "I thought we were going to look at your work," he said. "Incidentally, these donuts are very good. If I break my leg in the bush some morning, it's nice to know your co-pilot can cook." "Co-pilot?" she said, looking at him. "Oh Conk! You're kidding. Would you really teach me to fly? I'm sure I could learn before the fall. I'm serious." He came over to her, and pulled her in close. Her hair had that clean soap smell again. He clasped her hands, and held them low, and moved his lips across her forehead and down one cheek and up the other side, mouthing softly: "It's a very, very secret society, Miss Saltonstall. Very hard to get into. It will cost you. It will cost you big." He moved his hand up her back and toyed with the bra clips. "I don't have a lot to pay with, mister," she said, "but I can wash the dishes. But we won't start advance deposits in here this morning, will we!" "I'll work out a payment schedule as soon as I get back to the base," he said, releasing her. "In the meantime, what else do you have to show me?"

She took him on a tour of the room. She explained maps of old hunting territories of n'Daki Menan, she talked about some of the photos in frames, of Chiefs Whitebear, with his huge white moustache, and Pashawonaby, grim and sad-looking in a worn vest. There were slightly fuzzy pictures of the old Hudson's Bay Company Post in the 1870's, taken from the lake, with men lounging on the steps, some smoking pipes. There were pictures of old canoes. There were miscellaneous faces, of young and old, smiles, frowns, straight hair, pigtails, in bobs, dimples, staring eyes, wrinkles and bulging cheeks, bare arms and fur-covered bodies, men and women in fur-lined parkas on the frozen lake with dog teams. She got out the pictograph photos, and told him of her conclusions about what each picture meant. She told him about Ashton's note about the hypothetical panograph, "a larger story in pictures." "Have you asked them about it?" he said. "I think Chief Philip knows something about it," she responded, "and Harold too, but they're not saying much at the moment. I'm biding my time. We'll see."

They returned to the table. "The loons aren't just out there in the lake," she said; "they're in here too. I'm surer every day that they played a larger role in their ancient religious myths than we've suspected. The Montagnais to the northeast elevated the beaver to an important god. It was their family symbol for health and survival. It was called Amiktayah, the great mother of all beavers. Amiktayah provided food and clothing, and blessed their teepees and log houses. The more I study the Wendaban myths and the pictographs, I'm beginning to think the Ashwagane had a loon goddess, for she appears to be feminine." "You mean Henrietta may be an old goddess of some sort?" he asked. "How come?" "She's a bridge across time," she replied; "about three thousand years of it or maybe more. And for the same reasons you're so interested in them. They are great travellers, but they have territorial homing instincts, like the Ashwagane. For their adroitness at fishing, so they are abundant suppliers of a food staple. For their family habits. They stick together and put a lot of attention on training and protecting their young, just like the Ashwagane. The Ashwagane are probably the most family-oriented group of all the Algonkian nations. And for their communication skills. Rita came up with a horn, last week, a small slender horn made out of a bison antler. I wonder what calls they practiced? The loons let each other know where they are, as far as six miles away on a calm night, and not only that, but you've shown me that they can actually tell one another whether they're in trouble, or lonely, or want to get a whole group together to talk things over. They dominate the sounds of n'Daki Menan over all other creatures. So the Ashwagane would want their blessing and inspiration on that, too. Travel, food, family security, communications—what more could you ask for in your patron saint?" He stared at her. He felt an excitement, he didn't know why.

"And what about the mating games," he said. "You've seen them placidly swimming around, but remember the one chasing the other across the water last week? Wait till you see them in their spring mating games. They're unbelievable in their power, their fury you might almost call it. So throw in some sex, too." "Good," she said, "that would be a part of it. The Ashwagane's most important tribal ceremony was the Majukimo, a spring fertility ceremony. We'll see a modern version next week. So maybe the loon was their symbol of sexual vitality." "I'd never thought of Henrietta as Madonna," he said. "I'll bet Henry has," she said, smiling.

She got out the volumes of the recent Wendaban researches. She showed him an original line drawing of an archeologist's recreation of a log house, and how one of their more permanent campsites might look, and pictures of the artifacts found in excavated sites. "There's some rudimentary evidence of agriculture," she said, "but it is something I'm working on. They had a rich knowledge of medicinal juices from plants and barks, and their mythology shows a great reverence for plant life. Rita has turned up a stone implement that she's sure was used for digging or preparing the ground. But we're not sure, and we don't know what they grew. I suspect it was natural plants already found in the forest, but whether they had discovered how to grow them from seeds is still not determined. It wouldn't surprise me, though. The Ashwagane's intelligence and ingenuity continue to amaze me each day. They are a fascinating people. I can see why the Montagnais and Cree might want to league with them, not just to work out their hunting territories, or for defense, but for everyday down-to-earth useful information. The Inuit were better hunters of wandering herds, but the Ashwagane had them beat in family matters, like clothing and medicine. It is a real challenge to try to work it all out."

He sat quietly for a minute, his legs stretched out, gazing out the window, his left hand cradling his chin. The tiny tick of the battery-run clock made out of polished pine was all that could be heard in the hushed room. The ticking of time. But his mind was adrift in a timeless fantasy where Henrietta was hung by the neck over a roasting fire, while savage devils danced round in glee. "Did they eat the loons?" he asked. "There's no evidence of that," she replied. "I suppose if you get hungry enough you will eat anything. But the Ashwagane did not eat their gods like some native cultures, to get some of the gods' vitality and power inside them. Ducks and geese, yes; loons, no. The Ashwagane were the gourmets of the Algonkian peoples; the loons were too fishy, I'm sure."

They were quiet again. "What about your past, Conk?" she asked. "I've known you for six weeks now and you have never mentioned it. I have told you a bit about the old Saltonstall line, the good parts, anyway. What about your family? Can you tell me something about them?"

He got up and walked to the end of the room, and returned. He sat on the edge of the long reading table with his hands gripping the edge, his legs dangling. "I don't know a great deal about my past," he said, looking at her. He told her of his early memories of his father, who was French Canadian, of his learning to fish, and of a young mother, a blurred image in his memory. She was English, but he did not know from where. She died when he was nine. They lived in Gawa, two hundred miles northwest of Achinike. His older sister, Elsa, helped raise them, and he managed to stay in school until he was fifteen, because she wouldn't let him quit earlier. His father didn't seem to care. He was very easygoing. He worked in the local pulp mill. Their house was small, of wood, two bedrooms, livingroom, separate kitchen and an outhouse. He spent a lot of time helping his father cut wood which is how they heated the house. He had two younger brothers and one younger sister, but he didn't know where they were now. When he was sixteen, and had quit school, he worked in a local store, then the following year he went to Kimberley

Falls, eighty miles further south, to work in a lumber mill. He hardly got home at all. He later heard that his father had died, but he didn't go back for the funeral. His older sister had written him about three years ago, from Montreal. He had meant to reply, but somehow he didn't do it. He had the letter somewhere in his apartment. He had a flight up to Gawa a few years ago, and he had looked for the old house, but it was gone. There was a new brick one in its place, but he didn't go to the door to see who was living in it.

"Do you have any pictures of them?" she asked. "Or any mementos, like a ring, or bracelet or something?" "I have only one picture," he said, "of my mother. She's dressed in a big fur coat and smiling." Suddenly he wanted to change the subject. The whole thing was becoming messy. He jumped down onto his feet. "Do you realize we haven't had coffee yet?" he said. "Do you treasure your picture of your mother?" she asked. "I don't think I have seen it in your apartment. Is it framed? Do you look at her often?" He walked over to the window. He thought he could feel a moistness in his eyes at the corners. "God damn it!" he thought. "Where's she pushing me now? Jesus!" He deliberately turned round to her and raised his voice. "I know where it is, and, yes, I look at it from time to time. It's just a photo, you know. I can't help her now. If you don't make us some coffee, I'm going to expire on the spot, and then how are you going to explain a two-hundred-pound corpse on your library floor, dead from no apparent cause!"

They were soon sipping coffee. "What do you think of the Wendaban Land Claim?" she asked. "You must make a lot of trips to Sand Island with all these lawyers and government people coming and going." He looked at her. "Now what," he thought; "what's she going to needle me into now?" "Yes," he said, "I hear a lot about it, but I really don't pay much attention to it. They have their job to do, I have mine. A lot of people are pretty pissed off with the caution; it's canned a lot of development we really need. Prospectors, for instance. They're madder 'n hell. They can't register a claim. And all this business about saving the land for the next generation. I don't know. There's an awful lot of it. Timber, iron, copper, hunting, bush camps, cottages. This place could boom if it weren't for the damn caution." "Would you like to be a part of it," she asked; "invest in it, own some of it?" "I've already invested all I'm going to for now," he replied; "I own half the Airways. That's enough for me. And it's growing. We had to add Bill a few years ago, and Ted says we're to the stage where we're going to have to lay on another plane and pilot soon."

"And what about Henrietta," she said. "Would you go to bat against more development in case the loons left? Maybe your son will not be able to see any loons. He'll just chuck all your old photos; not relevant any more. Too bad. No more loons." He looked at her. "My son? What are you getting at, Cathy? I don't know whether I'll have a son or not. That's all up in the future somewhere." "Oh, is it?" she said. "Suppose I told you I was pregnant." He looked at her for several seconds. "Jesus! Cathy, how could you be?" he asked. "You mean we made a mistake? We've been so careful."

She came over and jumped up on the table close to him, and took his hand. "I'm not pregnant, that I know of," she smiled. "I don't think the mistake will be a leaky condom," she said, "but the commitment. You're so unattached. You have no past to think of, no thoughts for the future." He felt her eyes getting deep inside him. Her voice was quiet. "I can't seem to reach your soul, Conk. You commit yourself to yellow bird and the safety of your passengers, but what else? You have no commitment to people or groups, not to your own family, who got you so far into life, not to the Wendaban, not even to protecting the land you love and that nurtures you. Isn't that what love is, a giving of yourself? Please help me to work this out, Conk. I would have to have that picture of your mother on my little front stage just to stay alive. She's me and I am her. I could not live without a past. It's emotionally inside me. Can you understand that?" They heard the key in the door. Giselle's voice rang out. "Hi," she called; "another day in the life of the Wendaban, another Shagonash piss-off." Catherine put her arms around his neck and kissed him hard on the lips. "To be continued," she said to him in a whisper, putting her index finger on the tip of his nose. He wouldn't smile. "I'll see you tomorrow night," she said.

As he taxied out to the open lake, the rain was beating down hard. Both his clothes and the cabin were clammy cold. He turned on the windshield wiper. There was grey haze ahead, but he knew he had at least four miles of open water. He looked at the gauge; the engine was warming. He made the usual preparations, and squinted ahead again. "It's a good thing we know where we're going, Cloudie," he said. "But I have such a long, long way to go." He put his hand on the throttle knob. His left hand had hold of the wheel. He was about to pull it out for full throttle, but he paused. His head suddenly slumped down on his left hand, and he wept.

iii

She was not having her usual good morning. Try though she would, she could not focus the kind of

attention she wanted 'on her work. His pained face at the
end of their meeting would not go away. "I was too hard
on him," she thought. "I set him up for it. Such things
need to be led up to gradually, very gradually," she said
to herself. "But damn it, he's got to talk to me about these
things. Still, it was mean of me." It was almost time for
lunch. She thought she would go early. Giselle stuck her
head in the door. "The phone's for you, Cathy," she said.
"You can take it over there by the filing cabinet. Press the
number one button." "Hello," she said; "this is
Catherine Saltonstall." "Oh, Miss Saltonstall," the voice
said, "this is Freda at the Air Base. Conk asked me to call
you. He's just taking off for Sand Island and wonders if
you could meet him at the front dock in about fifteen
minutes." "Thank you, Freda," she said; "I'll be there."
"That's great, then," said Freda; "I'll let him know.
Goodbye."

Her mind skipped into high gear. Now what! Had she
so provoked him that he was going to give her a blast?
Was he going to tell her that it was all over? No, she
thought; their relationship was too strong for that. Maybe
he was going to cry on her shoulder and ask for her help.
Maybe he would want to take her to Montreal and try to
locate his sister. "That's ridiculous," she said; "he's
probably just got a package for someone and wants to
save himself a trip up the path."

It was still grey but the rain had stopped. It had
warmed up. As she watched the yellow bird taxi towards
her she was sure she could see someone in the passenger
seat. He cut the prop. As they started to swing alongside,
she was sure it was a woman. The wing was too high for
her to grab but she reached out for the strut and swung
Cloudie parallel to the dock and pulled her in with all her
might. She knew from past experience how heavy she was

in the water. The door opened and before she could utter a word the big girl had jumped from the top rung of the ladder onto the pontoon and onto the dock and threw her arms around her with such force that she let the strut go. "It's fantastic!" she screamed. "My God, he's everything you said he was. Where's my hunk? When's the next ballgame? Geez it's so good to see you, Cathy." She gave her another bear hug. Conk was tying up the plane and soon had the two large bags on the dock. "I suppose I'll take them up to Harold's for now?" he half said and half asked. As he passed them he smiled and said, "If you asked me, I'd say you have your hands mighty full. Mighty full." "You've got that right," Catherine flashed back at him, smiling. The research intensifying, a love affair to get back on track, the Majukimo coming up, and now Zellie Rabinovitch, on the prowl, from the Bronx, "Ne Yauk." "It's faaaaaantastic," Zellie was saying.

Chapter XI
MAJUKIMO

i

The Majukimo had been a long time in the planning. It was Chief Philip's brainchild more than two years earlier; he had nurtured it, revised it, enlarged it, until it had grown in his eyes into the major social and cultural event of the Wendaban year. It was part of the Council's attempt to reinforce in the life of Sand Island the old Indian ways. A few in the Band had caught his vision of the importance and potential of the Majukimo as a ritual of deep cultural significance in these days of negotiation. Others saw it as little more than a festival of fun and games, like their winter carnival when men in shirtsleeves and clouds of frosty breath cut through logs with big handsaws, one man on each end, to see which team was fastest, and ladies in red, white and green striped Hudson Bay parkas encouraged with claps and shouts cold little minnows through ice crystallized water in a tank to the finish line. A few were indifferent; the Majukimo would be another drain on their energies in a long, hot summer.

It began as a simple resurrection. The ancient Ashwagane Majukimo was a ceremony of initiation and thanksgiving held in late spring after the new crop of youth had returned to the summer villages from their ritual days of testing, when, alone in the wilderness, with patches of snow still in the gullies and deep recesses of the forest, they proved that they could survive and trap and hunt and bring back food and fur. The ceremony welcomed them home and gave thanks to Manitou for another annual rebirth, for the warming and lengthening of the days, for tiny alder sprouts which the moose would eat, for the new poplar trees which the beaver would chew on and grow fat, for the greening of the blueberry bushes and their little white blossoms which would turn into the bears' and birds' and long-haired girls' dainty delights, and for the return of the great-necked birds and ducks, some of whom would stay with them all summer, some of whom would rest in the marshes and bays before travelling on, some of whom would end up roasting over red-hot coals. If the boys had done well, the feast which concluded Majukimo into the early hours of the morning would be plentiful. If they hadn't done well, the older men would look perplexed and wonder if food would be in short supply this year, or whether the young boys were not yet sufficiently trained to the demanding skills of the hunt. If beaver and duck and moosemeat (and, from the southern hunting grounds of n'Daki Menan, venison) came back in short supply, the men would scurry for their canoes and the communal feast would go on as planned with large, succulent lake trout—namekoss.

The new Majukimo was to be adjusted for the political exigencies of the moment. The original ceremony of dance, song and feast was to be preserved with all the attention to its purity which the organizing committee of the Band Council could insist on. Three moose, cut into quarters, one hundred pounds of beaver meat, and two hundred pounds of fish, were waiting in unidentified freezers, along with eleven plucked mallards and seventeen teals. As long as no fee was charged, such a public feast of nature's illegal bounty could be allowed once by the government staff of Achinike with Head Office approval; they would look the other way. However, they wanted the beaver called beef, the moose, pork, and the duck, chicken. But Chief Philip put his foot down. There would be no little frauds in this rejuvenation.

Officialdom thought it best to compromise: all food and
native drink would be called by its Ashwagane name:
amik, kinuze, sheesheeb, papaski, neebeeshabo,
buckwayjigan, ininissip. Let those who were interested
find out what they meant.

There had been months of planning. Precise
information on the Majukimo was sketchy, so imagination
and invention were called upon. Masks were made for all
the clan animals—Nagik the otter, Mank the loon, Makwa
the bear—as well as for the thunderbird, Nanabush, and
the evil Wendigo. The story of the Ashwagane, from
earliest times to the present, was sketched out for a
pantomime dance. Costumes were sewn, choreography
and mime painstakingly created, with the help of two
teachers of dance from Almaguin. In the ancient
Majukimo, the pipe of brotherhood was lit and handed
from the Chief to the second Chief, elders, women and
men, and finally to the initiates. Chief Philip wanted to
use one of the old original pipes, but decided they were
much too fragile, so recreations were carefully crafted by
a potter in White Falls from local clay from n'Daki
Menan.

The guest list grew and grew. From the beginning, the
Council agreed to invite all members of the Band
officially recorded in the green leather-bound book in the
Band vault, some seven hundred and forty-nine half-
breeds and métis as well as full-blooded members, not
only living on Sand Island but scattered across the
country. Let this be a new occasion of coming together, a
rejoicing and celebration of their new links with the past
and hopes of preserving themselves into the future, a
holding of hands and smoking of pipes.

Then the concept grew bigger. Why not invite the
local Shagonash? Let the whites watch, taste, smoke and

dance too. What a fine opportunity for public relations, to invite Mr. and Mrs. Shagonash onto their one little piece of acknowledged Indian territory, present them with a day of events and ritual, and stuff them with nature's unpoisoned food prepared in dishes as exotic as would be found in the South Seas. "Many of the white people see us as non-aligned, uncooperative, defensive if asked to help, grasping if asked what we want," Chief Philip said to the Council; "Here is an opportunity for us to open our arms to our white brothers and sisters as we have never done before in the history of n'Daki Menan. If they understand us better, they might agree with us more." The Council pondered; they added up the cost (including the garbage pickup); they assigned the catching and hunting of the extra food needed; they added events; they calculated the stress of one thousand visitors to Sand Island, and looked appalled. Every man, woman and child would have an assigned task to perform: guide, hauler of huge pots and builder of temporary seats, wood cutter, cook, cleaner of fish, actor, dancer, player of instruments, sweeper, server, deputy-constable, docker and stacker of boats, taxi driver, sewer of costumes, singer of songs, drummer. The Council declared that on the day of the Majukimo, Saturday, August 6, no drinking of beer or alcoholic beverages of any sort would be allowed anywhere on Sand Island except as served in the official feast. Bottles in private homes must remain unopened. Anyone found transporting such liquids, or detected in any state of intoxication, would be charged and fined, and at the constable's or deputy-constable's discretion, given the luxury of listening to the Majukimo festivities from behind the bars of the Sand Island jail.

Originally the Mank, or loon, was but one of several birds and animals in the dance. But Chief Philip changed that at the last minute. He had welcomed periodic progress reports from Catherine whenever she wanted to talk to him, and by mid-July she had seen him twice in his office. Her primary reason for the second visit was to see if he could shed any light on the Ashton panograph. Had he heard of it? Did he know where it was? Yes, he had heard of it. He said that they knew there were still undiscovered rock paintings in the homeland but that they had not been able to muster specific funding for detailed search. She had the sensation that there was something odd in his face and eyes as he told her this, but this look quickly passed. She said that her research was suggesting that the loon played a deeper symbolic role in Ashwagane mythology than had been recognized, and she was sure that the mask Rita had discovered was a loon. But it was still too early for her to come up with a specific hypothesis; she needed more evidence.

That night the phone rang at Harold's and Chief Philip wanted to talk to Catherine. "I know it's getting late, with the Majukimo only three weeks away," he said, "but could we work the loon more prominently into the ceremony? I've been talking to Giselle and she thinks we could. Arthur says he can make a new mask. Talk to Giselle and tell her what you have in mind for how they figured in the overall picture, and let's see what we can come up with."

So, unannounced to anyone but Giselle, she worked up a statement on the loon as a clan goddess, and the writers worked it into the story and the choreographers into the dance. Angele already played a minor role in the chorus of Indian women, but because she lived with Catherine, and could learn from her, she was given the loon's new role. She was very pleased and Catherine thought Arthur required her for unnecessarily long periods of time for the mask fitting.

One night after Angele had been at rehearsal in the recreation hall, she asked Catherine further about her loon dance. On her last visit to town Catherine had found an earplug for Harold, and the late evenings in the little bungalow were now new times of bliss, punctuated by his high-pitched squeaks of joy, grunts of outrage, and the inevitable chuckles. Angele was already in bed and Catherine had just come in and closed the door.

"Cathy," she said, "I think I'm really getting into the loon dance. But I'm still not sure exactly what we're trying to say. The tough part is trying to do both the energy and the soft part." "Can you tell me more about your difficulty," Catherine said, looking over at her. Angele's long black hair was swept to one side on the pillow. The scar above her right eye was pink and angry-looking. "Well, Giselle has been pushing me on the first bit where I run back and forth waving my arms with the cloth wings, as if I was on top of the water. She has been trying to get me to weave my body more, to do some bumps as she calls them, to try to suggest that I want to have sex or something. It's hard to do. I'm not sure what the point is. I mean, I know loons have to have babies and have their mating and all that, but my dance seems to be more out of a girlie show where the women dance on tables. Loons don't do that. I know Grandpa won't like it."

Catherine undressed and got into bed. She decided to leave the overhead light on for awhile. She talked to Angele about what she knew of theatre, ritual, interpretation, about how Indian ritual was theatre and ballet, about how human beings had to pull their understandings of the animal world over into the human realm, because they were communicating to other humans, but at the same time, push the merely human world over into the animal world, because it was the animal they were trying to imitate, and blend them in a dance of make-believe or fantasy. "No, loons don't really belly dance," she said, "but the females do attract the males in all sorts of ways that are pretty sexy for loons. Have you ever seen the Swan Lake Ballet, Angele?" she asked; "or a movie of it?" "No," Angele replied; "maybe someday. Will you tell me about it?" "Maybe someday we'll see it together," she said. "Wouldn't that be fun? The music and the swan's dance are wonderful. Fantasy at its most beautiful. Are you going to college in Almaguin? I'm sure Swan Lake would come to the Arts Centre there." "No," said Angele; "I can't leave Grandpa. He needs someone to look after him." "Have you talked to him about it?" she asked. "Oh yes, he wants me to go to teachers' college and then come back here to teach." "What a wonderful idea, Angele," she said. "Then you could be like Giselle and train the young children in the dances and language of the Ashwagane." Angele didn't reply right away. "I would like to become a teacher," she said; "But who would look after Grandpa? I couldn't leave him." "We'll talk more about that, Angele," she said. "I think we should get the application forms sent here this summer so you can send them right in even though you are a year away from attending. Then you will be assured an early spot. They'll be so glad to have a bright young Ashwagane girl coming to their college. Early registration will get them all excited about you. After the interview I'll bet they just stamp "admitted" on your file before they even see your final grades. I'll coach you. You can tell them all about the loon dance. I'll speak to the Chief. We've got a year to figure out arrangements for Harold. We'll find a way."

Angele was silent. Then she said, slowly: "Cathy, if we spend so much time on our past, how are we going to deal with our future? I mean, Chief Philip's offices are full of computers, and I've had only a bit of work in them up at school so far. There's the new math, and the new nutrition, and now we're talking about a new treaty. Arthur says the forest management studies he's been doing are very hard to figure out. But we've got to know all these things, don't we?" "Of course you do," she answered. "And you will. But you have to know about your past and who you are and where you came from so that you can deal with the future. They're not two separate things, Angele. They're both part of each other. Can you feel that inside you, in the loon dance?" There was no answer. Catherine got up and turned off the light. "Goodnight, Angele," she said. She hoped Angele would reply. "Yes, I think I do feel it, sort of," said Angele, in the darkness. "Goodnight, Cathy."

ii

Harold, Angele and Catherine had quickly agreed on the grey afternoon of her arrival that there was no room for Zellie in the little house. No one knew how long she would stay, but Catherine said she was determined to have her packed up within a week, or a few days after Majukimo. Angele offered to move out to a friend's if that were the case, but Harold had a better idea. He went to the phone, and within the hour Catherine and Zellie were moved into the vacant apartment over the store. Harold insisted that preparation and eating of meals would remain at his house. He was intrigued by their new guest. The store apartment with its large bed and pull-out sofa would give them a more comfortable place to sleep. Zellie lost the toss and got the sofa-bed.

Catherine had her usual mixed emotions. She was happy to see Zellie and unload her new experiences on her, but she fretted over the time she would have to take away from her research to entertain her friend. Zellie had always been a tonic in little doses; what would she do to her as a steady diet?

But Zellie and the Wendaban had other ideas. "You just carry on," she said to Catherine; "don't you interrupt your studies or your Conking for me for one second. I'll have some meals and evenings and ballgames with you, and we'll have some good talks, and Conk has already asked me to join you for a flight. I'm going to swim and study the beach situation, and otherwise look around, and Harold says he can fix me up with plenty to do. And then there's this Majukimo thing on Saturday—that sounds like a blast." Zellie was taking up just where Catherine had left her: Miss Independence, USA, have bikini, will travel.

Harold was on the phone again. His regular contacts were all busy preparing for the Majukimo, but they would do what they could to invite Zellie over and show her the island. "What kind of a hotel are you running over there, anyway?" asked Giselle. "Have you requested a tourist permit from the Chief?" After listening to several of Harold's telephone conversations, Zellie plunked herself down on the floor in front of the old man's painful knees and lightly put her hands on them, and looked up at his grey crewcut and wrinkled face with the biggest blue eyes and thickest, reddest lips he had ever seen, and blinked her long eyelashes up and down and said in a quiet voice: "What about Sammy Osatig? Is he doing anything, Harold? Could he show me around?" Harold was immediately on the phone again. Sammy had to chop wood for the rest of the day, but he was going fishing tomorrow, and would be home before the ballgame. Would that be any help? "Would you like to go fishing?" Harold asked her, putting his hand over the mouthpiece. Zellie said she knew nothing about fishing but understood from Catherine that it had some great moments. Harold returned to his conversation with Sammy. "She's not to pay anything, mind you," he said. "She's my guest and I want you to show her your favorite spots and get her some fish. Mix it up, Sammy, some bass and pickerel, and some deep trout fishing. You'll have to supply all the lines and bait. And pack a good shore lunch. Show her the works. No booze, Sammy. You be good. I'll hear all about it when she gets back. You treat her as if she was the Duchess of Kent." Sammy apparently agreed.

Zellie was fully occupied for the next three days. The fishing had gone so well that by the time of the ballgame they were good friends and she was raving about her day. "It was fantastic," she said to Catherine as they sat in the stands. Conk had a late flight so couldn't join them. "Sammy's quite a guy," she said. "He played it real cool and concentrated on showing me how to fish. What gorgeous country! I'm falling in love with it already, Cathy. I told you it would be great. I don't think I'm going to want to go home. Anyway, I wanted to show him some things too. It got so hot after lunch I had to have a swim. 'Sure,' he said, 'You go right ahead. Won't bother me.' I dove in right off the boat. I'd worn my suit underneath just in case. It's fantastic, Cathy. You can see your whole body, the water is so clear. He could see it too. He was bothered, I could tell. He tried not to let on, but I knew he was watching me all the time. I thought maybe he'd strip and come in too, but he didn't. Of course, I had to stay in my suit to dry off. At one point he had to come over and show me how to hold the line. I faked that I was having trouble. I was sure he wanted to take me in his arms, but he didn't. He just played it real cool, Mr. Matter-Of-Fact. He asked if I was going to the game. I said I wouldn't miss it for anything. He seems a bit shy. But he's very nice. And that body, Cathy, my Gaaaawd!''

"Speaking of bodies," she said, "look who's at bat. It's Mr. Muscles." Zellie was quiet and just stared, her large blue eyes fixed on the object like a laser beam. "Maybe she's trying to beam something into him," Catherine thought. Then she was on her feet, jumping up and down. "Yes! Yes! Go! Go!" The ball soared high and far out and the centre fielder ran back, back, but it was a foregone conclusion for the ball didn't just clear the fence, it sailed over it and fell into the trees. The crowd was roaring. "I've never seen one go out that far, before," said someone up behind them. "Somethin's got him charged up tonight!" Zellie grabbed Catherine's hand and pulled her up to jump with her. They looked like the Bobbsey twins skipping over an invisible rope. "Isn't that fantastic!" Zellie yelled. "It's just so faaaantastic." Catherine said something to the effect that Zellie was never at a loss for words and wondered if a week was going to be enough. "This could become serious," she thought to herself.

Sammy hit two homeruns, a double, and struck out once, the Wendaban Bears won 8-4, and he asked her if she'd like to go for a walk around the island after the game. The following day he took her on a tour of his trap lines and Harold was puzzled why he'd be checking his trap lines this time of year, but said nothing. That night Zellie reported that she had been kissed, and Catherine lectured her on Indian-white relations and the sensitivity of it all right now, and Zellie agreed and said that she was absolutely right but that she need not worry, because she and Sammy were very sensitive people. Catherine had the distinct feeling that Zellie would go home with another trophy in her memory.

iii

After a lapse of eighty years, the resurrection of the Majukimo was smiled on by the great god Manitou. All day Friday boats and planes buzzed in and out of Sand Island, and as the sun rose Saturday on a clear day, the traffic intensified. A large yellow twin-engined government plane made two trips, bringing government officials, serious-looking men and women with black briefcases and black cameras. The press and television crews arrived, the one by water taxi, the other with Conk. The cottagers started arriving before noon, and Arthur was one of several assigned to take their boats around to the beach at the back bay and stack them on the sand as close together as possible. At 1:00 p.m., he would join the Warriors' display. By noon the three groups had arrived: the Ashwagane, returning for communal renewal, the government, praying that all would go well for their sakes, and the tourists, wondering what it was all about. All were in a festive mood.

The hard work of the Majukimo Committee for over a year had paid rich dividends. The library was open and set up with displays. Giselle and a group of volunteers provided tours and explained the long history of the Wendaban's claim to n'Daki Menan. There was hardly an inch of wall space uncovered. Carefully chosen pictures and maps were arranged chronologically from the archives, and one of the offices was set aside for a slide show which automatically began on the half hour. Matt had supervised the reconstruction of a log house from the mid-eighteenth century, including a root cellar, bear grease lamps, open pit fires and closed ovens, axes hewn from wood and stone, clay utensils and bowls, demonstrated by men and women in native dress of summer loin cloths and light moosehide jerkins.

Rita had flown down and assembled an exhibit in the Church. The warm colored light filtering through the round windows of red, yellow and blue panes of plain glass fell on tables of artifacts over three thousand years old, and the vestibule had drawings on the walls of what an Ashwagane village might have looked like one thousand years before the birth of the man who gave birth to the Holy Christian Church. By 3:00 o'clock the lineup into the Church extended down the steps and along the path all the way down to the boardwalk.

Although helpless to do more than watch, Harold had supervised the planning of the large tent of the "N'Daki Menan Community of Life." Borrowing from among their own and from government agencies and museums as far away as Almaguin, Harold's group had created a tightly-knit display to drive a naturalist wild. The Community of Life—animals, birds, trees, fish, ducks, plants, geese, insects—were frozen in their brilliant colors in what seemed a fragmentary moment. The brown moose with his five-foot rack of antlers hovered over the grouse, a hummingbird hung poised to insert its long beak into a wild rose, the black-eyed beaver eyed each passer-by from atop its house of twigs. Nothing was behind glass or ropes; there were no plaques. Only a few people were allowed into the tent at once, to mingle with the community of life as if they were all people in a park. Seventeen animals, twenty-four birds, ducks and geese, nine fish, fourteen flowers and bushes, ten different trees—the Community of Life seemed poised patiently awaiting some magic hand to lift the spell and release them to life again.

Angele and Arthur had gone up to the Infirmary on Thursday and brought down to the house a recently-purchased wheelchair. Harold spent Friday trying it out and with much reluctance agreed that it probably meant the difference between his being able to remain at the exhibit he had worked so hard to create, or not. So he sat parked conspicuously at the entrance to the Community of Life all Saturday afternoon, and smiled and welcomed and chuckled and explained and pointed with his crutch. Angele stayed beside him in case he tired, but he was in rare form. Try though she would, she could not restrain him from wheeling into the tent to discuss something with a curious observer. He especially liked the children and followed them into the tent as if he were a young wolf tracking a scent. Many little faces and big eyes looked at the wonders of the homeland that day, and dreamed they were young Indians on a treasure hunt, a magical game of hide and seek deep in the woods with animals all around them, watching them, chattering at them, stalking them; but Harold was with them and they were safe and would return to their homes tired but happy.

The Warriors had petitioned the Majukimo Committee late in June to have an outdoor display of the martial arts. The Committee was not disposed towards them; the martial arts of the east had nothing to do with the old Ashwagane practises. They said no. Sammy Osatig was chosen their spokesman for an appeal and appeared again before the Committee. The display would be a crowd

pleaser, he said. It required practically nothing in the way
of extra expense or volunteer labor. Modern societies were
recognizing the need for healthy exercise and the
non-mechanized arts of self-defense. Tai Kwan Do
schools were springing up all over North America in
answer to these needs. If the Ashwagane had a proud past,
why not show that they were part of the new present? The
Warriors were a small presence within the Band to act as
a watchdog, a helper should times of trouble come along,
a self-instructed disciplined group to show that the native
community would no longer tolerate deliberate acts of
racism or humiliation. The Warriors wanted recognition,
wanted to come forward out front and show their skills
and dispel rumor and misconception. They too treasured
their Indian past, but they were ready to protect it. The
Wendaban had always defended n'Daki Menan; the
Warriors represented modern Wendaban determination.
They intended no ill-will to anyone.

The Committee huddled. They were split. The Chief
cast the deciding vote. Sammy had been persuasive. Philip
could see their point. Tai Kwan Do would join the
Ashwagane rituals on the grass of Sand Island Reserve.

So now they were dressed and ready to begin at 1:00
o'clock. There would be no announcements or running
commentary, no introductions, no chairs. Ropes sectioned
off the performance area, beside which was a tent. The
Warriors came from the tent onto a large mat spread over
the grass inside the rope. They were dressed in moosehide
loose-fitting leggings, some with yellow, others with green
silk sashes. Their chests and feet were bare. They
performed two, then four at a time. They bowed politely
to each other and the audience after each set in which they
threw or knocked each other to the ground.

At first Zellie just watched. She wanted to clap when Sammy first came out. After bowing to Arthur with a smile, he suddenly pivoted on his left leg so as to turn his back to Arthur, but as he did so his right leg shot out and up and caught Arthur squarely in the chest, knocking him over in an instant. Arthur seemed very blasé about it all and got up as if he had just leaned down to tie his shoe. No one clapped. Zellie clapped, then several joined in. "Isn't he fantastic," she said to the man standing beside her. The man replied that he thought they were quite good.

By 2:00 o'clock Zellie was taking over as usherette, commentator and general hostess to the growing crowd. She longed for a microphone. Her "fantastics" were scattered among explanations of who was doing what to whom, and why, and how, and the skill required, though her sole introduction to, research in, and knowledge of Tai Kwan Do was but one hour old. As she warmed up, she began to call for the audience to watch for what would happen next, the shift of a hand, turn of a foot, bend of the head, whirl of the body, like a radio announcer whose listeners relied on the words alone. As her voice grew louder the crowds grew thicker. Those now standing at the back could only hear, they couldn't see, but the more they heard the more they wanted to wait and work their way forwards to see such fantastic stuff. "Let's have a big hand for that great performance," she was now shouting. "C'mon folks, how about it," and the cheers that went up could be heard all the way up to the ballfield. The more Zellie yelled, the faster the Warriors leaped, whirled and kicked and the louder the shouts went up. "What's going on down there?" asked Chief Philip as he attended to some last-minute details at the ballfield. "Sounds as if the Warriors are going off to war."

iv

The main events came in the evening. The ballfield was the only place on Sand Island big enough to hold the crowd, and it had been transformed into an aboriginal amphitheatre. Extra stands had been constructed, wood for a large bonfire was in place in front of second base, extra lights with home-made tin shades stood at first and third bases to light up the area between them, and a tent to house the performers was erected to the right of a small stage in front of home plate.

At 7:00 o'clock sharp the church bell rang, the call for the meeting of the Wendaban and their guests. As they filed up the path the spectators heard the steady muffled beating of a single drum in a slow rhythm. Before the path opened out into the ballfield there was a bear's head lashed to a pole and adorned with colored beads of rust and yellow corn and torn pieces of long blue cloth. Catherine's heart was beating faster than the drum. She was nervous. She had thrown herself into the preparation for the Majukimo and worked hard with Giselle and Angele to integrate the loon dance into the story. In the final week Angele had caught the spirit and had made great strides in her performance. She prayed she would do well; it would give her young student so much self-confidence.

By eight o'clock the crowd was assembled, the stands jammed, some sitting on the ground in the outer field, the rest standing behind them. A second drum had joined the first, the steady beating rhythm making an hypnotic effect. The crowd was hushed, as if in a church before the service. Suddenly the beating stopped. A baby was crying, the single sound in a sea of faces.

Chief Philip stepped to the microphone on the stage. He welcomed them. He talked of the long-ago past, present today in the Church, and of the new days ahead for the Ashwagane people, of the challenge of preserving the Community of Life in n'Daki Menan. Then he lowered the microphone. An old man in a wheelchair was lifted onto the back of the stage and slowly moved forward. He wore a moosehide jerkin with a single row of red and white beads down each side on the front. A single falcon's feather rose from a headband of light tan hide. Harold stopped and looked at the hushed crowd. Chief Philip adjusted the microphone so that it was only inches from the old worn face, then retired from the stage. A muted drum began a single slow, steady beat, as if coming from far away. He began, in the Ashwagane tongue, musical, chanting, as if in some old song of long ago, raising his pitch slightly, dropping it down, falling in with the slow rhythm of the muffled drum. Then he changed to English. "Our mighty Manitou, we come for your power." His voice was slow but powerful. "Protect our children and give them your strength. Give us the wisdom of our land and all its creatures. Sharpen our arrows for the days ahead. Sustain us with the bounty of this first hunt now concluded by our youth. Help us welcome them as new adults of the Wendaban. Give us the eyes of the owl to see in the dark. Give us the strength of the bear, the speed of the loon, the foresight of the beaver. Help us prepare for our unborn and their days of the hunt. Revive the soul of the Ashwagane." A long howl as if from many wolves went up from the tent, then the drums exploded in sound, three of them, beating a heavy, staccatoed pounding beat. She felt Zellie's arm tighten against hers. "Isn't it fantastic," she whispered to Catherine.

She saw Conk weaving his way through the crowd standing behind the screen back of home plate. She waved, and he finally saw her in the dimming light. She and Zellie were packed in tight in the stands, but they could make room somehow for another. She motioned him to come up. She had a sudden thought to put herself between him and Zellie, who would undoubtedly be heating up as the night wore on. "How ridiculous," she said to herself. He was soon beside her. He looked exhausted. He had come down in the boat; he'd have to be back home by midnight, he said. They had a full day coming up beginning at 7:00 a.m. He had logged thirty-nine hours flying in the last four days, exceeding department regulations, and Bill and Ted had been right behind him in number of hours in the air. Tonight they had locked up at 6:00, walked away and let the phone ring. Sunday and Monday were already booked heavily, and Ted was getting worried about the toll taking its effect. She smiled and took his hand and held it tightly and kissed him on the ear.

The sun was falling below the horizon; long dark shadows deepened across the field. Two young boys dressed only in loin cloths appeared with torches and danced around the stacked wood, chanting in Ashwagane: "an tapawamo manitokiwak mitewin nintasimikowin." They lit the twigs at the base and the mound was soon ablaze. The setting sun behind home plate streaked the sky in red, pink and yellow, but the field was in semi-darkness. The fire threw flickering shadows of red and orange and black over the dancers. The portable lights with tinted plastic filters of red and pink snapped on and off, following the performers as they came forward to dance. The drums were rising to crescendos, then softening to muted beats, then falling silent, only to begin

again. Voices rose in choral chants; single songs in
strange haunting accents of Ashwagane drifted across the
field. The audience was soon in darkness, the round orbed
faces of those in front flickering like masks of pale
firelight. A song in English talked of the long fight for
justice, and two guitars, a flute, a saxophone and the
chuck-a, chuck-a of mud-turtle rattles joined in. The
saxophone had a solo. She thought of Glenn Miller and
Tuxedo Junction and the warm dreamy, creamy nights of
Amherst and balloons and shuffling feet, but there were
new plaintive notes here, a wail of lamentation, a sad cry
of the reeded instrument she had never heard before.

Suddenly Wendigo and Nanabush darted out from the
tent. The ugly large-eyed black and red mask of evil
Wendigo glared at the tiny eyes of the trickster. Wendigo
was screaming in a high-pitched voice, Nanabush laughing
with glee. They pretended to fight, each claiming the same
territory, but Nanabush was too cunning and fleet of foot
to be caught. He suddenly raced into the shadows at the
back of the field, leaped over a little boy sitting in front,
and disappeared in the dark crowd. Wendigo turned a
somersault, then screamed his way back into the tent.

It was Angele's turn. Catherine squeezed Conk's hand
tightly. The loon swept across the field before the blazing
fire, the white rows of beads on the neck of the mask
catching the fire's glint. Then she stood still. The drums
ceased. The audience was hushed. Single notes of the
muted flute began. The wings slowly rose high, then the
body began to weave, slowly back and forth, then faster,
and faster, throwing its shoulders into a whirling,
thrashing motion, back and forth. The drums began. A
second loon came forward and they danced opposite each
other, hopping from foot to foot, like two boxers looking
for an opportunity. It was Arthur. Then a cry pierced the

night. It was a human voice, imitating the sharpest of all the loon's calls, a high soprano livid shriek: "Whee-oh-whee whee-oh-whee whee-oh-whee." Now it was Conk's hand that squeezed hers. "Who can that be?" he whispered. "Jesus! they're good. Sounds like the real thing." "I don't know," she said; "I didn't know it was planned. I've never heard it until tonight." Zellie leaned over to them. "It's fantastic," she said.

Other dancers now came out and joined the loons. Majukimo was rising to its climax. The drums began beating slightly faster, louder, the guitars and saxophone joined in, the flute began to play arpeggios. All the dancers came forward, chanting, raising and lowering their bodies, circling the fire, then spreading out into little groups who ran swooping, close to the audience on all three sides of the field, rejoining the main circle, the girls with their arms curved in circles. Two youths came forward dragging the carcass of a deer, symbolic of the ending of the hunt. The girls circled them, then enclosed them, bending their arms in the air. They were initiated. A yell went up. The drums pounded. The girls swooped aside and the boys raced to the fire where they stopped, curving their bodies back and forth, hands held over their heads. She could feel Zellie's contagious rhythm; her rear end had been pushing rhythmically against Catherine's for several minutes and her body was now beginning to sway.

Suddenly Zellie could stand the pent-up frenzy no longer. She jumped to her feet, then clapped her hands over her head to the beat, swaying, and began to sing, not in audible words, but a low guttural chant from deep inside her. She was a cheerleader at an Ashwagane Majukimo. A young white man sitting in the front row down on the field, after looking up at her, jumped to his feet too, and pulled up the woman beside him. "You've got the right idea, lady," he yelled at Zellie, and they began to dance and sway.

It caught on. The crowd, hypnotized for almost an hour of drums and dance and incantations, now joined in. They began to clap. Groups struggled to their feet and started to dance. Zellie was already down on the field and lost in the crowd. The young men brought fresh wood and the dying fire leapt up again. The drums pounded on. Conk pulled Catherine to her feet. "If I were Zellie, I would say this is turning into some faaaaaantastic affair," he said. "C'mon, let's go!" and they started down to the field through the swaying stands. As she stepped onto the field, she saw to her left one of the government men. His coat was off and the tie so loosened that it resembled a scarf on a western cowboy. He was clapping his hands and throwing his hips around in very suggestive motions at the government lady opposite him. He had the spirit. No one could accuse him here of sexual harassment. He would report to the authorities in Toronto that the Majukimo was very successful.

Then she saw Zellie. She had found Sammy among the choral dancers, and was dancing with him around the fire, flinging her arms around as if attacked by flies. She was wearing Sammy's headband. Catherine stared. If Madeleine Zukawitz could see her now. "I wonder how you could get that into a computer?" she thought.

The night was far from over. The performers and spectators danced for another half hour, but eventually exhaustion took its toll. The microphone crackled. The feast was now ready. The crowd started to drift down the path towards the recreation hall.

The women of the Wendaban had outdone themselves. The entire hall was taken up on three sides with long tables covered with quilts of beaded design. There were no electric lights tonight; the hall was lit by candled chandeliers, in direct contravention of the Achinike fire marshal's orders. Arranged on the quilts was the feast, in dark brown clay bowls and platters, with wooden spoons and ladles for serving. Such a gourmet buffet had never graced the tables of n'Daki Menan. As she surveyed the hall, she was sure all the former Chiefs were turning over in their graves. The Wendaban had prepared the greatest Majukimo feast ever held in the homeland.

The table along the left side of the hall held plates of cold moose meat, cut in slices, as well as a steaming roast leg of moose attended by a young man in beads and headband, to carve it. There was beaver, in dark brown chunks in a big bowl, and more in a second bowl, beaver stew with rich dark gravy. Braised geese and ducks were garnished with sprigs of cedar and sumac and there were plates of breast meat already sliced. There was a bowl of rabbit stew, a long slab of sanded pine wood, resembling a breadboard, stacked with frogs' legs, smoked venison with bread stuffing on another large platter, and plates of grouse breasts. Giselle had rigged up a barbecue with oak embers, and was frying up dandelions, stems and flowers, garnished with pepper, from a huge pile on a table beside her. "They're delicious," she called out to Catherine, "and there isn't a yellow dandelion left anywhere on the east side of the island. Hooray!" There were two bowls of moose liver and heart for the venturesome. Harold had told her to be sure to try some moose heart for he was sure it was the most delicious meat in all the world. "Oh oh!" said Conk as they took their places in the long lineup. He put his hand to his forehead. "I'd better phone Ted to cancel the early morning flights. I'll never make it."

Catherine's eyes, however, were on the table across the back of the hall: seafood à la Wendaban Ashwagane. In the middle of the table, propped up on a large flat piece of rubbed maple and surrounded by sprigs of wild plum, was a lake trout—head, tail, fins and all. It would easily run twenty pounds she was sure. It was the lord of the table. There were platters of pickerel, whitefish, small- and large-mouth bass, pike, speckled, lake, and brown trout, some fried, some baked with a bannock stuffing; the whitefish fillets were smoked. There was a large steaming bowl of burbot soup with vegetables. "That's ling," Conk said to her, pointing at it; "and if you can get past the stink of filleting them, you've got something as good as lobster." The platters of fish were garnished with sprigs of water-cress and the tender green sprouts of wild bilberry.

Finally, along the third side of the hall, was a table of greens, breads and drinks. Bannock was served either sliced or as a small muffin. There was hot maple syrup for the bannock. There were pitchers of steaming mint and anibiwanagek tea. The previous summer, Chief Philip had made a special plea to the youth to gather an extra-large harvest, and to the ladies to brew bigger-than-usual batches, and the results had been secreted away and guarded with care in basements and closets. Now, twenty-nine litres of blueberry wine in corked bottles waited under the table, a bottle at a time placed above. And there were pitchers of clear cold water from Lake Achinike. June Friday stood beaming over fifteen blueberry pies, which wouldn't last long. She had had her children, Joey Commanda, and the Pashawonaby girls picking wild raspberries for the past three days, but with one for me and one for the bowl, only three heaping bowlsful made it to the festive table. The Pashawonaby girls, standing beside her, had instructions to spoon them out only five to a serving.

They ate silently at one of the tables outside on the lawn, surrounded by a gulping, laughing, chatting, frolicsome crowd. Zellie had disappeared. They walked down hand in hand to the boat, the noise of the Majukimo gradually falling away behind them. They were exhilarated, exhausted, relieved, pensive. They would have to sacrifice lovemaking tonight. She knew he was already thinking of the first morning flight, only six hours away. Responsibility; duty; professionalism: that was what both their lives had been, in such different ways, and would continue to be. Their lips and bodies met in a long embrace. He stroked her hair and kissed it gently and slid his hand in the old familiar way up the nape of her neck, cradling her head as if he were holding a baby just born. They could barely see one another in the moonless night. The sky was so full of stars she thought she could reach up and pick one and it would never be missed. Their slow caresses said all that needed to be said. The beating drums had receded into the quiet lull of their warm tired bodies as they swayed back and forth gently on the dock. "I can taste a little fish," was all he said and he kissed her again. Each knew they were deeply in love.

She had left the light on outside the door to the apartment stairs and it guided her up the short path from the boardwalk. There was another light on upstairs. Zellie's bed was empty. She left the lights on and undressed. The evening had cooled, but the upstairs rooms still held the heat of the day. She wanted to lie naked under one sheet, to feel her body still tingling from the pounding drums and the touch of his lips, to run her hands down her arms and across her breasts. She would have to write Dawson and tell him. The time had come. She would write him in the morning. Should she cut him off, or do it in such a way that he would see that she wasn't sure of the future? It was wrong to ask him to wait, out of the question. That would be pure selfishness, a pandering to her longing for the secure. Could she ever live with him on a rebound from Conk? She didn't think so. The guilt. The memories. Wouldn't it be better to start all over if she had to? What was her future? Would the Wendaban hire an anthropologist? Did they need bush pilots in Boston? She turned and cradled the pillow and rubbed her cheek against its soft coolness, and kissed it, and fell asleep.

v

There was another light on, somewhere, and sounds. She thought someone was humming. She was so drowsy. She was too full of fish to care. She tried to open her eyes. The newer light went off now but there was still a yellow color coming through the door onto her ceiling. The other light must still be on, she thought. "Is that you, Zellie?" she called out weakly. "Oh Cathy," Zellie said from the other room, in a husky voice, "I didn't want to wake you but I've so much to tell you. My God, Cathy, wasn't it a fantastic evening?" She came and stood in the doorway in her nightie, which hung down barely to her thighs. Cathy blinked at her. "Can I come in and sit on the bed for a minute?" she asked, and then she was sitting close and Catherine could smell perfume and smoke from her hair.

"Cathy, you won't believe this, but I think I'm in love. We were swept away. I mean all those drums and that dancing! He's so casual, so carefree, such a magnificent creature of whim. Oh Cathy, we made great love—all the way!'' "Oh no!" Catherine thought to herself, trying to focus her mind; "I knew it. Oh no!" But she said only, "Zellie, you didn't! I cannot believe after our talk that you would." She had no more than said the words when her lady of the Bronx began her story, and the passionate words poured forth with amazing energy. Zellie described it all, how beautiful and deep and rich, the when and where and how, sparing no details, of the hard parts, the soft parts, the vital parts. As she was talking Catherine wondered what it would be like to be a priest listening to such a confession. Would he call out to her that she need not go into such detail? "Stop, stop," would he cry? "No need to tell me everything." Would he dig his nails into his palms and look at the ceiling of his little box and quietly curse? Would he feel compassion for such a poor lost lamb? Would the devil's tigress need special dispensation and therapy? Would he run fleeing from the confessional and fling his cassock into the fire? "Oh, the burden of being a Puritan!" she said to herself.

She was still drowsy but was becoming slowly embittered. Uneasiness was changing to despair, then anger. This was all she needed! Coming into such a different society, she had won their respect and their help. Now, a very white extroverted sex maniac, calling herself her friend, arrives on the scene and within five days rapes the local ball hero. "Oh no," she said to herself, "My dear Zellie. Why did I write her. What have I done?"

Zellie was looking at her, a big grin on her face. Catherine could see her large triumphant breasts silhouetted through the nightie; they had always been the apples of her eye. She wanted to run her hands over her own to make sure they were still there. "Zellie," she said, "I've always envied you your zest for life, but this time you have gone too far. There could be nasty implications over this. You have blown your usual sensitivity, in my view. A white nymphomaniac comes onto a red Reserve and enjoys their hospitality, then screws the first big red man to come along. It's the old plot all over again. Shagonash has been screwing Ashwagane for centuries, taking everything they have to offer. Why stop now! We can just pray he doesn't talk too much.''

Zellie got up and went to the end of the bed, looking down at her. Behind her the livingroom light filtered through the fuzzy ends of her dishevelled blond hair. Catherine prepared herself for a blast. She had never attacked Zellie so viciously before. Why now? What was the real reason? Should she try to recant a little? But she did feel some truth in what she had said. She thought she had not said it very well.

"Catherine Saltonstall," Zellie said, "I can't believe what I hear. You just amaze me. First of all, who screwed who? You make it sound like a rape. The very word sends daggers through my soul. You know that. This was mutual lovemaking. We both wanted it, we both agreed to it without saying so in so many words. I mean you don't go into inter-ethnic niceties when your passion's up. If you have to ask permission you shouldn't be doing it. There was no question of anyone taking advantage over the other. And we weren't taking; we were giving. Then you've got your politics and anthropology and love all mixed up in the wrong proportions and priorities. Sure I'm a white Jew and he a red Indian. So what? Is this the United Nations? Love is above all that crap, you know that. We were two unattached red-blooded human beings wanting to enjoy the love we would make, and that's all that matters. A bit of heaven in a screwed-up world. Anyone who suggests that I was trying to inflame whatever problems there are perceived to be between whatever bloods are involved here is in for a tongue lashing from me! I hope he does talk! It was worth talking about! What's there to hide? And don't talk to us Jews about taking advantages! We've had our bumps from those taking advantages. You Anglo-Saxon types haven't got that lily-white a record, you know. But let's not get into that." She was silent. She stood there. Because Zellie's face was backlighted Catherine couldn't see whether she was scowling or smiling. Then Zellie came over to her and bent down and put a little kiss on her forehead. "Speaking of love, Cathy, I grow fonder of Conk every time I see him. He's a great guy. But for you, Cathy. Just for you." She went out and the light flicked off and Catherine heard her getting into bed. Her heart was pounding. Zellie had just knocked in the winning run. Was there another game left in the series? There had to be, she thought.

Then Zellie's voice came out of the darkness. "Oh, and incidentally, as we lay there after the first time, and he had his arm around me, he asked if I'd like to hear a bedtime story. 'Sure,' I said, 'Why not?' So he said that once upon a time there was this huge loon. I was really kind of pooped, trying to save everything I had for a second round, but when I heard him say loon I thought of you and I perked up and tried to concentrate on what he was saying. Anyway, this big mother loon was full of babies. She was so full of babies she couldn't fly. But the babies stayed inside her. When it came time to head south she knew she was in trouble. Now she had noticed this big good-looking beaver swimming around all summer, so she went over to his house and knocked on the door. Sammy called him Mr. Kanick or Swamick or something like that. Anyway, she told Mr. Beaver all about her difficulty and asked him if she could stay in his house for the winter until she had her babies. She knew the beaver swam into his house under the water, so she said she would swim out under the ice all winter and bring them back all the fish they needed. Mr. and Mrs. Beaver talked it over and agreed to let her in. So she spent the winter in the beaver house, and had her babies, and provided them all with fish all winter. When the spring came and the loons arrived, here was big mother with her babies already there swimming around waiting for them. She called a big pow-wow and told all the loons that they should be friends with the beavers. She wanted them all to live happily ever after. In the Community of Life." She giggled. "I just added that last part now. Isn't that cute? Anyway, I couldn't figure out what Sammy was getting at, and I was so tired I panicked for a moment because it all got mixed up in my mind and I thought that maybe I was the loon and was already pregnant and he was the beaver and that this was the way an Indian asked you to marry him. But he only said it was a neat story for kids about love between different animals. And he mentioned something about that I should tell it to you. So there you have it. And just remember who told it to you—your old nympho from Ne Yauk."

Suddenly she was wide awake. She bolted upright in bed. "Zellie!" she said loudly, "are you sure you are not just making this up to get back at me? I've got to know more about that legend, if that's what it is. Where did it come from? Don't you see? My goodness! Amik, the beaver, is a major icon of the Montagnais to the east. If I'm right and Mank the loon was the family goddess of the old Ashwagane, then there's the clue we've been looking for. They were leagued in the old days. Oh Zellie, please talk to him tomorrow. You are in a much better position than I am to see if he just made it up or if he got the story from somewhere. We've got to trace it, Zellie. Will you try? Please? Zellie?'' There was silence. "Zellie! Are you listening?''

All she could hear was heavy breathing and a choked snore. Zellie was in dreamland, skipping hand in hand with her hero across endless fields of green ballparks towards the setting sun. "Oh Zellie! You are impossible!'' Catherine said as she snuggled back into the pillow and pulled up the sheet. She had a little burp, and the taste of whitefish was back in her mouth. She lowered her voice to a whisper. She knew no one was listening. ''You're just fuckin' impossible.''

Chapter XII
ASHTON'S CAVE

He pushed her off, jumped on the pontoon, and climbed up into his seat. The canoe was strapped on the other side. Whanga whanga whanga whanga. Little puffs of grey-blue smoke sputtered out from the exhausts as the engine caught. "Let's go!" he said, patting the dashboard.

He had been looking forward to this afternoon for days. Getting the Majukimo visitors off Sand Island on Sunday and Monday along with the regular bookings had pushed them all to the limit for a second week. "We've been in the air more hours this week than any other since I started keeping records," Ted had said as they closed up Friday night. "I'm going to have to screw around with the numbers a bit before our next inspection. Either we slow down, or get another plane." "We'll slow down," he said. "Late August always slows down until hunting season."

She had been very cooperative, he thought; but then, she had Zellie on her hands until she finally got her bundled off for home. They had agreed they were both exhausted and would try to catch up on their sleep and wouldn't see each other until Saturday. They would spend the afternoon down the lake with a shore supper, and catch the dance in the evening at Sand Island. He had the bag packed, and the diving gear and light and camera and the minnows in the plastic bag with the rope. He was determined one more time.

Since his first attempt, they had tried twice more to film them diving, at Henrietta's Bay. Catherine had helped him. She paddled the canoe and tried gently to manoeuvre Henry over to where the bag of minnows and Conk were waiting below. "Come on now, Henry—or are you

Henrietta?'' she would say. "Over that way a little more. Shoosh!'' and she would flick her paddle at him. Henry would say nothing, then dive. And just as she thought her part of it was going well, Henry wouldn't surface for the longest time, and then he would call to her from the other side of the canoe, from half way down the bay behind her. "I don't know who is more obstinate,'' she had said, "you, or Conk. Getting you diving on film is going to have to wait for a chance meeting.'' After Conk surfaced, she had said to him, "You've got the wrong loon cast for the part. Henry is too much the quiet loner type. What you need is a show-off, an extrovert. Are there no Zellie loons around?''

So this afternoon, they were extrovert hunting. "There's a big bay to the north, just beyond the cliffs. There are several loon families in there,'' he said to her as Cloudie started to climb. "Let's give it a try. There's a place to cook at the end of the bay.'' "I'm my usual game self,'' she said to him, smiling. "Incidentally, how did it go with Zellie yesterday?'' "No problem,'' he said. "We just barely made the train. I won't tell you about her parting kiss. It will just make you jealous.'' "All right,'' she said, looking coy; "I'm not the jealous type anyway so it doesn't matter, does it!'' "You know damn well you are and it was a very big, long kiss,'' he said. "I thought for a minute it was going to be a French one and I wasn't sure what I should do if it was. But it wasn't. She said I helped make her visit something special.'' "I'll bet she did,'' said Catherine. "But don't pay too much attention to her kisses. She always travels with an unlimited supply, as if she were a permanent candidate for re-election.'' He laughed. "What else did she say?'' she asked. He looked at her. "What a dumb question,'' he replied. "She said it was all quite fantastic." Catherine laughed. "I do not know how she does it," she said. "Every time she uses that word you think it's the first time you have ever heard it used properly. It's amazing." "It's fantastic," he said, grinning at her. He was glad to be back with her again.

As they circled, she counted seven loons spread out along the shoreline. Three were young ones, already half grown, but still staying close to their parents. "Look," she said pointing, "They are all diving now, leaving the chicks on the surface alone. All the adults appear to be fishing. Good. We have something nice for them."

By the time Cloudie was secured and the canoe unloaded, the loons had worked their way closer to the rugged shoreline. They nestled the plane into some trees beside an imposing cliff of sheer rock, jutting up from the water's surface twelve feet high. "What an ideal surface for a painting," she said. "But I don't see any marks." "Not even some graffiti," he said. "You'd have to do it from a canoe. I should hang some of my loon photos here. A natural gallery wall, and the rent is right."

They laid their plan. He dove and when he surfaced he said there was about thirty feet of water, so they added some rope to the minnow bag. She stripped to her swim suit, and paddled out beyond the loons. She would try to move them in towards him, gently. He waited till he could see her trying to move them shorewards, then dove and placed the bag and let the weight fall to the bottom. He figured he was about forty feet out from the cliff. The sky was a high white overcast; not a brilliant day, but plenty of light for pictures, he thought. He checked his watch and swam off about twenty feet from the bag. The minnows were their usual lively selves, the water clear, visibility good. "One of these times," he said to himself.

Suddenly he caught the blurred motion off to his left. Then it was distinct, the sleek body, slightly hump-backed, he thought, head extended away out in front, the speckled white back a blur of creamy froth. It was diving down on a long slant line, then it veered over towards the minnow bag. His heart began to pound. He started following it with the camera. But just as suddenly it veered off to its left, then dove deeper, darting over to where he was suspended, ten feet below him. He squirmed around with his flippers to aim the camera downwards. It was too dark. He could barely see the loon. It swam in a tight circle, then headed for what he was sure was the shoreline. He had forgotten to turn on the light. "God damn it!" he muttered as he switched it on. Intuitively, he snapped his flippers and turned himself in its direction and tried to follow it. It was heading towards the cliff he was sure, unless he had got his directions turned around, diving deeper into the black depths. "Anywhere you can go, I can go also," he said. The water was practically black as he dove. He had lost sight of it but the light picked up its bubbles. Now the bubbles started to rise. He realized it was pitch black above him. "He's surfacing," he thought. "But we must be in a cave. Or else, someone has thrown a thick blanket over everything." He aimed the beam directly above him and was sure he could see the line of the water's surface. But the water was now perfectly still. He surfaced very slowly in case he hit dark rock above. He broke the surface in inky blackness. He took out his mouthpiece. He flashed the light around on the placid surface. The loon was sitting twenty feet from him, staring at him, jerking its head around but keeping its one red pellucid eye fixed on him, brightly dull in the light's glare. He splashed the surface with his hand and heard the dull heavy echoes all around him. They were in a cave. "Now what,'' he said to the loon. "I hope you're going to lead me out of this mess.'' He flashed his light around. "Out of this . . . out of this . . . mess . . . mess . . .'' came back at him from the rocks. He turned his light to the right. His heart stopped. "Oh my God!'' he whispered under his breath. The light picked up the little piles of bleached skeletal bones, each lying in a heap, pile by pile, with some skulls on the floor of the rock. They were human, he was sure. One pile still had its head perched on top, as if the frame had just slowly collapsed and lowered the head gently to rest on top of the bones. Its teeth were intact and grinning at him in the darkened light. He heard a gentle swish and turned the light around and the loon was gone. He shuddered. Suddenly he felt cold. He had no fear of fear, but his heart was racing. It was the excitement, he knew, the unexpected, the strange and unforeseeable. He knew he could get out. He had lots of air and a light. He had discovered an old graveyard of some sort. He wanted to tell Cathy. Maybe he should start back. He looked at his watch. It had been fifteen minutes since he first dove. They had agreed he would stay down for thirty minutes.

He had a few minutes left. He would take a closer look. He shone his light against the rock cliff. The edge of the shelf was about twenty feet in front of him about a foot above the water's edge. He could see the wide shelf running along the water's edge in both directions, then the wall of sheer rock rose high above it into inky blackness. He switched off the light. He wanted to conserve the batteries. He swam over until he could feel the rock shelf with his hand. He lifted himself onto the rock ledge, sat for a moment to catch his breath, then turned and switched on the light against the rock. "Jesus!'' he said slowly. "Look at that!'' "Look at that. . .'' came whispering back at him from the blackness beyond, as if from a mocking audience sitting in an amphitheatre around him. The lines were clear, crisp, distinct, as if painted yesterday, dull reds, rusty reds, black, and yellowish reds. He could see fish rib cages like the ones she had shown him in the library, and there was the thunderbird and something that looked like a turtle with a long tail. There were figures of people, and canoes, he thought, birds and a skull-like face. He turned around and pointed his light down the rock surface toward the bones. "My God! There's twenty feet of this stuff," he said in a whisper. Before the echo returned he suddenly jumped up and yelled at the top of his lungs: "We found it! Cathy! Cathy! The God damn panograph. This is it!" He did some little jumps, shaking both arms in the air with the light wildly flashing its beam around into the upper darkness. The echoes thundered. "Found it . . . damn panograph . . . is it . . . is it . . . is it . . ." Suddenly he had to tell her. He had to get out fast, as if it were a dream, a bubble, and he wanted her in on it before it disappeared. He had to get her into the cave, today. He remembered he had laid his camera on the ledge. He picked it out in the light's beam. He'd leave it behind. He lined himself up as best he could at right angles to the rock face, and tumbled in backwards with the light on.

As he surfaced he could see her sitting languidly in the canoe, about two hundred feet offshore. Before she could spot him he dove and swam out until he located the bottom of the canoe above him. He glanced at his watch. He was seven minutes past the deadline. He intended to scare her, and tried to shoot up through the surface like a rocket, and he was sure he did because she looked scared and she threw up her hands but all she said was "Goodness!" He grabbed the gunnel of the canoe, unhooked the light from his belt, and swung it up into the canoe. He wrestled with the tank on his back, holding himself up with his left hand, and almost tipped the canoe, and he got it unhooked, and he swung the tank up into the canoe also. "Come forward and lean against me as I get in," he said. "What on earth are you doing?" she yelled as she eased herself forward and to the far side. "You will put us both in the lake. Have you lost your mind?" He pulled himself up, and could feel the little craft tipping dangerously under him, but in another second he was inside on his back and his legs with the flippers on were sticking up in the air. He debated taking them off, but he reached out for her and put his arms around her waist and pulled her down on him. His neck was propped up against the middle cross-brace of the canoe so it was painful and awkward and he tried to cradle their bodies sideways into a prone position between the thwarts, but his legs wouldn't come down, inside. There just wasn't enough canoe. "My mother warned me about rape," she said, smiling down on him, "but not from a big hairy ape like you." He managed to get his head up off the round aluminum thwart that was starting to press against the bloodstream in his neck like a dull knife and he pulled on her shoulders but could only get his head up high enough to be level with her breasts, so he kissed them over and over, suit and all, and fell backwards, trying to turn his neck so it wouldn't bump into the thwart again, but he couldn't crook it sideways enough and he hit it exactly in the same old painful place. She could see his predicament but she couldn't feel his pain, for now his legs, one still sticking, bent, out over the gunnel with the flippered foot dangling, were sending shooting objections into his brain, howling at him that he was dangerously close to dismembering himself. "I take it you got your pictures," she said. "Or did you meet an uncooperative mermaid?"

She extracted herself from his arms, which were too numb to hold her anymore, and moved back to the rear seat. "If you ask me nicely, I'll take off your flippers," she said. He reached out painfully and extracted one flipper, which he tossed to her, then the other, which he looped over his head hoping it would land in the canoe, which it did. He was a free man. He got up on his knees. "As soon as my blood starts flowing again, I've got some news for you. But it's going to cost you a big long kiss. It's big news, so it's got to be a big kiss." She bent forward on her knees and he took her by the shoulders and got what he wanted. "I can't wait to see the pictures, Conk," she said. "Let's go back to your apartment tonight and put them on the VCR. Maybe we could start planning a film." He moved his hands down from her shoulders and took her hands, and looked into her eyes. They gazed at one another in silence. "Are you sure you are feeling all right?" she asked. "What happened down there? I can hear your heartbeat."

"Cathy," he said, "I'm sure we've found it. Your panograph. It's in a cave over behind that rock face. A whole wall full. And bones. Six piles of human bones." She stared at him expressionless. They squatted down in the bottom and he told her the story, of the loon coming over to him and circling below him and of his following it up into the cave. "We've got to get you in there," he said. "I left the camera in there. I've got an idea. C'mon. Let's go."

They paddled over to the shoreline beside Cloudie, and got out. He thought it felt so good to stretch. He explained his plan. He got some rope from Cloudie. He would experiment from the canoe on where the right spot would be for the shortest dive into the cave. He would measure exactly how many seconds it took him to make the dive and surface inside. Meanwhile she was to see how long she could hold her breath. She should do some stretching exercises with deep breathing between each breath-hold and see if she could lengthen it any. If they did do the dive, he would go first with the light, with a rope attached from his waist to hers. If any problems developed he could have her back up to the surface "in no time." She nodded her head.

He donned his tank and flippers and paddled out and located the minnow bag, and retrieved it. She watched him dive and resurface, over and over, out in front of the rock face. Looking at her watch, she held her breath until she thought she would pass out: forty-seven seconds. She stretched, did some pushups, tried again: forty-five seconds. By the time he returned, she was at forty-eight seconds. Would it be enough, she wondered.

"I've got the right spot picked out," he said as he pulled the canoe up onto the shore. "The minnow bag is just below the surface to mark the spot. I can dive down and be surfaced inside the cave in fifty-one seconds. How are you doing?" "Well," she said, "with a bit more adrenalin I might make it. I'm up to forty-eight seconds here on shore." "For three seconds, you'll do it," he said. "I'll pull on the rope as soon as I surface. That will help a bit." He paused. "Now wait a minute. I'm using my flippers, which gives me more speed. But I'm dragging my tank along. I'll try it with one flipper, and no tank. You take the other flipper." They tried several dives out in the lake, gradually increasing their submerged time. Then he dove again into the cave, and came back. "It will work," he said breathlessly. "One flipper and no tank: fifty seconds." "It's a go," she said.

As he surfaced inside the cave he prayed all would go well. She was strong, in excellent shape, a good swimmer and diver. He pulled on the limp line. Then he felt her below. The light was on at his belt. Treading his feet with all his force, he pulled and pulled and suddenly she was beside him in the darkness. "Are you all right?" he whispered. He could hear her gulping the air. "Yes . . . I'm fine," she gasped, "But there wasn't . . . anything to spare. . . Thanks for the pull." "The pull . . . the pull. . . " echoed back at them. He reached for her hand. "Come with me slowly," he whispered into her ear. "I'll switch off the light. We've got to conserve power. I'll feel my way over to the shelf. But I want you right beside me." "Don't worry," she whispered; "I am not going anywhere." He reached the ledge, and she felt it with her hands and pulled herself up and sat on it. He pulled himself up beside her, and they untied the rope. "I'm right beside the bones, I think, Conk," she said. "I just put my left hand out and I think I felt them." He switched on the light. She was right. A skull glared up at them from just beside her leg. She tightened her grip on his hand. "Are you scared?" he asked. She looked at him. "Not any more than you are. I trust the ghosts are all asleep," she whispered. "Asleep . . . asleep . . . asleep . . ." the cave whispered back.

Hand in hand they slowly walked across the rock face, examining it bit by bit in the small arc of the light. "My heart's pounding faster than on the dive," she whispered to him. "Dare I quote an authority and say that this is simply fantastic?" She paused. Her grip tightened on his hand. "Oh Conk!" she said. "Point the light up there. Look! Oh Conk!" She turned to him and put her arms around him. "Please hug me a little for a minute." He could feel her shaking. "Is there anything wrong?" he asked. She pointed up, but said nothing, then gradually started breathing deeply, in gulps. The trembling started to subside. "There," she said as he aimed the light, "the great Ashwagane mother loon. The one in Sammy's story. See it, across the top? She stretches out over half the picture. I was right. Dr. French is right. See how her left wing is sawtoothed into the beaver's tail? He is facing east, she straight ahead. He's Amikgane, patron saint of the Indians to the northeast. All his power is in his tail. All her power is in her wings. Dr. French has been right all along. They were in contact, so long ago. The Montagnais—Naskapi. Oh, my God! Here's proof."

She started examining the pictures closely. "Look, Conk." She moved a step to the right and gently pulled his arm holding the light towards her. She was still breathing heavily. "Look at this," she said. The silence for a moment was stunning. "I have never seen anything quite like this before," she whispered. She raised her hand and gently passed it over the rock, the modern skin barely grazing the ancient ochre. "This color is magnificent, protected all these years in here. This man is chasing a woman. She is a woman all right because of the pointed breasts. See? But what is she chasing? She arched her hand back and forth like a little windshield wiper gently trying to shove aside an invisible speck of dust. "It's an animal. Maybe a wolf or coyote. Must be a wolf. I have not seen anything like this before." She studied the figures closely. "They're beautiful," she said. The light was weakening to a brown dimness; she slowly moved to another set of figures. "These figures are different, in a different hand, I am sure. There have been at least two artists at work here, Conk. Wouldn't it be nice to think that one was from northern Quebec, and one Ashwagane, each painting his Sistine Chapel. Can we bring in more lights, Conk? Maybe stronger ones? There are probably all kinds of ceremonial relics in this cave. We will have to get Rita in here. She will go wild. Goodness, what a find! I can't believe it." ". . . believe it . . . believe it . . . believe it . . ." faintly echoed back.

"And photos," he whispered. "If I can get more lights in here we can photograph each segment in detail, then patch them all together in a composite on a wall. We can reconstruct an exact replica of this in a museum." Her voice grew a little louder. "Do you realize this is only the third panograph discovered in the whole northeast?" she said. "Northeast . . . northeast . . . northeast . . ." the cave replied. "This cave was probably the meeting place for the chiefs and medicine men, and here they buried themselves, an inner sanctum just for popes and cardinals." He wished he had a tape recorder. "Cardinals . . . cardinals . . . cardinals . . ." It wasn't the information he wanted, not the echoes, but her voice, the sound, not the sense of it, for he knew he was sharing an original moment with her and it was she who was the original for him more than the panograph. Her breathless excitement thrilled him, was contagious. He would get more lights, better cameras. They would return over and over to the secret cave, explore it fully, study it, get everything she wanted. What a project, he thought. He looked up. There was the red eye, for sure. There was no doubt about it.

They were exhausted. They sat down on the ledge, their feet dangling in the water. The light was very weak now and he turned it off. "I want to save what's left in it for the trip out," he whispered. Suddenly they both heard it and she clasped his hand tightly. "What was that?" she whispered. "Over there, by the bones." He switched on the light. They could see nothing. He turned it off again. "It sounded to me as if a bone may have rolled off from on top of another one onto the cave floor,'' he whispered. "Maybe our voices and these echoes dislodged it. I don't know." He paused. "We should be going soon."

They sat silently in the darkness. "Cathy," he whispered, "how old do you think these pictures are?" "Rita will have to make a judgment on that," she whispered; "but from the way the rib cages are drawn on the animals, I'd guess it's in the same era as the pictographs—about three thousand years ago. We could get accurate carbon readings from the bones." "Bones . . . bones . . . bones . . ." barely whispered back at them. "But then," she said, "they are sacred, aren't they!" "Are you asking me or telling me?" he whispered. She was silent. "I would not want to disturb their spirits," she said. They were silent again.

A minute passed. "It's very old, Conk. Very old history," she whispered. He thought her voice sounded deeper, a bit far-off. "Not Greek, not Roman or Italian, not English or American," she whispered, "and not imported. Here . . . then . . . and now. Canadian. Beautiful original art as old as the Elgin Marbles—but not transportable. Buried here forever, Conk, forever fresh. And aboriginal." The echoes faded again to silence. "Aboriginal," she breathed again, slowly, barely audible. She slowly whispered out the syllables: "Ab-or-i-gin-al, the origins. This cave, Conk—it speaks not just to Ashwagane origins but to ours too, for we were all aboriginals once. Maybe, deep inside, something survives, if we will hear it. Who knows?" She was silent again. Then, as if an unbodied voice came from inside the rock, she whispered: "Vital, religious, mythic—wonderful." Was she in a trance? he wondered. He could feel her breathing heavily again, in soft gulps. The faint tremor had returned too, a nuance of shimmering in her soft skin pressed close against him in her shoulders and legs. He had the odd sensation again of something passing into him from her. They were too tired and excited, he thought. But he too felt strange—to have touched such ancient time. Weird, he thought. His dormant imagination awakened. Could he hear a call, an old voice in his mind's ear, from far away and long ago? What was it saying, what music whistled through what darkened trees on that magic chase on the bare rock behind him, now released into the fantasy of his dreaming? He saw the red eye across time with the same horrifying question he thought he had seen in the closeups of Henrietta's face. He couldn't shake off the feeling that his and Catherine's sexuality was somehow bound up with the experience of the cave and its link with ancient time. Now and then were blended in his mind. What was time? he wondered. He looked at the tiny incandescent figures on his watch glowing in the dark. What did they calculate anyway? Both he and the Indian on the rock were chasing a woman and they were not so much running from or towards each other as they were reaching after an animal who wouldn't be caught. What did it all mean? This was a cave of death, but the pictures were so full of life. Confusing, he thought—but not in the sense of being lost. It was a nicer kind of being suspended with her in a warm dark mystery. It was a gentler kind of not knowing, of hardly even knowing that he could ever know or even care to know. He thought he would like to sit here beside her in the quiet ponderous darkness of time forever.

"Conk," she suddenly whispered; "how did we find this? Who is the key player? I guess what I am wondering is, why us? Ashton could not get more than a hint of it, and nothing has surfaced in sixty years since. Let's call it Ashton's Cave. Chief Philip and Harold know it's here. I am sure of that. But I don't think they are going to tell me. So why us, all on our own?"

He thought for a moment. "Well, it wasn't Cloudie, because we could have come down by boat. And I was trying to shoot the stupid loon on film, so it wasn't me." "I guess it was the loon then," she whispered. "Strange. But I suppose there are lots of minnows in here." "No, stranger still," he whispered back, "because they don't fish in the dark. They have to see them to catch them. So why did he circle under me and then come in here?" "It was a he, was it?" she asked. "Can't be sure," he whispered. "It's so hard to tell anyway, and I was so busy trying to line it up in the viewer." "It was a she, I am sure," she whispered; "a descendant of the Great One up there on the wall." "No," he whispered; "there's another one. It was Henry. He is today's daddy loon for all the lake. The sex has changed in three thousand years. He's the boss. He knows what's going on. So he said to himself that he'd frustrate us down in Henrietta's Bay so that we'd go elsewhere for our pictures. Then he flew up here and talked to this loon about what to do when we got here. So it was really Henry." "No, the sex hasn't changed; very interesting theory, though, Professor Seguin," she whispered in the darkness, snuggling close to him. "And if it was Henry, how did he plant in your mind to come to this particular bay today?" He could feel her eyes on him. "Now we get into the deep stuff," he whispered, putting his mouth against her ear. "It was really you. You're the new priestess, the new shaman. Or is it shamaness? You've woven your magic spell over Cloudie and me and Henry and Harold and the whole damn caboodle of us. We're all your victims. You brought us here. Voodoo, voodoo, vampire, vampire." He hissed the last words. They turned to each other and her kiss was very French and the roof of his mouth was burning. "Was that as good as Zellie's?" she whispered. "Who's Zellie?" he whispered back. "But we've got to go. One more of those and I won't have energy left to dive, Miss Vampire. We'll tie ourselves together again, and you follow my light down, and when I get to the canoe I'll pull like crazy. Vampires get heavy in the water, I'm told." He turned on the light. They each put on a flipper and tied the rope around their waists. "I'll come back for the camera later, with my tank on," he said. "Tank on . . . tank on . . . tank on . . ." echoed back. It suddenly occurred to him that he hadn't taken one picture. "Let's go," she said, poised for the dive.

Chapter XIII
ICHABOD

i

When Thrumpington Saltonstall first set foot in the New World, he was already a few years too late to be considered part of that first pure errand into the vast and howling Massachusetts wilderness, to establish a shining city upon a hill whose white light of Truth would eradicate the heathen darkness, and whose soldiers would either convert the dark souls of the Indians, or wring their necks. Each succeeding generation had somehow slid further away from that high commission, until the latest in the direct male line, John Saltonstall, read of the original errand into the wilderness with the same interest as he found in Snow White and the Seven Dwarfs.

Not so, however, for his consort, brought into the Saltonstall line by way of holy matrimony. Lydia was still fanning the last dying ember. Perhaps there were young American boys and girls who, below the levels of their consciousness, had harbored a fantasy of escaping to live with the Indians. Lydia's mature bosom harbored no such thoughts. To the contrary, to rescue her only child from captivity among the wily snares of Satan's crew had become a growing passion and now that Catherine had been away for almost two months, it was a daily, nagging preoccupation. All suasion had failed; how could one use force?

Then an occasion presented itself. Dawson Penhurst III had recently come for dinner. Lydia's heightened sensitivities detected behind his usual suave and gentle demeanor a note of dismay. Something was amiss, she was sure. She finally drew out of him that his most recent

letter from Catherine contained the catastrophic news that
her heart had been stolen by another lover. No, he was not
an Indian, but from Dawson's meagre evidence she
suspected it was someone almost as bad. Dawson agreed
that the name Seguin sounded decidedly French Canadian.
"My God!" she said to herself. "A Catholic!" Dawson
had not been two minutes out the door before she lit into
her husband with the force of a sledgehammer. He quickly
realized it would be fruitless to protest.

The ability of American troops to mobilize quickly
and set off for any corner of the earth is well known. This
same spirit of no-nonsense determination resulted, not
twenty-four hours after that informative dinner, in John
and Lydia Saltonstall's being on a jet bound from Boston
to Toronto, with connections early the following morning
on the *Northlander* train for Achinike. John had insisted
on delaying for at least a few days. He would need time to
make arrangements at the office, and their travel agent
would need time to put together a suitable package of
arrangements. But Lydia's dander was up and his
insistence got no further than the amazed travel agent's
confirmation of plane and train reservations, the plane to
leave in four hours! "Catherine will look after us once
we're there, I'm sure," Lydia had said.

They were comfortably settled into the first class seats
of Air Canada's Flight 701 from Boston, which departed
earlier than the American Airlines flight by one hour, and
United by a full three hours, when she suddenly turned to
John and said, "Isn't Toronto an Indian name?" John
looked up from the *Financial Times* and pondered. He
looked at her over his dark-rimmed glasses and replied,
"Yes, I suppose it is." He turned back to his paper and
was about to relocate himself in Cecil Zadaski's most
recent defence of Federal pressure on interest rates, when

he put down the paper and turned to her again. "But then," he said, "so is Massachusetts." He returned to his article thinking the remark might occupy her thoughts for several minutes, but it worked for the rest of the flight.

All went well until the train pulled into Huronia City, sixty miles north of Toronto. As luck would have it, the cars were suddenly invaded by twenty-five very unusual-looking youths, barely in their teens, and the train was delayed for the loading of baggage and canoes. For years, the largest youth camp on Lake Achinike had sent its maturest veterans of the camp north for a six-week trip, over the watershed and down into the sparkling rivers running into James and Hudson Bay ("the North Pole" as the campers called it in letters home). Section Two went west for a month. Now they were experimenting with a new Section Three, a two-week trip for the less experienced. It had gone south, along the rivers heading from the outlet of Achinike down towards the great lake of the Huron, and through bays and sounds down to a system of rivers and canals that would lead them back inland to Lake Balleydown and Huronia City. Their trip was now done, and they were boarding the train to return to camp.

The new trip had had its problems. While the northcountry basked in sunshine, the south had experienced an unusually rainy summer and the rivers were swollen, swift, their currents and rapids unusually strong. Two planned short portages had grown into five. Days of rain had dampened more than clothing and bedding. The humid air kept the bugs healthy and hungry. The last week had failed to live up to the camp's brochure descriptions of "wilderness canoe trips." The rivers and canals ran beside four-lane highways with transport trucks and wafting diesel fumes, and through meadows of grazing cows and bleating lambs. In several places rivers led into lakes and canals alive with power boats, houseboats, and jet surf craft which whistled through the flotilla of canoes like careening race cars. Even the leaders had become demoralized. The bedraggled youngsters who boarded the train were anything but a tribute to wilderness camping. They had retreated back into something akin to escapees from a wartime prison camp. They smelled of unwashed bodies, "Bug Tough" mosquito dope, mildew, rancid cheese, and tobacco. Their raid on the lounge car's limited supply of nuts, gum, lifesavers and chocolate bars resembled a one-hour sale at Macy's bargain basement, including a fist fight. Their loud uncouth language laced Lydia's ears. She scowled at John. Then she heard them say they were from Lake Achinike. She scowled at John. She had not expected to find the border of barbarism only sixty miles north of the city whose new baseball team Catherine liked best as Red Sox opponents. They had one hundred and sixty miles still to go, and in spite of the conductor's continuing assurance to her questions, that the air conditioning system was working, the stench got steadily worse.

At Achinike Station, the twenty-five mildewed converts to the wilderness and their baggage and canoes alighted on an already crowded platform, and John and Lydia pushed their way into the station. They had made it! There was no one to greet them, no arrangements made, no one knew they were coming. John had wanted to get in touch with their daughter and ask her to have them met, but Lydia had prevailed again. "If there's anything we shouldn't know, it will be swept under the rug by the time we get there," she had said. "No, John, we must just walk in on them and see what is going on. I insist." "So now what," he said to her as they pulled their luggage against the wall so it wouldn't be trampled on. "The phone," she said, pointing. "There's a Chamber of Commerce in every Canadian town, I've been told. They practically run the place."

The Chamber told her there were two ways to get to Sand Island, by plane or water taxi. She immediately ruled out the plane. She had noticed a picture of one with peculiar-looking gull wings in a color advertisement for "Lake Islands Airways" on the station wall, and the idea of entrusting their lives to such a small-engined affair was out of the question. The girl at the water taxi office explained that their one boat was already on a call but would be back in about half an hour; then it could take them to Sand Island. Lydia asked her to reserve it; they would be down to the taxi dock shortly. The town's only taxicab was engaged getting the campers and their gear down to the airbase, and would be tied up "for the best part of forty minutes anyway, ma'am," the voice on the telephone said. John shrugged his shoulders. "This is all your idea," he said. Each took a suitcase and started trudging towards the water taxi office at the main dock.

When they arrived, Lydia was out of breath, but she collected herself. The girl at the counter looked sheepish. A tall muscular Indian was leaning against the far end of the counter. "I was hoping you would have a coffee, or snack," the girl said. "When our taxi arrived at its destination, another party there engaged it to take them to the southern end of the lake. I'm afraid it won't be back now for well over an hour, maybe even two." The young girl pursed her lips as if she had just noticed a fly in her soup. Lydia tried to be pleasant. She wanted to sit down. "Well, we'll just rest, then look about a bit," she said. "We're from Boston, and this is our first trip to your lovely north. May we leave our bags here?" "Of course," the girl replied. "Would you like your ticket now? That will be $54 for two."

At the word "Boston," the Indian's ears picked up. It was Sammy Osatig. On his trips to town he liked to come in and chat with the taxi secretary because she let him dock his boat right outside the door while he was shopping. He came over to Lydia, winking at the girl. "S'cuse me, missus," he said, "but I heard you're from Boston. I have friends there." His "friends" were really one—Zellie—and she had asked him to visit her any time in the future. So he could use a contact and a free bed in Boston. "I've been shopping and I'm just going back to Sand Island. I'd be glad to take you, for $20." Lydia tried to smile. Her first contact with the Devil's children was turning out rather unexpectedly. He was pleasant, rather interesting-looking she thought; she couldn't detect an alcoholic odor, his jeans and hide vest were clean, his eyes clear, he wanted to be helpful, he would save them well over an hour—and $34. "I don't believe I caught your name," she said. "Sammy," he replied. "Everyone knows me as Sammy." She looked at John. He shrugged. "That would be very kind of you," she said. "We're going to Harold Kenebek's house. Do you know him? Do you know Catherine Saltonstall, who lives there?" "I'll deliver you right to their door," said Sammy. John handed over an American $20 bill. "You keep the exchange," he said. Sammy took their bags.

When he saw Sammy's sixteen-foot aluminum boat with a twenty-five horsepower rather worn-looking outboard motor, John had reservations, but Lydia whispered to him, "Catherine says it's only fifty minutes by boat to the Island, so we will just grin and bear it." She was as cheerful as she had been in several weeks. She was nearing her only child, with helping hand outstretched. John looked across the bay to the closest island. A plane was just about to take off. He noticed the tips of the trees bending under a brisk wind, but when he looked down at the water, it was only slightly ruffled. The last time he was on a boat was three years ago, he recalled, the ferry to Martha's Vineyard to visit the Spencers. He tried to remember if he had ever been in such a small boat as Sammy's; he was having trouble recalling. He was sure he had not. Sammy threw the two bags up front, and seated them on the middle seat, facing backwards toward him. "You won't get so much wind in your face this way," he said. He handed each of them a dirty red cushion. John could not make out the printing in the middle, it was so worn, but across the bottom of one was the smudged word "Airways."

Sammy did not normally start his motor before shoving off from the dock. That had always seemed to him too Shagonash. He untied the boat, pushed it out as he climbed in, and the wind caught them and they were drifting out towards the bay. After the sixth pull without success, Sammy stood up and stretched. John noticed that every time he leaned over for another pull, Sammy's jacket raised just high enough to reveal the outline of a small protruberance in his right hip pocket. John was sure it was a flask or small bottle. He also took inventory and noticed that there was only one gas tank which, he assumed, was full, a paddle with a piece chewed out of it, and no further life cushions. Three passengers; two life preservers. He assumed their captain would honor the age-old convention of passengers first in times of trouble, but he decided not to ask, nor mention anything to Lydia.

Sammy returned to pulling his outboard cord, again without success. "If he has to paddle us back, I guess it would be the right thing to do to request my money back," John thought to himself. Lydia seemed oblivious to any difficulty. Sammy turned round to them. "I've been havin' trouble lately," he said; "but it's just an adjustment. The carburetor!" and he turned and unlatched the engine hood and ripped it off and threw it on the floor at their feet, barely missing his two plastic bags of groceries tucked in by the gas tank. Over the years, a gelatinous mass of black goo of oil and grease had collected under the lower lip of the cover at the back, and as it crashed to the floor, a colloidal blob could no longer hold on. It sailed through the air and landed on Lydia's silk stocking. John saw it land, and winced, but Lydia was oblivious, because she was looking across the bay to the air base where another plane was taxiing out towards them, praising herself for avoiding this noisy, high-risk means of travel.

Sammy got the motor started, but left the hood in the bottom of the boat. John knew nothing about motors, but he knew that if his car engine, or Lydia's, sounded the way Sammy's did, he would get it in for a tune-up immediately. It coughed for a few seconds, was irregular in the pitch of its whine, and there was a distinct clanking noise. Unless trolling, Sammy had two speeds, stop and full throttle, and with the speed handle twisted up as high as it would go, the motor gradually speeded up and the boat surged forwards in hesitant jerks, then levelled out. Lydia rejoiced that they were going to beat the plane out of the bay.

She was unpleasantly surprised when she discovered the greasy oil running down her leg, but the greater surprise lay ahead. The town had settled at the northeastern tip of Lake Achinike for good reason. The small bay laced with islands provided good protection from the wind for the docks and boats. Once out of the channel leading into the bay, however, boaters discovered fourteen miles of unimpeded lake, and if the wind was blowing strongly, as it now was at thirty-three mph, the water could become very rough. Lydia and John were soon aware that things were not what they might be. As the front of the aluminum boat hit each wave, it leaped up, then came crashing down again. The suitcases jammed themselves up against the middle seat. Lydia took one bump by leaving the cushion entirely and jolting back down onto it again. Her lower jaw snapped against her upper. She grasped the side of the boat with both hands. She yelled at Sammy: "Slow down, slow down. This is too rough for us," but Sammy only grinned and yelled back, "If I slow down, it'll get worse and last longer."

After two miles John and Lydia were visibly shaken. John wanted to crouch down on the floor; he thought he would be seasick. Even Sammy was mildly concerned. The wind had come up much stronger since he had come down in the early morning. He debated turning around, but he needed the $20 and wanted to get home. "What the hell," he thought; "I don't control the wind. It still beats swimming."

But he was under some stress. It was obvious his passengers were suffering. He needed a drink. He decided to try to cover up his first swig by turning around and reaching out behind the engine as if to check something, but as he tried to raise the bottle to his lips, leaning sideways, a wave pitched the boat, the rye spilled down his chin and dribbled onto his shirt, and he almost fell out backwards. He clutched the engine just in time. He knew they saw him. What else could they look at? "To hell with that," he said to himself. He wrote off the free bed in Boston. If he wanted a drink, he'd damn well have one. It was his boat. Twenty bucks was a bargain to Sand Island.

He didn't owe them anything. He had tried to be helpful. So it didn't work—big deal! Too bad! He smiled at them and took another swig. He didn't offer them the bottle because something told him that would be adding insult to injury. He'd just run his own show. Lydia's kidneys were now painful, as was the back of her neck. Another crash jarred her buttocks. She looked at John. He was turning green. He tried to lean out over the side before he puked, but some of it ran down the inside of the boat, and then there was another jarring crash and this time flecks of vomit, caught by the wind, sprayed back over Sammy's face and vest.

He slowed right down, pushed up between them, threw their bags into the back of the boat, swaying dizzily as his six-foot-three pitched with the waves, helped John turn around and lie frontwards in the bottom of the boat, with his back against the middle seat, returned to his seat and was going full throttle again, all within twenty seconds and not a word spoken. Out came the bottle again, and now he kept it in his hand. Lydia couldn't bear to look at him, and turned frontwards too, and now flecks from John's next puke caught her in the chest. She was in agony now, and with another crash to the cushion she couldn't hold it any longer and wet her pants. Sammy's eyes bulged as he saw the liquid running down the back of the seat, and he took two more swigs. The bottle was almost empty. They had seven miles to go.

A battered crew arrived at the front dock of the Sand Island Reserve in the little aluminum boat. John had recovered somewhat, but his back was very sore. He was still lying in the bottom of the boat, propped up against the seat, his legs numb. Lydia was hard-pressed to know where she hurt most. Her neck was aching, her buttocks inflamed and raw, her stomach and kidneys tense with pain. Sammy's bottle was empty, floating in the bilge of vomit and water.

Getting the boat docked was the final blow. The front and both sides of the dock were full of bouncing boats and the only berth was along the north side at the shoreline. To manoeuvre against the wind Sammy knew he needed some speed, and he hit the dock with a hard whack and ran the nose aground on the rocks. He did not see the sharp dock spike sticking out just under the water's edge by the shore, and Lydia heard the ripping sound as they hit the dock, and looked down and saw the gash and the water running in. But this final indignity was of no consequence or meaning to her. She stared at it blankly as if it were routine, as if she had just noticed a spot of dirt on her new gardening gloves.

Sammy tied the back of the boat to the one free dock ring and lifted the baggage out onto the dock. The stench of the vomit in the bilge was potent. John slowly got up. His trousers were soaked. He looked at Lydia. Spumes of upchuck dotted her coat and blouse as if she had been standing in front of a fan blowing porridge. His color had returned somewhat. "That was quite an adventure," he said to her weakly, trying to smile. "Could the plane have been worse? Well, at least we didn't run out of gas. I was worried about that, out there." He crawled up onto the dock. She sat there silent, scowling. She was too painful, too wet, too beaten, to move. Her anger had dulled; she was morose. She sat looking off across the lake as if she were blind and deaf. He opened his suitcase, and immediately smelled new trouble. He had tried to wrap the bottle of Jack Daniel's carefully in his underwear, and had worried the whole trip that it might break. But it wasn't the liquor that had broken; it was his new bottle of Eau du Sauvage after-shave lotion which Lydia had given him on his last birthday. It had cracked down the side of the bottle and the entire contents were reeking in his shirts, pajamas, kimono, slippers, ties, handkerchiefs, underwear, socks, and tan shorts. "I'm going to have to find laundry facilities by evening, Lydia," he said. She moaned. "I trust Catherine will be able to help us," she said, laconically. "Where is Catherine?" Suddenly she snapped up her head and looked directly at her husband. "John, I don't think I can take this. I want to go home now! And we're taking her with us! Are we agreed?"

ii

After Sammy had the boat tied he headed straight for the Band Office and breezed past Giselle. "Sammy, you've been into that stuff again," said Giselle. "Have you been sick? You stink! Get out of here!" She stood up. "Hey, you can't go in there in your condition," she shouted after him as he went into the library. "Get out of there!" she yelled.

Catherine returned with him to the boat. Lydia was walking around on the dock carefully, as if she had just been asleep for a week. John had the bags placed side by side near the path, and was sitting forlorn on the ground beside them. She kissed her mother on the cheek. From the smell and the look of their clothes she surmised the situation. "Have you been paid?" she asked Sammy. "Yes, Miss Saltonstall, I have been," he replied. "Well, you put their bags in the boat and take them to the store, please, Sammy. We'll put my parents upstairs in the apartment." Sammy put the bags into the boat and headed for the store. She took her mother and father, one in each arm, and headed down the path.

Within half an hour she knew the whole story from John. Lydia remained silent. They changed their clothes and Catherine threw the soiled ones into the apartment's little wash-and-spin-dry machine. Her mind was racing. Her mother's first encounter with the Wendaban would have confirmed her prejudices, making it all the more difficult to show her the truth. It was the peak of the tourist season; could she find them suitable accommodation on the lake? They were depressed, humiliated and physically sore. Why hadn't they flown in? It had not been a conspiracy nor the fault of any one person. But Sammy should have turned back; but then, she figured, when money is tight and you get some, you want to keep it. Why did it have to be so windy? It was all the little things that just ganged up. Conk would never have let such a mess develop. He was a pro. He would have looked after the niceties, like meeting them and taking their bags and helping them up the ladder and telling them about the elastic band. He would have had Freda tip her off that they were coming, so she could meet them. There were clean puke bags in all the aircraft. The way it happened was all so wrong, so needless. It was their fault too. They should never have got off the train unannounced, unprepared, with no one to ease them into their new environment. It was not like them. They should have known better.

She phoned the station. The southbound *Northlander* was due at 6:15 p.m., arriving Toronto at 11:45. It was now 3:05. She phoned the water taxi. It was available. She made up her mind. It would pick them up at 4:30. They would have time for a cup of tea and a muffin in town. Perhaps she would stay with them for a few days in Toronto, and try to put the record straight. Perhaps she would see them home to Cambridge. It would be for only a few days. Then she would be back. There would be long talks. They looked so tired, depressed, old. She must look after them until they got home. She would not bring Conk in on it. It was not the right time for them to meet. Perhaps getting home for a few days to reflect would do them both good. She would be back; she wanted to come back; she had to come back. She would leave him a letter. He would understand. It would be only a week. "You both have a rest," she said. "Daddy, you can use the sofa bed and mother, come with me to the bedroom. There's a lovely bed in here. We'll have you both feeling fine in no time. I am going to pack, and write a letter, and I will pick you up here in an hour. We'll be on the train tonight." Lydia tried to smile. "Thank you, Catherine," she said. "Thank you dear."

iii

When Angele got home from the store Harold told her the story. Catherine had packed up her things, but her computer was still in the library. She had left them each a letter. Angele read hers. Catherine would be back in about a week. She phoned Conk. He flew right down. He looked tired and agitated, Angele thought. She handed him his letter. He sat at the table to read it.

Tues., Aug. 23

Dear Conk,
Something very sad has happened. My mother and father arrived in Achinike at noon for a surprise visit, and somehow ended up in Sammy's boat for the trip. It was too windy. He got sloshed, they got sick and very sore.

Mother is beside herself and daddy seems quite shaken and helpless. I hadn't realized how old they are getting. I have made a decision to see them home without further incident. I want to get some warm clothes for the fall anyway. I'll be gone barely a week. I don't know how I can bear being away from you for even that long. Please try to understand my concern. Give my love to Cloudie. I'm having serious reservations about going back to Ashton's Cave, so please don't buy any lights or cameras on my account. But we will get into that later. In the meantime I'll miss you terribly. I love you very much.

Cathy

He put the letter down and walked over to the window. Children were splashing water on one another from a small blue plastic pool beside the next house. He turned and looked at Angele. He thought she looked very sad. "Did she leave her clothes, Angele?" he asked. "No," she replied. "She seems to have taken everything. But her computer is still in the library." "Thanks, Angele," he said. He walked to the door. Harold had his earplug in. He waved at him and went out.

He pushed Cloudie off and climbed in. "God damn it!" he said. "She sends you her regards. They came up here to get her and Sammy played right into their hands. It just went like clockwork and they didn't even have to work at it. They'll try to hold her, Cloudie. You bet they will. She might never come back. She's a hostage to her God damned past! Well, we'll see about that, won't we! Are you up for a trip to Boston, old girl?" He flipped the switch and Cloudie replied: "Whanga whanga whanga whanga." Then they both exploded into sound at once. As Cloudie spluttered and caught, he slammed his right fist down on the dashboard so hard it made a permanent dent. "Jesus Christ!" he shouted.

iv

She threw herself on her bed. She gazed at the two suitcases standing unopened on the floor where she had put them four hours earlier. Life could be such a drag, she thought. She glanced up. Marilyn's flossy smile was ridiculous. "That thing is coming down, soon," she said to herself.

She reflected on the whirlwind last twenty-four hours. Odd, she thought, that it was her mother who had been so morose, so visibly shaken and pommelled by her experience that she had retreated into a shell which had closed, leaving her distant, disdainful, almost oblivious to her surroundings. She had never seen her mother like that. But it had been John she had pitied more, John to whom her heart went out so longingly. It had been his look that persuaded her to bring them home. She had been used to his shrug; it was his way of coping. "Don't ask me, I just work here," was his typical body message where Lydia was concerned, his way of allowing her that territory which he had long ago decided was hers by conquest and cunning, if not by right. But the bewildered look on his face on the dock, and later in the apartment, was different—had scared her. It was as if the always reliable Saltonstall power of charm and knowledge and tradition and assurance was no longer relevant. It had not been the puke on his clothes nor the pain in his groin; it had been the bafflement. His response had not been a way of coping but a childlike signal that he was incapable of coping. For the first time in her eyes he appeared lost and powerless. She had never seen such psychic alienation in two people. And all from just a bumpy little boat ride. What had happened? What rite de passage had this failed to be?

She had wanted to get some take-out food but Lydia had insisted on throwing together a salad as soon as they arrived from the airport. Catherine had done all the talking during dinner. She had decided during the flight home that she would not apologize directly, but only obliquely, that she would emphasize the irony, that they had suffered so quickly in the land of God's aplenty. She talked of Angele and of her feeling so comfortable and welcome in the little house, of Chief Philip's generosity, of the new dig and pictograph, of the rich dissertation shaping up, of the challenge of interpreting and conjecturing and re-living, of reaching back into time for the truth, of Henry and Henrietta and the babies, of the Majukimo and its inspiring evening of mythology and dance, of Cloudie, and of Conk. She painted with rich colors and bold strokes, she put her heart and soul on the table with confidence and joy. She invited them into the bright sunshine of her recent life. She had been more fully alive in the last two months than ever before.

But they would not understand. She knew that, as she talked. They would not see, could not hear, refused to accept. They assumed she was deluded by initial intoxication. Their earlier fears were confirmed. She had slipped away from the girl she once was; she had traded a life of stability and tradition and grace for a mess of pottage. Now that she was home again, the wandering child might rediscover her former values. She felt they expected her to feel guilty. She had not a grain of guilt in her body.

She heard the livingroom clock strike. They had gone to bed early. Bong. Bong. Bong. She counted ten strikes. She got up and heaved the smaller of the suitcases onto the bed, opened it and rummaged around until she found it. She went to her desk with the book and took her pen from where she had last put it down only two months ago, only an eternity ago.

Cambridge, Aug. 24.

It was proper that I should have come home. They needed me, and knowing that, I have brought them home. The clock has just struck as it has for years gone by. But it sounds so strange, so unfamiliar.

I had thought that home was a place of security, of love and assurance. I think now that home is less a place than an understanding, a feeling, perhaps a conjecture. You take home with you, inside, but you cannot always come back to it again, for if you have changed, it will have changed too. My old home has changed because I have changed. I am new growth Saltonstall. Insecurity has the advantage of freshness and life and challenge. I see now that too much security is a bad thing, if it holds you back from life. I was pensioned off to the old ways before my time. The most secure place in the world is a remote dungeon lost to all memory, or a grave. But the sky is very insecure and requires diligence and care. Our gull wings will carry us only so high, for so long.

I have tasted love, deep and fresh and free. It has no past and perhaps little future. Its only home is in the heart. Perhaps it may find a home then create a home. I have been pulled and stretched and set free as a bird. I feel it so intensely here, back in my cage. But I can only test the height of that sky, that freedom, by the closeness of my cage. They measure each other. Emily knew that. Now, so do I. He has pulled me up into freedom, but my umbilical cord is endless and will not snap. If only I could pull him into me. If I could only show him a new home, down from the sky but up from the dungeon.

I think Emily did want to dive out into life that day, to jump free of the old house and grab onto me and shout, "Catherine, rescue me, take me away." Her soul could fly so high but she knew her body was a living corpse and she was smelling death. She didn't jump. But I have. And now, homeless, I long for a new home, bright, sunny, roomy, free, but secure and assured and somehow attached. Shall I ever find it?

Chapter XIV
BOSTON

i

He had not wanted to come. "The busy season, and I have to take time off," he had said to himself. Ted's eyes had asked why, but he never said a word of reproach. "What a sterling pair of partners," he thought.

He closed his eyes and listened to the big jet's hum, so quiet compared to Cloudie's raucous noise. But then, hers was more intimate, and besides, he thought, you could never get this big tub to do what she does! He fingered his plastic glass of Canadian on the tray in front of him, then leaned forward and looked out the little window. "What boring flying!" he thought.

He settled back and put his hand to his wallet. The rest of his traveller's cheques were in his suitcase. "I'm going to need $2500 in U.S. $100 bills," he had said to the bank manager in Achinike. "Why don't you take traveller's cheques?" he asked. "We probably have the Yankee cash this time of year, but you'll find the cheques much easier to manage. Incidentally, you have only $1400 in your account, so I'll have to put through a small loan for you." "What?" he snapped. "There was $2700 there last week and I've had a pay cheque since then." "Oh," said the manager, "we took out another certificate for you. You know our arrangement. Whenever we figure you are comfortably over $1000, we transfer your funds into another certificate. You're pushing forty-five of them now, I believe." "Do whatever you have to do," he had said, "as long as you have everything ready for me to pick up this afternoon." "Yes sir, Mr. Seguin," the manager had said; "everything will be ready."

The voice on the airport's direct line to the Sheraton Downtown said they had a lovely room for him and the lady at the Hertz counter said she had a nice new Chev Celebrity waiting, just for him, washed only an hour ago, just for him, and because it was Monday he would have an extra free one hundred miles on a four day rental. "Just for me, today?" he asked. "Just for you, Mr. Seguin," she replied, handing him the application form. "Do you have any extra specials for pilots, from Achinike, Ontario?" he asked. She looked at him. "From where, sir?" she asked. "Do you have an En Route card?" "Achinike," he said. "And you can call me Conk. You know, Canada's great northern sportland, the land o' God's aplenty. I'm sure you've heard of it." She had a puzzled look on her face but she had been on the job for over a year and was well versed in all sorts of games. "Conk," she said; "that's a very special name, isn't it! Why of course we do. Here it is right in my computer. I just had to find it. How about that! It's amazing. Leave it to Hertz! It says right here that pilots from Agonawa, Ontario are entitled to a free Hertz complimentary Good Customer Card, which will speed up all future rentals anywhere in the world, and act as a credit card for you." She smiled at him. "I'll give you that with your name printed on it when you bring the car back." "I knew it," he said. "All the world loves a pilot, even from Agonawa. But it's Achinike," and he spelled it for her. "A-c-h-i-n-i-k-e. Here's my card. Next time you're up, I'll take you flying. Just for you." He smiled. She smiled. He noticed the ring on her finger. "I wonder how many flirts like me she has to put up with in a day," he thought to himself as he grabbed his bags and headed for the car rental lot.

He was obviously not used to Boston traffic. Horns blared at him. "Get a donkey, buddy," a cab driver yelled at him as he passed Conk on his right side. He was trying to follow a city map spread out on his knee. The one-way streets were going the wrong way. A pair of tanned female legs in red pumps crossed in front of him at a light, and he followed them up onto the sidewalk. The light turned green but in his preoccupation, he failed to respond in the fraction of a second allowed in Boston. "Beep Beep." He glanced in the mirror. "Beep Beep Beep!" "For Christ's sake, shut up!" he said to the mirror, "or I'll walk back there and throw you the keys and you can drive both of 'em." "Beep Beep Beep."

The elevated pike proved tricky. He couldn't remember how he got on it, but now he wanted off, and three times he turned off, but the traffic was going so fast he didn't dare slow down, so he did not have time to watch carefully and figure things out, and three times he sailed up the opposite ramp and was right back on it again. The fourth time he turned hard to the left at the bottom and just about collided with a cement abutment. He jumped the curb and parked on the shoulder between abutments to study the map. "There has to be a way out of this mess," he thought. "Flying low through the islands in fog has nothing on this." Suddenly a police cruiser pulled up beside him with its red lights flashing. The cop came up to his window, which Conk lowered, and peered in. "Do we have a problem here, mister?" he asked.

By the time he was in his room his nerves were raw. He didn't have a plan. He didn't really know what he was doing in Boston. Had he come to rescue her, as with a bedsheet out of an upper-storey window in the dead of night? Was it to plead with her, or give her a piece of his mind? She had left so fast without making a lot of sense, and now he had done the same thing, as if he had been tied to her by a delayed bungee cord. "Knee jerks," he said to himself. "Time to settle down a bit and plan something. Knee jerks are dumb. I'm not here for a vacation. Time to make the move right now, as the song says, and I'd better get it right the first time. We should be back on the blanket in Keewaydin Bay."

He stared at the telephone. He looked up Saltonstall in the Directory. "Thirty-three Harrington Lane," it said. He had grabbed the address at the last minute from Freda's customer files. He had fancied himself going over to Cambridge and finding the house and parking across from it and just watching it, the way private eyes did on television. Somehow that wasn't his style, he thought. He dialed.

"Hello," she said; "this is Catherine Saltonstall speaking." "Hi!" he said. "Remember me?" "Conk!" she said. "How good to hear your voice. I was going to call you tonight. I could not get you last night." "I wasn't there," he said. "I was in Toronto." "Where are you now?" she asked. "Did you have a flight to Toronto? Are you still there?" "No, I'm here," he said; "in Boston. I'm at the Sheraton Downtown. So this is where the baked beans come from! And the craziest idiots I've ever seen behind a wheel. If I hadn't been a tourist with a sweet tongue, I'd have a $150 parking fine. I don't know who got the roughest deal, your mom and dad getting to Sand Island or my getting from the airport to the hotel. I'll tell you all about it sometime, if you're good. Just parking in the hotel's underground was an adventure." He heard her laughing. "Want some company?" she asked. "Why do you think I came here, anyway?" he responded. "I will be right down," she said. "In about an hour. What is your room number?"

They embraced and kissed. They caught each other up on events since they had been together. She tried to explain her actions and he kept nodding his head. He was trying to listen but was having trouble plugging his ears into his eyes which drank her in as if they had just opened after a long sleep.

"There's only one problem, Conk," she was saying; "and that's my parents. You are spared meeting Dawson, because he left a few days ago for an extended tour of Europe. He always wanted to do that, so now he's finally got his chance." "Without you," he said. "Without me," she said. "Let's not get into that. He will get along just fine. Maybe he will meet someone new." "Would you want him to?" he asked. She looked at him with a slight frown. "What does that mean?" she asked. "I have told you a lot more about Dawson than you have told me about your umpteen flings, I am sure. We cannot undo the past. We would not want to. But you and I have today and tomorrow to think of. We should discuss how best to meet my parents." She paused and looked at him. "Or, do you want to meet them? Is this a clandestine visit?" "She would pull a word like that on me," he thought to himself. He thought there was a cold, sad look on her face. "Is there any point?" he asked. "From all I know, they've already decided they're not going to like me. They'll see me as coming to rescue you, which is probably true, anyway." "Rescue me?" she asked. "From what? Where are the dragons?" She looked hard at him. "They're all over the place, here," he replied. "Correct me if I'm wrong, but your parents are worse than dragons, because they brainwash you while they hold you prisoner. This whole place is a brainwash. Liberty bells and Paul Revere greeted me as I got off the plane. I thought the American Revolution was over, but they were

shooting at me before I got through Customs. I don't
relish being the green kid from the boonies, Cathy. Think
of me, a bit. I've got some self-respect. Let's just hop on a
plane and you can leave *them* a letter this time and see
how they like it!''

"Conk, get hold of yourself," she said, bristling.
"First, the Liberty Bell is in Philadelphia. And I'm not a
prisoner, and not brainwashed, and nobody is shooting at
you. My past is inside me where it should be and I cannot
get rid of it any more than I could chuck out my lungs.
But I have broken any adverse grip it had on me. I am
freer now than you are, if only you knew it, because you
are becoming locked into some very strange prejudices."
She got up and started pacing the floor. "You probably
think that all you have to do is come down here and kiss
me and suddenly I will be all mush and we will make love
and I will hear the loons calling and all you have to do is
carry me over your shoulder through the lobby onto the
airplane bound for God's aplenty. Well let me tell you
something." She stopped and pointed a finger at him.
"You can't have my body without my soul, too. They go
together. You have paid too much attention to the one and
not enough to the other. And my past. That's part of me
too; take it, or leave it! When you decide that you can
afford the courtesy to meet my parents on their grounds,
and on their terms, and can afford the confidence to
explain to them why you and I should be lovers, and ask
for their support and understanding, and explain to them
why the life we have together in Achinike is worth more
than a few good fucks in the sunshine, then we can get on
the airplane and go back together. Think it over. You have
my number." She went to the door, and was gone.

He spent a restless night. He thought he must have looked up at the little red dot on the fire detector on the ceiling a hundred times. The digital clock face on the television registered twenty minutes at a time. "Jesus!" he thought. "So this is it. I come to get her and get my foot caught in a trap. She's laid it on the line and I either shit or get off the pot and move on." He knew what he wanted. He thought he knew how he might get it. "Opportunity only knocks once," he said to himself. "Really? Once! Just once!" He stared at the word long and hard. "Once. Only once! Jesus, don't blow it, Conk. Get it right the first time. Don't blow it." If it was only once, he wasn't moving on this time. He couldn't change overnight, but then she wouldn't expect him to. "Give me a signal and I'll throw you a line," was all she was saying. She'd help him. She'd give him all the freedom he needed. He knew that. "So body and soul go together," he said. God damn it, she was right. She had hit him where it hurt. "Okay, Catherine Saltonstall from five hundred years of fuckin' ghosts, hang onto your hat, woman! Give me one full day." He squinted at the digital. It was 5:45. He must have slept a little, he thought. He leaped out of bed and headed for the shower. "Let's go!" he said aloud.

By 7:45 he had had breakfast and had located three clothing stores, one in the hotel, two close by, and had checked them out. They wouldn't open until 9:00. He found a barber in the hotel, with a manicurist. "Good!" he thought. "Never tried one. No time like the present."

He went to the front desk. A young dark-haired girl with heavy eye makeup came over to him flashing a warm oriental smile. Yes, they had just the kind of suite he wanted: large livingroom with dark mahogany furniture, oriental rugs, adjoining bedroom and bath. "The small suites are $350 a night, the larger ones $600," she said. "I have one of each available for tomorrow night." "I'll take the smaller, just for tomorrow night," he said. "Then I'll want my old room back." She consulted her screen. "We don't have a major credit card for you, Mr. Seguin," she said, "so we will need an additional $500 deposit." He counted out the cheques and signed them. "You're sure you've got it right?" he said. "I'm in my room tonight, the suite tomorrow night, then back to my old room the following night, but I don't want to pay for two rooms tomorrow night." "Of course not," she said; "that's just the way my screen reads here. I've even punched in that we are to move your things into the suite for you." She smiled up at him. "One more thing, Mr. Seguin," she said; "the $350 does not include any services." "Either she's flapping her eyes at me or there's something stuck in one of them," he thought. "If you want a bartender and bar, they will be extra. Here, this is a list of the services and costs if you need them." He took the brochure and glanced at it. "Is the ice free?" he asked. "Of course," she replied. "That's all I'll need," he said. "I'm having only three guests." She stared at him. Her eyes stopped flapping. "Only three?" she asked. "Why do you need a suite? They are designed for parties of fifteen to twenty people." "It's all for effect," he replied. "I've got to pry my future wife loose from three hundred years of old Boston blueblood, and I want to look as dignified as we can make me. Do you follow?" "You bet I do," she said, her eyes growing big. "You don't need a suite; you need the Athenaeum Club! Good luck! We have just about all the services anyone could want in this hotel, but for that job I'm afraid you are going to have to fly on your own. It's a gorgeous room, though. It will help a lot." She paused for a second, looking at her screen. Then she looked back at him, her brown eyes shining. "But if it doesn't work, you can elope. I can fix you up with a gorgeous honeymoon suite in any of twenty-seven different cities in nine countries around the world right here at my little computer." Her face was beaming. He thought that if Catherine should throw him over he'd have to come back to this desk to see if there were any consolation awards. "Thank you," he said, smiling. "You have been very helpful. If we elope, all I'll need is a long ladder. We already have our honeymoon suite picked out at the Sheraton Henrietta." She looked puzzled.

He decided to start with the clothing store in the next block. Wellington's sounded very British; they should know what would impress a Saltonstall. But he was put off. The grey-haired salesman seemed uppity and stiff and the suits they looked at were intended for funerals or wakes, he was sure. He thanked him and left.

The clothing store off the hotel lobby was part of a major chain, so he expected run-of-the-mill treatment and product. To his surprise, the store struck him as more elegant than the one he had just left. The girl who came up to him had long blond hair and he thought she had just stepped out of a *Playboy* centrefold, but dressed to kill. "Jesus!" he said to himself. "What are they doing to me here? Why do I fall in love with every broad under thirty, and half of them over thirty? If I'm going to settle down, I've got to go to the doctor and see if I can get something fixed. This is bloody ridiculous." After ten minutes of chat and looking at suits, he decided she knew her stuff and he would take her into his confidence and he asked her to sit down, and he told her the story and how he wanted to look and for whom, when, and why. He wanted "the whole ball of wax," he said, suit, shirt, tie, cuff links, handkerchief, shoes, all to match. "I'll take you on," she said. "Of course you understand I can only fall back on how I'd like you to look if you were formally asking my mother's permission to marry me. My father has passed away. You want to look tailored, but in the new young fashions, not stuffy or prim. We need to convey youth and energy; the clothes have to say that, right? But in good taste. Let's see if I can come close to what you have in mind." For a fleeting second he thought of asking her mother. "One thing," he said. "I have only $500-600 to spend. I hadn't planned on getting a whole new get-up down here. Can we work within that figure?" She took her calculator, pencil and pad, punched some figures, crossed them out on her pad and punched again. "With tax, we can come within about $40 of that," she said, looking up at him with a quizzical smile. "It's a deal," he said. "Let's see how good you are. Northern bush pilot to Boston investment broker for $640. Everything to be ready for tomorrow noon." She had her tape in her hands. "We'd better get right to work," she said. He stood up and spread out his arms. He wondered if he was appearing too eager. Her perfume was getting to him. "This hotel is something else," he thought. "All the beautiful people in one spot! Whew!" He suddenly remembered he did not have deodorant on, and prayed he wouldn't perspire too much.

The barber was trimming all the right hairs that Conk asked him to—nose, ears, moustache. He talked about the poor Red Sox year, that the pennant was slipping out of their reach, and he was trying to listen, but his attention was on the manicurist. She had wanted to do his nails while he was having his haircut, but Conk said that he would wait until the haircut was finished. He had never had a manicure, probably never would again, he thought, and he wanted to concentrate on one experience at a time. She was well over forty he figured, maybe over fifty, but her skin was clear and soft-looking and her blue eyes sparkled. He couldn't tell whether her greying hair was natural or rinsed. It didn't matter. She wore heavy lipstick and lots of blue on her eyes, but her eyelashes were her own and there was no mascara. Her hands were large and veined. She had a deep visceral laugh, the kind that made you want to laugh too even though you didn't know what she was laughing at. Every husky word had a bit of a laugh to it, he thought. She should have been a circus clown, or the laughing lady outside the midway show.

"This is your first manicure, isn't it, darling," she said as she examined his hands. He liked the touch of her hands on his. It was a gentle but firm touch. "Such cuticles," she said. "You men! You're all the same! Such beautiful strong hands, but you don't take care of them." As she worked she asked him many questions and talked of her life. He expected her to start reading his palm or pull out some tea leaves or turn off the lights and they would gaze into a lighted crystal ball together. Her friendliness exuded from her hands into his and up into his spine. He had expected the big city to be cold, and for the second time in the day his spine was tingling from the human touch. He marvelled when he learned she was fifty-four. "How do you stay so young-looking, Sally?" he asked. She threw her head back and laughed. Her eyes were laughing, her nose was laughing, her hands were laughing in his. She looked into his eyes. "Because I flirt with every man who comes in here," she answered. Then she laughed again and he started to laugh. "I have been sitting on this stool for twenty-seven years, four more than him,'' and she jerked her thumb over her shoulder towards the barber who wasn't laughing, or even smiling as he concentrated on the head in front of him. ''I'm married with three children and five grandchildren. I've held God knows how many hands—with the lonely, the aching of heart, the rich and the poor, and I've been flirting the pains out of every one of them for all these years. I have men from down-and-outers to rich professionals who come in here for a manicure only three days after I last did them.'' She put her head back and roared. He looked at the barber. He was stony-faced. ''This has got to be an act,'' he said to himself. ''Can you believe it?'' she asked. '''What's to manicure?' I say to them. 'Never mind,' they say. 'For ten bucks you can pretend. But I want the full treatment.''' She roared again and he was sure the laugh was drifting out into the foyer and down the ivory marbled tiles, in and out of the dress shops and shoe and gift and tobacco and travel stores.

The barber now spoke up, still without a trace of a smile or emotion. ''But when there are no customers around, she's a perfect bitch,'' he said. Then he dropped his comb and scissors to his sides and he started to laugh and she joined in and then the stern-looking man in the barber's chair started to laugh. Conk joined in and felt his sides aching. ''It's quite an act you have here,'' he said. Someone walking by the store at that moment would have seen four laughing souls. The barber had learned to play straight man to her jocularity. The touch of her hands had given old Boston much joy over the years and they had just baptized their newest convert.

He had decided to wait until just before dinner to make the call. He thought they might be all together, which is what he wanted. Whether she had told them he was in town wouldn't matter. He suspected she wouldn't have, yet. He never wrote things out, but he had spent over an hour on his invitation if he could get Lydia's ear, and the final draft was lying by the telephone.

"This is the Saltonstall residence," the male voice said. It had to be John. "Hello," he said, "this is Conk Seguin speaking. Is this Mr. Saltonstall?" "Yes, it is," he answered. "Would it be possible to speak to Mrs. Saltonstall, please?" he asked. There was a pause. "You mean my wife, Lydia?" John asked; "not Catherine? Or do you mean Catherine?" "I'd like to speak to your wife, please," he said, "if it's convenient." "Just a moment, Mr. Seguin," John said. "I'll get her." His heart was beating faster than usual but he had good control. He was ready for the plunge.

"Hello," the voice said, "this is Lydia Saltonstall. You're Mr. Seguin, from Canada, I believe." Her voice was a bit harsh, he thought, but trying to be friendly. Perhaps only civil. "Yes. It's Conk Seguin from Achinike." He reached for the handwritten paper, but suddenly he decided not to read it. It might sound too wooden, rehearsed. He knew it by heart, anyway. "I am so glad to hear your voice at last, Mrs. Saltonstall. Catherine has told me a great deal about you both; I hope we can meet very soon. When I heard about your unfortunate experience up north, I wanted to come to Boston to express my regrets personally and to meet you." He paused, wondering if she might pick up the conversation, but there was silence. "I'm staying at the Sheraton Downtown, and last night I discovered they have a fine dining room and dinner menu which I can personally recommend. I wonder if you and your husband and Catherine could join me tomorrow evening for dinner. We could have a drink in my room, and a bit of a chat, then go down to the dining room. Catherine tells me you like rare roast beef, and if tomorrow night's is as good as last night's, I know you will enjoy it. Does that sound possible?'' ''It damn well better sound possible,'' he said to himself; ''I've got over 1000 bucks into it so far.''

''Catherine and John are right here,'' she said. ''Let me confer with them and I'll be back in a minute.'' He thought she would have muffled the phone in her hand, but she obviously put it down and he could hear their voices in the distance. ''That sounds just fine, Mr. Seguin,'' she said. ''We will have a good chance to meet at last. It's very kind of you. What time would you suggest?'' He could scarcely believe his ears. ''Jesus! Don't blow it now; keep the voice steady, matter-of-fact,'' he said to himself. ''I think about 6:00 o'clock here in the room would be good,'' he said, ''and I'll reserve our table for later. That will give us a chance to get to know each other. My suite number is 1101. I'll look forward to seeing you at 6:00.'' ''Very well,'' she said; ''thank you for the invitation. Tomorrow at 6:00, then. Goodbye.'' He heard the click. He heard his sigh. He heard his heart. ''By God, we did it!'' he said aloud. As he thought of the dinner bill, he decided tonight to go out to the diner down the street for a hamburger and fries. No gravy.

iii

He took another look around the room. On the buffet there was champagne chilling on ice for Catherine, Jack Daniel's for John, Glenfiddich scotch for Lydia, and two bottles of Molson's snuggled into the ice beside the champagne for himself. He had more chilling in the bedroom if John pulled a fast one and wanted some Canadian brew. Thank goodness water was the only mixer needed; it simplified things. The brown pitcher he had ordered up specially was full of water; the plate of assorted crackers and cheeses was garnished with pimento olives. He had put it together himself from the delicatessen next door to the hotel. Room service had asked three times if it had to be a brown pitcher because theirs were all clear glass or white or blue porcelain, but they finally produced a brown one. He thought brown fitted in better with the warm tones of the room. "Maybe they had to run out and buy one," he thought.

He had placed the chairs just so. Lydia and Catherine could sit on the chesterfield, which would hold four, and he and John in the upholstered chairs drawn up in front of the chesterfield, with the coffee table between. A second smaller plate of cheese and crackers was on the side table beside the chesterfield, under the Tudor table lamp.

He looked at himself in the mirror over the buffet, and then at his watch. It was 5:45. "She really has done a marvellous job in the clothing store," he thought, as he surveyed himself. After he had tried on several suits, they had agreed brown was his color, and she had finally selected a light pin stripe of grey and rust against a light cinnamon brown in a tight, soft weave of cotton. The shoulders were unpadded. The shirt was the lightest off-white he had ever seen, and the tie a conservative weave of light grey silk with deep red and gold narrow stripes, with matching silk pocket handkerchief. They had to compromise on the cuff links. She had tried to get him into gold ones, but he balked at the price so they settled for round imitation amethysts. They were the only fake thing on him. When he went for the shoe fitting at another store, he wasn't as taken with her suggestion as he was with the dark brown leather loafers in the window, and the bill jumped an extra $50. There were four pieces of

Achinike on him: his underwear briefs and jersey, his tan socks, and his watch. She had suggested another watch. His Longines with its large round black face and dials and wheels and pushbuttons was fine for a pilot and diver she was sure, but it really was too much machinery, too heavy and presumptuous for a Boston dapper dan. She suggested a simpler, tailored one in gold. He smiled at her.

He looked at himself for several minutes. He had thought that the last two days since their tiff would have been rough, but he was surprised at how gratifying they had become. He had made the big decisions. He looked at the new Conk, and rather liked what he saw. The old feeling of being trapped was gone. Either he had banished it, or it had just dried up and blown away. Maybe its last whimper had been drawn out of him by the manicurist. Five grandchildren and still so attractive! He adjusted his tie again without moving it. He had rehearsed what he wanted to say a thousand times. He had decided he didn't need to memorize the parts because they were inside him, now. It was what he wanted to say, not what he was supposed to say. He wet his finger and smoothed down an invisible hair over his ear. He knew where he wanted to go. He was thirty-one. He was ready. This was the once. Suppose he would drift on for more years, maybe all his life, flying and swimming and fishing and diving and photographing and getting into bed with the latest Crest smile with jolly boobs until it was time to go to work. For what? He'd had it all. It was a dead end. Pieces of temporary satisfaction called freedom, but nothing to plug them into, to give them coherence and meaning. Lots of jolts; no main line. No past. No future. Just now. Now he would try to roll them all into one. There was a knock at the door. He glanced at his watch: 6:04.

Catherine was in front, in a blue dress, her parents
behind her. She just stared at him for a moment. He
welcomed them and shook hands with Lydia and John,
and seated them just the way he had planned, and they
exchanged pleasantries. It was a warm evening but Lydia
had brought a light shawl of grey lace, and Catherine took
it into the bedroom. There were comments on what a
lovely suite he had and Catherine said something about
how good he looked in his new suit. He served the drinks.
Each took the usual, but he was careful to pour his beer
last, at the buffet, so what he brought over to where they
were sitting was a frothy glassful. For some reason he
thought he'd keep the beer bottle out of sight. Catherine
talked about the failing Red Sox as he had counted on her
to do, and the two hours he had spent that morning
catching up on what had been going on in the world of
baseball paid off, as he was able to comment casually on
what he thought they would have to do against whom to
stay alive in the pennant race which wasn't even a close
race yet. He had served the cracker plate from the buffet
once, but now Catherine passed it. He knew she was
trying to make it easy.

He tried to watch Lydia without obviously watching
her. She was at first quiet, a bit stiff, but he thought she
plunged into the cheese tray as if she hadn't seen food for
several days. He could see that she was studying him
carefully, every move, every word, though she tried to
appear casual. She was evaluating, he knew that. His first
sense was that $1200 worth of sofas and suits and oriental
rugs and the right booze had worked, for it gave the
message that he was trying, that he knew the score. There
wasn't a whiff of the boonies anywhere in the suite. She
could look under the carpet or scour the closets and she
wouldn't find so much as a pine needle. He could play
their game.

John started to ask questions about the Airways. How many planes, where did they fly, who were their "clients," what regulations did the government place on them, what were the taxes, what computer software was available, until he started to worry that Cloudie's world was dominating the evening. Once, he felt that John hovered on the edge of saying what a shame it was that they hadn't flown to Sand Island on that terrible day, but he didn't. They all thought it, though. He knew he was scoring points with John. Without pushing the issue, he was looking like a hard-working professional in a successful growing business of his own making. Lydia was munching, sipping and looking pleasantly interested. He decided she had not come to make war.

Then suddenly it was Lydia's turn; she just barged in. He wondered if his inner bewilderment showed on his face, or in his voice, for the unexpected was so unexpected that he felt unnerved. She wanted to know about the loons. Why was he interested in them, what was he going to do with all the fine photographs Catherine had told her about? Would he publish a book? She was sure he must publish a book. They didn't see loons around Boston but she hadn't really looked for them. Could he recommend a book for her to read about them? Just last month at the Ladies' Auxiliary they had a lecture on Ducks Unlimited and she had not realized what a dreadful plight some of the ducks and loons—she was sure he had said loons—were in because of acid rain and conversion of wetlands to industrial sites along their migratory routes.

So he told her about loons, all she wanted to know, and more. He was looking right at her and she at him and as he talked he said to himself, "Isn't she trying to meet me somewhere? Reaching out, opening a door? Or is she just enticing me to the guillotine? Killing me with kindness?'' He thought of Sammy in the boat. Was he evening the score? He needed another drink.

As he poured his second glass he glanced at his watch. He couldn't believe it: 7:30 already, and he hadn't got to the serious part yet. He returned to them, standing up with his glass in his hand. "I see that time is speeding by," he said. "We're due in the dining room, but I'm sure we have more to talk about. What's your pleasure? I can put them off for another half hour or so." He looked at Catherine. She was smiling. "Give me a signal," his eyes said. "We're just fine, Conk," she said. "The crackers and cheese and your hors d'oeuvres are delicious and I am sure dinner can wait. Why not see if they will delay it for us." "Good," he said, and went to the phone.

When he returned they were chatting pleasantly. He told them the reservation was delayed forty minutes, and offered to freshen their drinks. Catherine and Lydia said they would pass, but John wanted to try some Canadian brew. He returned with John's frothy glass and sat down. They looked at him. There was a lull.

"I hope I'm not going to put a damper on things," he said, "but I really would like to turn our conversation to some serious matters." He looked directly at Lydia. He kept his voice as soft and easy as he could make it. "My real reason for inviting you down here tonight, Mr. and Mrs. Saltonstall, is to ask your blessing on the relationship which has sprung up between your daughter and me." He paused, and looked at John, then back to Lydia. She looked very serious, but calm. Their eyes were rivetted on him. "I know you may have reservations; that's only natural. The truth is, I love Catherine very much and I know she loves me, too." He paused again; he was sure he was going to start hearing a tremor in his voice, but nothing had developed so far. There was sweat in his palms, though. He had put on lots of deodorant. "But love alone won't sustain a good marriage." Lydia winced visibly at the word, but her serious expression was unchanged; her eyes were burrowing deeply into him. "Bear up; give it to her," he said to himself. He did not look at Catherine. "I don't see that our separate careers need pose an insurmountable problem," he continued. "I suspect Catherine could get a position with the Wendaban Council when she has finished her degree, but if not, I am sure there will be a need for good pilots wherever we settle. I have a record of flying time and experience that would make me very competitive with other pilots in secure and profitable positions. I could retrain for different aircraft, and I have no problem with joining one of the larger carriers, like Air Canada, or American Airlines, and working my way up. Catherine loves her work and she'll make a superb teacher. I suspect ultimately we'll settle in a college community." He paused again, and took a sip. Could he settle in a college community? he wondered. It would have to be small, rural, with lots of good fishing nearby! The sweat in his palms was visible, he noticed. Was it on his brow? He was determined not to wipe it with his new matching handkerchief in his pants pocket. "Let it sweat," he thought.

"The truth is, Mrs. Saltonstall, I have come to realize I need Catherine very much in my life." Now he detected the tremor. "God damn it!" he thought. "I've led a fairly easy but rather routine, somewhat limited life," he continued. "It's been fun and I have what I consider a modestly adequate income and savings. But Cathy has opened up new possibilities." He could feel the sweat on his brow now. His arms were clammy. He leaned a little closer to Lydia. "I want to find my sister, and perhaps Cathy and I can go to Europe and look up some

Saltonstalls, and then we'll see if we can trace my father's line in France. My mother told me my grandfather had come over from Normandy. I was baptized a Catholic, but I don't practice churchgoing. I like to think I make a fair stab at the ten commandments, though I acknowledge I have some difficulty with the one about swearing. But I'm working on it." He leaned back, and tried to smile. Catherine got up and came over and stood behind him, and bent down and kissed his cheek. She whispered in his ear, "Where did the old Conk go?" He knew how impolite it was to whisper in such a situation, but he couldn't resist, and pulled her head back down and whispered, "I sent him off to play with the old Catherine, the imprisoned one." He looked back at Lydia whose expression was unchanged in ten minutes. Catherine was standing behind his chair with her hands clasped around his chest. He had saved the best until the last. He could feel sweat on the inside of his thighs.

"I would like to make one final point, Mrs. Saltonstall," he said. "If you will give us your blessing, I'd like to make you a deal." He put his hand over Catherine's. Lydia's face was stony cold and still expressionless. He thought she looked quite white. "Cathy has told me how much you would like a granddaughter. I want Cathy and myself to have each other just to ourselves for a year. Then, on the stroke of midnight on the 365th day from our wedding, we shall go about getting you that granddaughter. I have the feeling we are so healthy that you can just set your watch for nine months later. If the first is John, we'll keep at it until Catherine Lydia appears on the scene. And regardless of where we are living, we'll want you to visit us and play with the children, and with our free airline passes for anywhere in the world, we'll be popping in on you in Cambridge for all the holidays until you're sick of us." He stopped. He couldn't utter another word. He had cleaned his cupboard bare. He was sweating profusely. He was sure he could smell deodorant. She had goofed; the summer suit was much too heavy. Catherine bent down and kissed him again lightly on the cheek.

Lydia looked at John, then took her glass of scotch and drained the last dregs and placed the glass back on the table. "I see," she said in a dry voice. She was struggling. She looked at them long and hard without smiling. Then she held out her hand with the diamond rings and the diamond watch. "I believe you said last night, Mr. Seguin, that the dining room here serves very fine rare roast beef which you could personally recommend. If you would take the hand of a rather tired old woman and escort her downstairs, she would be very glad to try some of that beef." He reached for her hand. "I would be delighted, Mrs. Saltonstall," he said, and gave her hand a little squeeze, and raised her up. "Shall we?" he said. They walked arm in arm towards the door.

She looked at her father. He looked dumbfounded; he shrugged. "You have yourself quite a man," he said. "He's done more in two hours than I could in two years, against insurmountable obstacles." He offered her his arm. "Shall we?" he said. As they walked to the door which Conk had left open, she turned to her father and said in a low voice, "Daddy, do you have the feeling this is a rehearsal?" "I think it might be," he replied.

Chapter XV
SOUTHWEST 39 KNOTS

i

He had phoned Ted and things were fine, slowing down a bit. Yes, Ted said, he could take an extra day or two if he wanted. So she took him to a Sox game at Fenway and showed him how to get off the elevated, and they had dinner at Sweeny's at a different table, looking out onto the harbor. "Golden baked northern lake trout," the menu said, and they smiled over their secret that no one else at Sweeny's knew that night, about where to catch some excellent northern lake trout and how to cook them over an open fire, *au naturel*. They walked the Freedom Trail hand in hand, she providing all the commentary, and he was looking up continuously as much as ahead, and she had the impression he was photographing her more than the shrines, and they wandered through the colonial houses at Marblehead and looked at the old whaling grimscrews and splashed into the ocean at Wingarsheek Beach. She showed him her College and wanted him to meet Dr. French, but he was on holidays, and she wondered if she saw a bit of a smile on Waldo's face, but he replied he thought he looked quite serious. Zellie was away in New York. Cambridge seemed stuffy to her, a bit dead.

On the last morning before their flight, they drove out to Concord early and walked around Walden Pond as the sun rose. There were cigarette boxes and beer cans on the path, and they took a dip in the permitted roped-off bathing area, and when they came out to change in the pavilion he had a piece of dark green slime on his left shoulder. They opened Emerson's House with the day's first tour, and she tried to explain it all, about the Emersons and the Thoreaus and the Alcotts and the Hawthornes, and he promised he would try to read some of it when they got back, and he knew then that when they bought a house it was going to have to have a library in it, with some wall space left for loon photos he would insist.

"Funny," he said to her as the jet's hum lulled them into complacency; "I wasn't looking forward to a big city like Boston in August. I suppose I was dreading meeting your parents and wondering if you were coming back." He looked over at her. The auburn hair was glistening again in the sunshine from the jet's little window. She was smiling. "But I had a great time, Cathy. That's a hell of a town. Nice people. You won't have trouble getting me back there as often as you like." "Did you get anything out of the old houses, at Marblehead and Concord?" she asked. "Did you enjoy them? I mean, could you feel the old gentle ghosts walking around?" He paused, reflecting. "Well, sort of, I guess. I've got to work at it a bit. You'll help me, won't you? It's all so new to me. But I'd traipse through all that old stuff all day just to hear you explain their history. That's what makes it. That Emerson house was pretty nice. Lots of room. A paint job, new electric panel and fixtures, some new furniture, I could see us living in something like that. Course, it's an invitation to a family, isn't it! You'd have to fill up those bedrooms somehow. If a guy could pick it up for about sixty grand and fix it up." She smiled and snuggled into his shoulder putting her hands around his arm. "I'll write them when we get to Achinike and see what they say," she mumbled. "But don't hold your breath."

What he hadn't told her yet was that the morning after the dinner with John and Lydia, he went back to the clothing store off the lobby to thank the saleslady for her help and to give a progress report, and before he knew it, she was walking him over two blocks to her cousin's jewelry store. "He's got the best selection in Boston," she said, "and you are going to get a deal! I'll see to that." Whether he did or not, he did find the ring he wanted, one simple half-carat diamond in a plain silver band. She stayed with him the whole time while he looked over all the selections, not in a flirty way, but she was so interested, caring, even excited, and all she wanted to do, she said, was to be sure that her cousin knew the situation and would show him every possible ring he had that came close to what Conk had in mind. But he had the distinct feeling that she thought she was choosing her engagement ring. This time he phoned collect, and Ted went into action, and by 2:00 o'clock that afternoon the Boston branch of the Bank of Nova Scotia had $3000 in crisp U.S. $100 bills on the counter for him. No, he told them, he still wasn't interested in a credit card, thank you. Maybe later.

So he was pondering. He had the headphones on and was tuned into music of the 70's. He had been nineteen when Billy Joel came out with *The Stranger,* but it was still one of his favorite records, and with a bottle of red and a bottle of white racing through his senses like debating angels, he was trying to think of the right place and time to give it to her. Henrietta's Bay, early in the morning? No, something was wrong with that; he didn't know what, but it wasn't right. Ashton's Cave? Now there was an unbeatable setting. But how could he upstage three thousand years of secret history? No, that was too much competition. Sitting with a lot of dead bones wasn't a good place to get engaged. By the time the Captain broke in to say they were beginning their descent into Toronto he had decided on a quiet evening at his apartment, with a special candlelight dinner and two little filet mignons, thick and round in bacon strips, with small bottles of red and white. "Here's a little piece of Boston you can carry with you forever, Cathy," he would say. He smiled and looked down at her cuddled into his shoulder. She was asleep. She would like that very much, he thought.

ii

By late September the best-laid plans were being laid as best they could plan. They decided to announce the engagement formally in Cambridge during a visit for the American Thanksgiving in November, with a wedding in early April before the busy flying season. Meantime, she would wear the ring. Lydia, of course, would be in a flap about such short notice, but they were agreed Catherine would go home for March to assist the Cambridge ladies in preparing for the big event. He had talked it over with Ted and Freda and they were elated and wanted to be at the wedding for sure, and they started laying plans for an engagement party in Achinike after the planes were put away for freeze-up. Conk had their blessing for a honeymoon in late April. Catherine noticed European travel brochures starting to show up in his apartment, and they were soon decided on a week in England and a week in France. That would have to do for now.

She had written Dr. French and told him she was sure she could have a draft of the dissertation to him by April, so she would have the summer to revise and tidy it and add anything new that turned up, especially from Rita's dig. There was no mention of Ashton's Cave. If all went well, she anticipated a fall graduation. She had another talk with Chief Philip and he agreed the Wendaban could use an anthropologist for a year or two, and as soon as her studies were done he would pressure the Council to establish the position and he was sure they could get funding for it. They would know by early summer and she could begin in the fall. Rita would be very helpful. "We've been talking about establishing a Wendaban museum right here on the Island," he said. "Perhaps you could be its first curator."

She had been serious about learning to fly, and got her chance after they returned from Boston. Tuesday morning looning turned into flying lessons. She would start her ground school at the College in Almaguin in October. By the time of her first lesson, she had purchased two books on float plane flying from the bookshop on the highway, and Conk's mouth dropped open when, as he started to explain the features of the plane to her at their first lesson, she said, smiling, "Yes, I know," and then proceeded to tell him a few things, using technical terms he didn't know. He was speechless. "You and your books!" he said. "Why bother with teachers? Just jump in and fly it," and he turned to walk away. "Now Conky," she said, grabbing his arm, "I just know some terms and theory of what you're supposed to do under different conditions, but just in my head. I have no feel for it. Theory is only theory. Only you can give me the experience. You've given me quite a few experiences of feeling already. You're not going to quit now, are you?"

So he moved the pilot's seat back a few inches on the floor, and she sat in front of him between his legs at the controls, and he had his hands on hers on the wheel and the throttle and setting the gauges and winding down the flaps, and he sometimes had his hands on things that had nothing to do with flying but lots to do with feeling, and she just politely removed the large hairy hands, and once plunged Cloudie into a dive, and then he didn't do that anymore.

She learned quickly. "You are a true Stinson," he said to her as she effortlessly settled Cloudie down on her steps on her first landing by herself on a calm clear morning. When she had cut the engine to idle, she turned to him and said, "How so?" "Well, my memory may be fuzzy," he said as they taxied towards the dock, "but I believe it was his sister who talked Stinson into building planes. They made about eighty of these Reliants I think, in Detroit in the 30's. Until the Beaver came along, it was one of the best payload planes on floats. His sister was a pilot too. One of America's pioneer women pilots, I think. She could even have sat in the very seat you're sitting in now." He paused, looking out to where Ted was waiting for them. "Hey, how about Catherine Stinson Lydian Seguin for our daughter?" he said. "That sounds pretty New Englandy to me." Catherine was beaming, but not concentrating on the docking. "Too many names," she said, and then looked over at him, "but why not for the second? We could call her Stinsie." She cut the engine. Suddenly she leaned forward and groaned. She had not cut the prop soon enough, underestimating the speed of drifting into the dock on a windless morning, and Cloudie almost knocked Ted over as he tried to push against the strut. The left pontoon hit the dock hard. She threw up her hands with an "Oh my goodness!" She turned to her snickering instructor. "I guess she'll be a wild one, our Stinsie," she said smiling. "I'll bet she's flying by fifteen. Will Cloudie still be here, do you think?" She paused, looking down at Ted on the dock, who now had a good grip on the strut with his right hand, and was holding his nose with his left, looking up at her. "Stinsie Seguin, Miss Captain of the Clouds. Sounds pretty good to me."

"Providing she doesn't smash it up on her first docking," he said.

In mid-September she made her second trip by helicopter to see Rita at the site, and stayed five days to help her close it up till next summer, for Rita was due back on her campus by late September, and her student helper for the summer had already left to return to school. She had to leave Conk behind, but that gap in her life was almost compensated for by her long talks and growing friendship with the older woman. Catherine catalogued all twenty-one artifacts from the summer's dig, and they could both only speculate on the what and how of four of them, and they carefully packed them all to go back with Rita to her University for analysis. She photographed each from many different angles, including Rita wearing the half loon mask. Around the fire they talked into the long tired hours of the cold mornings, and she discovered by the time she got back to Sand Island that she had forty-seven pages of tightly handwritten notes on the dig and Rita's views on the ancient Ashwagane. The dig also strengthened Dr. French's thesis that there was substantial trading between the Wendaban and clans to the northeast as well as the south. They marvelled at how mobile these ancient people seemed to be without automobiles and airplanes. She knew that she would refer to Rita's work and ideas so often that maybe her name should be on the title page too.

They had made two more attempts to catch diving loons on film, one back with Henry and Henrietta and the two little ones which Catherine had named Mickey and Mouse and who were now almost as big as their parents, and turning lighter brown. But all they had to show for their efforts were blurred streaks and fuzzy lumps and some bubbles. "We've got to take this whole thing back to the drawing board," he said. It would be a long process to plan and photograph just what he wanted. The water by late September was getting cold, and Conk started to wear his rubber suit. As they were packing up the diving gear in the apartment one night, she said, "Why don't you start on your loon book this fall, Conk? The one mother wants to read. I am sure I can help you get started at least." The upshot of that conversation was that she would spend a lot of time living with him in the apartment during the winter. After she had done her writing by day, she could prod and help him during the evenings.

What he had not been able to understand was her attitude towards Ashton's Cave. After the discovery, he had investigated renting more underwater battery-driven lights, stronger than his, and decided that he would purchase another for his own use anyway. Photographing the panograph and exploring the cave had become an exciting project in anticipation, as important now in his mind as his diving loon project. He would get her a cold water suit. They would have lots to do before the ice set in. He was her instructor in canoeing, photography, flying, diving, fishing and loonology; she was his in Native Canadian and New England history, interpreting artifacts and pictographs, writing and mythology. It was becoming a compelling combination; their avocations were falling in love too, he thought.

The trip to Boston had postponed a second trip to Ashton's Cave, but after they had returned to Achinike he found her recalcitrant. She was not going back to the cave and she insisted on an oath of secrecy, that they would never, ever, on pain of death, reveal where or what they saw that day.

"But why, Cathy?" he asked. They had just cleared off the supper dishes from the little table in his apartment;

he had the hot water gushing into the sink and the suds were bubbling. "I don't get it. You come up here with a lot of general ideas and things to do and Indians to interview and all that. But you have one specific project from your teacher, to try to find more information on Ashton's note on the panograph. And so we discover the bloody thing itself, in all its glory. I'll never forget you that day. You were glued to that rock, like a little kid coming down to the tree on Christmas morning; your heart was pounding. I can still feel it. You were tracing things and pointing out this and attaching it to that, and making up a whole piece of history, as if you already knew the story but hadn't met the characters yet." He took out the glasses and set them upside down in the drying rack. "Never mind drying them," he said. "Once the water has run off we can put them into the cupboard upright. I fly the health inspector around a lot and one day we got into a discussion and he told me we probably put more germs back onto glasses and cutlery drying them than we took off in the washing. Ever since, I've never dried anything with a towel." She just looked at him.

"Do you remember what you said that day in the cave?" he continued, turning to her. "You said that something had gone wrong, you thought. That these two old strains of Indians on the rock had probably become separated even before we whites got here, and you wondered if we'd ever figure out why. Remember? And then you turned to me and said that this panograph might contain some clues, and that it was the most important discovery in the northeast in sixty years. So now what? Were you wrong, Cathy? Does it not matter anymore? Aren't you going to use it in your study? You surely can't be scared of going back there!"

"Of course I'm not scared," she said. "Well, if I don't have to dry them I might as well sit down." She hung up the dishtowel and sat at the table. "I know how strange this is all going to sound to you, Conk. No, I haven't changed my mind on its importance. In fact it's probably even more important than I realized then. With the information in the cave and from Rita's dig, we would have a stranglehold on three thousand years of history around here. Suppose carbon analysis of some of the earlier bones and Rita's artifacts were only a hundred years or so apart? In fact, they could be dead on, because the settlement that Rita is digging up was very sophisticated for its time, and I would bet it was they who were in on painting the cave. With the dig and the cave, it's as if someone had just washed the dishes and walked off the scene and then we walked in three thousand years later. All that is missing is the human voice."

"But I can't do it, Conk. I know from some little things I've picked up, intuition mostly, that Chief Philip and Harold know about the cave. I know they do. I've authenticated Sammy's story to Zellie, from Harold and Matt. It's a version of an older one that Ashton missed. And the proof is in the cave. But the cave's a taboo, Conk. That cave has been used down through the centuries by only the chiefs and shamen. It has been kept secret from the Band members, even from their Councils, for hundreds of years. It's a very, very sacred place. Harold will not break that taboo, for me, or Angele, or anyone else, unless for a new shaman. It's the last of their old taboos. To break it would be to deal their culture a cruel blow, and God knows it's already struggling enough. Think of it, Conk—the only important taboo left. Sure, it would be the centrepiece of my dissertation, photos and all. It would give me international fame. But am I going to

be the Shagonash to expose an Ashwagane sacred shrine
kept secret for all these years? Are you? The moment I
announce the panograph, my association with the
Wendaban is all but finished. I might as well clear out. I'd
be ashamed to meet Philip on the boardwalk of the Island.
I can just see the look in Harold's eyes—and Angele's.
And after all the hospitality I've received, and even the
possibility of a job with them? It would be academic rape,
Conk.''

She came over to him as he was putting the last dish
in the rack. She looked up into his eyes and took his
hands in hers and held her lips only inches from his chin.
''I'll have a good dissertation without it,'' she said,
smiling. ''I'll work in Sammy's story; I've got two
sources. That's enough to sustain my point. I've made
notes on the panograph and they're with my papers in the
library. But when the dissertation is finished, I'll destroy
them. In the meantime, my guess is that there are only
four people in the world now who know about Ashton's
Cave.'' She reached up higher on her toes and moved her
lips closer to his. ''And the two new ones will never tell,
will they! Our lips are sealed.'' And she sealed them with
a kiss.

iii

Wednesday, Sept. 28.

Last night we talked about Ashton's Cave. What irony
life throws at us. Madeleine thought I would find among
the Ashwagane little to warrant the time and effort spent
in my research. She questioned whether I could advance
even a little knowledge. And now, the great find, the
dream of an anthropologist's lifetime, and I reject it! What

knowledge I can advance must leave the most important knowledge I've discovered unadvanced.

But is it knowledge? Perhaps before it is knowledge, it is love. Certainly it is respect. Are they sisters, or does one turn into the other? Perhaps the most sacred mysteries cannot convert to measurement and analysis. Is that what the Ashwagane have taught me? Is that what I came here for? That is the last laugh, that I have come to see from my dissertation a seeing that no one else will see.

My handsome pilot is baffled. He is technology. He teaches me to lift us with mechanical wings into the freedom of the skies. He dives with bubbled air on his back, dragging me behind, with lights and cameras that see through water. He freezes spots of time in his photographs. He is so disappointed. He wishes to rise to the occasion. He wishes to reproduce the wall exactly, somewhere—the interlaced sharp details of the panograph and their exact colors and dimensions. Beautiful color reproduction for all to see. And now I implore him to bury it in his memory, for none ever to see. I implore him never to return.

For if reproduced once, why not everywhere? Museums all over the world could show that wall of rock in exact reproduction. But it would not suffice. The more it is reproduced, the more demand there would be to visit the original. They would swarm in on it, the researchers, journalists, photographers, tourists, painters, historians; it would be measured and squared, gazed at and catalogued and studied. Would not some chips appear, some bones depart? For it is the original that counts.

For the Ashwagane, that is the rub. I believe in museums and art treasures for all to wonder at, to feel their past in their bones. But for the world to gain this treasure, the Wendaban would lose more of their soul, now starting to heal. It is not a good tradeoff. We must all have our sacred places, buried in the woods somewhere, immune to the photocopier. We social scientists must be very careful. There are times when respect must take precedence. I thought how privileged I was to be allowed to gaze on the sacred rock. I wonder now if it was a curse. I shall leave it alone, let it sink into the dark recesses of memory and ultimately of death. Knowledge is easy to record, analyze and transmit. Love is another matter. My love for their love of the old bones outweighs all other considerations. Zellie was right. Love can get lost in professionalism and politics. It is mysterious, private, very original. You have to strike a balance, and I have struck mine. In this case I must not intrude, not even for the sake of knowledge, to which I thought I was so dedicated above all else. So be it.

iv

During the first week in October the fall colors are at their peak and the hunters arrive. Mountain ash, maples and blueberry bushes turn scarlet red, poplar to gold, birch to yellow, men's hats and coats to gaudy phosphorescent orange. The winds blow, dark clouds scud across angry skies, animals burrow and leaves fall. The first flecks of snow are in the air for a few minutes, then they are gone. Out come heavy red and black checkered wool jackets and high leather boots.

The phone rang. She looked at her watch. It was 6:45. Who would be phoning the Wendaban library at such an hour in the morning, she wondered. It must be Conk. "Hello," she said, "this is Catherine Saltonstall speaking." It was Conk. "Cathy, bit of a problem here this morning. Freda's down with the flu and we're jammed with flying hunters today. I hate to impose on you, but could you give us a hand? It would be just to answer the phone, book in the passengers, keep track of where the planes are and when they should be back, give us weather reports. Ted will be in and out to help you, but he'll have his hands full on the dock. Moving hunters is like moving the army. Almaguin says it's going to be a clear day—windy—but things should go like clockwork. The worst will be over by 4:00. Can I pick you up in twenty minutes?" "I'll be waiting," she said, "but it's going to cost you. Big." "I'll see what I can do," he said, and hung up.

She had planned a day in town, anyway. June had called her the previous evening. Would she like to go to town shopping with her? Their car was in for repairs but she could borrow Sammy's boat. She called June. "Hi June, it's Cathy," she said. "Change in plans. I am going to help Conk out at the airbase today and he is picking me up in a few minutes. But I would love a ride home with you if you're still planning on coming back around 4:00. I've promised Angele I would do the week's shopping and have supper started by the time she gets home from school." "That's fine," said June. "I'll see you in town."

The day went well until the accident. Pilots for forty miles around Achinike heard a new voice on their radios, and by 1:00 p.m. it was sounding sure of itself and friendly. She greeted the hunters and kept track of who was where, and with Ted's help squeezed in one more flight. At noon she managed to slip away for the fastest week's shopping she had ever done, and left the five plastic bags of groceries for Ted to pick up later and put in Sammy's boat. She raced back to the airbase. As she walked in there was no one in the office, but Conk was on the radio. She flipped the switch and figured she had grabbed it just in time, because he didn't ask where she had been. He wanted the latest weather and seemed very matter-of-fact. "The wind is out of the southwest at 39 knots, sir," she said.

She was to have met June at the taxi dock at 4:15. But events took a different turn. Just before 4:00, Tommy Wenjinabe was driving north into town in his new black car which he had just purchased in Almaguin. The seventeen-year-old Wendaban had saved and worked and scrimped and taken driving lessons after school, and now his dream had come true—a shining refurbished 1982 Chevy Impala. He couldn't wait to park it among the other Sand Island cars at the end of the access road, and he had bought a can of Turtle wax for the coming Saturday morning. He and Jimmy Pawatin would produce the shiniest car in the parking lot. He was in high spirits.

At the same time, driving into town from the north was a blue and grey half-ton with a camper cab, pulling a trailer containing a red four by four, gas cans, gun cases, helmets, and four long brown legs with black cloven hoofs, sticking up into the air. The small rack of antlers was roped to the top of the driver's cab, the trophy of success for all to see. Manliness personified. They had planned on a week in the bush, but had shot their moose within three days, and didn't have another tag, so they had decided to pack up and work their way homewards enjoying whatever sights might come along. If the day had begun with a little whiskey in the coffee, that was only to be expected on a chilly October morning in the wilds, and if the remainder of the 40-oz. bottle hadn't got put away but dumped into the other two thermoses with Pepsi and coffee, well, who was to know? They were so proud of their conquest; their wives would be so thrilled, the meat so good on the table all winter. It would be back to work in a few days without another outing until the annual ice-fishing jaunt in February. They were in a mood to celebrate. They were in high spirits.

The collision occurred in front of the hardware store. The hunters had pulled out, so they said, to avoid a pedestrian, but no one could remember seeing a pedestrian. They were going 25 mph they said, but George Garland who saw them come into town from his service station said he was sure it was more like 50. The hunter driving had blood on his face and a fractured arm, but he walked away. They all smelled of whiskey, and the driver couldn't pass the breathalyzer test. They were in trouble.

But Tommy Wenjinabe was in worse trouble. He had taken the brunt of the crash. He lay pinned in his demolished new car groaning, and by the time the police and ambulance attendants had him out, he was unconscious. The paramedic on the ambulance team said he needed immediate hospitalization. He figured most of the damage was internal, to the head. Conk had just returned from a flight, and within fifteen minutes Tommy was on a stretcher heading north to White Falls behind Cloudie's steady clatter. June was beside herself. The Wenjinabes lived next door. She would go along with Tommy until his mother could get up to the hospital. She asked Catherine to take her groceries home for her. Conk said that there were over three-foot waves on the lake, but if she just took it easy, she'd be fine. Ted took June's groceries to the boat. Now there were eleven plastic bags.

Sammy had repaired his engine, and she got it going on the third pull. There were two life cushions and a paddle. By the time she was out of the channel she could see that Conk was, as usual, right. The waves were big, but no bigger than she had been in before. She tried different speeds, but finally settled on the slowest. The little boat pitched and crashed about, but she had carefully sorted the groceries, and the eggs and bottles were back with her, where it was smoother; the nonbreakables were up in front for a bit more weight, including four cellophane packages of round multicolored balls of bubblegum for June's children. Conk had given her a pair of gloves, but she thought she wouldn't need them. She looked up at the sun and could feel its heat on her face, though the back of her neck was cold.

She was settling into the routine. She was about thirty minutes out of town already. Bash, crash, roll, bash, crash, roll—she would grin and bear it. She thought she was actually enjoying it. It had been a good day. She had learned a lot about Conk's business and she had been helpful. But she would be glad to get back to the library tomorrow. She breathed in the clear fresh October air; she held her head high. The waves sparkled. Suddenly she felt her feet wet. She looked down. There were four inches of water in the back of the boat. She was amazed. She had noticed the gash in the right front of the boat at the bottom, but Sammy had filled it with epoxy and it wasn't leaking at all when she left Achinike. Now the filler was entirely gone and water was gushing in, rather quickly she thought. It spurted up into a little geyser when a wave hit. She glanced around. There was no bailing can. Maybe, she thought, as the back sinks down a bit and the front comes up, the leaking will slow down or stop. She'd try it for another mile or so. But before the mile was up, she knew she was in trouble. There were now over eight inches of water in the boat and the leak was still gushing water. She thought she could probably find something in the groceries to make a bailer out of, but that would take time. It seemed best to head for shore. A boat or plane would come along before long.

She figured she had about a mile to go to the nearest island. She turned sharply to the right, heading straight for it, but abreast of the waves now. She didn't speed up. Instead of rolling with the first wave to hit her broadside the boat sluggishly tipped up only slightly because of the swilling weight of the water in it, and the wave crashed over the gunnel. She was soaked from her waist down. Some of the grocery bags were now floating. Instinct told her to speed up and she turned the handle up full throttle. The boat tried to surge forward, but it was too heavy to get up on plane, and it ploughed. As she saw the next wave coming, she leaned far out to the right to try to tip the left side higher. Not nearly as much water came in as before. She looked ahead. The island seemed only a little closer. She thought she could make it. The engine was roaring. She leaned out again as the next wave hit and again water came in. Now she saw that the transom was so far down in the water that the lake splashed in over the back on each side of the motor well when the back dipped into a trough between waves. She let go the handle. The motor continued to roar. She quickly moved to the middle seat. As she moved, the mass of water in the back surged forward as the weight shifted, and as the next wave hit, the bow was too heavy to lift and it took on the brunt of the wave's water. The boat careened to the left and the bow nosedived into the next wave. She was sitting in water. It happened so fast all she could do was watch it. Water was pouring in over the transom. The motor started to sink, sputtered, and quit. The back of the boat sank down beneath her. She was afloat in the lake. The grocery bags were sinking. The gas tank was barely floating, but got suddenly pulled down by its fuel line. The paddle floated away and bounced high in a wave. She knew aluminum boats had flotation, but Sammy's was old and waterlogged through countless days of being full of rain. The bow stuck out and didn't sink further. There was some flotation. The boat was hanging vertically in the heaving lake. The pointed bow disappeared under the next wave and bobbed up again in the trough. She reached for a floating life cushion but as she tried to tuck it under her chin she could not feel any lift. It was already waterlogged. The second one was gone. She knew she must decide in a second. If she stayed with the floating bow she would soon be too cold to hang on and she would still have to try to keep above the waves.

She started to swim. The first strokes were reassuring. She was cold and her teeth were chattering, but as she threw herself into the high arched arm movement and furious kicking she felt a tingling, warm sensation. She glanced ahead. The island beckoned in reds and golds and green, shining clear before her. She started to shout. She knew she had to charge up her system to its highest pitch of energy. "Yes, yes! Jesus! We can do it. We can do it! Come on! Come on, Cathy! Up down. Up down! Yeeoo!"

She had gone about a hundred feet, she figured, when she realized she was not going to make it. Her arms were strong, but the calves of her legs had numbed and she could no longer work her legs. She couldn't feel any sensation in her thighs. Her legs started to sink. She could feel her toes wriggling, then she lost sensation of her whole lower body. She thrashed her arms about. She would not quit easily. She fought off the idea. A wave crashed over her and she took in her first mouthful. If she could only get her legs to work. She put her thumb over the diamond on her finger and pressed hard until she could feel the pain. But she could not revive her system. Suddenly there was a sweet numbness in her brain. She was so sleepy. Needles of pain suddenly shot through, then they were gone. She was a huge rubber band. Zellie was smiling at her. "For what we are about to receive." Why were the bells ringing? Bong bong bong. She screamed at Dawson. "She's jumping, right down on me." Then she heard Conk. It was coming, the yellow bird, flying so low, right at her. "It rattles a lot, doesn't it," she said. He was smiling. She flipped the switch. "The wind is out of the southwest at 39 knots, sir," she was saying . . . .

Chapter XVI
THE LAST LAUGH

i

He was sitting in the back of the police boat in his black diving suit, his head buried in his hands. The lieutenant handed him a cup of black steaming coffee from the thermos. They had been diving for three days. There were four of them, two police divers, the lieutenant from Achinike, who drove and answered the radio, and Conk. The large cream-colored boat had POLICE painted in large black letters across each side and the top deck. Conk had refused to leave each day until darkness shut down the search. The lieutenant kept a careful log of the hours and depths, and on the second day when Conk was told he had done enough diving for that day, he would not submit, and they had to use force to restrain him.

They did not know where to dive. It was guesswork, miles of guesswork at varying depths, working their way in bands out from where they had found the boat, to the northeast, southwest, and towards the shoreline. But the police would persist.

They had found the boat the same evening. When Angele called Conk at 6 p.m. after Harold had checked the places she might be visiting, he flew right down, managing to land before grey darkness obscured the surface line of the lake. The girl at the water taxi office had seen her leave Achinike without apparent difficulty around 4:30. Conk phoned several of the lodges up the lake where she might have stopped. He checked with the police; no one had reported seeing a drifting boat. June verified from the hospital that she had filled the gas tank. Catherine had told Angele that morning she would have the dinner underway when she got home from school. Since she had left Achinike, no one had seen her. Something was wrong. By 8:00 p.m., it was dark, but Matt, Sammy and Arthur arrived in Matt's boat, and Harold said to take Angele's boat as well. Matt had a strong searchlight which operated off his boat battery and Arthur had brought another strong flashlight. "Giselle says there are two new heavy-duty lights down in the store, and that we should get them, Angele," said Matt. "Do you have a key?" Matt brought back the two new lights and extra batteries and soon they were equipped and ready; two boats would sweep four little rays of light across the sombre blackness of Lake Achinike. The wind had died down, but it was still rough; the night was cold and clear.

Without a shred of evidence to go on, they decided to take the lake's main arm which went to town, and divide it in two. The way the wind had been blowing, if she had had engine trouble she would have drifted down towards town and in towards the south shore. They parted at approximately the half-way point just out from Labelle Creek, Conk and Arthur working their way southwest in Angele's boat, Sammy and Matt, northeast in Matt's. They had agreed they would cruise at trolling speed out from the shoreline, sweeping their lights back and forth from the boat to the shore and along the shoreline. With the wind as high as it had been that day, they were agreed that a drifting boat would certainly have been eventually pushed into the south shoreline somewhere.

Conk spotted it at 10:15. But he didn't see what he was looking for. He had become convinced that she had had engine failure. He was looking for the boat tied to the shoreline. She was strong, and in excellent condition. She had never had any fear of the water, or the bush, or night.

She would act calmly, sensibly. As the wind pushed the boat towards the shore, she would have paddled hard and kept it off the rocks and eased it into a fallen tree or gently sloping bare rock, where she could pull it up, just the way they had done with Cloudie's pontoons many times. She knew they would come looking soon. He thought he would see a fire. Surely she had matches with her, after all his talk about emergencies in the bush. She would have seen some complimentary ones somewhere and put them in her purse. Maybe June had bought some with her groceries. She was adept now at making a fire. She wouldn't need an axe. He was momentarily expecting to see a little fire. She might be sitting in the boat instead of on the frosty rocks. Or on an old log. Three times now he had asked Arthur to stop the engine, and with his hands cupped to his mouth, he had hellooed into the dark shoreline as loud as he could. "Caaaaaathy!" The echoes reverberated out across the lake and bounced back from the shore along with the sound of the lapping waves. "Caaaaaathy!" There was no response.

As he swept his light into shore it picked up the dull silver glint of the bow poking up from the surface like a heavy, rolling tip of stone. The bottom of the boat, hanging down into the lake, had hit the bottom and stopped the boat from drifting further towards the shore. They pulled up to it. As they flashed their lights into the inky depths they could see a spot of dull red; the gas tank, now full of water and gas, was still attached by its line to the engine and was lying on its side on the bottom, two feet from the edge of the transom. He scoured the shoreline with his light. He shouted and shouted. Nothing. He looked out to the dark lake. If this was where the boat drifted to, how far out, how far up the lake, had it gone down. He was shaking. "Jesus!" he said softly.

They flashed their lights down the lake, on, off, on, the agreed-upon signal, and within twenty minutes Matt and Sammy had joined them. Little was said. They all went ashore and walked up and down for evidence of footprints or broken twigs—anything that might suggest someone had been there recently. If she made it ashore she might have fallen from exhaustion, he thought; she might be sleeping somewhere, might have set off on foot for Achinike. They split up and for two hours carefully inspected the shoreline for a mile in each direction, two abreast, through thickets, gullies, bushes, over large broken rocks. They replaced the batteries. Nothing.

When they returned to their boats, Matt attached his anchor to the end of a long rope and threw it into the lake beside the submerged boat and tied the other end to one of his bright new orange life cushions. It was too dark and cold to do anything more. It was 2:00 a.m. "If the boat shifts, this will mark the spot where we first saw it," said Matt. "That's all we have to go by. We'll get a crew and the police out here before daybreak." He confirmed Conk's fears. "The way that wind was blowing this afternoon and the heaviness of this boat hanging in the lake like this, I'd say it went down probably two miles further up the lake."

"You go ahead," said Conk. "I'll go north a mile or so and make a fire. I can prowl the shoreline and see if I can see anything. If she made it to shore she's got to be there somewhere. Maybe she got confused and headed inland instead of following the lake. I couldn't sleep, anyway. I'll see you in the morning." Matt came over and put his arm around him, and gave him his thermos. "Giselle made some chicken soup," he said. "There's some left. I'll have a good crew ready before sun-up. We'll see you then. You can come with me, Arthur."

"No, I'll stay too," said the boy. "Ask Angele to send me some breakfast." He looked at Conk and tried to smile.

By 6:00 a.m. there were nine boats and nineteen men and four women, including Angele, on the search. The Sand Island Reserve dropped its normal business and formed a plan, two to a boat, which systematically covered seventeen miles of shoreline of the mainland and islands, from the narrows outside Achinike, down the lake to Sand Island. Matt and Giselle were coordinators, Giselle staying at the office and the phones and walkie-talkies. June organized food and coffee shuttles. Harold took the tiller handle in his boat. Angele tried to persuade him to let the younger men do it, but there was no restraining him. If the will is determined, an old warhorse is unstoppable. Matt helped him down to the boat on his crutches. Harold would be invaluable, for he knew every rock, shoal and current in the lake. Chief Philip went with him and promised Angele that if the old man tired too much, he would bring him home. The police cruiser joined the search by 11:00 a.m., and the divers started at noon after mapping out a diving plan based on sweeps northwest from where the boat was found. Conk was still searching the mainland with Arthur.

All that was three days ago. There were now still four boats from the Reserve searching, including Chief Philip and Harold, who refused to give up. But now he knew she was gone. He had joined the divers on Thursday and refused to take any time off from the police boat. He was exhausted and growing ill. He was coughing. He could not understand, could not comprehend. Gradually he admitted it, bit by bit, to himself. When they got Sammy's boat out on Wednesday they saw the ugly open gash and then they knew. Sammy couldn't believe it. He had spent hours applying several coats of epoxy to the gash, with the boat high on the shoreline, and had left it out of the water for two days to make sure of a hard dry bonding. That was six weeks ago and it hadn't leaked a drop since. It appeared to have popped out, all of it, probably all at once. Why? He started to sob and he and Conk embraced, the tightening fingers of their grips trying to induce mutual strength.

He had to find her. They all knew that if she had sunk into a deep hole she would stay down forever. Parts of the lake bottom in the search area dropped down to three hundred feet. The deep water was so cold all year round that she would not float up. It was so dark in the deeper areas that two abreast, with the strong police lights, they could only cover six feet on each side of them; a little path of twenty-four feet through a trackless unending waste of cold dark silence. Were they looking in the right place? Where was she in this fathomless mass of cold black death?

His head buried in his hands, he heard a boat approach the cruiser. He looked up. It was Ted. Unknown to Conk, the lieutenant had phoned Ted and said he must come out and take him home to bed, stay with him if necessary. He had overreached his limit of endurance. They were worried. Ted must be firm.

"Hi, Conk," Ted said. "Freda and I were just talking to Doctor Grant in White Falls, and I'm afraid it's off to bed for you. Those are his orders. He had some pills sent down, and I've got them. You have to conserve what energy you have left or you are going to be very sick and will have to be hospitalized. I'm taking you home."

"Wise move," said the lieutenant. "We'll stay out here till dark. The two divers from Almaguin will spell our

324

guys off in half an hour. Get some rest, Conk. You are
going to be very sick if you don't. If you're feeling better,
you can join us tomorrow."

The cool sheets felt good but his head was on fire. He
had taken the pills and insisted Ted go back to the base.
Freda would be over at 5:30 to check on him and get
some supper. The digital clock beside his bed read 1:47.
He knew he should sleep. He wanted to sleep. But her
face would not go away. He knew he shouldn't punish
himself. The guilt was now intense. He had told her she
would be okay in the boat. He had never heard of the
gash. But if it hadn't leaked in six weeks, wouldn't he
have said to go ahead anyway? She was such a fine
swimmer. In Henrietta's Bay they had gone out and back
over a mile many times and he couldn't exhaust her.
Why? Why? If the water had been ten degrees warmer,
she'd be alive. He knew he shouldn't think of her final
moments, torturing himself, but he couldn't help it. He
lurched over onto his other side, then back again. When
was it she knew for sure? He tried to put himself in her
place. She would have fought it off to the end. What did
she think of? Who did she blame? Tears were in his eyes.
How he loved her. He wanted her in his arms one last
time. Please, oh Jesus. Would it have been quick? He
cried into the pillow and the raised fist came crashing
down on it. Why? Why?

The alarm was ringing. There must be a fire. Was it a
police car? She was watching one of those police series on
television. It was still ringing off and on. What was
ringing? "Just a minute," he groaned. He was so drowsy.
No, don't answer, he said to himself, let it ring. He got
one eye open and reached for the phone. "Hello," he
grunted. "It's Philip," said the voice. "I was just about to
hang up but they said you would probably be asleep, so I

let it ring. Did I wake you?" "I think you did," he said, "but I should probably be getting up anyway. What time is it?" He squinted at the digital. It was only 3:15. "We've found her," Philip said. "Harold and I. Not too long ago." There was a long pause. His hand was trembling. His lips felt as if they were two feet thick. He could feel the tears coming. "Where?" he asked. He could hear his voice becoming raspy. "Harold's hunch was right all along," said Philip. "She was closer than any of us thought. About a mile north of where the police are diving." He could hardly hold the phone. "Where is she now?" he asked in a weak voice. There was another long pause. "Conk, that's what I want to talk to you about. Can you come down? Are you okay to fly?" "Yes," he said. "A quick shower and I'm off. Where will I meet you?" "Give me at least half an hour," said Philip. "Up the north arm, in Woodward's Bay, there's a sharp cliff coming straight up out of the water. It's a landmark; you must know it." That's the cliff at Ashton's Cave, he thought. "I'll meet you right across the bay from that cliff, in about forty minutes," Philip said. "You'll see my canoe. Harold wants to see you too, but he's very tired and Angele and I have put him to bed. He was growling at us. See you later." The phone clicked.

ii

As he feathered Cloudie's prop and drifted in, the Chief was standing waiting for him by a tree fallen into the water. A dark green canvas-covered canoe was drawn up on shore. The Chief grabbed the strut and pulled the plane in gently and had it tied to the tree by the time Conk had climbed down and onto the log. They moved onto the shore and stood facing each other. Philip's face was serious, drawn. This had been hard on them all, he knew. They stared deep into one another's eyes for several seconds. He noticed that the Chief was in moosehide leggings and jerkin, and wearing moccasins. He had never seen him dressed like that. He wondered what was going to happen. Was something wrong?

"We were going to ask you, to discuss it," the Chief said. "But Harold changed my mind. He's in on this too. So it's too late. It's done; it's decided. You were going to marry her, so she's very special to you. But she's more than just yours. Harold and I have had several discussions the last few weeks about bringing her in on it, but we couldn't. Now she's gone." He paused. "She is very worthy." He raised his hand as if taking a pledge. Conk was shaking mildly. What was going on? "It's entirely fitting," the Chief said. He took a large red cloth from his pocket and approached Conk. "Trust me. It has to be this way." Then he blindfolded him.

He led Conk to the canoe and helped him to sit in the bottom. Once they had left the shoreline, Conk was sure they turned a complete circle in the lake. He heard only the sound of the paddle and the water lapping under the bow. It seemed a long time. Then he heard the grating of the bow on shore, and Philip was out, beaching the canoe. "Give me your hand," he said. "We're going to have to climb a bit, so be careful. I'll keep your hand. Stay close to me." He led him up through rocks and around trees and then he was told to bend down. Philip gently eased him forward with one hand on Conk's waist and the other on his bent head, and he knew the footing was very difficult for he could feel the sharp rocks biting into his sneakers. Philip took off the blindfold and switched on a flashlight. They were in darkness. "Come," he said, "and be careful. Watch your footing.'' They picked their way down through the rocks in the little arc of the light, which the Chief sometimes swung back of him so Conk could see better, and then they were on a rock shelf and he could see a flickering shadow coming off the rock ahead. He knew now where he was. They turned around a slab of high rock and they were in the cave. A bear grease lamp sent flickering rays of orange light into the shadows. She was propped up against the rock wall beside the closest pile of bones just where she had been sitting weeks before. A skull was two feet from her left leg. Her eyes were open. Her face looked relaxed, without pain. The lips showed a hint of a smile. The skin was clear but yellow-grey. Her hands were folded on her lap. Her red checkered blouse and blue jeans were still damp but no longer soaking. Her coat was gone. One foot was bare. The other had on a blue sock. He couldn't move, staring.

"We actually found her early this morning," the Chief said. "Harold is too crippled to help me. It's taken me most of the day to set this up. It's our tradition to come here only by canoe. It has taken time." He paused. He put his hand on Conk's shoulder. "Go," he said.

Conk went to her and crouched down and looked at her. He felt strangely relaxed and at peace. The shaking was gone. He sat down on the rock ledge beside her and gently put his left hand up under the nape of her neck and cradled her head in his hand and pulled her over to him, putting his other arm around her. She rested against him. She smelled of the water and weeds but he thought there was a trace of perfume. He must be imagining that, he thought. He gently brushed off a tiny smudge of moist mud from her right cheek with his thumb. He put his lips softly against her cold greyish brow and held her, swaying slightly. He heard the Chief come up, standing behind him.

"This is the most sacred place in n'Daki Menan," he whispered, just loud enough for Conk to hear him. "Until about a hundred years ago, some of the chiefs were buried here. They came of their own will, to die, when they knew their time was come, sitting down against this rock beside their last." He paused. He leaned down beside them, and touched his finger to her hair. "She was different," he said. "She would have made a fine Wendaban." The Chief stood up and backed away. "Somehow she knew we had gone wrong," he whispered, "that we had let go something we needed back, that it was our doing as much as her people's. I know that's what she thought. But there was never any blame or pity. I think that was it. I think that's why Harold wanted her here. What she represents is our link to the future. To honor our past with great respect. She knew only respect. She wanted to help us but knew she couldn't. She knew only we can do that. That is what makes her different."

He had been listening. He heard the words, less for their meaning than for their rhythm, flowing through him and into her; or was Philip the conductor, and they flowed from her through the Chief into him? He looked at her. He kissed the cold lips without pressing too hard and started to tremble again. A little yellowish dribble came out of her lips. He wiped it off with his handkerchief. He reached down and put his thumb on the ring and held it there for a moment; from the Yankee finger it would come to rest on Ashwagane rock forever. He felt the hand on his shoulder. "We must go," the Chief whispered. He gently placed her up against the rock. He refolded her hands on her lap. He backed off, without taking his eyes off her. Something inside him said goodbye, but he did not move his lips. "The light will burn out in a few hours," Philip said. ". . . few hours. . . few hours. . ." whispered the cave.

They turned to go. Then they heard a quiet sliding sound. He looked back. She had fallen over onto the closest bones, her head propped up on them, her open eyes staring up at the panograph. He started towards her. The grip on his arm was firm. "Leave her," said the Chief. "She has taken her final position for eternity." ". . . eternity. . . eternity. . ." quietly echoed the cave. Conk turned and rushed forwards into the darkness.

Outside, blindfolded again, he knew dusk was closing in. He could feel the temperature dropping. They were soon beached across the bay, and he could see again. The Chief looked at him. "I guess it's too dark to fly home," he said. "It's getting risky," replied Conk. "You can stay with us, tonight," said Philip. "I'll see that you get over here early tomorrow for your plane. If Harold is awake, maybe the three of us can have a good talk." Conk nodded. "Thanks, Philip," he said. He walked over to Cloudie. He climbed up onto the pontoon and reached in for his emergency bag under the back canvas seat: dried food, some kindling, clean underwear, soap, toothbrush and paste, razor, aspirin, iodine and bandages, comb, matches, one can of Molson's Canadian. As he closed the door he put his hand on the strut and held the cool aluminum tightly for a moment. "Take care of her this first night, Cloudie," he whispered. "It's going to be our roughest one. I'm leaving her in your care. See you in the morning."

They paddled out of the bay and curved south towards Sand Island. The October sun was setting and the horizon's yellow was deepening to orange and pink. He turned; the north star was already a point of cold white. The Chief was talking to him from the stern, saying that after some time had elapsed he would ask the Band to formally adopt her as a Wendaban. Did Conk know of anyone who might assemble her research and tidy it up? Could Rita do it? He would write Dr. French. Angele had said recently she would like to be an anthropologist and he would encourage her. He wanted Conk to encourage her too.

He listened to the words but new feelings were struggling in his aching body. He couldn't figure out why he was feeling so strong. Suddenly he heard her. She spoke to him as if she were sitting beside him. "Why not do the book, Conk, the one mother wants to read." "Yes," he said to himself, "yes." He could feel strange strength surging through him. "Yes," he said to her. He would start tomorrow. He would sort through his pictures, start writing some text. He would go through her notes in the library. She had shown him where she kept them. She had already written many pages which were in his apartment. "Yes, Cathy," he said. His heart was pounding. He felt the paddle bite the water with deep, strong strokes. He couldn't believe it. He had that strange feeling again that she was inside him. He could feel her voice. "Henry and Henrietta," she was saying; "we'll tell their story to weave the book together, of their meeting at the spring flypast, their courtship, the babies and their summers on the lake, their diving and flying and calling, the long trips south." The story would be full of his pictures. He would work in the early myths somehow, describe the ancient loon paintings and the story on the rock at Ashton's Cave, and no one would ever know where they came from. He would respect her wishes. Always. The secrets of the cave would end with him and he would never return. She was safe. No one would ever know.

He looked ahead. The lights of Sand Island were twinkling in the distance. It would be his and her book, by them, about them. He paused in his paddling. Miles away, high in the northwestern sky, beginning to descend for the night's rest, the ancient bird sent out its faint far-off tremolo, calling to locate its mate. "You will have the last laugh in our book," he said, looking up to the orange-dark sky. "Henry, I know you agree to that," he said to himself. He started paddling. "Isn't he a she?" she said. He smiled. He paused for a stroke, then resumed paddling.